WITHOUT A SHADOW OF DOUBT

WITHOUT A SHADOW OF DOUBT

An Olivia Penn Mystery

THE OLIVIA PENN MYSTERY SERIES
BOOK V

KATHLEEN BAILEY

First hardcover edition: November 2025
First paperback edition: November 2025

ISBN (hardcover): 978-1-956270-19-8
ISBN (paperback): 978-1-956270-18-1
ISBN (e-book): 978-1-956270-17-4
ISBN (audio): 978-1-956270-20-4

Editing by Serena Clarke at Free Bird Editing
Proofreading by LaVerne Clark at LaVerne Clark Editing
Cover design by ebooklaunch.com

Published by:
Rhino Publishing LLC

www.kathleenbaileyauthor.com

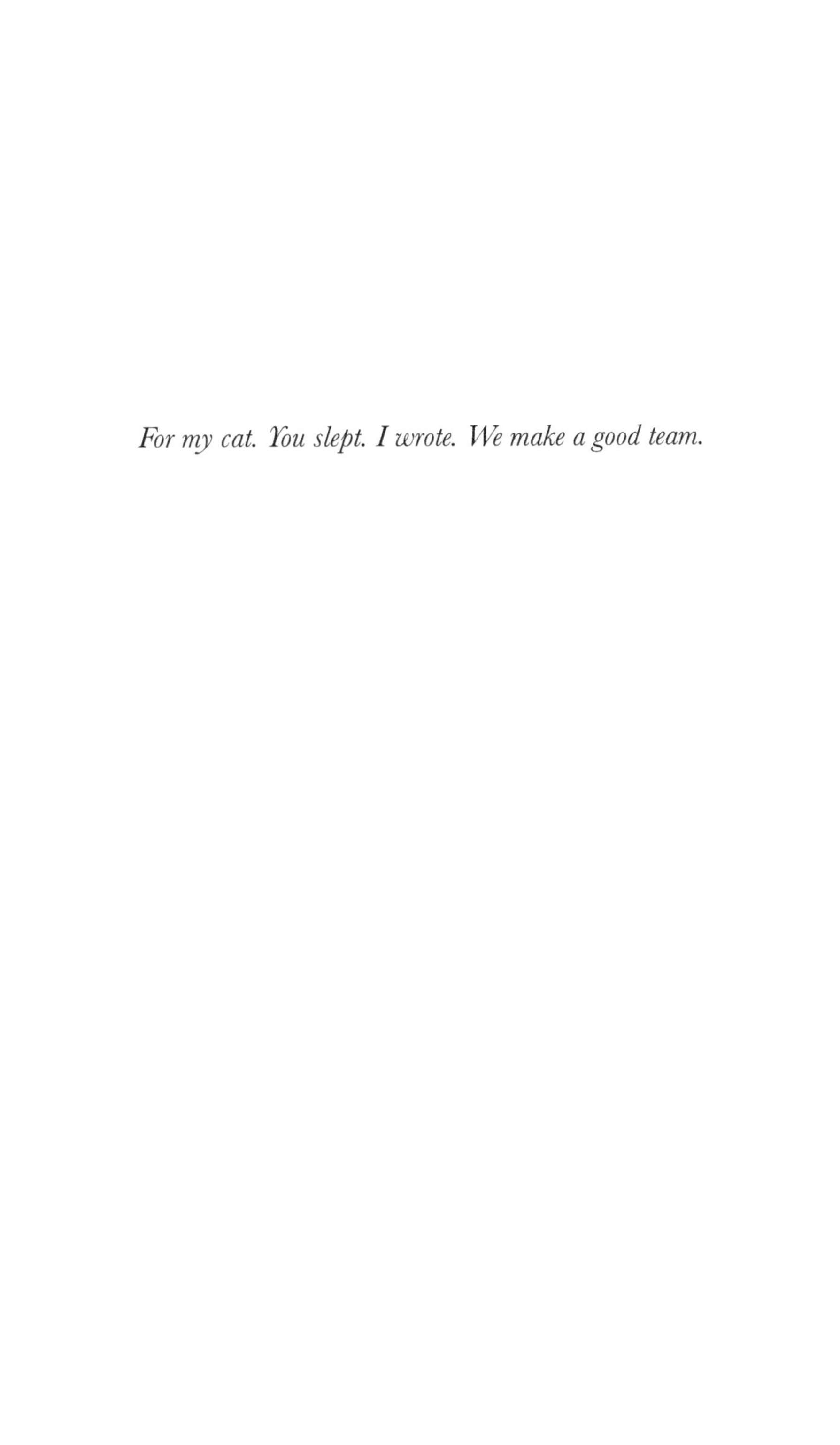

For my cat. You slept. I wrote. We make a good team.

Our lives are fashioned by our choices. First we make our choices. Then our choices make us.

— ATTRIBUTED TO ANNE FRANK

CHAPTER 1

Olivia Penn stood frozen on the sidewalk bordering the town square, her gaze locked on the two brutish men squaring off. One brandished a claymore, and the other gripped an axe and a small, round shield. A crowd had gathered to watch the spectacle, one unlike anything the normally quiet town of Apple Station had ever seen. This was a place for festivals, not midday duels between lumberjack lookalikes wielding battle-worn weapons, ready to inflict devastating injuries.

The larger man's scraggly beard hung over his barrel chest, and his bulging biceps were easily twice the size of Olivia's calves. He bellowed something unintelligible, possibly in an ancient language, then slammed his sword against his opponent's shield with a resounding *thwack*. The sound jolted Olivia as the axe-wielding man stumbled and fell backward.

A collective gasp swept through the crowd as the

fallen man scrambled to evade another strike. But his opponent was too quick. The claymore came down again, pinning both the shield and the man beneath it. Trapped, the defeated fighter curled into a fetal position as the larger combatant thrust the sword toward his opponent's side, stopping just short of a fatal blow. The victor stepped back, raised his arms, and unleashed a triumphant roar. Applause erupted from the onlookers as he basked in glory. He reached down to help his opponent to his feet, and the two exchanged a hearty bro hug before turning to wave at their appreciative audience.

"That was intense," Olivia said, glancing at her long-time friend Sawyer Weston beside her.

"Seriously, how much do you think that claymore weighs?" Sawyer replied, tipping back his black cowboy hat.

She eyed the massive weapon. "At least five pounds. Maybe more."

"And those dudes in the kilts?"

The pair of combatants were now posing for photos with giggling children poking at their flexed biceps.

"Two-fifty, maybe two-seventy-five."

Sawyer took off his hat and fanned himself, giving her a few playful swipes for good measure. She flashed him a grateful smile, though the gesture was more wishful thinking than anything. The midday sun was relentless, and they would've needed an industrial-strength fan to feel any real relief. At least the humidity was low. Ninety degrees in Apple Station still beat sweltering heat and soupy air, especially for the first Tuesday in August.

He settled his hat back onto his head. "I hope it cools down before the Highland Games open on Saturday."

"Is this the first time your family is hosting them at the ranch?"

"Yep. They're usually held in Marshall, but the venue was already booked for the weekend. When the organizers reached out to us, we jumped at the opportunity. You planning to come?"

"I am. Will you be around?"

"I'll be helping out on Saturday, but Sunday I'm heading south to pick up a horse we're taking in at our stables."

She slipped the elastic tie from her ponytail, took another from her pocket, and used both to fasten her blonde hair into a loose bun. "Gypsy is getting a new friend. That'll be nice. It's been way too long since I've driven up to Berryville to visit my favorite mare."

"Tell me about it. Almost borderline unacceptable," he replied with a wink. "Gyps says she misses you *berry*, *berry* much. She's chomping at the bit for some trail time with you."

She laughed at his quick-as-a-whip charm. "How could a girl say no when you and Gyps conspire to get me to hoof it up your way?"

"That'd be mighty *neigh*-borly of you," he teased, tipping his hat. "First cooler Sunday we have, I'm holding you to that, ma'am."

"Deal. How's life been at the ranch?"

"Busy with all the preparations for the weekend. The rental company delivered the tents, chairs, and assorted whatnots yesterday. We'll be setting everything up between now and Friday. A few vendors have already rolled in with their trailers, and some competitors dropped off their equipment this morning. You should've seen this tiny SUV driving up to the arena with one of those long poles strapped to the roof."

"A caber," she supplied.

"Yeah, that. Talk about a road hazard."

"I'd say a caber is slightly over the baggage limit for a flight."

A sharp, rapid-fire *rat-a-tat-tat* interrupted their conversation as four members of the pipe band launched into a snare drum performance with impeccable precision. A bass drummer pounded out a steady rhythm, soon joined by the piercing wail of bagpipes that filled the air with a lively march.

Olivia instantly imagined heavy mist rolling across a loch as she watched the performers. All wore white dress shirts with ties, black vests, and green tartan kilts. Glengarries sat atop their heads, each hat adorned with pompoms, ribbons, and side-pinned badges. Marching from the gazebo to the center of the town lawn, the band formed a circle around the bass drummer and played a tune that enchanted the crowd, whether they had Scottish roots or not.

With the Highland Games set to take place just

twenty miles up the road, Apple Station had transformed over the past week into a temporary Scottish burgh to attract tourists. Allen's Tavern offered nightly specials on imported Scottish ales, while Jillian's Cafe stocked its bakery case each day with shortbread, Dundee cakes, and scones. Tales and Treasures, the town's family-owned bookstore, had created a charming window display of Scottish crime fiction, Highlander romances, and Celtic folklore. Daisy's Feed and Saddlery had even hung the Saint Andrew's Cross, Scotland's Pantone blue and white national flag, outside the store, while a sale sign boasted thirty percent off tartan horse blankets.

"That's impressively loud for three bagpipers," Sawyer remarked. "Do you have any Scottish ancestry?"

"A wee bit on my mom's side. What about you?"

"Not a drop."

She took in his outfit—jeans and a long-sleeve button-down shirt, ready for full-on ranch work despite the heat. "If you wore a kilt, you could probably pass."

He rubbed his chin, pretending to consider it. "I don't know about that. Although it might be cooler, especially if I went commando."

Laughing, she scrunched her nose. "Maybe stick with the jeans."

The band finished playing to enthusiastic applause.

She glanced back at the saddlery across the street, where Sawyer worked part-time repairing tack. "Will you be in the shop this afternoon?"

"Nah, I'm driving back to the ranch. What've you got going on?"

"I have one more stop, then I'm heading home. I wrote my columns this morning so I could take the rest of the day off."

"Uh-oh," he said suddenly, pointing toward the gazebo. "I don't think that's part of the show."

A few men dressed as Highlanders were shouting at each other. Two burly men restrained a third, holding him back as he yelled at a hulking figure in a red tartan kilt and a black T-shirt.

"This could get ugly fast," she said.

"Medieval, even. Especially with the *Braveheart* battle-field arsenal lying around."

Another broad-shouldered man stepped into the chaos, wielding a claymore. He planted the sword in the ground between the feuding men, forcing them apart. After a few sharp words, he scolded both sides. Following a tense pause, the aggressors begrudgingly shook hands and dispersed.

She recognized the peacemaker. Craig Campbell was a friend of Preston's who had come for the Highland Games with his son Gavin and daughter Kirstie. Olivia had met the Campbells briefly on Sunday when she had brunch with Preston at the Apple Station Inn, which was owned by his mother, Bev. They'd arrived over the weekend for an extended vacation ahead of the event.

"Wonder what that was about," Sawyer said.

"No idea, but I hope it's not an omen." She fanned

her T-shirt against her skin. "I'd better get going. It was good to see you. Don't work too hard in this heat. Stay hydrated."

"Yes, ma'am. Text me on Saturday, and we'll meet up."

After a hug and a few goodbyes, they went their separate ways.

Her last stop before heading home was a quick visit with her dear friend A.J. at his general contracting office. She followed the sidewalk toward Blossom Avenue, where his suite was located.

She passed a family seated on a bench and couldn't help smiling at the sweet summer scene. Two young boys in ball caps and sunglasses sat sandwiched between their parents. Mom and Dad were enjoying fish-and-chip takeout from the Wee Chippy food truck parked near the gazebo. The brothers each tackled a swirled vanilla-and-chocolate ice cream cone, the soft-serve melting in sticky streams down their tiny hands.

That's going to be an ooey-gooey mess.

Farther down, the next bench stood empty except for two mourning doves, which fluttered to the ground as she approached. Looking ahead, she slowed, nearly stopping. Staring straight at her from the bench just beyond sat someone she never expected to see anywhere near Apple Station again.

CHAPTER 2

Carolyn Shaw was the only person Olivia knew who could sit leisurely under the blazing summer sun in a pantsuit and still look as cool and unfazed as an iceberg. Olivia had first met Carolyn in May, under peculiar circumstances. Short on manpower, Carolyn had recruited her to go undercover at a carnival to help bring down an animal trafficking ring. That involvement had led to the startling revelation that Olivia's good friend Sam was an operative for Carolyn's government-sanctioned, black-budget team. Carolyn also happened to be Sam's mother-in-law, likely the reason Sam had joined the team after her husband Aaron was killed in combat and she left the Marine Corps.

Carolyn sat with one leg crossed over the other, her arm draped casually along the back of the bench. Her ivory linen jacket hung open, revealing a black silk blouse and a glint of layered gold necklaces. Dark-tinted cat-eye sunglasses perfectly complemented her close-cropped auburn hair. She swirled a plastic cup and took a sip through the straw as Olivia neared.

From the moment they'd met, Carolyn had struck Olivia as someone who commanded every room she entered. Poised, intelligent, and decisive, she always seemed three steps ahead of everyone else. In high-stakes situations, she could be downright intimidating. But here, in this neutral setting, Olivia approached her casually, like an acquaintance she'd bumped into while enjoying the town's festivities.

"Carolyn, I'm surprised to see you here. Did you come to watch the events?"

Without so much as a hint of an expression, Carolyn replied in her posh British accent, "Heavens, no. How such nonsense passes for entertainment utterly escapes me."

Well, I enjoyed them. Olivia's spidey sense tingled as she looked around for Sam or any other team members. She wanted to press on, but her curiosity was piqued. What was Carolyn doing here, sipping lemonade instead of orchestrating a covert operation to bring down some shady organization?

"Is it work, then?"

Carolyn set her drink on the bench. "I'm here because of you."

That wasn't at all what she'd expected. Olivia stared at her for a moment, then glanced around again. "You came to Apple Station, to the middle of town, and have been sitting in this heat waiting for me to walk by?"

"And to take care of some related business."

Carolyn's matter-of-fact tone made it sound like a perfectly reasonable agenda.

How would you know I'd be here this afternoon? Then it dawned on her. She'd mentioned it to Sam. "Okay … so what did I do?"

"Nothing yet. Have a seat. I have a proposition for you."

And just like that, Carolyn was calling the shots again. Olivia hesitated, then sat down two feet away, her mind churning. Maybe Carolyn wanted to use her the same way she had before. Playing a faux reporter had been a one-off, something she'd agreed to because Sam's life had been at risk. That didn't mean she was looking to make it a freelance gig.

"What can I do for you?" Olivia asked.

"I'll be to the point. I want you to come and work for me."

Her mind tripped over the words, and she had to replay them. *What?* Background laughter from a group of teens felt like a cued-in sitcom soundtrack. She opened her mouth, but no words came. When Carolyn offered no immediate elaboration, Olivia shook her head. "Work for you? I don't understand. You know I'm an advice columnist, right? I don't have Sam's skill set."

Carolyn's lips curved up in something close to amusement. "Of course you don't. If I sent you into the field, we'd probably lose you on the first day."

She wanted to be insulted, but there was too much truth in the statement to argue, so she let it slide.

"I need a research analyst to provide intelligence reports to the operatives. As you're aware, one of our former analysts was a mole. His actions nearly cost lives and could have led to the dismantling of the unit. I know exactly who you are, what you've done, and what you're capable of. I want someone outside our usual recruitment circles. A fresh set of eyes. Someone who thinks unconventionally."

Olivia studied Carolyn for a long moment before standing. Had it been anyone else, she might've thought it was a prank. But Olivia had never heard Carolyn crack a joke, and she understood that the out-of-left-field offer was dead serious. Much too serious, in fact. She'd come into town to watch the events and see A.J., not to consider changing careers.

"I'm flattered, but I don't think I'm the right person for the job. Thank you, though." She took a few steps past Carolyn.

"I can double your salary."

She stopped mid-stride. *Double? How does she know what I make?*

If Carolyn had simply said she'd pay her more, Olivia would've kept on her way and tossed a polite "no thanks" over her shoulder. But double? That made her pause.

She turned as Carolyn stood. Before Olivia could even ask whether the offer was in U.S. dollars, her focus shifted entirely. Because aside from Carolyn, the last person she expected to see on a random Tuesday in Apple Station was the man walking toward them.

Rhett cut an unmistakable figure as he strolled along the sidewalk. Dressed in jeans and a form-fitting black T-shirt, he was a different kind of strongman than the Highlander types milling around the town square. He was all muscle, no gut, with a six-pack his tee didn't try to hide.

She had first met Rhett in October when he was posing as a golf instructor at Whispering Meadows Country Club. But in December, she'd learned it was a ruse. That was also when Sam revealed she had some kind of history with him, including a friendly fire incident in which he'd shot her. That part, Olivia still didn't fully understand.

"Olivia, long time no see," Rhett said, throwing an arm around Carolyn's shoulders.

Olivia nearly gasped on Carolyn's behalf. The dictionary definition of an odd couple: Rhett, an all-American, babe-loving jock, and Carolyn, a stern British woman of a certain age. Yet, to Olivia's shock, Carolyn tolerated the half-embrace without so much as an attempt to cripple him.

He took a bite of a small pastry wrapped in a napkin. "Scottish sausage roll. No idea what's in it, but damn, that's good grub."

Carolyn remained unfazed, but Olivia felt the need to state the obvious. "I take it you two know each other?"

He pulled Carolyn closer and kissed her on the cheek. "Yeah, you might say that. Right, Mum?"

Holy—Mum? Olivia's brain sputtered, then it clicked. Sam and Rhett. Sam and Carolyn. Of course. She looked between them. "You work for your mom? I thought you were a security consultant."

He took another bite of his roll and swallowed in three chews. "I did some private contracting on the side. Turned out to be a bad decision."

"I should say so," Carolyn commented dryly.

Then the second bombshell hit her. "That makes you Aaron's brother. And Sam's brother-in-law."

"Correct-o," he replied.

Olivia went full-on deer-in-headlights, stunned that Sam had never once mentioned the family connection.

"Think about my offer, Olivia," Carolyn said, composed as ever. "I don't extend it lightly, and I won't be kept waiting for a response." With that, she turned and walked away.

Rhett gave a dazzling smile and shot Olivia a finger-gun. "Later." Then he spun and easily caught up with Carolyn.

"Later," she muttered to herself, feeling like she'd just landed in *The Twilight Zone.*

CHAPTER 3

Olivia watched Carolyn and Rhett for a moment before slowly continuing toward A.J.'s suite. What if she hadn't taken the sidewalk? Had Carolyn truly been waiting for her, or was it just coincidence? Right place, right time? Would Carolyn have chased her down in three-inch heels if she'd used a different route? Or would Rhett have tackled her, holding her until his mum caught up? She laughed to herself, thinking if that had happened, those around the square might've applauded, assuming it was part of the Highland demonstrations.

The job offer had caught her off guard, but Carolyn had clearly been planning this for some time. That thought gave Olivia pause. Capriciousness wasn't a trait she associated with Carolyn. Exacting, prepared, and determined were her calling cards. An invitation to join her team was likely the result of hand-picked selection, not application.

Over the past year, Olivia had been involved in four police investigations, each tied to her in some personal way. Sleuthing intrigued her, and her efforts had helped solve several murders. But she wasn't an expert in intelligence or national security. With no background in legal studies, how could she possibly be qualified to work as an analyst in Carolyn's world? Still, she turned the idea over in her head.

She enjoyed writing her advice column, but with her editor Angela soon leaving to become an innkeeper in Vermont, working at the newspaper wouldn't feel the same. Olivia had been considering a career change for a while, just not a complete overhaul.

In June, her friend Cassandra had accepted a job at Olivia's paper in D.C. and was now a few weeks away from leaving her position at *The Apple Station Times*. Olivia had considered stepping into the vacancy as a temporary fix until something more suitable came along, though it would probably mean cutting her salary in half.

And then there was another possibility, one that Carolyn's unexpected offer had pushed to the forefront of Olivia's thoughts. Private investigator John Mack had expressed interest in working with her in a more professional capacity. They'd met in December, and though their early encounters had been rocky, she'd gained a new appreciation for him after his daring actions to help her in May. Mack, as he preferred to be called, already had an assistant, but he'd hinted at bringing her into the business. What exactly he had in mind, she wasn't entirely sure.

The idea intrigued her enough that she'd fallen down a rabbit hole of research on what it would take to become a registered PI in Virginia. The training requirements were surprisingly achievable. What she didn't know was whether Mack's veiled offer had been sincere or simply the result of heightened emotions after their brief partnership in taking down the animal trafficking ring. They hadn't spoken since May, which only muddied her sense of his intentions.

Setting the questions aside for now, she crossed Blossom Avenue and peered through the window of A.J.'s office. He stood near the door, a phone pressed to his ear. She tapped on the glass a few times, catching his attention. Smiling, he gave her a thumbs-up and waved her in.

She stepped into the suite, greeted by a cheerful chime and a blast of cool air. The space was uncluttered, furnished with only the essentials: desks, file cabinets, and a coffeemaker beside a mini fridge. Most of the heavy-duty work happened in the back shop, where A.J. stored his equipment. A yellow moon cactus in a red pot sat on the windowsill, a small but noticeable addition. He didn't know a pansy from a petunia, so someone special must've inspired the feminine touch.

Dressed for the job in khaki carpenter pants and a white T-shirt, he was a little taller and a few years older than Olivia. Whenever they got together, they still acted like the kids who had grown up next door to each other.

"Thank you, that's great," A.J. said into the phone. "I'll gather what I need and should be able to start Thursday … Sounds good. Thanks. Bye." He lightly tossed his cell onto a pile of folders and clapped. "Yahoo!"

Grinning like he'd won the lottery, he cha-chaed over to her, grabbed her hands, and twirled her once around.

"Whoa there, Fred Astaire," she said, laughing. "At least buy me a drink before you spin me."

He let go only to wrap her in a bear hug, lifting her off the ground.

"Oh, jeez," she squealed. "What's gotten into you?"

"You're my lucky charm. Lucky Liv, that's your new name." He set her down and rubbed her head like he was summoning a genie from a lamp.

She playfully flicked his hand away. "You're messing up my hair."

"I thought messy buns were a thing."

"I don't even want to know why that's on your radar," she teased. "I take it that was a good phone call?"

"A very good one, Ms. Penn. I've been doing some work for Peter Tillerman on his farm. He's got an enormous property. A big old house, two barns, and stables. He wants me to be his go-to handyman for repairs. That means steady business. And as a town council member, he has a lot of friends. If anyone asks him if he knows a guy who can—fill in the blank—guess what?" He jabbed a thumb into his chest. "I'm that guy."

"You are *that guy*. That's great. I'm really happy for you."

"And it's all because of you."

"I wouldn't go that far."

"So, to what do I owe the pleasure of your visit? Because if you need something fixed, my schedule is about to get crowded."

"Hey, now. I've known you longer than just about anyone. I'm pulling rank for your services."

He gave a theatrical bow with one hand over his heart. "And you'll always have them."

She leaned against the desk as he straightened. "I was in town running errands and stopped to catch a bit of the show on the square."

"I could hear the drums and bagpipes from in here."

"There was a mock battle and almost a real fight between some pro-wrestler types in kilts." She glanced at the moon cactus. "Are you and Soph going to the Highland Games?"

He pressed his lips together at the simple yes-or-no question. She caught the hesitation and smirked. "You two aren't fooling anyone."

"What do you mean?"

"You know what I mean."

"Hypothetically, if I knew what you meant, how would you feel about that?"

Over the past few months, Olivia had sensed something developing between him and her best friend, Sophia, though neither seemed eager to bring it up with her. She didn't push. The elephant in the room was obvious, but that didn't make addressing it any less awkward. She knew the day was coming when she'd be asked for her opinion.

She shrugged. "It's none of my business."

"But I feel like it kind of is. She's your best friend, besides me, of course. I didn't know what you thought about us sort of …"

"Dating?"

"We've just gone out casually a few times."

"Call it what you want, but if you two hit it off, that's fantastic. Paige was the first special someone you really saw a future with, and it's okay to date again. You deserve to be happy. So does Soph. Though what she sees in a lunkhead like you is beyond me."

His mouth rounded into a perfect *O*. "What? My charm? My good looks? My ability to put up shelves?"

"True. I wouldn't have batted an eye at Preston if I thought he couldn't use a set of tools," she joked. "You know I'm kidding. But if things between you two become more serious than casual get-togethers you haven't started calling dates yet, you better be good to her."

He stepped closer and wrapped her in a hug. "Thanks for the blessing. I would never want to do anything that would put us at odds."

"That would never happen." As they pulled apart, she gave him a reassuring smile. "Soph must be out-of-her-mind excited for the playground dedication on Sunday. Is everything ready?"

"After the final inspection tomorrow, we're good to go."

Over a year ago, A.J. had learned he was the heir to Grove Manor, a sprawling estate outside of town that had been abandoned for decades. The property, once known for its extravagant parties, had fallen into disrepair and gained notoriety after their friend Paige Warner was killed there.

When A.J. became the legal owner, he tore the manor down and cleared part of the land. He built a home for himself and worked with local authorities to plan, construct, and finance a special needs playground. Sophia had lobbied town officials for years to fund one for the community. The nearest large-scale inclusive playground was over two hours away. Yet, many of the parents of the children she saw at her physical therapy practice made the trek regularly. As for the rest of the property, A.J. had resisted the big payday of selling it off, except for a small parcel on the far edge of the lot, which he sold to a woman he'd never met.

"Are you entering the naming contest?" he asked.

"Is it still open?"

"If you've got fifty bucks for a raffle ticket, then yes. But you'll need to get your entry to Maria soon. She's vetting the names to make sure they can be used legally."

"I'm stopping by Soph's clinic tomorrow evening to

help with some things, so I'll give it to her mom then. Did you get a good response to the contest?"

"Beaucoup. Apparently, bragging rights for naming a playground are a hot commodity."

His cell rang. He stepped over to the desk, picked it up, and answered. "A.J. Matthews General Contracting … Yes, Mr. Pickens, I just spoke with Mr. Tillerman … That was nice of him to say … What do you need done?"

He smiled at Olivia and gave her a thumbs-up.

She waved and whispered, "Bye."

As she turned to go, he reached out and ruffled her hair, mouthing, "Lucky Liv."

With her and Preston going strong, an intriguing job offer on the table, and a fun weekend ahead at the Highland Games, she couldn't help thinking maybe he wasn't far off the mark.

CHAPTER 4

After arriving home shortly before five, Olivia strolled across the sun-scorched lawn in front of the porch. A robin landed on the rim of the birdbath, then hopped into the basin, flapping its wings in a lively splash. She'd refilled the bird feeder yesterday, but it was already half empty. The pole-mounted baffle hung lower than usual, hinting that a squirrel had made an ambitious leap to raid the seed.

Her father, William Penn, stood near the far side of their colonial-style house, inspecting the garden. Wearing a red ball cap, black mesh shorts, and a yellow wicking T-shirt, he could've passed for an athlete training for the Virginia Senior Games. Since taking up baking over the winter, he'd approached it with Olympian focus, even donning performance gear to stay cool in the heat of the kitchen.

Torrential spring rains had delayed the planting of

their summer garden until early June. Her father eagerly anticipated the growing season every year. Though she handled the heavy labor, he spent days planning the layout and selecting seedlings from local nurseries. Planting was always a backbreaking day for her, but the joy he took in watching the garden flourish made all the aches and pains worthwhile.

"How's everything looking?" Olivia asked.

He gently straightened a cherry tomato stalk inside its cage. "Great. I watered this morning, and some of the tomatoes need to be tied up again. I swear they grew overnight. We're in for a big harvest. You did a fantastic job with the planting."

"You say that every year. I'll tie them before I go to Preston's."

He moved down a few more rows, and she fell in beside him.

"No, I can do it. I'll pick those Early Girls tomorrow. Look there." He pointed to the base of a beefsteak plant. "Something's been digging at those roots."

She nudged the displaced soil back into place with her shoe and pressed it down. "Probably a squirrel or a chipmunk."

He reached toward the base of a Better Boy tomato plant, plucked a few sucker shoots from near the bottom, and dropped them onto the lawn. Then he straightened, testing the wooden stake to make sure it was firmly anchored in the ground.

"Did you get all your errands done in town?"

She pinched a pair of suckers from a Roma plant and tossed them behind her, knowing she'd catch them the next time she mowed.

"I did. I caught some of the Highland demonstrations. I saw Preston's friend Craig from a distance. He's the one I told you about who I met Sunday at the inn. He had to break up a fight between some guys who were involved in the event."

"What were they fighting about?"

"I don't know, but it didn't come to blows. Just a lot of yelling." She glanced at a nearby row. "Those Celebrities look really healthy."

"They always do well for us. When are you leaving for Preston's?"

"Not for a while," she said, as they neared the back of the house.

"I wasn't sure if these cucumbers would be okay on this side, but they're growing like crazy."

"That front corner gets the brunt of the afternoon sun, but shade hits this spot early. Moving the patch out of the midday heat helped." She looked up at the cloudless sky, then toward the other end of the garden. "Preston is stopping by the inn after work, so our dinner plans got pushed back a little. I have time to make you something to eat before I go."

He waved her off and adjusted his cap. "Don't bother. I've already decided I'm ordering a pizza. Is this the week you have to drive into D.C.?"

"No, it's next week. I'll meet Angela's replacement in

person on Tuesday. He won't officially take over until September, but they're starting the transition."

"Do you know anything about him?"

She bent down, yanked out a clump of crabgrass creeping into the garden's edge, and tossed it aside. "Not much. Angela says he has good credentials. She knows him professionally, but not personally." Olivia had thought about looking into his background but never got around to it, figuring she'd find out soon enough. Joking, she added, "Maybe I'll just quit. We could be two retirees, spending our days tending the garden."

"Why not? Sounds like a good life to me. But you might be the only retiree living here."

She turned to him, narrowing her eyes. "What do you mean?"

"I've been thinking about something for a while. I'm considering going back to work."

Stunned, she blurted, "Why would you want to do that? I thought you liked retirement."

"I do, especially with you here. But lately, I've been thinking about how I could put my time to better use."

"You mean like volunteering somewhere?"

He pointed at the A-frame cucumber trellis. "We might need to add a cage on both sides so the tendrils from those end cukes have something to climb." He glanced back at her. "No, I mean actual work."

"I ask again, why would you want to do that? Why be obligated to go to a job after you've spent your whole life working?"

"It'd keep me out of trouble," he said with a light laugh.

Thrown by the idea, she was momentarily at a loss for words. He'd never said anything about being unhappy with retirement. In fact, he seemed healthier and more content than he had in years. "I wouldn't want you to take on something too demanding or stressful."

"If it were, I'd quit. I don't need to work. I've just been thinking about it." He wiped his brow. "Come on, let's go inside. It's hot out here."

They went up the back porch steps and entered the house through the kitchen door. Willow, June Warner's cat they'd been caring for since January, was loafing on the table.

"No, Willow, not on the table," she said. "You're not even pretending to follow the rules anymore, are you?" She picked up the white cat and set her gently on the floor. "Does she do that when I'm not here?"

"Sometimes," he replied, taking a seat.

"You shouldn't let her."

As much as she hated to admit it, the cat's time in the Penns' household was likely coming to an end. She'd originally agreed to look after Willow while June visited family in North Carolina for three months at the start of the year. But when June followed up that trip with an Alaskan cruise, they'd been happy to continue caring for the cat since she'd settled in so well. The longer Willow stayed, the harder it was to imagine letting her go. She felt especially bad for their beagle Buddy, who'd grown fond of his playmate. The thought of him losing his friend made her heart ache.

On Thursday, she was going to June's house to pick up the cat's monthly supplies. At first, Olivia had politely declined June's generous offer to keep providing food, treats, and toys, but she'd insisted. Helping to care for her late daughter's beloved pet, even in a small way, brought her comfort. Olivia couldn't argue with that and gratefully accepted her kindness.

Last week, June had texted to confirm Thursday's pickup, adding that she wanted to discuss something about Willow. The message left Olivia with a sinking feeling that her time with the cat was running out. June hadn't taken Willow back in the spring because her house was being painted. But the work had been finished for two weeks now, so there was no reason the cat couldn't return to live with her.

"Do you want anything to drink?" she asked.

"I'll take a root beer."

She grabbed two sodas from the refrigerator, popped the tabs on both cans, and set one in front of him.

"Thank you."

Buddy padded into the kitchen and greeted her with a few playful barks.

"Hey there, Budster," she said.

"I walked him while you were out."

She glanced at Buddy's bowls. He had devoured his morning meal, leaving only two pieces of kibble behind. "Let's get you something to eat."

Buddy went over to his water bowl and lapped up a generous measure as Willow meowed for Olivia's attention. She refilled Buddy's food dish and treated Willow to her favorite squeezable snack. When the cat finished, Olivia tossed the empty packet in the trash and washed her hands, looking out the window at her office in the backyard.

Formerly her mother's writing cottage, the one-room outbuilding had become both her workspace and a place of solitude whenever she needed time to think. Carolyn's offer drifted back into her thoughts. Though she wasn't ready to discuss the specifics with her father, she was eager to get his impression.

She dried her hands with a tea towel and sat across from him at the table. "Since employment is the topic du jour, I got a job offer today."

"Doing what?"

"I'm not entirely sure, but it involves mostly research."

"Is this something you applied for?"

She shook her head and took a sip of soda. "No. It just sort of happened when I was in town. I ran into someone I know, and apparently, she's hiring."

His face tightened. "Is it in Apple Station?"

Carolyn clearly knew a lot about her, and some of that had to come from Sam. Before making the offer, Carolyn must've known that Olivia had no intention of leaving Apple Station, not even for double the salary. If relocation were part of the deal, the decision would be easy. She'd been so caught off guard by Carolyn that she hadn't thought to ask. Though Sam traveled often, her living next door suggested they were based nearby.

"She didn't exactly say, but she didn't say it wasn't, either. I'll find out more, but it pays very well."

"Then maybe you should look into it, if it interests you."

"It does, and I know someone who can fill in a few of the blanks." *And tell me why she didn't warn me about the offer, or that she's related to Rhett.*

She pushed back from the table and stood, soda in hand. "I've got to clean up and change clothes."

He pulled his phone from his pocket and tapped the screen. "I'm going to get my order ready for dinner. Bella's has an app now. Oh, look, they've got a 'Two for Tuesday' special. Buy any large pizza, get a second one free. You can't go wrong. I'm doing that."

"You refuse to do online banking or electronic bill pay, but you have an app for the local pizza joint?"

"I also have apps for Burger Bistro, The I-Screamery, and Taco Town."

"Wow, Dad, really making the most of modern technology."

"If you sign up for an account with Sweet Moe's through their app, they give you a free brisket sandwich. Then, if you delete your account and the app, you can reinstall it and receive the same deal."

"Let me guess, you know this from personal experience?"

"I've gotten three free sandwiches so far. No one cares or questions it."

"I think I've already heard more than I wanted to." She shook her head, laughing. "I'm going to get ready."

With that, she left the kitchen, letting thoughts of job offers and gaming fast-food apps fade as her mind shifted to the romantic dinner awaiting her and Preston under the stars.

CHAPTER 5

"I saw Craig in town today," Olivia said to Preston as they rocked gently side by side on the back-porch swing at his house.

Wrapped in beige siding, his modern Craftsman-style home blended rustic charm with polished design. It featured wide overhanging eaves above both porches and a gable roof with slate-gray shingles. His nearest neighbor was well over a baseball toss away, and the house sat far enough from the road that passing traffic was never heard inside. The modest home suited him. It was roomy enough for one, with space for more, should that day ever come for them. For now, she was content to spend the occasional evening there or have him over once a week for dinner with her and her father.

"He wants to get together for dinner sometime this week," Preston replied.

"That sounds nice. How often do you see him?"

He draped his arm across the top of the bench, his fingertips grazing her shoulder. "Not very often. Winston-Salem is only about a five-hour drive, but it's hard for either of us to find the time."

"When you get a weekend off, we could take a trip down there. I've never been to that part of North Carolina. I'm sure it's nice." She shifted slightly, turning toward him. "You mentioned on Sunday that his wife didn't come because she was sick."

"Yeah. She's had something wrong with her lungs for years. She was doing well for a while, at least holding steady with medication. Craig says her condition has worsened, and now she's being evaluated for a transplant."

She leaned into his side and let out a weighted breath. "Wow. That's heavy. How old is she?"

"Both she and Craig are forty-five. Gavin is twenty. Kirstie is eighteen."

"They had kids young. We were in high school when Gavin was born. Is his wife originally from Scotland too?"

"No, she's from Alabama. They met when he came over on a student visa to study at UNC. He'd planned to go back to Scotland, but they ended up getting married a week after graduation."

"Scottish and Southern accents in the same house. That's a colorful linguistic upbringing for the kids. It must be hard for them, watching her health decline."

"And stressful. If she ends up getting a transplant, her medical expenses could skyrocket."

"Is someone staying with her while the rest of the family is here?"

"Her mother came up from Florida. Craig wanted to bring the kids for the week since they don't get away much anymore. Plus, it gives him a chance to visit his aunt." He glanced at her. "You know that nice Victorian house on Raven Lane?"

"Of course. A.J. and I used to make a special trip there when we went trick-or-treating."

"That's his aunt's house, Fiona Campbell."

"Oh, Mrs. Campbell. I didn't make the connection when I met them on Sunday. Campbell is such a common name."

"Craig has his mother's maiden name. She kept it when she married his father, and they passed it on to him to keep the Campbell name in the family."

"I don't really know his aunt, but she always gave out the best candy on Halloween. If we went there late and she still had a lot left, she'd give us double the loot."

He removed his arm from the back of the swing and planted his hands on his thighs. "Speaking of late, it's half past seven already. I better get the grill going and the food on, or we'll be eating at midnight."

They stood and went down the steps. He'd already set the picnic table with a blue-and-white gingham cloth, glasses, dishes, and silverware. At its center, a bud vase held wildflowers from the field behind his house. The sun was dipping toward the horizon, carrying away the day's sweltering heat. Early twilight streaked the summer sky in cooling pastels, setting the stage for their romantic dinner under the stars.

"Are you sure you want to eat outside?" he asked. "It could get a little buggy."

"It'll be fine. It's such a lovely evening. What can I do to help?"

He gave a charming smile, revealing a dimple beneath his short-stubbled beard. "Your man has it all under control. Sit back and watch the magic happen."

She burst out laughing. "Who knew you had such hocus-pocus up your sleeve? Here I thought I was just getting dinner, but apparently I'm in for a sleight-of-hand supper show. I hope it doesn't turn out to be an illusion."

"Do you doubt the culinary wizardry of Preston the Magnifico?"

"Oh, jeez. That's a lot to live up to. Now my expectations have doubled."

"Prepare to be amazed. I'll grab the food from the fridge and fire up the grill. There are citronella candles in the shed that'll help keep the mosquitoes away."

"I'll get them. Is the shed open?"

"Yeah. Should be on one of the shelves."

"I'm on it," she said, heading toward the side of the house.

"Watch out for snakes in the corners."

She stopped dead in her tracks and spun around.

"Nope. I'm out. I'll take my chances with the mosquitoes."

He laughed, holding up his hands. "I'm only kidding."

She didn't move.

"Really. I promise, no snakes."

She narrowed her eyes, took a few cautious steps backward, then turned.

"That I know of," he added.

Ha-ha, Mr. Magnifico. A magician and a stand-up comic. What a combo.

Once she got to the shed, she opened the door, stepped inside, and pulled the chain on the overhead light. The single bulb cast little illumination, but it was enough to get the job done. She nudged a paint can a few inches across the concrete floor with her foot, hoping the scuffing noise would warn any lurking snakes that she wasn't one to mess with. Satisfied she'd made her presence known, she headed to the back to look for the candles.

The shelving unit stood about two feet from the wall. Beside it, in the corner, sat a six-foot-tall locker, pulled out slightly farther. There was no telling why he'd grouped certain tools and parts together on the shelves. His haphazard organization reminded her of the junk drawer in her kitchen: random, yet functional in its own way.

A bottle of mower oil, wearing a small orange funnel like a hat, sat atop a roll of duct tape that pinned down a stack of receipts. The whole thing resembled a piece of toolshed modern art. No doubt, Preston would argue he knew exactly where everything was, just as she did with her kitchen's junk drawer.

Scanning the shelves, she figured the citronella candles would be easy to spot. She was looking for big, round jarred candles, but maybe he'd meant smaller votives instead. Several boxes were stuffed with cords and parts she couldn't begin to identify. She pushed aside a few repurposed coffee cans, then stilled when something hit the floor behind the unit.

She tried peering behind it, but the locker blocked her view. Dropping to her knees, she pulled out her phone and turned on the flashlight. After moving a few items on the bottom shelf, she aimed the light toward the back, where a small padded envelope lay on the floor. It was too far to reach, and though it wasn't exactly an emergency, she wanted to retrieve it.

Setting the phone down, she stood and tested the weight of the locker. Bit by bit, using alternating angles of pull, she created enough space to squeeze between the locker and the shelving unit. Then she knelt on the floor and shimmied into the narrow gap. *He'd better have been joking about that snake. Because if I were a snake, this is exactly where I'd be hiding, waiting to sink my venomous fangs into someone who clearly doesn't belong here.*

She reached blindly, skimmed her hand along the floor, and found the envelope straightaway. As she pulled her arm out, the back of her hand brushed against something near the wall. Wiggling backward, she set the envelope in front of the shelves and picked up her phone. With the flashlight still on, she crawled forward again, wanting to see what else was behind the locker before grabbing it.

A coil of vinyl tubing lay tangled on the floor. She guessed it had probably fallen off a shelf at some point. When she grasped the tubing, one end sprung free, striking something with a sharp metallic *ping*. She aimed the light toward the source: a large copper pot with a pipe column rising from its center. The contraption stood about three feet tall, and next to it sat another copper pot and a box containing more coiled tubing and a thermometer.

Her mind assembled the pieces instantly. She'd never seen one in person, but thanks to late-night reality TV, she knew without a doubt she was looking at a deconstructed moonshine still.

"Hey, Liv," Preston called as he stepped into the shed. "Liv, are you in here?"

She scrambled backward out of the narrow space and popped up, holding the vinyl tubing.

"I was looking for the candles and accidentally knocked an envelope off the shelf," she explained. "I moved the locker to reach it."

His gaze shifted to the envelope on the floor, then to the tubing in her hand. "I remembered I put the candles in the garage after the last time I used them."

"Okay, cool. Well, you're right. No snakes. Just this

vinyl tubing and ..." She glanced toward the corner. "What looks very much to me like a still."

He stepped closer and rubbed the back of his head, looking every bit like a man who knew he'd been caught.

"Are you doing that legally?" she asked.

He shook his head. "It's not mine."

"If it's not yours, then—" The realization struck. She gasped, managing only one word. "A.J."

He lowered his hand and nodded.

"That's A.J.'s still," she said slowly. The events from two Mays ago came rushing back: Paige's death, the secrets behind Grove Manor, and A.J.'s reckless decision to make a few quick bucks by illegally distilling moonshine with a shady partner. After Paige's murder was solved, A.J. had avoided charges for lack of evidence. Police had searched the dense forest around the manor for the still, but nothing was ever found.

"It is."

"What's it doing in your shed?"

"You weren't supposed to see it. *Nobody* was supposed to see it."

She stared at him as the pieces fell into place. Only one explanation made sense. "You took it, didn't you? Why would you do that? And why do you still have it?"

He stepped closer and reached for the tubing in her hand. She let go, and he placed it on a shelf.

"It's not exactly easy for a police detective to throw away a still. I can't put it out for trash pickup, and I can't take it to the dump. They have cameras, and that's footage I don't want to be part of. I figured I'd keep it here until I could get rid of it some other way."

"How did no one know you took it? You even kept it from Payne, your boss. The chief of police. You could've been fired. Or charged."

"I accepted that as a possibility, but I doubted it would come to that." He let out a deep breath and relaxed his stance. "When we searched the woods after what happened at Grove Manor that day, everyone was assigned an area. I found the still but told the deputies the section was clear. Later that night, I went back and removed it."

"Why did you do that?"

He reached for her hand and held it lightly. "Because after everything that had come out about Grove Manor and Paige's death, I knew A.J. had just done something stupid. He needed someone to look the other way. As long as he didn't get into any other trouble, I let it go."

"But you didn't even know A.J. back then. Why would you take such a big risk for him?"

"I didn't do it for him." His thumb brushed her knuckles. "I did it for you."

She held his gaze, speechless for a moment. "But you didn't even know me that well. And from what I thought, you didn't like me very much."

"I knew A.J. mattered to you. I wasn't sure if he was just a friend, someone you were interested in, or something more. But after I saw what you did to save Cassandra and catch Paige's killer, I wanted to help you.

Your friend had been murdered, A.J. was under suspicion, and you almost lost your life. Taking the still felt like one small thing I could do to ease some of what you'd been carrying."

Floored, she stammered, "I—I had no idea. I never even suspected."

"That's how it was meant to stay."

She stepped closer as he rested his hands on her waist.

"Are you going to tell A.J.?" he asked.

"I don't see how that would serve anyone," she said, settling her hands on his shoulders. "I can't believe you took that risk for me when you didn't even know me."

"Since that day at Grove Manor, I wanted to get to know you more. Not a day went by that I didn't think about you."

Her smile came before his words even sunk in. "Then why didn't you say something sooner?"

"I asked around about you. I heard different things. Somebody said they thought you were seeing someone in D.C."

She shook her head. "I wasn't."

"I didn't know that then. Or if you might end up moving back to D.C. or New York eventually. I knew I hadn't made the best first impression, and if you ever thought of me, I figured it wasn't in a flattering way."

"I thought of you. A lot." Her smile grew, and her pulse quickened. "I didn't think I could love you any more than I already do, but now … now you've given me a reason."

"I like the sound of that."

He drew her closer, leaned down, and kissed her gently. She wrapped her arms around him, but he suddenly pulled away.

"What's wrong?" she said.

His eyes went wide. "Do you smell that? Oh, no. The chicken."

He spun and bolted out of the shed, calling back, "To be continued."

She laughed, watching him go. "To be continued," she echoed under her breath.

After repositioning the locker, she picked up the envelope and set it on a shelf. Then she turned off the light, stepped outside, and closed the door.

By the time she made it back to the picnic table, Preston stood with his hands on his hips, staring down at a platter of charred chicken.

"I'm afraid it's a goner," he said.

"We could call it extra crispy."

"That's great if we were supposed to be having fried chicken. I'll order a pizza."

"You don't have to. We still have the potato salad."

He pulled his phone from his pocket. "I'll get it delivered from Bella's. You want mushrooms?"

"Sounds good."

Thirty minutes later, a pizza box sat on the table in front of them, citronella candles flickering by their feet. It was nearly nine, and though that was usually closer to her bedtime than dinnertime, she didn't care. They were eating under the stars, and the lightning bugs were putting on a dazzling summer show.

Just as they both started on their second slice, his phone rang. Being a cop in a small-town department meant he never truly went off duty. More than a few of their dates had been interrupted by official business, and she'd accepted that would always be a part of their life together. But calls this late worried her the most. Cops rarely received good news after dark.

He reached for his phone on the table and tilted it toward him. "It's Craig. I was supposed to call him back earlier."

Relieved it wasn't the department, she teased, "I think you're in trouble."

He held the phone to his ear. "Hey, Craig. Sorry I didn't—" His expression shifted as he stood, switching instantly into cop mode. "Slow down. Are you sure? … Okay, get out of the house. Don't touch anything. Call nine-one-one. Stay nearby to direct the officers, but keep safe. I'm on my way."

He ended the call and began hastily clearing the table.

"What's going on?" she asked, rising to her feet. "Don't worry about this. I'll take care of things if you have to go."

"Thanks. Craig went to his aunt's house and found

the front door open." His jaw tightened as he shoved his phone into his pocket. "Fiona Campbell is dead."

CHAPTER 6

After Olivia blew out the candles, she stacked the plates, silverware, and napkins on top of the pizza box and carried the pile inside. She wrapped the leftovers in foil, stored them in the refrigerator, then returned outside for the tablecloth, the bud vase, and the glasses. The night hadn't gone as she'd hoped, but learning what Preston had done to help A.J. on her behalf more than made up for another evening cut short by his off-hour official duties.

She was already considering ways to get rid of the still and had even thought about taking it with her. No one was likely to see it at either place, but it made more sense to hide it at her house. She made a mental note to research trash facilities in nearby counties, knowing some were less strict about monitoring what got dumped. From her time in D.C., she also remembered that theater companies sometimes welcomed prop donations. She imagined a stage crew would gladly accept a genuine still, no questions asked.

Once she'd finished cleaning up, she locked the house with her key and tossed the pizza box into the trash bin outside the garage. Preston had hurried off, knowing nothing more than what he'd already told her. Craig had found Fiona's front door open, which seemed suspicious, but she wasn't going to assume the worst.

Fiona's house was iconic in Apple Station. Located close to town, the Southern Victorian featured a wrap-around porch, tall windows, and a steeply pitched roof. White siding, light gray shingles, and steel-blue shutters gave it a timeless warmth and charm.

Olivia often passed Fiona's on her way to and from town. The yard and shrubs were always meticulously maintained. Flowers bloomed in abundance through spring, summer, and fall. In winter, strings of twinkling white lights adorned the pines at the edge of the property, the eaves, and the lamppost by the sidewalk.

Fiona was often outside, sitting on the porch or walking around the yard with a cane. Olivia guessed she was in her late seventies and appeared to live alone. At her age, and with mobility issues, a medical emergency or a bad fall seemed a plausible cause of death.

Sliding behind the wheel of her Expedition, she fastened her seat belt and started the engine. As she pulled her phone from her pocket and set it on the center console, the screen lit up with a missed text. She usually kept the phone in "Do Not Disturb" mode when she was with Preston, silencing all calls and texts except from a few emergency contacts, including her father. She'd always answer if he called, no matter what. He rarely interrupted her date nights unless it was urgent, like last week, when he accidentally hit the wrong button on the TV remote and lost the sound. After twenty minutes of trial and error while she guided him over the phone, the volume finally returned, prompting him to declare her a genius.

Mack had sent the text about thirty minutes earlier, around the same time Craig had called Preston. That he'd reached out to her at all was unusual. She hadn't spoken to him in nearly three months, and he'd never initiated contact.

She opened the message and read: "Go to my office now. The key code for the building is 5863. The office code is 4862. The code to get behind the desk is 3861. In the bottom drawer of the end cabinet take the file labeled Winters."

What?

She reread the text, figuring he must've hit the wrong contact. She dialed his number, but the call went straight to voicemail. Without leaving a message, she hung up and texted, "Did you mean this for me?" Then she set the phone down on the passenger seat, pulled out of the driveway, and headed home.

There was no logical reason for Mack to have sent her that message. More likely, he'd meant it for his assistant, Nolan Pierce. But why include the access codes?

Surely Nolan already knew them, unless Mack had changed them without telling him. She'd met Nolan in December and learned he handled most of the background checks for Mack's cases. At nine thirty, it was well past business hours, even for a PI. If Mack needed something from the office, why contact her instead of Nolan? Maybe he wasn't available. Maybe Mack had a new hire. Or maybe the message was meant for someone else entirely.

Dismissing it as an accidental text, she pushed it out of her mind and turned her attention to tomorrow's agenda. She planned to spend the morning and early afternoon writing copy for her column. That evening, around seven, she would head to Sophia's clinic. She'd promised to join Sophia, along with her mother and grandmother, Maria and Josefina, as they baked goodies for Sunday's playground dedication. Olivia doubted she'd be much help in the kitchen, but for her, it was mostly an excuse to visit Sophia and her family. Whenever the three generations got together, it was always a good time, full of unfiltered, no-holds-barred conversation.

About halfway home, she glanced at her phone and tapped the screen. A photo of Buddy and Willow appeared, but still no reply from Mack.

That's just so odd.

It had to be a mistake. But if she'd received the message, that meant Nolan, or whoever Mack had intended it for, hadn't. Curiosity niggled at her. She pulled onto the shoulder, leaving the car running with the lights on for safety. Picking up the phone, she reread the text. It still didn't make sense, but it was clear Mack wanted someone to go to his office immediately and retrieve that file.

Mack wasn't careless. If anything, he was always thinking several steps ahead. As a PI, he had to anticipate scenarios and react quickly to changing circumstances. She called him again. Same result. Straight to voicemail.

When she'd asked for his help back in May, he'd agreed despite having no personal stake in the matter. He'd put himself in harm's way and walked away with a bloody nose and a sprained knee for his trouble. What if Mack had intended the message for her? He had to know she'd find the request strange. But if he'd sent it expecting her to act, could she really ignore it?

She glanced at the clock. Nine forty-five. From here, it would take less than thirty minutes to get to Winchester. She exhaled sharply, drumming her thumbs on the wheel. Headlights filled her rearview mirror as a car approached, then sped past.

I wouldn't be breaking and entering. He gave me the codes, and I have his written permission.

The longer she debated, the more curiosity turned into concern, and that would be enough to keep her up all night if she did nothing. Checking her mirrors, she made a U-turn and headed north to Winchester.

Within half an hour, she pulled into the parking lot of the red brick building where Mack's office was located. The area was well lit—great for safety, but not so great for keeping a low profile. She hadn't expected anyone to be around, but the empty lot didn't put her at ease. There had to be cameras on the premises, maybe even real-time security monitoring. But armed with the key codes, she shouldn't trigger any alarms when she entered. If she ran into anyone, she was ready with her explanation.

She got out of the car with her phone in hand, locked up, and hurried toward the front, keeping her head on a swivel. At the main entrance, she keyed in the code, opened the door, and headed straight for Mack's suite at the end of the hallway.

The gold "Mack and Associates" nameplate on the door was pure marketing. Nolan had once told her there were no other associates, but projecting the image of a larger firm was better for business. She peered through the narrow windows on either side of the door. A sofa, a table, and two chairs sat exactly as she remembered from her last visit. Without a second's delay, she entered the code, turned the handle, and stepped into the office.

Something felt off, as if she were walking into a setup. She'd half expected the codes not to work or to be blocked by some kind of security measure, like needing to hit the pound key before or after the numbers. The ease of it all left her wary, and she couldn't shake the feeling that Mack or someone else was orchestrating a trap.

She flipped the three switches by the door, lighting up the suite. Two floor lamps cast a warm yellow glow in the waiting room, while a bright white overhead light illuminated the area behind the glass-enclosed reception desk. She scanned the ceiling corners for cameras, then glanced through the window, certain someone might burst through the door at any moment.

Moving quickly, she crossed to the door that separated the waiting room from the back and entered the final code. The lock disengaged, and within seconds, she was behind the scenes at Mack and Associates. A short hallway lay ahead, but her target was to the right. The cabinet Mack had referenced stood just inside, across from the reception desk.

She crouched, opened the bottom drawer, and rifled through the files. Finding the one labeled "Winters," she straightened, turned, and set it on the counter.

Mack had asked someone to take the file, but she had no idea why. He'd given permission for it to be removed, but had he meant for *her* to do so? If security caught her, what would she even say? That a man she didn't work for had asked her to retrieve a file from his office after hours? The more she ran that story in her head, the less believable it sounded.

She trusted Mack to a point. But she wasn't about to involve herself further by taking the file with her. Instead, she opened it and, without reading the contents, photographed everything with her phone. There were about fifteen pages, including printouts, copies of public records, and handwritten notes. Once finished, she closed the folder and returned it to the cabinet.

The moment the drawer snapped shut, she hustled back to the waiting room, turned off the lights, and left the office. She checked the door lock behind her, then hurried down the hallway and out of the building.

As soon as she got behind the wheel, she pressed the start button and shifted into drive, fastening her seatbelt with one hand while speeding away. A quarter mile down the road, she turned into the well-lit lot of a big-box store. After parking near the back, she shut off the engine and turned on the cabin lights.

Opening her photos, she skimmed through the images of the file's contents. It appeared to be a background check on a thirty-two-year-old home health aide named Amy Winters. Born in Georgia, she'd lived in North Carolina, Maryland, and Virginia. She held a nursing degree and had ten years of clinical experience.

Olivia swiped through the images, trying to figure out why this file mattered so much to Mack. Nothing stood out until she read the top line on a page of handwritten notes. Amy Winters, who currently lived in Luray, had been employed for the past twelve months as a home health aide for Fiona Campbell.

CHAPTER 7

By noon on Wednesday, Olivia had completed two of the three columns she'd planned to write that day. Finishing them all would put her ahead of schedule. If she powered through the rest of the week, she could bank some columns and maybe even take time off soon.

Tomorrow afternoon, she had an online Q&A for work, the last one she'd be doing with Angela. The hour-long open forum was a rapid-fire version of her column, with readers peppering "Ms. Penn" with their most pressing questions. They had both expected Angela to be in Vermont by now, handling last-minute preparations for the grand opening of her B&B. But delays with contractors, along with an unexpected roof repair, had pushed her departure back and extended her time at the paper through August.

Olivia stood up and stretched, glancing at Willow napping on the cat tree by the window. The cat often accompanied her to the office on weekday mornings. She took a sip from her thermos, debating whether to save her third column for after lunch. Willow stirred, got up, and reversed her curled position before settling again. Other than a few pictures she'd taken of Willow, her phone had stayed idle all morning, making the stack of papers on her desk even more mysterious. Sitting down, she pushed her laptop aside and slid the pages in front of her.

Last night, she'd printed all the photos of Mack's file. He hadn't returned her calls or texts yet. Her call to his office that morning had gone straight to voicemail, suggesting Nolan was either with him or unavailable. Even if the message hadn't been meant for her, she would've expected at least a quick follow-up about the mix-up.

Still, there was no reason to overreact. Mack was known for limiting communication during active cases, sharing his whereabouts only with those on a need-to-know basis. She didn't flatter herself by thinking she was on that list.

The file had provided plenty of late-night reading. Mack hadn't told her to look through it, but he also hadn't told her not to. He had to know she'd read it, so she considered it fair game. A deeper dive had confirmed her initial impression: the file was a background check on Amy Winters. The level of detail was unsettling, tracking Amy's life from the time she graduated from college to the present. Mack or Nolan had documented every address and phone number associated with her since she was twenty-one.

Someone had commissioned the investigation, and Olivia wondered if that person had been Fiona or a member of her family. Amy had worked as Fiona's aide for about a year, yet the documents showed the research had been initiated in June. That didn't make sense. Why would Fiona, or anyone, hire a PI to look into Amy's past after she'd already been on the job for ten months?

With Fiona's death last night and no word from Mack, his urgent text wasn't feeling like a coincidence. But without context, Olivia couldn't begin to piece together how they were connected.

From what Preston had said, she got the impression Craig and his aunt hadn't been particularly close. Yet his name appeared once in the file. On a page of hand-written notes, there was a record of a call Mack had with him a month ago. Next to Craig's name, Mack had written "unaware."

She flipped through the pages again. *What did you want me to do with this?*

Nothing about Amy stood out to Olivia, except for her career change. Until two years ago, she'd worked as a nurse. Several hospitals and assisted-living facilities were listed among her former employers. Olivia knew nurses were underpaid, but still assumed their salary was higher than that of a home health aide.

Amy's last nursing position had been at a long-term care facility in North Carolina. Next to that note in the file was the name Gladys Henderson, along with a date of death that coincided with Amy's employment there.

She slid her laptop closer, opened a browser, and typed into the search box: "Gladys Henderson, obituary, North Carolina." The first page of results displayed obituaries for a few women with the same name. Scanning the snippets, she found one that matched the year of death in the file. She clicked the link and skimmed the obituary. It mentioned the care home where Amy had worked but said nothing about the facility itself, only that Gladys had been a resident there. She had died at the age of eighty, leaving behind two daughters. One lived in Texas, while the other, Linda Lacoste, resided in the same county as the facility.

There had to be some significant connection between Gladys and Amy. Was it just a coincidence that Amy stopped working as a nurse around the time Gladys died?

Next, Olivia searched the facility's name along with the terms, death investigation, lawsuit, negligence, and Gladys Henderson. Nothing relevant came up, so she set that angle aside for now.

Another thought struck her. Maybe Mack hadn't been the one who linked Gladys to Amy. Could Gladys have been a friend of Fiona's? If Gladys had known Amy, maybe her daughters did too. Olivia searched for Linda Lacoste along with the name of the county where she lived. The first half-page of results all pointed to the same woman, a principal at Homewood Elementary School.

Opening a mapping site, she entered the names of both the care facility and the school. A five-minute drive between the two all but confirmed she'd found the right Linda Lacoste. She scrolled back to the top of the results and clicked the link to Homewood Elementary. Navigating to the administration page, she found Linda's picture above the fold. Beside it were her bio and her contact information, including an e-mail address and a phone number.

She swiveled her seat and debated calling. But what would she even say? She imagined the conversation: "Hi, I know I'm a complete stranger, but do you have any suspicions that Amy Winters was involved in your mother's death?" *Yeah, that wouldn't work.*

A familiar *thump* interrupted her thoughts. Willow had jumped down from the cat tree and was sitting by the door, a telltale sign she wanted out. Olivia stood, shut her laptop, and went over to scoop her up. After turning off the air conditioner and lights, she locked up and carried the cat across the yard and into the house through the kitchen.

Her father sat at the table with a bowl of soup and the newspaper's crossword puzzle in front of him.

"Soup's on if you want some," he said.

She set the cat down and grabbed a banana from the crystal dish on the counter. "I'm not that hungry. I had a big breakfast."

"Did you find out any more about that job?"

Between her columns and Mack's cryptic message

dominating her bandwidth, she hadn't given Carolyn's offer much thought since yesterday. "Not yet."

"Are you going to?"

She wanted to speak with Sam first to get her take on the whole thing. How, and why, had Carolyn zeroed in on her as a recruit? "Maybe. I'm not sure if it's right for me."

"It can't hurt to talk to them."

"No, I suppose not."

She peeled the banana, broke off a piece, and popped it into her mouth.

"You were an English major. You should know this one," he said, tapping his pencil on the crossword. "I need a six-letter word for the clue 'a fleeting presence in Macbeth's reflection on life.'"

She finished chewing, then tossed the peel in the trash. "Shakespeare. *Macbeth*. 'Life's but a walking shadow, a poor player that struts and frets his hour upon the stage and then is heard no more.' Shadow."

"Ah-ha! That's it." He penciled in the answer. "If you don't think this research job is for you, you could always teach English. Not to young kids. I mean, like, as a college professor."

She set the banana on a napkin and took out a container of yogurt from the refrigerator. "Not really interested in that."

Carolyn's offer intrigued her, as did the idea of working with Mack. "Do you remember John Mack, the PI from Winchester?"

"I do."

"In May, he hinted at the two of us working together. I don't know how serious he was, but he seemed to be."

"Doing what?"

"I'm not sure."

"Don't you need a license to be a PI?"

She pulled a spoon from the drawer, picked up her food, and sat across from him. "You have to be registered and complete a certain number of training hours."

"Seems like you've already looked into it."

"Just out of curiosity. I don't think Mack was offering a partnership. He has one assistant, and maybe he needs more help on that side of the business."

"That sounds interesting, but it's a small company. Probably no health care or retirement plan."

"Yeah, I know."

"Have you talked to him about it?"

"No, and he doesn't seem to be reachable right now. He texted me last night." As she ate, she told him about Fiona's death, Mack's message, and her trip to Winchester. From past sleuthing, she'd learned that keeping her father in the loop whenever she got involved in police matters was the best policy. When she finished, she asked, "Did you know Fiona?"

"No, but I know the house you're talking about. I used to see her out in the yard with a young woman, probably your age. I bet she was the home health aide. Why do you think Mack wanted you to take the file?"

"I don't know. It's possible he texted me by mistake, but I don't think he did."

"Is Fiona's death suspicious?"

She stood, tossed her trash in the bin, and wiped her hands on a towel. "I haven't talked to Preston about it yet."

"You can shut the stove off. The soup's plenty hot."

She turned off the burner, rinsed her spoon, and put it back in the drawer.

"So, you've got a missing PI who might be connected to Fiona's death," he said. "Sounds like something interesting to look into. If you need help—"

"Hold up, dear Watson," she cut in. "This could be much ado about nothing. I'm going to wait it out. I think Mack will reach out to me at some point. I called his office earlier, but there was no answer. Maybe I'll try again later."

"Well, what about that other job? When will you find out more about that?"

"I don't have any contact information for them, but I know someone who does."

"Then you should talk to them and get the number."

"I think I will. I'll be out for a while." She stepped over and kissed him on the cheek. Then she left through the kitchen, walked around to the front, and crossed the yard, heading for Sam's house.

CHAPTER 8

"I'm not keeping you, am I?" Olivia asked, stepping into Sam's house.

A duffel bag and a backpack sat just inside the entrance. As always, Sam was dressed with a tactical edge: ranger-green pants, a black T-shirt, and sturdy boots with lug soles, ready for any terrain.

"I have a few minutes," Sam said, closing the door behind her.

They crossed the living room and sat on the sofa.

"What's up?" Sam asked.

"I saw Carolyn in town yesterday." Olivia waited for a reaction, but Sam gave nothing away. "Does she live around here?"

"Recently she's been spending more time nearby, but she still travels a lot."

"I imagine so." She rubbed her hands together, then got to the point. "She offered me a job."

Sam nodded slowly, unsurprised.

"You knew?"

"Yes. We discussed it."

"Why didn't you say anything to me?"

Sam gave a small, almost apologetic shrug. "Not my place or my call. I know you used to be a beat reporter, and when the opportunity came up to start your advice column, you felt it was the right time to switch gears. Back in May, you said you were thinking about another change. I asked if you'd be open to something completely different, and you said yes."

"And working for Carolyn was what you meant?"

"Correct."

Olivia shook her head. "It's definitely different. At first, I thought she meant I'd be doing the kind of work you're involved in. She shut that down fast and basically said I'd be a goner on day one."

Sam laughed softly. "I wouldn't say that. But no, that's not what she had in mind. And you make my job sound more dangerous than it is. Sticky situations are few and far between."

"I guess I'm flattered she even considered me. I get the sense candidates are recruited and thoroughly vetted. I doubt Carolyn is placing help-wanted ads. She probably knows things about me I've forgotten. But I don't have experience in national policy or legal matters. I don't think I'm qualified."

Sam folded her arms. "You are. The job isn't about policy. It's about research."

"What exactly does that mean?"

"As an analyst, it means gathering data, spotting patterns, and making connections. Analysts act as a think tank, providing the field ops with the intel we need. Honestly, I don't know anyone more qualified or someone I'd trust more than you."

That sounded like weighty work. The occupational hazards went far beyond fielding e-mails from disgruntled readers or missing deadlines.

"We make tactical decisions based on the analysis we're given," Sam continued. "You'd be a researcher, assessing intelligence to evaluate risks, develop contingencies, and forecast outcomes. Mostly, it involves staring at a screen and writing reports. It's not a normal nine-to-five, if that's what you're looking for. Things happen off-hours, and you might be on call. But there's a lot of flexibility. You see I'm home a good bit. We don't always have active ops running. Sometimes we're just monitoring situations long term."

This was a far cry from what Olivia was doing now. Her job was relatively stress-free, especially since moving back to Apple Station. She'd only considered writing-related opportunities, aside from Mack's roundabout proposition. But she had to admit that the sleuthing she'd done over the past year had sparked something in her. Though she could've done without her life being in peril, the investigations had energized her and put her in the zone.

"I'd be lying if I said I wasn't interested. The work

sounds fascinating, and Carolyn said she'd double my salary. I'm not sure if she meant that literally, but that's a very generous offer."

"You were already on her radar before we discovered the mole in May. I told her about you after I'd gotten to know you better and saw how effective you were at investigating when you had skin in the game. It's a big change, and I wasn't sure you'd be interested. I know John Mack floated the idea of you joining his firm, and that seemed to get your attention."

Olivia nodded, exhaling slowly. "You're not wrong about that. FYI, Mack seems to be missing."

"What do you mean?"

"Maybe 'missing' isn't the right word." She gave Sam a condensed version of yesterday's events.

When she finished, Sam asked, "Do you want me to see if I can find out anything?"

"No, not yet anyway. It hasn't even been twenty-four hours. But it's weird. You know what else is weird?"

Sam raised an eyebrow. "You considering a job as an analyst on a black-budget team?"

"Fair point, but no. Something even weirder. Rhett is your brother-in-law, and you never told me. What's up with that? I thought he was a private security consultant."

"Valid point. But you've met him. Would you want to claim him as family?" she joked. "Kidding aside, he's a solid guy. Rhett and I hadn't crossed paths much for a couple of years until December. He'd been working mostly overseas, gathering foreign intel. He kept floating the idea of partnering up, but after my time in the Corps, I preferred life stateside. Carolyn reassigned him in January after finding out about his freelance work. She shut that down fast, and we've been working together ever since."

Olivia stood and went over to the mantel, where a framed picture of Sam's late husband sat. "Did Aaron and Rhett have the same father?"

"Yes. Rhett is older. They're both from Carolyn's second marriage. Their father died of cancer."

Olivia studied Aaron's photo. With his sparkling eyes and bright smile, he looked like a Top Gun pilot. "That actually makes me feel a little sympathy for Carolyn. Were they born in the U.S.?"

Sam got up. "Yes, both were raised in San Diego."

"Every time I looked at this picture, I thought there was something familiar about Aaron." She turned toward Sam. "Now I see it. It's because he looks like Rhett."

"They do look alike, especially their eyes."

"I saw Rhett yesterday. I was floored when he called Carolyn 'Mum.'"

"I can imagine." Sam looked at the photo for a moment. "So, now that you know more about the job, what do you think?"

"I'm just not sure I'm right for it. It might be more intense than what I was looking for."

"That's understandable."

"I also don't want to leave Apple Station if that's required."

"It's not."

"Do you have an office nearby?"

"Actually, I was heading out there before you showed up. Would you like to come and take a look?"

She jumped at the chance to get a peek behind the curtain of Carolyn's operation. Her third column could wait. Since Sam had already been on her way out, they left after Olivia got her car.

As she followed Sam, Olivia tried to guess where they were going. She kept an eye out for office buildings, industrial parks, or discreet retail spaces that could serve as a front for their operations. She didn't know how many people were on Carolyn's team or what kind of setup they used. For sure there would be a high level of security in the building. She'd probably have to go through a checkpoint and get a visitor's badge before reaching the lobby.

But after twenty minutes of driving, she was no closer to figuring it out. They were on the road that would take them past the new turnoff to A.J.'s property. From that entrance, he'd built three roads during the playground construction to keep traffic separate. One led to his house, another to the playground, and the third stretched to the far end of the property, where the other home-owner lived. Since the buyer had funded that road's construction, A.J. hadn't objected to the land being cleared. The private road could serve future development if he ever decided to sell more parcels.

She considered voice-dialing Sam for a hint about their destination, but Sam's brake lights answered for her. Sam turned onto the road leading to A.J.'s property. Confused, Olivia sat up straighter as she followed, wondering if they were meeting Carolyn at the playground for some reason.

At the fork, Sam veered onto the road Olivia had never traveled. In a beat, the fog lifted, and the realization jolted her like thunder on a cloudless day. The home, the road, the mystery buyer A.J. had never met. Carolyn.

Olivia's stomach flipped. Carolyn must've targeted the property as soon as he took ownership, possibly even before. How much did she know about its history? Had Carolyn been watching her all this time? Olivia wasn't sure if she felt blindsided or impressed. Maybe both. If Carolyn had gone to this much trouble to stay out of sight, what else could she be hiding?

Trees bordered the two-lane asphalt road, which cut across mostly flat terrain. As they drove farther, Olivia glanced into the forest, certain security cameras had to be hidden somewhere.

She followed Sam around a gentle bend where the dense forest thinned, revealing a wide clearing. There, nestled at its edge, stood a stunning ranch-style house. The sprawling home had multiple wings and a stone exterior that blended rustic charm with modern elegance. Large windows, wood accents, and lush land-scaping gave it a warmth worthy of a magazine cover.

They drove around to the back of the complex and parked alongside two black SUVs and a white Mercedes. Once out of her car, Olivia took in the quiet, almost eerie serenity of the area. For a place so tucked away, it seemed surprisingly accessible. No warning signs, no gates, no obvious security measures. Then again, there was only one way in and out. If any curiosity seekers made it this far, the sheer sight of the estate-like home would scream private property.

"Let's go to the front," Sam said. "That'll give you a proper introduction."

They followed a walkway around the building.

"How long has this been here?" Olivia asked.

"It was completed about three months ago. The building itself went up quickly, but we couldn't use it until Carolyn had the tactical infrastructure in place."

At the entrance, Sam keyed in a code on the panel beside the door. With a quiet beep, the lock disengaged. She opened the door and motioned Olivia inside. "Come on, let me show you around."

Stunned, Olivia took in the space, which looked more like a luxury home in Aspen than the base of operations for a black-budget team. She'd been expecting cold and utilitarian, not natural wood beams, soft lighting, and upscale finishes. As they walked down a hallway, Sam gestured to various rooms, naming them in turn: office, conference, kitchen, tactical, communications.

Olivia tried to absorb it all, but the setting clashed so starkly with what she'd expected that most of Sam's words got lost in the dissonance. It felt more like a ski lodge than a classified operations hub. An armory next to a kitchen that smelled like pumpkin spice? That was going to take a minute to process.

"As you can see, things are pretty quiet around here," Sam said. "What do you think so far?"

"I don't know about working here, but I could definitely live here."

Sam gave a small smile. "You and Carolyn could have late-night girl chats then."

"Does she stay here?"

"Since construction was finished."

Sam led her through the kitchen and dining room, then into a large open space overlooking a stone-paved patio with a firepit. A saddle-tan leather sectional faced the floor-to-ceiling windows. On the couch sat someone Olivia already knew.

The last time she'd seen Mark, he'd been posing as a Mormon, checking in on her after she'd tried to reach Sam through an emergency contact number. A laptop sat open on the coffee table in front of him. When he glanced up at Olivia, his expression was less than welcoming.

Thinking he might not recognize her, Olivia said, "Hi, Mark. We've met before. I'm Olivia Penn. You came to my house."

He looked at Sam, hesitant.

"It's okay," Sam assured him. "She knows."

His face softened with a smile. "Sorry. I remember you. It's just that we've never had a visitor here."

A sharp whistling tune drifted in from the dining room. Olivia turned as Rhett entered. When he saw her, he stopped mid-melody and stared. No flirtatious charm. No easy grin.

"What's she doing here?" he asked.

"Carolyn wants her to join the team," Sam replied.

Rhett's eyes narrowed. "As what?"

"An analyst," Sam said.

Mark shot up from the couch. "Really? That'd be awesome. I'm so swamped with work."

Rhett's expression shifted from suspicious to pleased in a second flat. He flashed a grin and winked at Olivia. "That would make this place even more charming. Welcome aboard."

"I'm only looking around," Olivia clarified.

Before Rhett could respond, Carolyn entered from the adjoining hallway, and the room went silent.

Sam turned to Carolyn. "I brought her to show her the setup."

Carolyn gave a small nod. "Very well. Carry on." She disappeared into the dining room, heading toward the front of the complex.

"Wow, Carolyn must really like you," Mark said.

Rhett checked his watch. "Sam, we've got the meeting in five."

"I'll be there. Go ahead, get ready."

Rhett looked at Olivia. "Good to see you again. Two days in a row. How about we make it three?" With another wink, he walked off.

Mark picked up his laptop and closed the screen. "I'll see you in there," he said to Sam. Then, to Olivia, he added, "I hope you join us. If you've gotten this far, Carolyn has already made up her mind about you."

Once Mark left, Sam looked at her watch. "I have this meeting in a couple of minutes. It should last about half an hour. You can stick around, and I'll show you more when I'm done."

She shook her head. "No, I don't want to take you away from your day. I think I've seen enough."

"Alright. I'll walk you out."

As they made their way to the front, Olivia took one last look around. She couldn't have asked for a better working environment. Gorgeous setting, close to home … and close to A.J.'s house. That raised a complication she hadn't considered. She'd only learned about the true nature of Sam's work out of necessity. If she accepted this position, what would that mean for her? Who could she even tell? Would she have to keep this a secret from her father and Preston? What about A.J. and Sophia, her two best friends? Sam had kept her own work a secret from Olivia. But Olivia didn't want a job that required lying to the people closest to her.

As Sam opened the front door, Olivia's phone buzzed with a call. She slipped it from her pocket and checked the screen. Preston.

"I'll let you get that," Sam said, nodding toward the phone. "We'll talk later."

"Sounds good."

After a quick goodbye, Sam closed the door as Olivia answered the call.

"Hey there," she said.

"How are you doing?" he asked.

"That's a layered question."

"Are you at home?"

"No." She glanced around, admiring the stone exterior. A hawk screeched from its perch on the roof. "I'm at … Sam's office, if that's what you want to call it."

After a long pause, he said, "I'm not sure I want to know why you're there."

"Yeah, I'm not sure you do either. How are you?"

"Busy and tired."

"Late night?"

"Yeah."

"What happened with Craig's aunt?"

"It's not good. Hold on." His voice lowered for a moment as he spoke to someone in the background. Returning to the line, he said, "Let me call you back. I need to talk to you about something."

"I'm near town. I can stop by the station."

"I'm actually at the inn right now."

"Even better. Want me to come by?"

"Yeah. I'll wait here."

"Can I buy a vowel? What's this about?"

"I need you to tell me everything you know about John Mack."

CHAPTER 9

Ever the entrepreneur, Bev had transformed the Apple Station Inn for the week, sparing no expense in decking it out for the Highland Games. For the past month, she'd flooded social media, targeting D.C. dwellers and Northern Virginia suburbanites with the promise of an authentic old-country experience for a fraction of the cost of flying across the pond.

Stepping into the lobby, Olivia felt swept away to eighteenth-century Scotland. St. Andrew's Cross flags adorned every corner, and amber-stained whisky barrels flanked the front desk. The usual artwork of rural Virginia landscapes had been swapped for paintings of Scottish castles, rolling hills, and family clan crests. A round table covered by a blue, green, and yellow tartan cloth showcased a set of bagpipes and a bodhrán, while lively piped-in fiddle music filled the air. The dimmed lights allowed the temporary faux-gas lanterns mounted on the walls to cast a flickering glow, even at midday.

A pot of Scottish tea sat beside the French roast and decaf carafes on the coffee cart. At Sunday brunch, Olivia had learned that the tea had a rich, malty flavor, much stronger than Earl Grey. A card by the pot suggested pairing it with cream and sugar for an authentic taste, which she agreed was the best way to go.

Several guests milled around the lobby, admiring the artwork, while a young couple browsed a souvenir table outside the dining room. The display featured tartan scarves, miniature terrier figurines, shortbread tins, and postcards of the Highlands.

A woman stood at the unattended reception desk with a suitcase resting beside her. Olivia guessed Preston might be in one of the offices in back, possibly speaking with Bev. Rather than risk interrupting, she decided to wait for Zoey, the inn's usual weekday concierge, to return for confirmation.

As she approached the desk, the woman turned slightly toward her. "Nobody seems to be around."

"The front is always staffed," Olivia assured her. "Someone will be here shortly."

The woman, likely in her mid-fifties, wore a gauzy cream duster over jeans and a white T-shirt. "Well, it's certainly charming," she said. "Very *Outlander*-chic."

"Are you here for the Highland Games?"

Shaking her head, the woman reached into a basket beside a vase of heather and thistle on the counter and picked up a Loch Ness Monster keychain. "No, but that explains this. I thought it was an odd souvenir for a small town in Virginia. I'd expect more Bigfoot than Nessie."

"Maybe next year," she replied with a laugh.

When the woman turned fully toward her, Olivia did a double take, locking in on her eyes. One was green, the other blue.

"Heterochromia," the woman said with a knowing nod. "The eyes, right?"

"Sorry for the not-so-subtle stare. They're stunning."

"No need to apologize. I get that all the time."

"I guess you would. So, are you vacationing?"

"Not exactly. I just needed to get away from the world for a while. Unplug. Go off the grid, so to speak."

"I can understand the feeling. Apple Station is a good place for that. There are lovely shops in town to explore, all within easy walking distance."

"I don't plan on venturing out. I think I'll stay in and get caught up on my reading."

"That's what I'd like to be doing too. My TBR pile is practically a skyscraper. If you run out of books, there's a great local bookstore nearby called Tales and Treasures."

"Thank you. I'll keep that in mind."

Out of the corner of her eye, Olivia caught Bev coming down the stairs. "Here's your help now," she said, stepping aside to give the woman space to check in. "Enjoy your stay."

Bev crossed the lobby and gave Olivia a welcoming smile before rounding the desk to assist the guest. A few moments later, the woman wheeled her suitcase toward the stairs and headed up to the second floor.

Olivia stepped up to the counter, admiring Bev's commitment to going all in with her wardrobe. She wore a mid-length red and green tartan kilt and a white blouse adorned with a silver Celtic knot pin. A matching plaid shawl draped her shoulders, and a black beret sat atop her head.

"Business is booming, Bev."

"We haven't been this booked in ages. And these men competing in the Games? My Lord, they can eat. This week is going to be more profitable for the restaurant than the holidays were. Will you be coming to the whisky tasting tonight?"

"I don't think so. I'm not much of a drinker."

Bev tilted the basket of keychains toward her. "Did you see these? Aren't they adorable? Take one."

"They are cute. Thank you," Olivia replied, picking one out. She dug her keys out of her pocket and attached the trinket to her ring. "Where's Zoey?"

"She's taking care of some deliveries. Did you need her?"

"No, I'm here to meet Preston. Is he around?"

"He's in my office, looking at security footage."

"Did something happen?"

"Not here. You may not have known her, but Fiona Campbell was found dead last night in her home."

Olivia leaned over the counter, lowering her voice. "I was with Preston when her nephew called after finding her. What's the connection between the security footage and her death?"

"I'm not sure. Preston didn't say."

I wonder whether it involves Mack. "Did you know Fiona?"

Bev nodded. "Wonderful woman. She came here to eat once or twice a month."

"Alone?"

"No, usually with her aide. Fiona seemed to get around okay with a cane, but I got the impression she just liked having the company."

"Are you talking about Amy Winters?"

"Yes, do you know her?"

Olivia shook her head. "Only by name."

"She must be heartbroken. If you didn't know better, you'd think Fiona and Amy were mother and daughter."

Olivia glanced over her shoulder, sensing someone had come up behind her. "I'll let you go. Good to see you."

"Haste ye back!" Bev said. "That means come back soon. And don't forget, try to make it tonight for the tasting. We'll have lighter libations for the teetotaler-minded."

"I'll do my best to haste back," Olivia replied with a smile before heading for the rear of the lobby.

She slipped through the door to the back, treading lightly toward Bev's office and peeking around the doorframe to make sure Preston was alone.

"Hey there," she said, stepping inside.

He looked up from the computer screen, then rose and came around the desk to greet her. They fell into a hug that could've lasted forever, as neither seemed eager to let go.

When they finally separated, she said, "You look stressed."

He rubbed his forehead, his expression heavy, as if carrying a load.

"What's wrong?" she asked.

He closed the door, then motioned for her to join him. "Have a seat."

She sat in a chair across from him at Bev's desk. "If this is a bad time, I can come back."

"No, it's fine. Thank you for coming."

"Why do you want to know about Mack?"

He dragged a hand down his face. "Early this morning, around five, the station received a call about a car found in a ditch off Old Mill Highway. We ran the plates. It's registered to Mack."

She shot to the edge of her seat. "Is he okay?"

"We can't locate him. There's no answer at his office in Winchester. I sent a deputy to his home, but no one was there. His neighbors say they haven't seen him for a few days. The airbag had deployed, and the car sustained substantial damage. But we didn't find any blood or signs of injury."

Her stomach tightened. *Did he send the text before or after the crash?* "He must've called someone to pick him up."

But then why did he ask me to get the file instead of coming to help him?

"Maybe. We found a phone about halfway between the road and the forest line."

"Is it his?"

"We're not sure. It's locked and has no ID. We'd need a subpoena to access the owner's information from the carrier. But since there's no evidence of a crime, that'd probably be denied."

"What about just calling his number to see if it rings?"

"We found his business card at Fiona's house with an office number listed, but it's not a match."

She pulled her phone from her pocket. "Lucky for you that you have connections." After finding Mack's number in her contacts, she texted it to him.

His phone lit up on the desk. Tilting the screen, he raised an eyebrow. "Should I ask why you have his number saved?"

"You never know when it might come in handy. Like now. He could have more than one phone, but that's the only number I have."

"Thanks. I'll check it out."

"What do you think happened to him?"

Preston leaned back. "Someone picked him up, either somebody he called or maybe a passing driver. We're not sure when the crash occurred."

"He could be at a friend's house."

"That's possible. The forest around where his car was

found is like a jungle. When we searched the tree line, we found what looked like a fresh trail of trampled foliage leading into the woods. We followed it for about twenty yards, but then it stopped. There are trails back there, so I called several neighboring police departments to see if I could get a K-9 unit to search, but all the local teams are tied up."

She sank back in the seat. "Why would he go into the woods after he crashed? That doesn't make any sense."

"I agree, but I want to follow up on that trail. A friend of mine at the Page County Sheriff's Office put me in touch with someone from their volunteer search and rescue team." He picked up a sticky note from the desk and glanced at it. "Summer King. She has a golden retriever that my friend says has helped find missing people. She's in North Carolina this week for training with her dog, but when I called, she said she'd drive up right away. They might not arrive until late today. If that's the case, we'll wait until tomorrow morning to search."

Questions popped into Olivia's mind faster than a firecracker's fuse. Why did Mack crash? Where was he? Was he okay?

Knowing it was time to fess up, she said, "I have something to tell you about Mack." She walked Preston through last night's events, then explained what she'd found in Mack's file. He listened without interrupting, and when she finished, she asked, "Do you want me to give you the printouts?"

"Hold off on that for now. We may have to access that file through the proper channels. Using you as the source wouldn't cut it legally, especially if Mack is involved."

"Involved in what? How did Fiona die?"

"We don't know yet. Craig found her in the hallway on the second floor. There were no signs of trauma, but she could've fallen and had internal bleeding. Based on her physical appearance, the paramedics suspected a heart attack. The medical examiner might have preliminary results in a day or two. The full report, including toxicology, will take four to six weeks."

"From what you said last night, it sounds like there was a break-in?"

He nodded. "Craig found the door open. There were no signs of forced entry, but a small table near the entrance had been knocked over. A few minutes before Craig contacted me, the station got a call from Fiona's closest neighbor, about thirty yards from her house, reporting they'd heard gunshots."

"But she wasn't shot."

"No, but we found two bullet holes in the wall by the door and casings on the steps."

"Then who was shooting at who?" she said rhetorically. "And if Craig found her upstairs, that makes it unlikely she was involved in a struggle downstairs. So if the door wasn't busted, someone either picked the lock or had a key."

"Or Fiona didn't lock it. There's no deadbolt on the door. Just a standard keyed lock and a chain."

Was Mack there last night? He couldn't possibly be involved in her death.

"Why do you think Mack contacted you?"

She felt guarded, not wanting to cast suspicion on Mack, but circumstances weren't looking good for him.

"Do you really think he's involved somehow?" she asked.

"The only thing connecting him to Fiona until now was his business card. But after what you told me, along with the wrecked car and the fact that he's nowhere to be found, he's a person of interest."

"I've been trying to figure out why he reached out to me. Now that he's missing, I don't know what to say. I thought I'd hear from him today."

"I know what you two went through in May at Spring Hills, but how well do you really know him?"

The truth? Not very well. She wanted to believe there was no way Mack could be involved in Fiona's death. But without him available to explain himself, there were too many questions.

"I can't see him hurting anyone," she said. "Your mother told me you were reviewing security footage connected to Fiona's death. Does it involve Mack?"

Preston pressed his lips together, hesitant to answer.

"I understand if you can't tell me."

"You know I trust you. Mack pulled you into this for a reason, and if he contacts you again, I need to know about it." His jaw tightened. "There's something else. When I asked Craig about his timeline last night, he told me he was at Allen's Tavern until seven, then came back here until he left for Fiona's house. But remember in May, when my mom upgraded the security system? She installed an extra camera in the lobby to get a clearer view of the front entrance. The footage shows that Craig didn't return to the inn until after we released him from the scene. That wasn't until around ten."

"He lied to you?"

Preston nodded, his frown as grim as a funeral procession.

"You don't really think he had anything to do with her death, do you?"

"I have to consider all the possibilities. It's my job."

"But why? What motive would he have?"

"Money. I asked if Fiona had any other relatives. Turns out, she had none. Craig is her sole heir. He stands to gain the most from her death."

She read his eyes, finishing the thought for him. "And he needs the money for his wife and family."

CHAPTER 10

The office door swung open, cutting off Olivia and Preston's conversation.

"I didn't realize you were still in here," Bev said, stepping inside. "I'll let you two be."

Preston clicked the mouse a few times, then stood and came around the desk. "I'm done here. I have to get back to the station."

"Did you find what you needed on the footage?" Bev asked.

"Unfortunately, yes."

"I'll walk out with you," Olivia said.

After saying goodbye to Bev, they left the office, passed through the lobby, and exited the inn. Once on the sidewalk, they turned to face each other.

"I'm parked around back," he said.

"I'm down the street. What are you going to do about Craig?"

"I don't know yet."

"It seems like a stretch to think he'd be involved."

"But with no signs of forced entry, Fiona could've let him in. I'm sure she had valuables. If he needed money …"

She took his hand. "I know you have to consider every angle, but do you really believe he's capable of harming his own aunt?"

"I don't know. With the gunshots and Mack missing, the trails are leading in different directions."

"For what it's worth, I don't think Mack could be involved."

"He contacted you for a reason. If he reaches out again—"

"I know. I'll call you right away." She squeezed his hand, then let go.

"Okay, I should be off."

"Be careful."

They exchanged a hug and a quick kiss before parting ways. Olivia turned and headed toward her car parked near Carol's Comforts. Passing the newspaper suite, she glanced in the window. She had no set schedule for going into the office to write her weekly pro bono advice column. Truth be told, she could easily finish the short feature from home, but she enjoyed catching up with her friends. As long as she gave Ellen, the newspaper's editor, something by five on Fridays, subscribers would have her folksy two cents to entertain them over the weekend. Today, Cassandra sat at her desk, and

Cooper, Ellen's son, stood near the front door. She hadn't planned to stop in until later in the week, so she kept walking, thinking of getting home to wrap up the work she'd started that morning.

As she approached Carol's Comforts, Dorothy Peabody stepped out of the boutique gift shop with a small brown bag in hand. Dorothy and her husband, Floyd, were familiar fixtures in town during the spring, summer, and fall. The retired couple often grabbed coffee from Jillian's Cafe, sat on a bench near the square, and struck up conversations with anyone who passed by.

Dorothy dressed to the nines, regardless of the weather. Today, she wore a floral-print dress, a pale pink three-quarter-sleeve cardigan, and carried a small straw handbag. As the town's unofficial documentarian, she always had a story to share, preserving Apple Station's history for younger generations.

When Olivia got closer, she smiled and waved. "Mrs. Peabody, nice to see you."

"You too, Olivia. It's been ages. How have you been?"

"Good. And you and Mr. Peabody?"

"Well, you know how it is at our age. Something is always cranky or acting up."

"I hope that's not why Mr. Peabody isn't with you today."

"Floyd dropped me off, and he's picking me up in an hour. I'm meeting my garden club at the inn. One of our members passed away last night. Fiona Campbell. You probably didn't know her."

"Actually, I did hear about her passing. I didn't know her personally, but I'd often see her outside when I drove by her house. She always had the prettiest azaleas in the spring."

Dorothy nodded. "And hydrangeas too. She was a member of the Blooming Belles for as long as I've been."

"That's the club's name?"

"Yes. It was her idea. I was shocked when another member called this morning and told me she'd died."

The door to the gift shop opened, and they stepped aside to let a customer exit.

"I'm sorry for your loss," Olivia said. "It sounds like you were close."

"Fiona was a good friend. When you get to be my age, your circle just keeps getting smaller." She lifted the bag slightly. "I bought a sympathy card for her home health aide."

"Amy Winters?"

"Yes. Do you know her?"

Surprised the card was for Amy and not Craig, she shook her head. "Have you met her?"

Dorothy tucked the bag into the outer pocket of her purse. "Many times. I visited Fiona about once a week, and Amy was always there. She's very sweet."

Olivia already knew the answer, but she asked anyway since Dorothy seemed to know Amy better than anyone else right now. "How long had Amy been working with Fiona?"

"About a year, I'd say. After Fiona broke her hip, she needed extra help around the house. She insisted on keeping her bedroom upstairs. I told her she should've moved downstairs. It would've been easier and safer, but she said she was fine. What can you do?"

"Do you know how Amy came to work for her?"

"When Fiona got out of the hospital, the rehabilitation facility put her in touch with a home health company. They sent a young woman at first, but she left soon after she started. That girl knew Amy and connected her with Fiona."

"Does Amy work for the same agency?"

"No, she doesn't work for a company. She's an independent contractor."

Maybe that's why Mack was looking into her background.

"I should be getting to the inn," Dorothy said. "The other Belles are probably there by now. We're getting together to figure out something nice we can do in Fiona's memory."

"Of course." While Dorothy was on a roll, Olivia wanted to tap the well before it ran dry. "Do you mind if I walk with you?"

"Not at all."

They turned and slowly made their way toward the inn.

"Since Amy isn't with an agency, she must have a

solid résumé and good references to work as an independent contractor," Olivia said.

"I'm sure she does. Fiona was careful about hiring people. She always did her research. I know she interviewed three landscaping companies before choosing one. She didn't think she needed much help, but having Amy there for part of the day gave her peace of mind."

"I met Fiona's nephew on Sunday. He's in town for the Highland Games."

"I've never met him. If he ever visited before, Fiona never mentioned it. She spoke fondly of him, though. I know his wife has some medical issues, and Fiona said that it was hard for him to get time off. Still, living alone at our age isn't easy. I have Floyd, and between us, we manage. On days when Amy couldn't come or was sick, I'd go over to see if Fiona needed anything. This winter, Fiona spent a week in the hospital with pneumonia. She gave me a key so I could take care of her cat. She insisted I keep the key in case something like that happened again. She just adored that cat. I don't know what will happen to her if she turns up."

"What do you mean?"

"Just before Floyd dropped me off, we stopped by Fiona's house for a few minutes. Amy pulled in right after us, and we talked for a while. She was heartbroken about Fiona. I asked if she'd heard anything about what had happened, but the police hadn't told her much. She came to check on the cat but was afraid it might've gotten out last night with all the police activity."

As they neared the inn, Olivia slowed her pace, trying to prolong the conversation. "Was Amy at Fiona's every day?"

"Mostly. She usually came around noon and stayed until Fiona had dinner."

"It must be hard on Amy. She lost someone she was close to, and now she's out of work, unless she has other clients. I imagine it's hard for a contractor to find steady work."

They arrived at the inn, and Dorothy stopped beside the sidewalk lamppost, prompting Olivia to do the same.

"She'll be okay for a while," Dorothy said. "Fiona made sure of that."

"How so?"

Dorothy leaned in a little and lowered her voice. "You didn't hear this from me, but Fiona left Amy money in a life insurance policy."

Wow. That's really odd. "How do you know that?"

"Fiona told me. She asked me one time if Floyd and I had a policy. Floyd always had one, even after he retired. She said Amy felt like a daughter to her, and since she had no other family besides Craig, it was something she wanted to do. Amy isn't married, and she lives alone. I'm sure she doesn't make much as an aide."

"I wonder why Fiona didn't just leave her money in her will."

"I asked her the same thing. Policies aren't cheap at our age. She said, this way, Amy would get the money right away. She wouldn't have to wait for probate, and no one could contest it." Dorothy switched her purse to her other arm and let out a quiet breath. "Fiona was very generous with her money. She was always writing checks to charities. This was before your time, but she paid for the town's gazebo. Every year, she helped cover the upkeep of the flowers around it. She also helped fund the renovation of the children's wing at the library."

"I had no idea. I didn't know she'd been in Apple Station that long."

Dorothy nodded. "She had a very interesting life. She was born in Scotland but moved here almost forty years ago. Her family owned a famous distillery, and when they expanded to the U.S., she came here to help run things. Eventually, another company bought the business, but by then, she'd lived in the area so long she decided to stay."

"She never married?"

"No. She had one sister, Ruth. That's Craig's mother. She died about five or six years ago. People here don't realize how much Fiona did for the community. Your paper ought to do a piece on her."

Dorothy couldn't possibly mean her paper in D.C., so Olivia assumed she was referring to *The Apple Station Times*.

"Maybe they will. I'll ask Ellen McCarthy about it."

"Oh, that would be wonderful." Dorothy waved at a woman approaching, then whispered, "That's Helen. She's a Blooming Belle. Every spring, she tries to plant phlox, and I tell her the rabbits are just going to eat them. She won't listen." Dorothy raised her voice. "Hi,

Helen. Sad we have to bring the Belles together under these circumstances."

"You're right about that," Helen replied.

"I'll let you go," Olivia said. "It was good to see you. Thanks for speaking with me."

"You take care, Olivia," Dorothy replied.

The two Belles headed toward the inn's entrance.

"How are your phlox doing this year?" Dorothy asked.

Helen grunted. "Those darn rabbits make me so mad. They ate them clear to the ground. I swear this is it. I'm not planting them anymore."

Olivia turned, smiling to herself as she imagined them having the same conversation next year.

As she walked back to her car, her thoughts returned to Mack. What did it mean that he had a file on the beneficiary of Fiona's life insurance policy? Had Fiona hired him? If so, why? Did she have concerns about Amy? Had something happened that raised a red flag, something serious enough to warrant hiring a PI?

She thought, too, about Gladys Henderson. Mack's note in the file listed only a date of death, not a cause. Now another older, vulnerable woman connected to Amy was dead. One could be a coincidence. But did two deaths make a pattern?

Both Craig and Amy stood to gain financially from Fiona's death. Preston had been right to question her about Mack. Truthfully, she didn't know him all that well. She'd first met him when he was chasing reward money for the return of a stolen sapphire. Just as Preston had to investigate Craig's potential motives, she had to consider whether Mack had any financial stake in Fiona's death.

Mack was smart, always several steps ahead of everyone. She believed his text, the wrecked car, and his disappearance were all connected. But what had he intended for her? Did he want her to take the file and use it to point a finger at Amy, or to keep it out of police hands? Could he and Amy be working together? When he texted, was he asking for help? Or was she being drawn into something bigger?

He wouldn't play me. Would he?

So many questions, but no answers. She couldn't ignore any of it. Her concern was for Mack. And she'd do exactly what he would in this situation. Follow the trail. Thanks to Dorothy, she now had a plan for how to do that without raising suspicion.

CHAPTER 11

The newspaper office struck Olivia as unusually quiet for three o'clock. By now, the staff would typically have returned from their morning assignments to write, polish, and file stories for the next day's edition. But only Cooper and Cassandra sat at their desks, while Brad rummaged through a cabinet at the back of the open workroom.

Cassandra glanced toward Olivia by the door and rose slowly, still typing on her laptop. She stayed hunched for a moment as she finished, then straightened and came around the desk.

"Hey, Liv. And here I thought today was going to be boring. What did the cat drag you in for?"

Olivia gave Cooper a small wave from across the room. "I need to speak with Ellen about something."

"Do tell."

Unsure whether the police had classified Fiona's

94

death as an official matter, she kept the sensitive details to herself. "Did you know Fiona Campbell died yesterday?"

Cassandra zipped up her ruby-red cardigan, fending off the chill in the office-turned-icebox, and nodded like it was old news. "I saw it this morning on my CloseBy app. It's a local community forum for happenings, gossip, and gripes between neighbors. Someone posted about seeing several police cars and an ambulance at her house last night. Later, somebody updated the thread, saying she'd died."

"Did you know her?"

"Not really. I interviewed her years ago for an article about her garden club."

"Have you heard anything about what may have happened?"

"Hmm … *may* have happened? No, but I detect some suspicion in your once-upon-a-time journalist voice. What about you? Unofficially, of course."

"I'm not sure. The police are waiting for the medical examiner's preliminary report."

"I love that my best confidential informant is dating a detective. So, two plus two means there were no obvious signs of trauma. Okay, she was in her seventies. Maybe a fall? A stroke? A heart attack? Is she the reason you want to talk to Ellen?"

"Give that girl a prize. I just spoke with Dorothy Peabody and hadn't realized how much Fiona had contributed to the community. I wanted to see what Ellen thought about doing a feature on her. I know *The Times* doesn't run obits, other than the one-line death notices, but it seems like she deserves more of a tribute."

"Yeah, that sounds good. Want me to bring it up with her?"

"No, I'll do it, but thanks."

"While you're here, can I show you something?" Cassandra asked, returning to her desk. She sat and opened a browser on her laptop as Olivia joined her. "This is one of the apartment buildings in Georgetown I'm thinking about. The condos in the area are out of reach right now."

Olivia leaned down for a better view and used the mouse to scroll to the bottom of the page, checking the address. "I thought I recognized that building. That's right near where I used to live. It's still an expensive neighborhood."

Cassandra clicked on an apartment photo, opening another window with the floor layout and unit details. "I know. The rent is even higher than I conservatively estimated. The square footage isn't anything to plan parties around, but I don't need a lot of space. If the job works out long-term, I can look for something bigger down the road once I've saved more. The building is close to work, and that's worth two checks in the pro column. The other apartments I was considering are in Virginia, which would mean driving in and dealing with rush-hour traffic. I could take the Metro, but it's still about a ten-minute walk to the office."

Olivia straightened. "Which is fine when the weather

is nice, but if it's raining or freezing, that ten minutes will feel like thirty. And in winter, you'd be walking to the Metro after work in the dark. It's a fairly safe area, but still not ideal. If this apartment fits your budget, it seems like a good choice."

"That's what I needed to hear." Cassandra leaned back and swiveled her chair, glancing around the office. "I'm really going to miss this place. Even you, Penn."

Olivia laughed, placing a hand over her heart. "Thanks. I'm touched."

"I'm serious. Truthfully, I'm both excited and nervous about the whole thing. I'm not sure I'm ready."

"You are. This is what you've been working toward for years. You'll do well. It's just another stepping stone to something even bigger."

"Your lips to God's ears. Honestly, I thought Paige would've made the leap before me. She was such a talented writer."

"Yes, she was. But so are you."

Ellen came out of her office and went to the copy machine, waiting for a document to print.

"I'd better catch her while I can," Olivia said. "We'll talk more later."

Ellen returned to her office, and Olivia crossed the room, knocking on the door before entering.

Ellen rounded her desk and sat down. "What brings you here today?"

"Do you have a minute?"

Ellen waved her in, and Olivia took the seat across from her.

"Did you hear about Fiona Campbell?" Olivia asked.

Ellen put on her glasses, picked up the top sheet of her printouts, and skimmed it as she spoke. "Cassandra told me. It's sad. She was a wonderful person."

"Did you know her?"

Ellen nodded, setting the paper down. "I'd see her every year at the St. Luke's Christmas luncheon. It's held on the second Saturday in December to thank volunteers. Fiona was on the committee that handled the church's flower arrangements."

"I know you don't run obituaries, but I was speaking with Dorothy Peabody, and she wondered if you might publish a piece on Fiona's life and contributions to the town."

Ellen took off her glasses and swung them gently by the stem as she mulled it over. "That's a good idea. I'll put Cooper on it."

Olivia leaned forward. "Do you mind if I do it?"

"Was she a friend of yours?"

"No."

"Then why?"

Olivia wasn't about to mention Mack, but she knew she needed a solid reason. Ellen had a razor-sharp instinct for detecting nonsense and could sniff out a story from ten miles away on a country road.

"I have a personal stake in it."

Unmoved, Ellen pressed. "What's that?"

"Fiona was Craig Campbell's aunt, and he's a good friend of Preston's."

Ellen leaned back, waiting. When Olivia didn't elaborate, she pushed further. "Is there anything else I should know? Or will I find out later?"

She'd expected this and knew exactly how to pique Ellen's curiosity. "It's possible. If there's more to Fiona's death, the police won't share much publicly yet. But if we keep an ear to the ground, we could stay ahead of developments if, in fact, her death wasn't due to natural causes."

Ellen considered it, then set her glasses on the desk. "Your connection to the nephew, plus your special relationship with a member of the police, could be useful if foul play is involved. You might get more from the family than Cooper or any other reporter would. How exactly do you plan to keep your ear to the ground?"

"I've already spoken with Dorothy Peabody, who knew Fiona well. She said Fiona was very close to her home health aide, Amy Winters. Apparently, they had something of a mother-daughter relationship, so I want to speak with her."

Ellen stayed quiet for a few moments, tapping her fingers on the desk—a sign she was weighing the idea, looking for angles, or anticipating legal pitfalls. When she finally stopped, she scooted her chair forward. "Okay. Talk to the aide and the nephew. Find out about the funeral. We'll run a piece on Fiona, maybe a day or two beforehand."

"Thank you."

Ellen pinned her elbows on the desk and folded her hands. "Olivia, if you're interested in more of this kind of work, even part-time freelance, I can pay you. With Cassandra leaving, we're short-staffed, and I haven't found any qualified applicants. I can't match the big outlets, but you'd have the freedom to pick what you want to cover."

Supplemental income, like free dessert, was hard to turn down. Olivia had grown to enjoy writing her local column, but maybe that was because it came without pressure or obligation.

She pushed up from her chair. "I don't know if I'm the right person for the job."

"I know you're overqualified. I wouldn't ask you to cover council meetings, potluck dinners, or high school football games. You could tackle regional issues and investigative pieces, focusing on bigger stories. Just think about it."

The idea wasn't entirely off-putting, though she probably could've lobbied for similar work at her own paper in D.C. "Thanks for the offer. I'll think about it." With that, she left the office and returned to the workroom.

Before she could head for the door, Cooper intercepted her by the copy machine.

"Are you going to be here a while?" he asked.

"No. I stopped in to speak with your mom. Did you need something?"

He shook his head and took a sip of soda. "Just curious, that's all."

"Your mom told me last week you'll be filling in more for Cassandra when she leaves. How are you going to manage that with your classes? They start this month, right?"

"Yes. I've decided to take fewer credits per semester, but that's okay. I'll be gaining experience by continuing to work here. I'm glad I chose Shenandoah over George Washington. Besides saving a ton of money, commuting lets me stay in Apple Station." He glanced around the room. "It's going to be quiet without Cass."

"We'll all miss her, for sure. But just think, she's moving on, and down the road, she'll be able to help you with her connections. Someday, you could follow in her footsteps, if that's what you want."

He smoothed down his yellow, black, and red tartan tie. "Hopefully."

She pointed to his Celtic knot tie tack. "I see you're getting into the Highland spirit. Are you going to the Games this weekend?"

"I think so. Maybe Saturday. On Sunday, I'm going to the playground dedication. I bought two raffle tickets for the naming rights to double my chances."

"At fifty bucks a pop, that makes you a big spender. Any hints about what you'd name it?"

"No spoilers, but I made a spreadsheet of potentials and narrowed it down to a few favorites." He held up his hand, emphasizing each word. "Cooper's Super-Duper Colossal Kingdom of Fun."

He said it with such a straight face that Olivia couldn't tell if he was joking, so she played it safe. "I see where you're going with that. Remember, it needs to fit on a sign and be easy to reference."

"Good point. Cooper's Troopers Playground also made the list."

Though equally perplexing, at least it was more concise. "Were those your top two?"

"I had plenty more golden nuggets, but like I said, no spoilers. You'll just have to wait and see if I win."

Cassandra came over from her desk. "Excusez-moi."

"Well, good luck, Cooper," Olivia said.

"Cheers to that," he replied, raising his can. Then he turned and walked to the back of the suite, where Brad was writing on the whiteboard.

Cassandra's voice dropped to a conspiratorial tone. "Okay, Penn, what's going on? I just saw a new CloseBy post about a deputy outside Fiona Campbell's house. A police presence doesn't scream natural causes. You know more than you're saying. Deal me in."

"Look, I don't know anything for sure. I can't go into specifics, but there's reason to believe her death is suspicious."

"So what's your stake? I thought you didn't know her."

"I didn't, but someone I know did, and he reached

out to me yesterday about a matter directly related to her. Now, suddenly, he can't be found."

"Crikey. The more you talk, the more tangled this web gets. Did you tell Ellen?"

"Not exactly. I'm not even sure what's happening. It could be something or nothing."

"Police at her house isn't nothing."

Olivia lowered her voice. "Do me a favor. Keep this between us for now. I heard her aide was there earlier, and I want to catch her before she leaves."

"Gotcha. This could be one last story to send me off in style."

After saying their goodbyes, Olivia left the office and headed to her car. Truthfully, she didn't have a handle on any of it. Mack's disappearance could be unrelated, but it didn't look good. If Fiona's death was tied to a break-in and Mack was involved, the next question became whether he was a suspect or a second victim.

CHAPTER 12

Fiona's driveway stretched from the street to the side of the house, ending at a cement walkway that ran from the front porch to the detached garage. This summer's rains had been sporadic, with weeks passing without a drop. Still, the lawn remained shamrock green, and the flowerbeds popped with every color of the rainbow.

Olivia parked behind a Cadillac sedan, a silver compact, and a police cruiser. Even before she and Preston were a couple, she'd been friends with a few of the department's deputies. Over the past year, she'd become casually acquainted with several more, though she didn't know them all. She'd hoped to catch Amy alone, but depending on who else was here, gathering information might prove difficult.

She followed the walkway to the front, where neatly pruned boxwoods lined the wraparound porch. A few of the bushes had been shaped into whimsical topiaries, including a perfect replica of a cat adorned with a collar of pink silk flowers.

Once on the porch, she knocked and waited. A few moments later, Deputy Cole Lee opened the door. He was a friend, and though she'd still have to tread carefully, at least she could buy herself a few minutes. Next to him stood a woman about her age, dressed in jeans and a yellow T-shirt with the sleeves pushed to her elbows.

Olivia gave a warm smile. "Hi, Cole."

"Hey, Olivia," he said. "If you're looking for Detective Hills, he's not here."

"Actually, no. I didn't come to see him." She turned to the woman. "I'm Olivia Penn. Are you Amy Winters, by chance?"

"I am."

"I'm sorry about Fiona," Olivia said.

Amy sighed, her eyes at half-mast. "I'm still in shock. The police contacted me last night, but coming here, I still expected to see her."

"Dorothy Peabody told me how close you two were. Someone I know is good friends with her nephew. I free-lance for *The Apple Station Times*, and the editor wants to run a piece on Fiona and her contributions to the community. I plan to speak with Craig Campbell, but since you knew her well, I was hoping to get your insight too."

Amy glanced at her watch. "Fiona was very kind to me. She wasn't just a client—we became friends. I don't mind answering a few questions, but I'm short on time. I came by to grab my things and do a quick search for Shadow."

"Is that her cat?" Olivia asked.

"Yes. I haven't checked the whole house yet. She could be hiding somewhere inside. With all the activity here last night, I'm afraid she may have gotten out."

Olivia looked at Cole. "I take it you didn't come just to help with the search."

"No, but I'm going to look outside here. I came to let Ms. Winters in so she could collect her belongings."

"Does that mean the police haven't released the house yet?" Olivia asked.

"Chief Payne is waiting for Fiona's lawyer to verify that Mr. Campbell is the executor of her will before we officially release anything."

Amy checked her watch again. "I'm sorry, but I really have to get moving. Deputy, is it okay if I go back in and gather my things?"

"Yes, ma'am."

Not sure she'd get another chance to speak with Amy, Olivia offered, "I can help look for Shadow while you get your stuff, if that's alright with you, Cole."

"Fine by me."

"Thanks," Amy said. "Another set of eyes would be great."

"I'll be right out here if you need anything," Cole added.

"Thank you, Deputy."

Olivia stepped inside, taking in the space. A small

table near the door held an empty silver valet tray and a glossy black ceramic cat figurine. Straight ahead, a long hallway led to the kitchen, with two doors along the right wall. To her left, a sitting room opened through a wide entrance. A few feet away, the staircase rose to a landing, then turned left before continuing to the second floor.

"My stuff is upstairs," Amy said. "You can look up there if you want. I already took a quick look around down here. I filled Shadow's bowl with dry food and changed her water. I also put her carrier on the porch, just in case she's outside and comes back. Maybe she'll recognize it as a safe place. I thought about leaving food out, but I read online that it's not a good idea. They say it attracts predators, and Fiona told me foxes come through the yard almost every night."

"Is Shadow microchipped?"

"She is. Hopefully, if someone finds her, they'll take her to a vet or a shelter to get her scanned."

Amy started up the stairs, and Olivia followed. Each step on the wooden boards creaked like a ghost ship adrift at sea, its hull groaning with every rise and fall.

"I take it Shadow is a black cat?"

"Yes, with yellow eyes. She always hides from strangers, but once she's comfortable with you, she's affectionate."

"I have a cat at home, so I know a thing or two about hiding places."

At the top of the stairs, Amy stood by the railing and

pointed down the hallway. "They found Fiona right there outside her room."

"Did the police give you any idea of what happened?"

"No, only that there were no signs of trauma. They said it looked like there had been a break-in, but they didn't share many details. I can't help blaming myself."

"Why is that?"

Amy inhaled deeply and let out a heavy breath. "Maybe if I'd stayed, Fiona would still be alive."

Olivia understood grief-induced guilt, but Dorothy had said that Amy typically left in the early evening. "I heard Craig found her around nine. Were you usually still here then?"

"No. Fiona always ate dinner at six, and I'd leave when she finished. But I left early yesterday. She had another visitor and told me it was okay to go."

Another visitor? Someone besides Craig?

"But if it was a break-in, it happened well after you'd normally be gone."

"I suppose so."

Thinking Amy must've already told the police about Fiona's visitors, Olivia cast a leading question. "It must've been awful for Craig to find her last night. Did he come earlier in the day?"

She shook her head. "No. A friend of Fiona's sister flew in from Scotland and stopped by."

Interesting. "Maybe she has some memories of Fiona she'd be willing to share. Is she staying in town?"

"I'm not sure."

"Maybe Craig will know. I'll ask him. What's her name?"

"Winifred Fraser. She came with her great-niece, Clare."

Olivia nodded. "Fiona must've been happy to see someone she knew from Scotland."

"I guess. She thought Winifred might visit, but she hadn't expected her yesterday. Fiona always told me when guests were coming, and she didn't mention anything about them stopping by. When she saw Winifred, I could tell she wasn't exactly thrilled. They came late in the afternoon."

"Huh, that doesn't sound like she was necessarily happy to see them. Am I reading that right?"

Amy shrugged. "I only know what Fiona told me about Winifred. They spoke on the phone a few times over the past year, and after each call, Fiona always seemed upset. Yesterday, she said Winifred must be 'desperate' if she came all the way here."

Desperate about what? That's weird.

Maybe Amy lacked a filter, or perhaps the shock of Fiona's death had lowered her guard. Either way, Olivia intended to press for as much information as she could. "All this way? Did she mean Virginia?"

"I think so. I didn't ask Fiona why she'd come. It wasn't my business, but I offered to stick around. I didn't want her getting worked up. But she knew I had a meeting with a loan officer in Luray and told me not to worry, just to go ahead and leave."

"I'm sure if Fiona had felt uncomfortable, she would've asked you to stay. So Winifred was the other visitor besides Craig?"

"No, her accountant came earlier, around three. He'd been here before, but Fiona was taking a nap when he came, so he left."

Learning the accountant's name could be useful. If Fiona trusted him with her finances, he might've known her better than most. "I bet Fiona used the accountant from town. The one with the office next to the barbershop," Olivia said, tilting her head and pausing as if trying to recall a name. "I think it's Paul …"

Amy shook her head. "No, it was Jim or … Joseph— no, wait. John. That's it. John Mack."

Olivia kept her expression neutral, willing herself not to react. "Yes, that sounds familiar."

Things had just gone from bad to worse for Mack. He had tried to see Fiona the day she died. Why? Had he come back later that night? Preston hadn't mentioned Mack being here. She understood Preston couldn't share every detail of the investigation, but did he even know?

"Did you tell the police about Winifred and the accountant stopping by?"

"Winifred, yes. I didn't mention the accountant because he never saw her."

Amy glanced at her watch. "I'm sorry. I need to grab

my things and get going. You can look around anywhere you want."

They walked down the hall, and Amy stopped in front of an open doorway.

"This was her bedroom. Maybe check in here. It was one of Shadow's favorite places." She pointed to the end of the hall. "Fiona let me keep some clothes and a bag in the spare. Sometimes I'd stay overnight if she wasn't feeling well."

"Are you sure it's okay for me to look through her room?"

"Oh, yes. She'd want Shadow found. I'll just be a few minutes." With that, Amy headed down the hallway.

As Olivia stepped into the room, her thoughts spun and bobbed like painted ponies on a carousel. Why was Mack posing as an accountant? Did Fiona know who he really was? Was he trying to hide his identity from Amy? Or had Fiona been the one keeping secrets, hiring a PI to dig into Amy's past? Too many questions, all pointing in different directions. For now, with only a few minutes, she had to push them aside and focus on finding the cat.

She turned on the lights, revealing a spacious bedroom tailored for both Fiona and Shadow. A cat tree, a scratching post, and a cardboard box suggested it was one of Shadow's favorite hideouts. The carpeted floor was free of tripping hazards, and the burly furniture looked hand-hewn from solid oak. A glider chair and a small table stacked with books sat by the window over-looking the front yard. Olivia imagined it would be a perfect spot to read before bed. The walls were adorned with paintings and photographs of rolling Highland hills and rugged coastlines where jagged cliffs met raging seas.

"Shadow?" she called out, hoping the cat might stir at the sound of her name. "Are you in here? Shadow?"

She crossed the room to the open closet, scanning from top to bottom. Blankets and boxes lined the upper shelf, probably too high for a cat to reach, but she jostled them around anyway, just in case. Dropping to her knees, she checked the floor, pushing aside bags and storage bins tucked under the hanging clothes.

Then she scooted a few feet from the closet to the dresser. Though the gap beneath it wasn't comfortably wide, she knew from experience a determined cat could squeeze into impossibly tight spaces. Willow had proved that to her more than once. Peering under the dresser, she found nothing but a brush and a tube of lipstick. She picked them up and set them back on top, guessing Shadow had swiped them off at some point.

Still on her knees, she inched closer to the bed and lay flat on her stomach. Something small rested in the center beneath the box spring. She shimmied sideways, reached blindly, and grabbed it. Even before withdrawing her arm, she knew by touch alone that it was a toy mouse, identical to the ones scattered around her own home.

She stood and went over to the dresser, placing the toy beside the brush. A glass jewelry case with silver beveled edges caught her eye. Inside were three exquisite brooches. One featured a prominent emerald encased in delicate gold latticework. Another was a cameo pin, its raised profile set against a coral background. The third was heart-shaped with a border of diamonds and a single drop pearl in the center.

Behind the dresser, several framed pictures hung on the wall, along with an old iron cross. Elaborate scroll-work covered its surface, and a dark patina mottled the bottom half. It looked like the kind of antique someone might pick up at an estate sale for a few bucks, only to later discover it was a museum-worthy artifact.

Next, she checked the bathroom, where a small bowl of water sat on the tile floor near the door. Finding it still full wasn't a good sign. She crouched, picked it up carefully, and emptied it into the sink. After placing the bowl back, she refilled it with fresh water from a half-gallon jug on the counter.

Back in the bedroom, she lifted the hinged lid of a wicker hamper, pulled a rumpled blanket from the cardboard box, and checked between the headboard and the wall. No Shadow. She hadn't expected to find the cat there, but it was worth a shot.

A five-by-seven photo of Fiona holding the cat in her lap sat framed on the nightstand. Beside it rested a large, well-worn Bible. The dark brown leather cover was heavily scuffed, its gold-embossed lettering nearly faded away.

She sat on the edge of the bed, picked up the Bible, and opened it to the title page, scanning to the bottom. If she still had her game for converting Roman numerals, she gathered that a press from Edinburgh had printed the Bible in the late 1600s. As a book lover, she was in awe. It felt like touching history. She probably should've been wearing gloves, but if Fiona had kept it on her nightstand, she must've read from it often.

The next page was filled with handwritten genealogy, documenting generations of Campbell family births, deaths, and weddings. Many names were accompanied by references to churches and kirkyards, likely indicating burial sites. Fascinated, she read through the earliest names and notes, which included a marriage between a Fraser and a Campbell. Common surnames, she thought, much like Brown, Johnson, or Rodriguez in the States.

"Did you see any signs of Shadow?" Amy asked, approaching from the hallway.

She closed the Bible, set it back on the nightstand, and stood. "I found a toy under the bed and a couple of things knocked off the dresser. They're both signs a cat had been in here at some point. But her water bowl in the bathroom was still full." She turned off the lights and stepped into the hallway.

"Shadow spent a lot of time in there," Amy said, adjusting the strap of her overnight bag.

Together, they went downstairs. At the bottom, Amy paused, looking around as if taking it all in one last time.

"I'm really going to miss coming here," she said. "It never felt like work. I try not to get too attached, but it's the nature of the job."

With only a few moments left to talk, Olivia angled for insight into Amy's background. "How long have you worked as an aide?"

"About two years. But before that, I was a nurse."

Bingo. "Oh, that's a big change. I mean, it's a similar field, but I'd think nursing pays more. Not that money makes a job better, but still."

"No, you're right. I loved patient care, but it was everything else that came with the job."

As Amy opened the door, Olivia said, "Would it be okay if I contact you again if I have more questions about Fiona?"

"Yeah, sure. Let me give you my number."

They stepped onto the porch and stopped in their tracks. Nearly two dozen men in full Highland dress stood in the yard, looking up at them.

CHAPTER 13

Given the variety of tartans, Olivia gathered several family clans were represented. Each man wore a white shirt, a black tie, and a vest, with kilt hose pulled up to his knees. Sporrans hung from their waists. Some were simple leather pouches, while others featured decorative tassels, metal plates, or intricate clasps. Parked cars lined both curbs in front of the house. Two men from the group stood at either end of the short street, stopping traffic in both directions. As vehicles approached, they walked between them, exchanging brief words with the drivers.

Olivia and Amy descended the steps to where Cole waited, his uniform campaign hat held over his heart.

"What's going on, Cole?" Olivia asked.

"Mr. Campbell has organized a memorial for his aunt."

Olivia, Amy, and Cole moved off to the side as Craig

stepped to the front of the quiet, solemn gathering. He opened a small softcover book and read a psalm, a scripture passage, and a Celtic blessing. Then a man with bagpipes came forward and began playing "Amazing Grace."

The haunting hum felt ancient and mournful. A few waiting drivers got out of their vehicles and stood at attention. Tears welled in Olivia's eyes, the melody stirring memories of her own mother's funeral. The neighborhood fell quiet, as if holding sacred space for the memorial.

When the bagpiper finished, all stood in silence for a few moments before Craig turned to thank everyone for coming. Several men in the group offered their condolences while the street slowly reopened in both directions. After the last well-wisher had left, Craig approached Cole, Amy, and Olivia near the porch steps.

"Deputy, thank you for allowing us to stop traffic for a few minutes," Craig said.

"I think everyone understood. We have good people in this town. Do you need to get into the house now?"

"No. I just wanted to do this before we all got busier later in the week."

"You can drop by the police station tomorrow to pick up the key. Detective Hills says the approval should come through soon." Cole turned to Amy. "Did you get your things?"

She patted her bag. "All in here."

"I'm heading off, then," Cole said. He jogged up the

steps, locked the door, and came back down. "If you need anything else, call the station."

"Is it okay if I stop by to look for Shadow again?" Amy asked.

"If it's okay with Mr. Campbell."

Amy reached out to Craig, and they shook hands.

"We've never officially met. I'm Amy Winters. We spoke several times on the phone."

"It's nice to put a face to the name. Thank you for everything you did for my aunt. I know she was quite fond of you. And I don't mind at all if you want to come back to look for her cat. I'm only in town until Sunday, so if we can't find her by then, we'll just have to hope someone takes her in."

Olivia glanced between Craig and Amy. One was Fiona's heir, the other, the beneficiary of her life insurance policy. Did each know that about the other? Amy had left unusually early yesterday, and Craig had been the one to find Fiona dead. If Olivia were a true crime devotee, she might've suspected some kind of nefarious plan between them.

"Okay, folks," Cole said. "Take it easy."

They exchanged polite goodbyes as he left.

"It's good to see you again," Craig said to Olivia. "I wasn't expecting you to be here."

Before she could explain, Amy interjected. "I have to be on my way. If I get the chance, I'll come by tomorrow and look around for Shadow."

Olivia pulled out her phone and opened the notes

app. "Can I have your number? Maybe we can talk again later."

"Yeah, sure," Amy said, adjusting the tote strap on her shoulder. She took the phone, entered her number, and handed it back. After a quick goodbye, she headed to her car, leaving Olivia and Craig alone.

"That was a lovely memorial," Olivia said. "I'm glad I was here. I'd stopped by to speak with Amy. Our local paper is running an article about Fiona that I'm helping with. Since Amy was close to her, I thought she'd be a good person to talk to. I'm sorry to say I didn't know your aunt well. I used to come here trick-or-treating because she was so generous."

"That sounds like Fiona."

"Have you made arrangements for her yet? The editor wants to run the piece before the funeral."

Amy started her car, and Olivia watched for a moment as she backed the silver compact out of the driveway and onto the street.

Craig loosened his tie and wiped the sweat off his forehead. "After my mum died, Fiona made her own final arrangements and shared them with me so there'd be no guesswork or scrambling when the time came. She wanted to be cremated and have her ashes interred next to my mum's in Scotland. Since there won't be any services here, we're holding another gathering at the inn's restaurant tonight. I'm hoping for a good turnout. You and Preston should come. The more, the merrier, especially since she didn't have any other family."

"I have something going on earlier in the evening, but if it's not too late, I'll come by. Are you still participating in the weekend Games?"

He nodded. "I'm carrying on. I think that's what Fiona would've wanted. I'd planned to go with my kids on a day trip down to Williamsburg tomorrow, but we decided to stay in town. I'm going to try to settle as many of her affairs as I can before I leave on Sunday. I'll have to come back to take care of the house and get it ready to sell, but I don't want to be away from home for too long. My mother-in-law is staying with my wife, but she's leaving Monday."

"Have you heard from Preston about what may have happened?"

"Not yet. I haven't talked to him since last night. It seems like someone broke in. The door was wide open, and the table by the entrance had been knocked over. I don't know if anything is missing. I can't understand why anyone would want to harm her."

And Olivia couldn't imagine that Craig had anything to do with Fiona's death, but he wasn't as visibly upset as Amy had been. Maybe it was just his personality, or perhaps he hadn't been that close to Fiona. The latter could explain why he'd come to visit her at nine. He might not have known she'd normally be in bed by that time. Equally, though, coming at that hour could've been strategic, providing him an opportunity to enter the house when she'd be alone.

"Amy told me Fiona had a visitor yesterday," Olivia

said. "She was a friend from Scotland who came for the Games. Winifred Fraser."

"Sure, I know her well, but I didn't realize she'd come by to see Fiona. My mum and Winifred had been friends since they were kids in Scotland. They were the same age, but Fiona was a few years younger."

"Has Winifred been to these Highland Games before?"

"This is the first time I've seen her at any I've attended."

"Maybe it had something to do with Fiona, since the Games were so close to her home."

He nodded. "Could be. She's staying at the same inn we are. Her great-niece Clare traveled with her. Clare and my son are the same age and good friends. They play those online games together. When I arrived on Sunday, I ran into Winifred, and we had a nice conversation about my mum."

"Have you kept in contact with her since your mom's passing?"

"No. I always meant to reach out again. The last time we spoke was at the funeral. I know she and my mum were very close. In fact, she said my mum was supposed to have left something for her, some kind of personal keepsake. She said there should've been a note about it. I looked all over, but I didn't come across anything. I felt bad that I couldn't find it."

"That's too bad. What was it?"

He shrugged. "She didn't say exactly. Just that it was

something personal. I looked through all my mum's papers. There was nothing in her will about it either."

Olivia smiled. "Sounds mysterious. How were you supposed to know what to look for?"

"You got me. I thought maybe I'd missed something, but time passed, and Winifred never followed up. I always meant to ask Fiona about it, but honestly, it slipped my mind."

"Perhaps she asked Fiona herself."

"That would make sense. She didn't bring it up when we spoke on Sunday, so maybe she forgot all about it too. I don't know how much insight she has into Fiona's later years, but she might have some childhood stories that would interest you. She'll be at the gathering tonight."

Olivia doubted that Winifred's first trip to the Highland Games, given their proximity to Fiona, was pure happenstance. But what exactly did that mean? Fiona had expected Winifred's visit, but she hadn't been particularly thrilled about it. They must've spoken recently for her to have anticipated the face-to-face. Now that Olivia knew Winifred believed Craig's mother had promised her something, she wondered if Fiona had ended up with it instead. That might explain why Craig never found anything. But would she really have flown across the Atlantic just to get it?

Amy had mentioned that Fiona had called Winifred "desperate" for coming all the way to Virginia. If Fiona had something of her sister's that Winifred believed was hers, it was likely personal. Still, what could be valuable enough to fly over three thousand miles, drive two hours to a rural Southern town, and show up unannounced at Fiona's door? The whole scenario seemed unlikely. Maybe.

Craig was mentioned only once in Mack's file, but the nature of the phone call between them was unclear. There was no way Craig could know about her connection to Mack. Preston would never share case details with him, especially since he was under some suspicion. So she took a cue from Amy's story, hoping to find out what, if anything, Craig knew about Mack.

"Amy told me Fiona's accountant came by yesterday before Winifred," she said. "A guy named John Mack."

Craig's expression stayed neutral, showing no sign of recognition. "I didn't know that. I guess I should track down his number and see if Fiona had any accounts I don't know about."

"That sounds like a good idea." With no follow-up to the dead-end response, she added, "Well, I've taken up enough of your time. It was good to see you again."

After saying her goodbyes, she promised to try to attend that night's gathering for Fiona and headed for her car.

She couldn't take Craig's blank reaction to Mack's name at face value. Mack had probably spoken to him while posing as someone else. She knew he could slip in and out of aliases as easily as a stage actress changing costumes between scenes.

Craig's account of Winifred's relationship with his

mother and Fiona left her with more questions. Perhaps Fiona hadn't even been the intended target. Maybe it was just a burglary gone wrong. A random break-in was possible. It was just as plausible, though, that the intruder had come looking for something specific, something they knew had value. And here was Winifred, having traveled all the way from Scotland, showing up at Fiona's door the very day she died.

CHAPTER 14

Olivia strode down the hallway to Mack's office, her steady pace in sharp contrast to her rushed exit the night before. Judging by the cars still dotting the lot at five-thirty, she wasn't the only one with late-day business in the building. Now that she knew more about Fiona and Amy, she'd returned to search for any additional files on them. Craig had been mentioned only once in Amy's background check, which made her suspect Mack might've kept a separate file on him. After talking to Craig, she was even more determined to find out who had hired Mack to investigate Amy's past. To piece it together, she had to retrace her steps, starting with a return visit to his office.

As she neared the lit suite, her plan unraveled faster than a sweater caught in a kitten's claws. No one had answered the phone earlier, so she'd assumed the office was still closed. A flicker of hope sparked that Mack might be back, alive and well, but her sixth sense told her otherwise.

She opened the door and stepped inside, finding the waiting room empty. Nolan was sitting behind the reception desk, but the moment he saw her, he jumped to his feet. Dressed in jeans and a T-shirt under an unzipped hoodie, he looked like a college student who'd barely dragged himself to a Monday morning class after a wild weekend.

She wasn't sure if he'd remember her, since their interaction in December had been brief. But before she could speak, he skipped a greeting and blurted, "Do you know about Mack?"

Catching the urgency in his voice, she followed his lead and dispensed with the pleasantries. "What have you heard?"

He stepped to the side and opened the door to the back. "Come around." After she did, he plopped into his chair. "The police told me they found his car wrecked off Old Mill Highway, but there was no sign of him. How did you find out?"

She wasn't about to admit she'd been there last night or mention Mack's text. But she needed an inroad with Nolan. Right now, he knew more about Mack than anyone else she could talk to.

"I heard it from the police too. I was worried about him, so I came here hoping he'd show up or that I'd find you and you'd tell me he was safe."

Nolan ran a hand over his head. "I wish I could. I

know he trusted you. He told me about what happened at the army base in May. I'm so glad you came. I'm *freaking* out."

Back in December, Nolan had been measured and guarded. Now, his rapid, unfiltered thoughts revealed that he, too, had been thrown for a loop by the past twenty-four hours.

"When was the last time you talked to him?" she asked.

"I've been out of town since Friday. I drove up to New York to visit a friend for a vacation. The last time we spoke was Thursday, right before we closed the office. I came in this morning, then the police showed up. He had two client appointments today. He never misses appointments. Ever."

"Did you try calling him?"

"First thing I did."

"Does he have multiple phones?"

Nolan nodded. "I tried all his numbers. I hope he's okay. Why wouldn't he call me?"

She leaned against the counter and folded her arms. Her attention drifted to a daily planner beside a laptop with a screensaver displaying spirals narrowing toward their centers in a slow, hypnotic rhythm. "What about family?"

He swiveled his seat toward her. "He has a sister in Chicago. I thought about calling her, but I didn't want to be the one to break the news if something has happened to him. I figured the police would contact her if she needed to know anything."

The desk phone rang. He jumped up, grabbed the receiver, and answered before the first ring ended. "Hello … Oh, hi, Mrs. Thomas." He glanced at Olivia and sighed, his shoulders slumping. "Mack is out of the office right now. I'll have him return your call as soon as he can … Okay, bye." He set the handset down and sank back into his chair. "I was hoping that was him."

She subtly scanned the workspace for cameras. Last night, she'd been so focused on getting in and out quickly that she hadn't considered whether there might be surveillance behind the desk.

"Do you have any guesses about what could've happened?" she asked.

He lifted his hands, palms up. "No idea."

"Is there any way to tell if he has been in the office? Do you have cameras or a way to check if his key code was used?"

He shook his head. "Our clients pay for discretion, and cameras put people off, especially given the sensitive nature of the work. The building has security, and we use access codes to get in. There's no way for me to tell if Mack was here, unless he left something behind: trash, a file, anything on his desk. But when I came in this morning, the office looked exactly the same as it did when we closed Thursday."

Now that she was certain he didn't know about her visit last night, she steered the conversation toward the reason she'd come. "Did you know Mack tried to see Fiona Campbell yesterday?"

He hesitated, then said, "Yesss."

"She was found dead last night. Possibly murdered, though there were no signs of trauma."

His mouth dropped open wide enough to catch a dragonfly. "What? Oh, jeez. Oh, man. This is bad. How do you know he went to Mrs. Campbell's house?"

"How do you know?" she countered.

He gestured toward the planner. "It was on his schedule for this week."

"I spoke with Fiona's aide, Amy Winters, earlier today. She was at Fiona's house with the police, gathering her belongings. She said Fiona's *accountant*, John Mack, tried to see her yesterday around three. So he was lying to Amy about who he was. Was he also lying to Fiona?"

Nolan stood up and paced sideways as if unsure where to go. "No. It wasn't like that at all. Mrs. Campbell hired Mack to check Amy's background. He said Mrs. Campbell introduced him to Amy as her accountant, so he just rolled with it. He wished she hadn't used his real name, but it didn't seem to raise any suspicions."

"Why did Fiona hire him?"

"She had recently made Amy the beneficiary of her life insurance policy."

"Did she have concerns about Amy?"

He wrapped his arms around himself. "I don't know. That was between Mack and Mrs. Campbell. I helped with the background check, mostly looking into Amy's past jobs. I spoke with Mrs. Campbell on the phone a few times, but I never went to her house. She seemed nice. She had even invited me to come with Mack once, but he said she had a cat, and I'm allergic."

"Do you know why he went to her house yesterday?"

He let his arms fall to his sides. "Probably just following up on his report. The police were asking about him too. They questioned me about his movements over the past few days, but like I said, I've been out of touch. They kept pressing me about his relationship with Mrs. Campbell but never said why. I figured it was just routine, trying to piece together his timeline. I had no idea she was dead. Do you think they're looking at Mack as a suspect?"

She didn't want to admit it, but it was possible. "In connection with her death? Not yet, as far as I know. Mack isn't a murderer."

"No, yeah, you're right. But it just looks bad. He goes to her house, she ends up dead, and now he's missing."

"Do you think he might've gone back there at night? Would he do something like that?"

Nolan sat down, resting his forearms on his thighs. "I guess it's possible. One time I had to call Mrs. Campbell to reschedule an appointment. Mack told me not to call after seven because that's when she started getting ready for bed. My grandma was the same. In bed by eight, up by four." He bit the corner of his thumbnail. "Ever since the police left this morning, something else has been bothering me about the car wreck."

"What's that?"

He straightened, silent for a moment, then cracked his knuckles. "The police said there were no signs of injury, meaning no blood. It's possible … that Mack could've staged it."

"Staged the crash? You think he wrecked his car on purpose? That's extreme. Why would he do that?"

"I don't know."

She unfolded her arms and took a few steps toward the desk. "We know he was at Fiona's in the afternoon, and sometime between then and five o'clock this morning, his car ended up in a ditch. It's only been a little over twenty-four hours since he was last seen. He could've called someone to pick him up and arranged for his car to be towed."

Nolan nodded. "That's true. I just don't get why he hasn't contacted me."

"Maybe he got injured and needed time to recover."

The front door swung open, and Nolan sprung up, stepping quickly toward the desk. A mail carrier entered, holding a stack of envelopes. He slid the mail through the slot at the bottom of the window, said a casual hello and goodbye, and left.

Nolan picked up the envelopes, flipped through them, and tossed the pile onto the desk, bumping the laptop's mouse. The screensaver flicked off, revealing a browser window open to the homepage of the care facility where Gladys Henderson had died.

He's following Mack's trail too.

She looked at Nolan, and he pointed at the screen. "That's a nursing rehab facility in North Carolina." He went over to the cabinet she'd rummaged through, opened the bottom drawer, and pulled out a folder. "This is the file I helped Mack compile on Amy."

She silently thanked everything holy she hadn't taken it last night.

He laid the file on the desk next to the laptop and opened it. "Amy was a nurse before she became a home health aide. There was a woman who died at that facility in North Carolina, which was the last place Amy worked as a nurse. Mack got her name from Mrs. Campbell, who got it from Amy. Mrs. Campbell wanted to know why Amy switched careers. Amy only said that after this woman's death, she left nursing altogether. Mind you, this is all according to Mack."

"Okay, so where are you going with this?"

He turned a few pages in the file. "I'm not sure, but …"

"But you have theories," she prompted. "Do you think Amy was involved in this woman's death in North Carolina?"

"It's possible. I'm going back through everything, trying to find any connection between Mack and Amy."

"What are you talking about?"

He puffed out his cheeks, reluctant to speak. "If Mack resurfaces or walks through the door, I'll deny ever saying this. But Amy was the beneficiary of Mrs. Campbell's life insurance policy, and Mack knew it. He told me

Mrs. Campbell had a lot of what he called 'heirloom-quality' valuables in her house. He'd been inside several times. He knew Amy wouldn't be there at night, and that Mrs. Campbell went to bed early."

She shook her head. "Mack is no killer."

"I agree. But maybe he went there to steal something, and in the process, Mrs. Campbell woke up and got startled."

She considered the possibility, recalling Mack's relentless pursuit of a stolen jewel for the reward money last December. "Then where is he? Disappearing only makes him look guilty. The safer play would've been to go about his normal routine. Besides, there weren't clear signs of a break-in, just an open door and an overturned table. Those could have other explanations."

"Maybe Mack was let in," he suggested.

"By Fiona?"

"Or Amy. They could've planned something together. Maybe Amy let Mack in and stayed in case Mrs. Campbell woke up."

That's not entirely out of the question. Amy could've returned to the house at night.

"Have you ever met Amy?" she asked.

"No."

"When I talked to her, she seemed sincere. She spoke fondly of Fiona."

"I would too if someone made me a beneficiary of their life insurance policy. I get Mrs. Campbell being grateful, but until a year ago, Amy was a stranger. Mrs. Campbell had family. A nephew."

"I have a hard time believing Amy would harm Fiona."

He leaned against the desk. "Maybe she didn't mean to. I don't know if Mrs. Campbell had any health issues, but if Amy was there last night, maybe something just … happened."

She thought of the brooches and the cross in Fiona's bedroom, wondering if similar valuables were elsewhere in the house. Nolan had raised some valid points, and she couldn't dismiss his theories outright. She didn't know Mack well, but she trusted him enough. Amy, on the other hand, was more of an unknown, someone with both means and motive.

Her attention shifted to the file on the desk. She'd read it multiple times since last night. Both she and Nolan had been following Mack's trail. The next logical step was to dig deeper into Amy's background, especially her connection to Gladys Henderson. But Fiona's death was still front and center, and Mack's absence couldn't be ignored.

"Does Mack own a gun?" she asked.

"I don't know. Why?"

"Two shots were fired inside the house shortly before Fiona's nephew found her."

His eyes widened. "Mrs. Campbell was shot? I thought you said there were no signs of trauma."

"She wasn't shot. She doesn't appear to have been the target."

"Then who was shooting at who?"

She shook her head slowly. "No idea. What I do know is that Mack went to Fiona's in the afternoon, shots were fired at night, and he wrecked his car for an unknown reason."

Nolan exhaled sharply. "Maybe more than two shots were fired."

She didn't want to think so, but deep down, she knew it was possible. "And at least one hit its mark."

CHAPTER 15

By seven o'clock, most stores in town had closed. Those still open catered to lingering diners, last-minute shoppers, and locals enjoying a slow evening stroll. A Scottish folk trio played on a small stage in front of the gazebo, their rollicking rhythms filling the square. Large speakers amplified the toe-tapping cadence of the guitar, frame drum, and fiddle. Townsfolk sprawled across the lawn, lounging on blankets or sitting in folding chairs. Many had brought coolers, pairing twilight picnics with the concert. Others balanced takeout plates piled high with fare from the Highland Grub food truck parked along Cider Lane.

Olivia stood on the sidewalk bordering the square, soaking in the festive scene. On the drive into town, she'd mulled again over why Mack had brought her into all this. With Nolan away since Friday, the idea that she was second on Mack's go-to list was almost flattering, assuming he wasn't using her for his own agenda. She'd followed the trail he'd left behind but didn't like where it led.

Fiona's death was tragic. Though Olivia couldn't quite believe Craig might be involved, Preston hadn't shown the same hesitation with his own friend. Now, after her conversation with Nolan, she had to apply that same caution to Mack. She considered him a casual friend, but his absence and the wrecked car were troubling.

Another theory crossed her mind: maybe Mack hadn't been the one driving. He could've loaned his vehicle to someone, or it might've been stolen. For all she knew, he might be lying low somewhere, unaware he was under suspicion.

Before leaving Mack's office, she and Nolan had exchanged numbers and agreed to stay in touch. They'd tried to reassure each other, but his suggestion that Mack, either alone or with Amy, might've returned to Fiona's house last night left her unsettled.

The fiddle player introduced their next song, "Lochaber No More," then launched into a mournful melody that evoked the sorrow of parting. As the music drifted through the square, Olivia turned, crossed the street, and walked half a block to Sophia's clinic.

Finding the door locked, she knocked on the window and waited as Sophia came from the hallway into the foyer to let her in. After a quick exchange of hellos, they proceeded to the back of the suite.

Once a commercial-sized kitchen for a bakery, the renovated space still served as a production hub whenever Sophia's mother and grandmother made large batches of baked goods for celebrations or charity sales. The stainless-steel prep island resembled an assembly line, cluttered with ingredients and mixing bowls in various stages of use. In the sink, a jumble of bakeware soaked in sudsy water. Nearby, a wheeled sheet pan rack stood beside the ovens, ready to hold trays of sweet treats once they browned to perfection.

Josefina was cracking eggs into a glass bowl while Maria rolled out dough.

"Hi, everyone," Olivia said.

Maria set down the rolling pin and came over, wrapping Olivia in a warm hug. "Hola, mija. Thank you for coming. I wouldn't blame you if you changed your mind after seeing this mess."

Olivia laughed. "This looks like controlled chaos, unlike the pure chaos my dad creates whenever he bakes. So I'm prepared."

As they separated, Josefina stepped to the counter, sliced a thin wedge of sponge cake, and set it on a napkin before offering it to Olivia.

"Tell me what you think," Josefina said. "I want the truth. I can take it."

Olivia already knew it would be delicious. She broke off a piece and popped it into her mouth. The sponge was light and fluffy, rich with a distinct vanilla-almond flavor. With Josefina's steely gaze on her, there was only one correct verdict.

"This is exquisite."

Josefina's face softened with satisfaction. "Gracias."

"What's the cake for?" Olivia asked.

"It's the final recipe, or at least the latest iteration, for Melissa and Kevin's wedding," Sophia replied, peeking into the oven.

"Mamá, how many more test cakes are you going to bake?" Maria teased. "You only have two more weeks."

"Hasta que esté perfecto."

Maria and Sophia laughed as Josefina resumed cracking eggs.

"It already is perfect, Mamá," Maria said.

"Have you seen Melissa recently?" Olivia asked Sophia.

"Just yesterday. On Tuesdays during the summer, I run motor play groups. It's kind of like a mini-camp for the kids. Mikey comes in on those days. I thought she'd be overwhelmed with preparations for the wedding, but she says everything is almost done. Are you and Preston going?"

"Yes. It's going to be so pretty having it at the farm." She finished the sliver of cake, tossed the napkin in the trash, and washed her hands. "What can I do to help?"

Maria nodded toward the end of the kitchen island, where ingredients were lined up beside measuring cups and a stand mixer. "You can make the dough for the next batch of Mexican wedding cookies. The recipe is in front of the butter. Those sticks should be soft enough to cream by now."

At the prep station, Olivia looked over the index card and sorted the ingredients. "These are for the playground dedication on Sunday?"

"Sí," Maria said. "These cookies keep well. Since we make everything in small batches, we have to start early."

"Always do small batches," Josefina added, whisking the eggs. "Tastes better that way."

Olivia started creaming the butter. "I kind of miss baking. My dad has completely taken over that side of the kitchen business."

"It's good for him to have a hobby," Maria said, dolloping balls of dough onto a cookie sheet.

"Work with your hands," Josefina said. "That'll keep you young."

Olivia added sugar and salt to the creamed butter, then turned the mixer on low. "He told me the other day he's thinking of going back to work."

"Doing what?" Sophia asked.

"He didn't go into specifics. I just don't want him taking on anything too stressful."

Maria placed the sheet pan in the oven. "That's why I still tutor. It helps the kids, but I don't have to be with them all day. It's like being a grandmother. Your grand-kids visit, and then you happily send them home."

Olivia added vanilla, almond extract, cinnamon, and flour to the bowl, then turned the mixer back on. "How many dozen cookies are you making?"

Maria winked. "Depends on when I turn the lights out."

Olivia stopped the mixer, removed the bowl from the base, and stirred the dough with a wooden spoon.

"That looks good," Sophia said over Olivia's shoulder. She reached around her, took the bowl, and brought it to Maria. "We're backlogged here," she added, glancing at Olivia. "Hold off on the next batch. The dough needs to chill a bit first."

"On standby," Olivia replied with a thumbs-up. She moseyed to the counter, swiped a cooled cookie off a wire rack, and took a bite before asking Sophia, "Are you all set for the playground dedication?"

"You betcha. A lot of the families I work with will be there. We should have a good turnout. Tori's bringing Tyler, and Melissa and Kevin are coming with Mikey. There's nothing like it in the area. A fully accessible playground where kids with special needs can play right alongside their friends. Very cool."

"Are you still selling raffle tickets for the naming?" Olivia asked.

"Sí," Maria replied. "Until you leave the clinic."

"What payments are you accepting?"

"Cash, check, or charge," Sophia said.

"Is it okay if I bring you cash on Sunday?"

"Since I know where you live, that'll be fine," Sophia joked. "I'll get you an official entry." She walked out of the kitchen and down the hall, while Olivia polished off her cookie.

A moment later, she returned with a piece of paper, a pen, and an envelope, handing them to Olivia before checking on the cookies in the oven.

"Cooper McCarthy told me a few names he was thinking about for the raffle," Olivia said. "They were real doozies."

"Did his entry pass muster?" Sophia asked her mother.

Maria smiled, raising an eyebrow. "Both of them did. You'll be quite surprised if his name gets drawn."

"What were the names?" Sophia asked.

Maria feigned shock. "Mija, I can't tell you that."

"You can, but you won't," Sophia replied.

"This is true," Maria said with a wide smile as she washed her hands.

Josefina came over to Olivia and handed her a napkin with a cookie on it. Olivia set down the envelope, the paper, and the pen as Josefina stood in front of her, waiting for a verdict.

The small cookie was round, crumbly, and coated in powdered sugar. She took a bite, and it melted in her mouth, buttery and nutty with just the right sweetness. "Mmm, this is fantastic."

"Ay, caramba," Josefina said, snatching the napkin and cookie from Olivia's hand. "I'll make them better. They need more almonds." She turned and went back to the kitchen island.

Olivia shook her head. "No, that's not what I said."

She looked at Sophia and whispered again, "That's not what I said."

"Don't worry about it," Sophia replied. "You could've told her they were the best cookies on the planet, and the only correct response would still be, 'They need more almonds.'"

At the counter, Olivia half-turned and jotted a name on the paper. She slipped her entry into the envelope and sealed it. "Where do you want this?"

"Give it to me, and I'll add it to the mix," Sophia said, taking the envelope from her before leaving the kitchen.

Maria pulled a sheet pan from the oven and slid it onto the cooling rack. "If you want, you can start putting those boxes together," she said, nodding toward a pile on the counter behind Olivia. "We're also selling some of these cookies on Sunday as part of the fundraiser. We'll pack them up on Saturday."

Olivia picked up one of the flattened boxes. After inspecting it for a moment, she figured out which ends to fold and which to tuck. She finished the first box, set it on the counter, and reached for another.

"How's Preston?" Maria asked.

"He's okay." *He'd probably be doing better if Craig weren't under suspicion in his own aunt's death.* "A friend of his came in for the Highland Games. He's Fiona Campbell's nephew. Did you hear she passed away yesterday?"

Josefina nodded and made the sign of the cross.

"Yes, we heard," Maria said. "She was a wonderful woman."

"Did you know her well?" Olivia asked, stacking the finished box.

Josefina sat at the dining table.

"Mamá, we've done enough tonight," Maria said. "I'll finish this last batch, then we'll go home." She looked back at Olivia. "I knew Fiona from my teaching days. She was the librarian at our school."

"I thought she moved here from Scotland to help run the family business," Olivia said.

"She did until the family sold it. Then she earned her library science degree. Sophia has one of those neighborhood apps on her phone, and she said people were posting about seeing police cars at Fiona's house last night. Some were even speculating she'd been killed. I can't imagine anyone wanting to harm her."

Josefina shook her head. "This is why you need to have children," she said to Olivia. "So you don't have to live alone when you get old. If she'd had children, this wouldn't have happened."

"Mamá, you can't rely on kids to take care of you these days."

"Sí, which is why you are such a good daughter."

"Fiona was always independent, and she used to be so outgoing," Maria said. "After breaking her hip, she didn't get around as much. Use it or lose it. Motion is the potion. Stay active. That's the key, right, Mamá?"

"Sí, and live with your children."

Olivia added another box to the stack. "Did you know her aide, Amy Winters?"

Sophia returned to the kitchen.

"That took a while," Olivia said.

"Phone call," Sophia replied, inspecting a tray of cooling cookies.

Maria pulled another batch from the oven. "I've never met her, but Sophia has."

"Met who?" Sophia asked.

"Fiona Campbell's aide," Maria replied.

Sophia gathered some dirty bowls from the island and carried them to the sink. "Yeah, right after Fiona got out of the hospital last year. She called me because she knew my mom from their teaching days. She wanted advice about a new cane. The one she had was hurting her wrist, so I got her a different kind and went to her house to make sure she was using it correctly. I met her aide in passing."

"Was she steady with the cane?" Olivia asked.

Sophia nodded. "She had pretty good balance for her age, but she was afraid of falling. Happens a lot with older folks."

"Why don't you head home, Olivia," Maria said. "I think we'll cut the night short. I can finish cleaning up."

"Are you sure?"

Maria lowered her voice, glancing at Josefina. "I want to get Mamá home soon. She's looking tired. Thank you for coming, though."

"Okay. It'll give me a chance to stop by the inn for a bit. Fiona's nephew is having a gathering for her."

"Did you know Fiona?" Maria asked.

"No, but Preston might be there." That was easier than explaining she really wanted to talk to Winifred about her visit with Fiona.

"I'm going with you," Sophia said. "That is, if you don't need more help here, Mamá."

Maria waved them both off. "Go ahead. I'll take care of everything."

After exchanging goodbyes, Olivia and Sophia left the clinic. The warm glow from the lampposts cast a soft trail of light across the quaint streetscape. The concert crowd had dispersed, leaving Jillian's Cafe, the inn, and the bookstore as the remaining hotspots of the evening.

As Olivia started toward the street, Sophia gently caught her arm.

"Wait up, Liv. I'm actually not going with you."

CHAPTER 16

"Okay," Olivia said. "So why did you say you were?"

"I'm going over to A.J.'s house," Sophia replied. "That was the phone call."

Olivia suppressed a smile and stepped toward the curb. "I see. Well, have fun."

"Wait, Liv. Hold up. I just didn't want to say anything in front of Abuela. You know what she's like."

Olivia held up her hands. "Look, you don't have to explain it to me. I understand about Josefina. She'd have you engaged by the end of the week if she knew. Like I said, have fun."

"You know … we've never really talked about this."

Knowing what Sophia meant, Olivia preferred not to make it her business. "Talk about what, exactly?"

Sophia pressed her lips together, glancing to the side.

Since she'd had "the talk" with A.J. yesterday, Olivia figured it was as good a time as any to deal with the other half of the equation. "If you're referring to you and A.J., that's not really for me to weigh in on."

"But I feel like it kind of is. I just didn't know if you felt weird about it."

She smiled, hoping to put Sophia at ease. "I don't. And how I feel doesn't matter anyway. At first, I needed a hot second to process it. You're like my sister, and he's like my brother. So I see it as my like-sister dating my like-brother, and there's nothing weird about that at all."

"Only you would come up with something like that."

"Just please, don't be a bridezilla," she teased. "Let your maids of honor choose their own dresses. The color choices can be yours, as long as peach or pink aren't in play."

"Now *you're* being weird. We've only officially been out three times."

Olivia used her fingers to make air quotes. "Officially."

"You know what I mean."

"Have you been counting the hours since you last saw him?" Sophia opened her mouth to respond, but Olivia cut her off. "I'm just kidding. Honestly, I couldn't think of two people who are a better match. And a bonus for me, it would make planning social activities so much easier if I could see both of you at the same time. Is it too soon to start thinking about a mutual Christmas gift?"

"Way too soon."

"Gotcha. I'll keep your clandestine meetups with you-know-who a secret from Josefina. What about your mom?"

"She knows and agrees it's probably best not to tell Abuela just yet."

"Got it. I'm happy for you. Look at us. A year ago, we were both single and pleased as punch to remain so. Now, though we're still paid-up members of the spinster club, I have Preston, and you're seeing what happens with A.J., albeit on the down-low."

"What's the world coming to?" Sophia said.

They embraced in a warm hug.

"Maybe better times," Olivia replied. "You and A.J. have to stay together, or things between the three of us will get extremely awkward."

"That's a lot of pressure, but I'll do my best not to turn this into a situation that requires 'Dear Ms. Penn's' help," Sophia joked as they pulled apart.

"You'd best be off," Olivia said. "Someone special is waiting for you. I'll see you Sunday, if not before then."

With that, they said goodbye and went their separate ways.

Olivia crossed the street and headed for the inn. The temperature had cooled now that the sun had fully set. Warm lights glowed from the shops still open, and a savory scent lingered in the air from the food truck that had served concertgoers earlier.

She entered the inn, finding the lobby buzzing with conversation as the guests mingled, sipped cocktails, and nibbled on finger foods. A boisterous song erupted from the dining room, carried by hearty bass and baritone voices. She caught a verse about a sailor's long voyage before the chorus swelled: "Home at last, home at last, my true love, I'm home at last."

Zoey sat on a stool behind the concierge desk, scanning the crowd. When she spotted Olivia, she gave an enthusiastic wave. Olivia smiled and waved back, weaving through the crowd as she made her way to the desk.

"Hi, Zoey. I've never seen it this busy in here."

"I know. It's wild, isn't it? Are you here for the whisky tasting?"

Olivia leaned over the counter so she wouldn't have to shout over the loud chatter. "No. I heard there was a small gathering for Fiona Campbell tonight."

"It's in the dining room."

"It's not a private event?"

"Bev initially offered Mr. Campbell the banquet room, but the crowd was too large. Now it's a complete free-for-all. Regular patrons, whisky-tasting attendees, guests for Fiona's send-off. At this point, I can't even tell who's who anymore."

"Alright, thanks. I'm going to see who I can find."

Zoey raised a fist in a triumphant gesture. "May the banter be braw!"

Olivia pondered that for a moment, taking it to mean something good. "Indeed."

Stepping into the dining room felt like walking into a wake at a Scottish pub. Men in formal Highland attire mingled with tourists and locals, creating a vibrant atmosphere everyone seemed to be enjoying.

Several tables that usually lined the near wall had been taken away, replaced by a portable bar and a buffet laden with appetizers for the whisky tasting. Every seat was taken, and patrons stood around chatting, eating, and drinking.

Preston stood at the far end of the bar, talking with a guest, but when he saw her, he excused himself and came over. They exchanged a quick hug and a safe-for-public kiss.

"I didn't know you were coming," he said.

"I saw Craig earlier today, and he invited me. I can't believe how many people are here. The whole lobby is full."

"My mom is thrilled." He nodded at the chalkboard sign propped on the bar, advertising the night's specialty spirits. "I just got an earful from a determined Scotsman when I suggested someone had spelled whisky wrong. I thought there was an E at the end."

"Never in Scotland."

"So I've been told, but I guess as a writer you'd know that."

"Maybe you need to spend some time in a kilt."

He smiled, shaking his head. "Not happening."

"At least your mom is getting into the spirit. She's looked quite festive all week." Olivia glanced around, then leaned in, lowering her voice. "Any more news about Mack?"

"No. Have you heard from him?"

She shook her head. "What about the search? Any luck?"

"Summer King got delayed and won't be here until tomorrow morning."

"Will the dog still be able to track a scent after twenty-four hours?"

He shrugged. "I don't know, but it's better than nothing."

"I found out something you may not know."

He placed a hand on the small of her back and guided her to a quieter spot near the dining room entrance.

"Okay, what is it?" he asked.

"I spoke with Amy Winters. She said Mack tried to see Fiona yesterday afternoon. She didn't mention it to the police because he never saw her. Amy turned him away since Fiona was sleeping."

"What time?"

"Around three. Another thing. Amy referred to Mack as Fiona's accountant. Apparently, Fiona didn't want Amy to know she'd hired a PI to check her background. Did you know Amy is the beneficiary of Fiona's life insurance policy?"

"How do you know that?"

"Dorothy Peabody told me."

He nodded. "Amy volunteered that information to us."

"I wonder if she stood to gain anything more from Fiona's will."

"According to Craig, he was the only heir. But Fiona could've had a new will drawn up that he doesn't know about."

"Amy might've known who Mack really was. Maybe Fiona hadn't actually been sleeping, and Amy turned him away so he couldn't speak with her."

"It's possible. She could've seen his business card in Fiona's address book."

Olivia glanced around the gathering. She wasn't ready to mention her conversation with Nolan just yet. He'd made some valid points, casting doubt on Mack's actions. But she wasn't convinced enough to push that angle, especially not with the police, when all she had was speculation.

"Mack could've discovered something troubling about Amy's past, and maybe Amy took action before Fiona learned about it," she said.

"It's a theory."

"Are you still considering Craig a suspect?"

"More like a person of interest. I have to."

"Mack had some kind of contact with Craig documented in his file on Amy. I spoke with Craig at Fiona's house this afternoon, and he acted like he'd never heard Mack's name before. Granted, Mack could've used an alias when he spoke with him. Did you try calling Mack's cell?"

He nodded. "Yeah. The phone we found is his, but

it's locked, and we can't pull any information from it. Here comes Craig."

She turned as Craig approached.

"Thanks for coming," he said to her.

"You have a nice turnout," she replied.

"I don't know how many are here for Fiona, but word is getting around. Quite a few people have offered their condolences and shared memories of her with me."

Spotting an opportunity for an introduction, she asked, "Is Winifred here?"

Craig scanned the room. "That's her, sitting alone at the table by the fireplace. Clare was with her a moment ago."

"Thanks," Olivia said. "I'll go over and say hi." She touched Preston's arm. "I'll catch up with you later. Good to see you again, Craig."

Leaving Craig and Preston, she wove through the tables and small clusters of standing guests. Winifred sat alone with a cup of tea and an untouched scone in front of her. She wore a crisp white blouse and a tartan scarf at her neck, her posture ramrod-straight and her demeanor dignified.

"Excuse me, Winifred Fraser?" Olivia asked.

She looked up. "Yes."

"My name is Olivia Penn. I'm a friend of Craig Campbell." *Sort of.* "He mentioned you'd known Fiona for a long time. Could I speak with you for a few minutes about her?"

She'd already decided against approaching Winifred

under the pretense of collecting anecdotes for the paper. With Winifred's reasons for coming to Apple Station unclear, Olivia felt it best to keep her own intentions equally vague.

Winifred assessed her for a moment, then gave a single nod. Olivia pulled a chair closer, angling it so she could be heard over the hum of the room, and sat down beside her.

"To Fiona Campbell," a man near the bar said in a raised voice.

Many lifted their glasses. "To Fiona Campbell," the crowd responded.

Olivia turned back to Winifred. "Craig organized a lovely memorial. I didn't know Fiona well, but I've learned that she funded a lot of projects and charities in town. Craig mentioned you knew her as a child in Scotland. What was she like growing up?"

Winifred paused, a faint smile touching her lips. "Fiona was kind, smart, and always very independent," she said in a warm, lilting Scottish accent. "I was closer to her sister, Ruth. Fiona was a few years younger than us."

"I see. Is this your first time visiting the U.S.?"

"No, I've been to Los Angeles, Orlando, and New Orleans."

"You've done some traveling," Olivia said with a smile. "Which place did you like best?"

Winifred took a moment to consider. "New Orleans. The food was unusual, but very good."

"Apple Station can't compete with New Orleans on the culinary front," Olivia said, grinning wider. "But we've got a few hidden gems. Did you travel here just for the Highland Games?"

"My great-niece Clare wanted to come and talked me into joining her. She's good friends with Craig's son, Gavin."

She doubted Clare's insistence alone was Winifred's only motivation. "I met Gavin when he arrived on Sunday. I imagine his family planned to visit Fiona sometime during the week. Did you stay in touch with Fiona after her sister passed away?"

Winifred took a sip of tea. "We spoke a few times over the years. Fiona came to Scotland for Ruth's funeral. That's where she's buried."

Olivia nodded. "Craig mentioned he'll be taking Fiona's ashes back there to inter them in the family plot with his mother."

"Fiona would've liked that. We were from a different time, when traditions and lineage mattered. Young people nowadays don't even know who their great-grandparents were."

"I was in Fiona's house earlier, helping someone look for her cat, and I saw an old Campbell family Bible with a genealogy that went back at least twelve or thirteen generations. There was even a marriage recorded between a Fraser and a Campbell."

Winifred gave a small smile. "Those are two very common names in Scotland. I'm sure many such marriages appear in both the Campbell and Fraser family histories."

A young woman in her early twenties approached the table, carrying a plate of hors d'oeuvres. She wore jeans and a T-shirt with a DJ panda on it. Setting the plate down, she glanced at Olivia before gesturing at the scone.

"Aunt Winny, you need to eat something."

"You must be Clare," Olivia said. "Your great-aunt and I were just talking about Fiona. I understand you saw her on Tuesday."

Winifred removed the napkin from her lap, placed it on the table, and abruptly stood. "Clare, walk with me back to our room. I'm feeling tired."

Clare linked her arm with Winifred's.

"It was nice speaking with you," Olivia said quickly.

"Thank you. The same."

With that, Winifred and Clare crossed the room toward the exit, leaving Olivia with the impression that something she'd said had struck a nerve.

CHAPTER 17

Thursday morning was unusually quiet in the Penn household. After a solo breakfast, Olivia tidied up, unbothered by her furry friends, who typically begged for treats while she ate. Her father had left a note on the kitchen table, saying he'd gone into town to run a few errands. In the living room, Buddy and Willow milled around, barely interested in playing. Maybe they sensed her gloomy mood. Shortly before ten, she planned to take off for June's house to pick up the cat's supplies, perhaps for the last time.

Olivia had known Willow since Paige adopted her as a kitten, and over the past eight months, they'd formed a special bond. The cat seemed more in tune with her moods than happy-go-lucky Buddy. Even her father had grown accustomed to having the cat in their home. Many nights, Willow would claim his recliner, and instead of shooing her away, he would settle on the sofa. The thought of Willow leaving saddened her, but she felt worse for Buddy. There was no way to explain to the beagle why his best friend wouldn't be around anymore. She'd browsed local animal shelters online, toying with the idea of adopting a cat, but she hadn't submitted any applications yet.

To top off the somber start to the day, her hope that Mack might contact her again was all but gone. Before getting out of bed, she'd checked her text messages and e-mail for any word from him. During breakfast, she'd scanned the local and regional news headlines but found no mention of Mack's disappearance or of the car wreck.

The Times was equally silent about Fiona's death. Either the police were keeping a tight lid on information, or there was simply nothing to report. Out of curiosity, she'd downloaded the CloseBy app to check the thread discussing the police presence at Fiona's house. A few recent posts mentioned hearing gunshots in the area on Tuesday night, but skeptics quickly dismissed them as fireworks. Despite the intrigue surrounding the events, there was no further speculation that Fiona had been murdered. The thread had gone quiet, and by yesterday afternoon, ten newer discussions had already pushed the topic farther down the forum, fading it from the community's collective focus.

She still didn't understand why Mack had pulled her into all this. Three names stood out in the file he'd asked her to take. Both Amy and Craig seemed unlikely suspects, yet each had something to gain financially from

Fiona's passing. While Amy stood to receive a windfall, Craig was under mounting pressure to cover his wife's medical expenses. Mack had linked Amy to the sudden death of Gladys Henderson, another patient in her care. Amy seemed unaware of Mack's true identity, and Craig might've lied about knowing him.

A glance at the clock warned her she was running late. Dread about her meeting with June had slowed her all morning. Now she needed to hustle. She grabbed her things and checked on Willow and Buddy one last time before heading out the door.

Twenty minutes later, she pulled into June's driveway and parked behind her car. Hanging pots overflowing with summer blooms adorned the porch, and the lawn was still thick and verdant despite the recent drought. The rhythmic *tch-tch-tch-tch ... shhhhhh ... tch-tch-tch-tch* of a pulsating sprinkler sounded from the side yard as a breeze coaxed harmonics from the wind chimes hanging from the porch eaves.

June opened the door as Olivia stepped onto the porch.

"I saw you drive up," she said with a warm smile. "Come on in."

Olivia went inside and said her hellos as June closed the door.

"Have a seat," June said. "Can I get you something to drink? Water or tea?"

She declined politely and settled onto the pebble-gray sofa, glancing around the living room. A large manufacturer's box featuring a picture of a cat tree leaned against the bay window. Beside it sat a basket of cat toys, many still in their original packaging. Even though she might have another month with Willow, it looked like June was preparing for the cat's return.

"The room looks so much brighter with the new wall color," Olivia said.

"I absolutely love it. I used similar tones throughout the house. It's completely transformed the space. How have you been?"

Not wanting to dive into everything that had happened over the past few days, Olivia simply replied that she'd been doing well before shifting the conversation. "I've been thinking a lot about Paige with the playground opening on Sunday. Are you coming to the dedication?"

"I am. At first, I wasn't sure if I wanted to. It's a great thing A.J. has done with the property. Right after Paige died, I went out there, and all I felt was grief. I didn't think I'd ever want to go back. But when the playground was finished, he invited me to see it, and I was really amazed. The whole area looks completely different. You'd never know the manor had been there. The memorial garden he planted for Paige is beautiful."

"She loved her playgrounds. She never outgrew them. When I lived in Georgetown and came back to visit, we'd always ride the swings at the town square for old times' sake."

June looked at the two shopping bags filled with the

cat's supplies by the door. "She loved Willow too. I can't thank you enough for taking care of her all this time. You've truly gone above and beyond for what was supposed to be a three-month stay."

"Really, she's been no trouble. I've enjoyed having her around."

"It's been a huge relief knowing she's with someone I trust and that she's attached to."

"She's become like a member of the family." Olivia pointed at the box by the window. "I see a new cat tree there. Willow is going to love that."

June nodded, her warm smile fading. "That's part of what I wanted to talk to you about today."

Before Olivia could respond, her phone rang, playing her father's ringtone. She quickly dug the phone out of her pocket. "Excuse me, this is my dad."

June slid to the edge of the sofa as if preparing to stand. "I'll give you some privacy."

"No, it's okay. Stay. I'll just be a second." She answered, "Hi, Dad. What's up?"

"Where are you?" he asked.

"I'm at June's house."

"Can you meet me in town?"

She glanced at June with a small smile. "What for?"

"Just meet me in front of the old hardware store."

Lowering her voice, she said, "Is everything okay?"

"Yes, just get here when you can. I'll wait."

She checked the time on her phone to gauge whether

she could make the trip and still be home in time for her afternoon Q&A with Angela.

"Okay, Dad. I'll see you soon."

After saying their goodbyes, they ended the call.

"Is everything alright?" June asked.

"Yes, if not a little mysterious."

"Well then, I'll get to the point."

Olivia braced herself for bad news.

June folded her hands and turned slightly toward Olivia. "After Paige died, I shut down for a long time. I didn't feel like going anywhere or doing anything. I thought if I laughed or even smiled, it meant I'd accepted she was gone. And I wasn't ready for that. In fact, I didn't want to be." She glanced toward the window. "Willow was a great comfort to me. She helped keep my connection to Paige alive. Every time I saw *her*, I saw Paige. I've been through loss before Paige, and I know grief never really gets better. But we do, over time. And I did, day by day. My trip to North Carolina in January helped me feel like myself again. After that, I started getting my life back, little by little. I think Paige would be happy to see me moving forward."

"I know she would. Paige would never want you to stop living because her life ended."

June nodded. "I've been thinking about all the things I've never had the chance to do and the places I've always wanted to visit. Europe, Japan, Australia."

"Wow, that's an adventurous itinerary."

"I don't have plans for any of those trips right now,

but you never know when something will come up. Like next weekend, I'm flying down to North Carolina for my sister's birthday. It's been over twenty years since I've spent her actual birthday with her, and I'm really looking forward to it. I could never just do things on the spur of the moment before." She paused, exhaling slowly. "I adore Willow, but I don't think it's fair to her to be moving back and forth or having people come and go from her life. She's already lost her first caregiver, and I want her to have stability. So, what I wanted to ask you today is … how would you feel about keeping Willow permanently?"

Olivia couldn't believe what she'd just heard. "Oh!"

"I have a new cat tree and some toys I bought that we never got around to using. And I'd want to help with her expenses," June added quickly.

"Oh gosh, no." She held up a hand, smiling freely. "I mean, yes! Absolutely, yes, I'll keep her. I meant no, you don't have to help with her expenses, but I'll gladly take the cat tree and toys."

June grinned and stood as Olivia did the same. She wrapped Olivia in a heartfelt hug, and when they separated, both had teary eyes.

"This has been weighing on me for a while," June said. "I didn't feel right asking since you've already done so much for me."

"When you texted that you wanted to talk about Willow, I thought it was because you were ready to take her back. I've grown so attached to her, as has our beagle."

"Are you sure your dad won't mind?"

"Not at all. He adores her. But seriously, you don't have to cover any costs. You've already been so generous."

"I still want to," June insisted. "Maybe she'll just get some very large boxes packed with gifts for her birthday and Christmas. I have her food and medicine in the bags. Would you like to take her other things with you today?"

"Sure. Can you help me carry the cat tree to the car?"

"I think we can manage."

Olivia made two trips, loading the bags and the basket of toys into the Expedition. She folded down the rear seats before they carried the cat tree out and loaded it into the vehicle. Then they said their goodbyes, and Olivia backed out of the driveway.

She'd been dreading her visit to June's that morning, but the unexpected turn of events had completely flipped her day. Maybe it was a sign of better things to come. Maybe Mack would show up out of the blue and prove he had nothing to do with Fiona's death. Still, as she drove toward town, she tried to temper her optimism until she learned what was so urgent her father had asked her to meet him.

On the drive into town, Olivia's thoughts raced as she considered everything she needed to do now that Willow was officially hers. Day to day, not much would change. Willow wouldn't even notice the difference. But knowing she was solely responsible for the cat kicked her full-on into mama-bear mode.

First, she'd schedule regular vet visits, then look into insurance plans. Willow had always been an indoor cat, and Olivia planned to keep it that way. She'd decided to place the cat tree in the living room, right in front of the window. A few more scratching posts, strategically placed, would help protect the furniture. Maybe she could rope A.J. into installing cat wall shelves. Willow had a knack for parkour, and Olivia figured the shelves would keep her active, engaged, and entertained.

Before she knew it, she'd reached town. Since it

wasn't quite noon, parking was plentiful near the cafe on Blossom Avenue. After finding a spot and locking up, she headed toward her father, who stood on the sidewalk in front of the old hardware store.

"You haven't been waiting out here in this heat the whole time, have you?" Olivia asked.

"No, I went into the cafe for a cup of coffee. But I figured you were about due, so I came out a few minutes ago."

"You won't believe this. June asked if I wanted to take care of Willow permanently. I said yes."

His brow creased. "Is June okay?"

"She's fine. She just wants more freedom to travel without feeling guilty about leaving Willow or shuttling her back and forth. She offered to help with Willow's expenses, but I told her that wasn't necessary."

"Oh, of course. She shouldn't pay anything if we're keeping her."

"I already said yes, but you're okay with that, right?"

He nodded. "Sure. Willow is no trouble at all."

"June also gave me a cat tree and some toys. I thought we could put the tree in the living room by the window."

"Willow will like that. That's one of her favorite spots."

"Great. I'm glad we're on the same page."

"There's something else I hope we agree on."

He stepped into the recessed entrance of the vacant

suite, and she followed. A faded carnival flyer from May still clung to the glass door near the handle. Over time, the wind had swept scraps of paper and other debris into the forgotten corners of the entryway.

He peered through the door into the dark, dusty space. "What do you think about this place?"

She glanced through the grimy glass. "What do you mean?"

"Do you remember when this used to be a hardware store?"

"Y … yeah."

"I'm thinking of reopening it."

She stared at him, stunned, grasping for another meaning of what he'd just said. Slowly, like the next victim in a horror movie, she turned toward the empty suite. "What do you mean, reopen it?"

"I've contacted the property owner about leasing it, and I've researched renovation costs."

She closed her eyes, grappling with his words. "You want to open a hardware store?"

He shook his head and wrapped an arm around her shoulders. "No. I don't know the first thing about hardware. Even better. I want to turn this into a bakery."

The words hit her like a punch to the gut, leaving her momentarily shell-shocked. Her thoughts scrambled to catch up, but nothing made sense. When she finally managed a breath, she stammered, "Are you out of your mind? What made you—when did you—what makes you think you know anything about operating a bakery?"

"The school in Oregon taught me everything I need to get a bakery up and running. They provided a blueprint, and I've been e-mailing the instructor for advice. She's been really supportive."

"Dad, you can't be serious. Opening a business is a full-time job. Owning a bakery is a far cry from making a few dozen cookies over the weekend."

"I'd hire staff to handle most of the work. I'd manage things behind the scenes."

She groaned and rubbed her temples, trying to soothe the headache coming on. "That would cost a fortune, and you don't have that kind of money. You can't risk your retirement funds on something so unpredictable. Most businesses fail."

"This one would be a winner," he said, letting his arm drop from her shoulders.

"I know you said you wanted to do something more with your days, but I thought you meant a part-time job. Or volunteering. This is … this is too much."

"It would be a lot, sure. But I wouldn't be doing it alone." He grinned. "What do you think of 'Penn and Penn's Bakery'?"

She gasped. If not for her vagus nerve, she might've stopped breathing on the spot. Her throat tightened as she struggled to swallow his words. As composed as possible, she asked, "Dad … who would the other *Penn* be in this scenario?"

His smile widened, only deepening her sense of

doom. "It would be great. We could work together. Think of how much fun that would be."

Her chin dropped to her chest as she shook her head. "No. No. No. I have a job."

"Which you've been thinking of quitting."

"Yeah, to find something in my field. Writing. I'm—a—writer."

"We would need menus." Before she could unleash the tirade rising on her tongue, he added, "I'm just kidding. Look, this town needs a bakery, and I want to make it happen. What about 'Penn's Sweets and Treats'? That was your idea, remember?"

"When was that my idea?"

"December. You said I'd found a new calling and should open a bakery. You even said, and I quote, 'Penn's Sweets and Treats.'"

"I didn't mean it literally." Between the heat and her shallow breaths, she felt lightheaded. "I need to sit down."

She moved to the window ledge in the shaded entryway and sank onto the makeshift bench. The elation about becoming Willow's full-time caretaker, and maintaining the household status quo, vanished like woodland critters scattering under a hawk's shadow.

She took a few calming breaths. *Let's just approach this rationally.*

"Dad, it's about the money. You can't invest your retirement savings in something with little chance of succeeding. I'm sorry, but that's the truth. The bank isn't going to give you a loan big enough to turn this place into a bakery."

"I left the best part for last," he said, stepping closer. "I wouldn't have to invest a dime or take out a loan."

She looked up at him, incredulous. His claim was more baffling than the Bermuda Triangle. "And how is that supposed to work?"

"On Monday, I went to the bank to talk to someone about getting a loan. And you're right. They weren't exactly jumping through hoops to give me money. So I left the bank and came back here to take another look at the suite. That's when a woman approached me and asked if I owned it. I told her it used to be a hardware store, but I had this idea to turn it into a bakery. We started talking about small towns and the importance of supporting local businesses. Then she told me she leads a group of investors who focus on backing small businesses in rural areas."

She held up a hand. "Dad, wait. Are you saying a complete stranger is willing to invest in this place based on an offhand conversation?"

"I know. It sounds too good to be true."

She sighed, realizing they'd crossed the line where she had to be the parent. "That's because it is. Doesn't any of this sound fishy to you? You didn't give her any personal information, did you? Please tell me you didn't fill out any forms with your Social Security number."

"No, but she gave me her business card." He pulled

his wallet from his back pocket, slid out a card, and handed it to her.

She took it and read the name: Jacqueline Delacroix. As she flipped it over, her stomach sank. "Are you serious? This is just a name. There's no phone number, no address, no website. Dad, this is a scam. I don't know the angle or how she plans to take advantage of you, but this is one hundred percent not legitimate."

"No, you're wrong. She was very nice and genuinely interested. This is what she and her investors do. They invest in small businesses in small communities."

"Scam." Her phone rang, and she welcomed the interruption. She needed a moment to regroup before going another round trying to reason with him. Pulling the phone from her pocket, she checked the caller ID. "It's Preston."

"Go ahead, take it," he said. "That coffee has run right through me. I'm going home. We'll talk more about this later." With that, he turned and headed for his car.

"There's nothing to talk about," she muttered to his back.

The call went to voicemail, so she hit redial as she stood.

"Hi, Liv," Preston answered.

"Sorry, I was in the middle of something."

"Is everything okay?"

Her father pulled away from the curb, giving her a quick wave as he passed.

"I can't even begin to explain. What's up?"

"Mack hasn't contacted you today, has he?"

She looked into the empty suite, then started for her car. "No. I really wish he would've."

"That makes two of us."

"What is it? Did you find something?"

"I'm afraid I've got bad news."

"Is it bad news about Mack?" Olivia asked as she slid into the driver's seat. She set the phone on the center console and switched to speaker.

"It's looking that way," Preston said, his voice tight as a wound wire.

She started the engine and cranked up the AC, only to be blasted by hot air. "What happened?"

"Summer King arrived this morning with her dog and went with us to the site of the wreck. The dog caught a scent near where we recovered Mack's phone."

She lowered the window to let out the stifling heat. Bagpipe music blared from the speakers flanking the stage in front of the gazebo. A small crowd was watching a group of young girls perform a traditional Scottish dance in full Highland dress.

"Do you think the dog was picking up on Mack?"

"Summer couldn't say for sure. The dog can detect

any human scent, but it followed a trail into the forest. Everything points to Mack. I can't see why anyone else would be out there, and we've been careful not to contaminate the scene over the past two days. The trail ended at a dirt road. Based on the dog's behavior, Summer thinks the scent disappeared there."

The air inside the cabin began to cool, so she adjusted the vents and raised the window. "Where does the road lead?"

"Heading east, it intersects Old Mill Highway about fifty yards from where we found Mack's car. Going west, it dead-ends at a trail that cuts deeper into the forest."

"What's your theory?"

"I think Mack got into another vehicle."

"How does that make any sense? He crashes his car, hikes into the forest, and then gets picked up?"

Nolan's suggestion that Mack had staged the crash now seemed less far-fetched. Maybe Mack wanted the police to think he'd wandered into the woods, only to reappear later after finishing whatever he was planning. But why? To buy time? For what?

"How sure are you about that theory?" she asked.

"Not very. That's why Summer and her dog are still searching."

"How reliable is the dog?"

"It's a golden retriever, and according to Summer, it has a solid track record. She's confident it followed someone to where the scent disappeared."

Muffled applause drew Olivia's attention to the stage,

where the little girls were making way for a group of older dancers. The AC kicked on full blast, so she turned it down, easing the Arctic chill blowing at her face. "Can the dog also find someone if they're … dead?"

"It's not fully trained for that, but if the scent is from a recent death, Summer said it might still react."

"Why would Mack go into the forest?"

"I don't know. Strange behavior, to say the least."

She leaned her elbow on the windowsill and rested her head in her hand. Now that Mack had likely been tracked to an exit point, she felt compelled to share what she knew. "Yesterday, I spoke with Nolan Pierce. He was just as confused as I was. But he suggested Mack may have staged the crash."

"Why would Mack do that?"

"Nolan said Mack told him about some heirloom-quality valuables he'd seen at Fiona's house. On Wednesday, while I was looking for her cat, I saw a jewelry box with three antique brooches and an old iron cross on the wall in her bedroom. I doubt Mack was ever in there, so she probably had other pieces like that on display elsewhere. Nolan thought that Mack might've had an interest in them."

"Huh. Makes me wonder how much time Mack spent in there."

"He wouldn't steal from her."

"I don't think Craig would either, but I still have to consider him. I should go. Jayden is shadowing Summer, and I want to see if the dog has picked up any other trails."

"Alright, be careful. I'll talk to you later."

They said their goodbyes and ended the call.

The joy she'd felt at June's this morning already seemed like eons ago. Quiet evenings after a ho-hum day, with Willow curled beside her on the sofa, looked like a good life compared to the roller coaster of the past year.

Her gaze softened as her mind drifted. Maybe she would be better off working with her father in a bakery. No murders, no mysteries, no mayhem. She could leave everything behind and lose herself in the hands-on work: mixing, kneading, and baking. Or she could manage the front of the shop, selling pastries and chatting with customers. Cozy and quaint—a quiet, Hallmark life.

She shook her head, pushing the intrusive thoughts away. There was no way she'd let her father get caught up in some scheme by a stranger preying on his trusting nature. Maybe she'd ask Sam to run a background check on Jacqueline Delacroix to see if she had any criminal ties. Olivia imagined investigating scams and fraud might be the kind of work she'd do if she joined Carolyn's team. Perhaps the scope involved international affairs as well.

I wonder if any travel would be required. I should've asked more questions. With double the salary, I could help pay for reno-vating the shop.

She shook her head, harder this time, ridding her

mind of her father's ridiculous plan and refocusing on Mack. Her thoughts kept circling back to the same question: what did Mack want her to do? She'd followed the trail to Amy, but so far, there were no glaring red flags, only a few caution signs. The mystery of Gladys Henderson still gnawed at her. And why had Mack put Craig's name in Amy's file? What was it that he was unaware of? Maybe that Amy was Fiona's aide? Or that she was the beneficiary of the life insurance policy?

Olivia wanted another chance to talk to Amy, hoping to learn more about any interactions she might've had with Mack or Craig. When they'd spoken on Wednesday, Amy hadn't seemed nervous, but she could be a stone-cold actress.

She picked up the phone and dialed Amy's number. No answer. Without leaving a message, she hung up and fastened her seatbelt, staring out the windshield at the old hardware store. How many times had she walked past the vacant suite over the years without giving it a second thought? Never in her wildest dreams had she imagined she and her father would have anything to do with it.

A sudden knock on the driver's side window jolted her. She turned to find A.J. inches away, palms pressed flat against the glass.

"Boo!" he said, flashing a mischievous grin.

She lowered the window. "You almost gave me a heart attack, moron."

"Situational awareness, Liv. I could've been some crazed lunatic trying to get into your car."

"Let's drop the 'could've been' and go with the present tense. You *are* a crazed lunatic."

He leaned on the windowsill, clasping his hands inside the cabin. "Whatcha up to?"

She exhaled slowly, resting her head against the seat.

"That complicated, huh?" he said.

"You have no idea."

He glanced into the back, then nudged her shoulder, causing her to lurch sideways. "What's that?"

"Hey, excuse you."

"Move. You're in my way."

"Wow. Imagine that. I'm just sitting in my car, minding my business. It's a cat tree."

"Thanks, Sherlock. I meant, why do you have it?"

"That wasn't your question. June gave it to me, along with permanent cat mom status for Willow."

"You don't say. Is she okay?"

"Yeah. She wants more freedom to travel without disrupting Willow's life."

"Does that make me Willow's uncle?"

She tilted her head, feigning deep consideration. "Maybe? Sort of?"

"Have you thought about a catio?"

"I've only been Willow's full-time, responsible human for about an hour. Forgive me for not immediately diving into zoning laws and building permits for her dream expansion."

"I'll build you one," he declared. "On the back porch. Or outside your office. Or both. I'll sketch out some plans." He rubbed his hands together, glowing with excitement. "I'm gonna love being Willow's uncle. She's going to be the most spoiled cat ever."

"You may end up becoming her favorite human."

He gave her arm a playful poke. "I could never replace you in her eyes."

"That's morale-boosting," she said dryly. "By the way, June is really proud of what you did with the playground. You know she's coming on Sunday."

"Yes. I thought she might pass, but once she saw it, she seemed okay." He paused, narrowing his eyes. "So you never answered my question. Why are you sitting in an idling car, showing an alarming level of situational *unawareness*?"

Her phone rang, and she glanced at the screen. "Hold on a sec."

He drummed his fingers on the windowsill. "No, take it. I'm sure it's important. I just wanted to say hi-de-ho. See you on Sunday, if not before. Stay out of trouble."

She smiled and waved. "Bye."

Turning on the speaker, she said, "Hello, Amy."

"Uh, yeah. You called my number?"

"Yes, this is Olivia Penn."

"Oh, hi."

"Do you have a few minutes to talk?"

"I'm sorry, but now's not a good time. I'm at Fiona's house, looking for Shadow, but I have to be at a client's in an hour."

"How about I come there and help you search?"

"Okay, that works."

"Great, I'll be right over. Maybe we'll get lucky and find her."

And perhaps a clue about what happened to Mack.

CHAPTER 20

All was quiet outside Fiona's house. The lawn had been freshly mowed, likely by Fiona's landscapers, who probably didn't know what had happened. The flowers were holding their own, though without rain or a hose, they'd soon wither in the heat. Patches of marigolds and zinnias basked in the full sun, while impatiens thrived in the shade near the porch. With no sign of Amy outside, Olivia went to the front door and knocked. She waited a moment, then was about to check around back when she spotted Amy through the sidelight window as she came down the stairs.

A moment later, Amy opened the door, managing a polite smile that couldn't mask her exhaustion. "I thought I heard knocking. Come on in. I was upstairs looking for Shadow."

"Any luck?" Olivia asked, stepping inside.

"No. Her food hasn't been touched, and none of the

litter boxes have been used. I think we can rule out her being in here. She must've gotten out Tuesday night."

"Maybe someone will find her and take her to a vet or a shelter to be scanned."

"Hopefully. I don't know who would look after her. I'm not sure if Fiona arranged for anyone to care for her in this situation."

Olivia glanced at the cat figurine on the table, then at the door, unable to imagine feeling safe at night without a deadbolt. *I bet Fiona didn't even use the chain half the time. If someone knew what they were doing, it'd probably be easy to pick that lock. To get in here, they'd hardly even need the—*

She looked at Amy. "Did Craig or the police give you the key?"

Amy placed her hands at the small of her back. "Actually, neither. I have my own. Fiona insisted I keep one so I could let myself in. She said either I take it, or she'd leave the door unlocked when she expected me. I didn't think that was very safe, so I agreed."

"I see. But I thought the deputy had to let you in yesterday."

Amy nodded slowly. "Yeah, about that. When I got here, I called the police station to see if I could get my things. I didn't want to go in if they hadn't released the house yet. They said I could, and a deputy would be right over to unlock the door. I didn't tell them I already had a key because, honestly, I wanted to keep it a little longer. I thought I might come back to look for Shadow. That way, if I found her outside, I could let her back in.

At least she'd be safe until someone could look after her. I'll return the key to Craig as soon as I can. I just don't have time right now. I still want to check the garage before I leave."

"That makes sense." *It could also explain why there was no sign of forced entry on Tuesday night.* "We can talk while we look in there."

After locking up, Amy led the way to the garage. She punched in a code on the keypad by the side door, and they went inside. Though large enough to fit a car, the space looked more like a storage depot. Paper bags, plastic bins, and cardboard boxes were scattered and stacked everywhere. Some had labels, but most were anyone's guess. With countless hiding spots and things to explore, it was a perfect playground for a curious cat.

"Is that Fiona's Cadillac in the driveway?" Olivia asked.

"Yes. As you can see, there's no room for it in here. She stopped driving around the time I started working for her, but she still loved going for rides in that car. She enjoyed being chauffeured. Sometimes, if the weather was nice, we'd drive thirty minutes just to get a cup of coffee."

Amy scanned the garage. "Shadow! Are you in here, sweetie?" When there was no answer or rustling, she frowned. "I didn't think it would be that easy."

"I'll check the back half," Olivia said, weaving her way toward the rear.

"Okay. I don't think we'll find her, but I figured the

police probably went through here Tuesday night, and maybe she slipped in. If I didn't look, it would bother me." She pushed aside a few bags to get closer to a shelving unit. "I'll have to find time to meet Craig and return the key. My schedule is crazy right now. I picked up a few shifts for a friend who's on vacation. The clients' homes are an hour apart and in opposite directions from where I live."

Olivia moved a few boxes to check behind a headboard propped against the wall. "He's leaving Sunday, but he'll be coming back to take care of the house. If you don't see him before then, you could mail him the key or give it to the police. They'll hold on to it and make sure he gets it."

Amy looked inside some open containers on a low shelf. "Yeah, that sounds like a good idea."

"He had a nice gathering for Fiona last night at the inn. It's just so terrible. He came here to have a good time with his kids, and then this happens. Did he get a chance to visit Fiona before Tuesday?"

"Not that I know of," Amy replied, pulling a drop cloth off an upright piano. "He could've come after I left on Sunday or Monday, but Fiona didn't mention anything to me. She figured he'd stop by during the week." She set the sheet on the piano bench. "Shadow?"

Olivia stood still, listening for any movement. When all stayed quiet, she pulled up the side lever on a worn-out recliner and slowly extended the footrest. Then she knelt and checked underneath.

"I don't think she's in here," Amy said, straightening some garden equipment.

Olivia got up and pushed the footrest down. She opened a wicker picnic basket sitting on the chair. "Was Fiona looking forward to Craig's visit?"

Amy went back over to the piano and covered it with the cloth. "I'm sure she was."

"I understand they weren't terribly close. Not that there was any bad blood, just that they didn't see each other often."

"That's true," Amy said, lifting the lid of a footlocker. "I try not to get too personal with my clients, but sometimes they share things with me, Fiona especially. She spoke fondly of him, mostly because he was her sister's only child."

Olivia peered into the well of four stacked tires. "I heard Craig's wife has serious health issues."

"Yeah, it's really sad. Fiona told me about her. She was helping with some of the medical expenses."

"That was generous of her."

"She didn't mind helping Craig out … as long as it was *really* for medical bills."

Olivia looked over at her, letting the words hang. When Amy didn't elaborate, she nudged her, knowing this might be the last chance she'd get. "Was there another reason Craig needed money?"

Amy glanced around the garage. "Something has been bothering me ever since the police contacted me, and I'm having a hard time shaking it. I don't know if

I'm seeing something that's not there, and I'm not sure if I should say anything to the police."

That got Olivia's attention like a rooster crowing at midnight. She took a few steps toward Amy. "If it's something about Fiona's death, you should tell them."

"I don't want to throw around accusations, especially when they're based on feelings alone."

"Feelings can be warning signs."

Amy exhaled slowly. "Last week, I overheard Fiona talking to Craig on the phone. I wasn't eavesdropping. She had the conversation right in front of me. When she hung up, she was upset and said she wouldn't give him any more money for gambling."

A flurry of questions flew through Olivia's mind, but she stayed quiet, waiting to see if Amy would say more.

"I don't know the whole story," Amy continued. "Sometimes people just say things when they're mad without realizing who's around."

"Did Craig ask for money often?"

"I don't know if he asked or if Fiona just offered. I know this might sound crazy, but … what if he had something to do with Fiona's death?" She paused, then shook her head. "Saying it out loud, I feel awful. You must think I'm terrible for considering that her own nephew could harm her. But you hear about things like this happening, even between much closer relatives."

"I don't think you're awful for considering the possibility." *And it sheds new light on Craig.* "The police have to investigate all angles."

Amy stepped toward the side door. "That means I'm a suspect too."

"Because you were her aide?"

"That, and Fiona left me money. I told her not to. It was a life insurance policy. I said the money should go to her family or a charity, but she insisted."

And that would make you a person of interest under the circumstances.

With Amy talking freely, Olivia offered a sympathetic ear. "The police can't think you had anything to do with Fiona's death just because of that."

"I also don't have an alibi for that night. I was at home alone. I know how these things work. But I had nothing to do with her death or the break-in."

Olivia joined her by the side door. "I believe you." *Maybe.* "Fiona must've really cared about you."

"I get attached to all my clients, but Fiona was different. It never felt like work when I came here." She checked her watch. "No luck with Shadow today. I have to go. I don't know when I'll be able to come back."

"You did your best. I drive by here often, so I'll keep an eye out for her in the neighborhood."

They left the garage and walked toward the driveway.

"Can I ask you something else?" Olivia said, not waiting for a reply. "When Fiona's accountant came to see her on Tuesday, how did he seem to you?"

Amy stopped by the driver's side of her car. "What do you mean?"

"Was he insistent on seeing her?"

Amy shook her head, unlocked the door, and opened it halfway. "No. He was friendly. Like I said before, I told him she was sleeping. He said he'd come back later, but I suggested he call ahead, since she goes to bed early."

As a last-second Hail Mary, Olivia lobbed one more question. "Did the police ask you if anything was missing from the house? You'd probably be the best person to notice."

"Fiona had a lot of antiques from Scotland. I'm sure some of them were valuable. But off the top of my head, I didn't notice anything of *hers* missing."

"Of hers? But you did notice something missing?"

"Something of mine was taken."

"What was it?"

Amy let out a long breath. "Sometimes I work nights or in areas even more rural than this. Most of my clients are older and live alone. One time, I was staying overnight at a client's house because she wasn't feeling well. She'd just come home from the hospital, and her daughter was flying in the next day. The daughter asked if I'd stay, just in case. I was happy to." She paused, pressed her lips together, then continued. "Around two in the morning, someone broke in. I locked myself and the woman I was caring for in the bathroom, then called the police. Everything turned out okay, but after that, I decided I needed a way to protect myself and my clients. So I bought a gun, and I've carried it ever since."

Olivia tensed slightly. She hadn't considered the

possibility that the gun fired Tuesday night belonged to Amy. "That sounds terrifying. I can understand the need for protection."

"Whenever I was here, I kept it in a bag upstairs in the spare bedroom. But on Tuesday, I had the bag in the living room since I'd planned to leave early. Between Winifred showing up and rushing to get out of here, I accidentally left without it. When the police came to my apartment to tell me about Fiona, they asked if she owned any guns. That's when I told them about mine, and then they informed me it was missing from my bag."

"I heard Fiona's neighbors reported gunshots Tuesday night, and that two bullet holes were found in the wall by the door. If someone stole the gun and was shooting at her at such close range, it seems unlikely they would've missed."

"I know."

"Was Fiona aware that you had the gun?"

"Oh, yeah. I told her upfront, and she thought it was a good idea. She was glad I had the extra protection when driving home late."

Olivia nodded, glancing to the side. If Mack was determined to see Fiona on Tuesday, Amy's roadblock that afternoon wouldn't have stopped him. He would've come back later, probably when he knew Amy wouldn't be there.

The intruder could've taken the gun. But Craig found Fiona upstairs, and the bullet holes were downstairs. Who was shooting at who? Was there a third person involved? Was Mack the target? Could Amy have shot at him? Was it staged?

"Maybe Fiona caught the intruder in the act," Olivia said. "Do you think it's possible she was the one who fired the gun?"

"Fiona used to be a competitive shooter in Scotland. If she were firing, she wouldn't have missed."

CHAPTER 21

After parting ways with Amy, Olivia drove home, her concerns about Craig lingering. The possibility that he needed money for both his wife's medical expenses and a gambling habit made his motives for theft, or worse, even more compelling. Craig finding Fiona now seemed suspiciously convenient, especially since he'd lied about his whereabouts in the hours leading up to her death.

She understood why Preston hadn't told her about Amy's missing gun. Selective sharing was part of his job. He wouldn't compromise the investigation just to satisfy her curiosity. But now that she knew, the revelation only muddied the waters further. Could Mack have been the shooter, or the one being shot at? No matter how she turned it over in her head, every possibility led to a grim outcome for him.

What if the shots, the missing gun, and the wreck were all part of an elaborate setup? She imagined the sequence of events: Mack went to Fiona's house late at night, then supposedly found himself on the wrong side of a gun. Later, he wrecked his car, perhaps to make it look like he'd been injured. But then, where was he? Could he be hiding? Was he covering up a crime, buying himself time?

She hadn't ruled out the possibility that Fiona was the one who fired the gun. She likely noticed Amy's bag in the living room and knew the gun was inside. If she'd heard someone in the house, she might've retrieved it, then gone to her bedroom to hide. Perhaps before she could, the intruder came upstairs. From somewhere on the staircase, she could've fired toward the door, putting two bullet holes in the wall and maybe hitting the intruder as well.

Olivia arrived home shortly after two, setting aside her speculation so she could focus on her upcoming Q&A chat. After parking, she got out, grabbed the basket of toys, and carried it inside. Willow jumped down from the window ledge to greet her but froze at the sight of the large, unfamiliar object in her hands.

"It's okay, Willow. It's all good. These are all for you." She set the basket on the floor, then went back outside and returned with the two bags of supplies. Wary but curious, the cat crept forward inch by inch toward the basket. Once close enough, she sniffed all around it, then stood on her hind legs to peer inside. The faint scent of catnip was all the encouragement she needed. She stepped back, crouched, and leapt straight in.

Olivia knelt, picked Willow up, and set her gently on the floor. She grabbed a fluffy kicker from the basket and rolled it a few feet away. The cat pounced, flopped onto her side, and clutched the toy in her paws, biting into it with delight.

"This is your forever home now. I'll always do my best to make it a happy one for you." She'd worried about how Willow would adjust after Paige died, but the cat had done okay. Her hope was that the same would be true for Shadow, if she was ever found.

The kitchen door creaked open, and Buddy padded in with her father close behind.

"Hey, Dad," she called.

Buddy trotted over to her. She gave him a few affectionate pats before he turned his attention to Willow's new toy, sniffing and pawing at it.

"I was outside playing fetch with him," he said, crossing the kitchen into the living room. "We weren't out too long. It's hot out there, and I didn't want him to overheat. Wow, that's a lot of toys."

"The cat tree is still in my car. Can you help me bring it in? It's in a box, but it's not too heavy. June and I managed."

"Let's do it now. I'll put it together this afternoon." He gestured toward the bay window. "You want it there in the middle?"

She stood up, nodding. "I think that'll be perfect. It'll give her a nice, wide view. I was also thinking we could hang a hummingbird feeder from the porch roof, right above the railing. That might bring some action closer to her."

"Sounds like a plan. I'll find one online."

They went out to her car, carried the box inside, and set it by the window.

"I bet this is at least six feet tall," he said as Willow came over to investigate.

"It looks impressive. And exciting for you, little kitty," she added, stroking the cat's head.

"Have you thought any more about my exciting news?"

"If you mean opening a bakery … I know it sounds like a fun idea to you, but it's a huge undertaking, especially in an area you have no experience in. The time and effort to renovate that suite and run the business would be enormous. You need to think about how you spend your days now. A venture like this would be more than a full-time job. Is that really what you want at your age? You'd give up all your freedom. And then there's the cost. It's just not a wise or realistic investment."

"I already told you, the money is covered."

"Did you give that woman your phone number?"

"Yes. How else is she supposed to contact me?"

"Ideally, she won't. Don't answer calls from numbers you don't recognize. If someone really needs to reach you, they can leave a message." She grabbed the basket. "I'm putting these upstairs for now. I have an online chat for work at three. Can you take these two bags into the kitchen? Just leave them on the table. I'll put the stuff away later."

"Okay. I'll start on the cat tree after lunch," he said as she went up the steps. "And if that woman calls back, you can talk to her yourself. Ask her anything you want. You'll see. She's the real deal."

"Jacqueline Delacroix," she called from the top of the staircase. "That name even sounds fake!"

She went into her room and reorganized the bottom of her closet to make space for the basket. Time would tell if stashing it there would be enough to keep the goodies hidden. Most of the toys were still in their original packaging, but Willow might pick up on the scent of catnip. If scratches appeared on the closet doors, she'd need to find a new hiding spot for the treasure.

Before going back downstairs, she looked up the local animal shelter's number and called. With Shadow still on her mind, she wanted to check if someone had dropped the cat off. After a brief search, the shelter worker confirmed Shadow hadn't been brought in, but they would post a missing-cat notice on the front desk bulletin board. Since Olivia didn't have Craig's phone number, she listed herself as the contact in case Shadow turned up.

When the call ended, she hurried downstairs to grab what she needed for a quick lunch: an apple, a container of yogurt, a spoon, and her thermos. Then she left the house, crossed the yard, and went into her office. After turning on the air conditioner, she booted up her laptop and popped in earbuds. As she settled into her chair, she dialed Angela's number.

"Hello, Olivia," Angela said. "I wasn't expecting you to call so soon."

"The chat starts in five minutes," she replied, peeling back the lid on her yogurt.

"I know. This is extraordinarily early for you."

"Ha-ha. Someone is in a funny mood today. Guess what?"

Angela paused long enough to suggest she was seriously weighing her options. "You're getting married."

"Wrong. Willow's owner asked if I wanted to keep her permanently, and I said yes."

"That's even better than getting married."

"I know, right?"

"I'm so happy for you. I know how attached you've become to that little furball."

Olivia logged on to the chat and took a bite of her apple.

"Can you believe this is our last one of these?" Angela said.

"I know. I'm a bit verklempt. It won't be the same without you."

"I'll miss them too, kiddo. I'm sure they'll resume once Jordan officially takes the helm. Did you decide yet whether you can come up to Vermont in October?"

"Yes, the first weekend of the month looks good for us."

"I'll finally get to meet this man of yours."

"Be nice."

"Aren't I always?" Angela replied with a chuckle. "Okay, looks like we're just about ready. I see you've logged on, and attendees are joining. You know, I've always wanted to be on the other side of this. To be 'Ms. Penn' spouting advice to a captive audience that is hanging on my every word. If I tried to sell my hard-won wisdom to strangers, I'd probably get an earful and a one-finger salute."

"Is it possible for you to post as me?"

"With admin access, I have all sorts of power."

"Let's do it, then. You be me. Take the questions and show me what you've got."

"You want me to answer for you?"

"Uh-huh," Olivia said, taking another bite of the apple.

"Okay, you're on."

Angela welcomed everyone to the chat as Olivia silently read the first question. The anonymous guest asked if they should feel offended about not being included on a weekend trip with friends.

Under Olivia's handle, Angela posted, "Yes."

"No, Angela," Olivia said quickly. "You can't just give a one-word answer. And for the record, that response should've started with 'no.'"

"This is payback."

"You're making me look bad. From now on, I want to see your answers before you post them. Send them to me in the private chat."

"My, aren't we getting bossy," Angela teased.

Olivia sighed and quickly typed out a more appropriate response, apologizing for any confusion and explaining she'd misread the question. Then she posted her own revised answer.

"Personally, I would've been offended," Angela muttered.

"Focus. The questions are piling up."

Olivia read the next one from someone asking about how to handle a cheating boyfriend. She braced herself, nervous about what her virtual doppelgänger might say.

After reading Angela's proposed solution, which involved hastening karma, Olivia jumped in immediately. "Absolutely not, Angela. That's inappropriate on so many levels, not to mention borderline illegal."

"Oh, come on. You're no fun."

Olivia quickly posted her own response. "Yeah, well, I'm supposedly the one answering these questions, and corporate would have me writing apologies up the wazoo if what you wrote went out under my name." She moved on and read the next question about seating arrangements at a wedding reception. After a long silence in the private chat, she said, "Angela? Are you going to answer that?"

"Shh. I'm thinking. This is harder than it looks."

When Angela's response finally came through, Olivia reviewed it, tweaked the wording, and copied it into the feed before posting.

"You're editing me now?" Angela asked.

"You need to be reined in."

"The next question could go one of two ways," Angela mused. "Long-term, say five or ten years down the road, I could see that situation going south. But in the short term—"

"I'd love to have a philosophical debate over tea and biscuits, as our friends across the pond say," Olivia interrupted. "But you've got to get in and out of these questions quickly, in four sentences or less."

"This is a lot of pressure."

"Welcome to my world." She read Angela's response, then posted it with no changes. "That sounded enough like me."

"This is exhausting. I'm out. You take over."

Olivia straightened in the chair, squared up to the desk, and fully resumed her official role. They carried on as usual for the next forty minutes until Angela ended the chat.

"And that's a wrap on the online version of 'Dear Ms. Penn,'" Angela said. "At least for now. I think Jordan will keep the status quo until he finds his footing. I'm sure he'll come up with his own ideas to impress the bigwigs with some innovative way to boost subscriptions. I've spoken with him a few times, and he hasn't mentioned any major changes. He's young, but he has experience. You'll be okay."

"I got a job offer," Olivia blurted. She hadn't intended to bring it up, but the words just slipped out. Over the years, Angela had become a trusted friend and a sounding board. She always called it like she saw it, even when it was hard for Olivia to hear.

"Oh? With another paper?"

"Yes and no. There's a freelance gig at the local paper, but that's not the offer I'm talking about. It's an analyst position."

"Analyst? For who?"

"A private company that provides logistical support for monitoring and developing strategies for system operations." The words spilled out faster than she expected.

I'm already sounding like Sam.

"That's … very different. What kind of operations?"

"They're related to law enforcement."

Angela let out a slow breath. "That's a hard left turn for you. I know you've been involved in some situations with the police, but those were by circumstance, not by choice."

"I agree," Olivia said quietly.

"I'm surprised. I knew you were considering a change, but this isn't what I expected."

"Me neither. It just kind of popped up."

"How do you feel about it?"

She swiveled the chair, gathering her thoughts. "I don't know if I'm cut out for it."

"Is this something you applied for?"

"No. Someone I know made me the offer."

"Well, in that case, this person must think you're qualified. Are you seriously considering it?"

With Angela moving on, Olivia felt the itch to do the

same, but she didn't want to leap at the first opportunity just because it was convenient. The high-stakes environment wasn't something she was sure she wanted or was ready for. But Angela, as always, had a point. Carolyn didn't make haphazard decisions. If Carolyn believed she had what it took, that was a resounding vote of confidence.

"I don't know," Olivia said. "It's an option. It would take me away from what I've been doing, in one way or another, for the past fifteen years."

"You're bound to have some trepidation. A career change is daunting. You could always do freelance writing on the side to keep your pen sharp. What's the salary like?"

"Good. The offer is double what I'm making now."

Angela sounded like she choked on something. "Double? If you don't take it, maybe I will," she joked. "What about work-life balance?"

"I think it'd be about the same, though with less flexibility. The more I think about it, the more unsure I feel. Doubt means no, right?"

"When it comes to marriage, yes. When it comes to eating that second piece of pie, doubt rides in the back seat." They shared a laugh before Angela continued. "I'll admit, this job offer is unexpected, but your leaving isn't. You've been thinking about moving on for a while, and actually … I already compiled a shortlist of columnists from smaller papers who could take over for you."

"Nice to know I'm so easily replaced," Olivia joked.

"The intrepid Olivia Penn is never replaceable. But we all move on. I'm doing it, and we both knew your time would come too."

Olivia's phone buzzed with a text from her father.

"You could be right about that," she replied.

"I just didn't want to leave Jordan high and dry in case you flew the coop."

She glanced at the message, silently reading: "There's a guy here, Nolan. Says it's urgent he speaks with you. What should I tell him?"

That's odd. Olivia texted back, "I'll be there in a few minutes."

Angela continued, "I think if you're interested, you should go for it. If it doesn't work out, you can always make a comeback. I've got plenty of connections, and I'll always help however I can."

"Thanks. That means the world."

"You got it. Listen, I have to go to a staff meeting. We'll talk more later. It's been a pleasure spending these afternoons with you, Olivia."

"Likewise."

"To new beginnings for both of us."

"I second that."

After they ended the call, Olivia turned off the air conditioner and lights. Then she locked the office and headed toward the house, hoping Nolan's visit meant he had good news about Mack.

CHAPTER 22

Olivia entered the living room, finding her father and Nolan chatting about Buddy, who was lying on a dog bed near the cat tree by the window. She didn't want to be rude, but she also didn't see the need to roll out the red carpet for someone who'd shown up unannounced.

"Nolan," she said flatly.

Her father rose from the recliner and started toward the kitchen. "I'll let you two talk. Honey, I'm running into town for a few things."

If they'd been alone, she might've asked whether his business had anything to do with Jacqueline Delacroix. But as it was, she had to let it go for now and focus on why Nolan was sitting on their living room sofa.

"Why am I not surprised you know where I live?" Olivia said, glancing over her shoulder as her father left through the kitchen door.

Nolan shrugged. "You're not hard to find. Even if

Mack didn't already have your contact information on file."

She knew Mack had investigated her background, but learning she had her own file in a PI's cabinet wasn't on her bucket list.

"Were you involved in compiling that?"

"Yeah. That's kind of what I do. For what it's worth, it was only because Mack was thinking of asking you to join us."

"As an associate?" she half-joked.

"Maybe. With a partner, he could take on more clients, and that's better for everyone. He thinks highly of you. I know he trusts you, which is why I'm here." He rubbed his eyes, then clamped his mouth shut before sneezing. "Excuse me," he muttered, then sneezed twice more. "My eyes are watering like crazy."

She looked over at Willow, perched on the top level of the cat tree. "We have a cat. I remember you said you're allergic. Would it be better if we talked outside?"

He popped up, already heading to the door. "Yeah, if you don't mind."

They stepped out onto the porch, where they both remained standing.

"I hope your visit means you've heard from Mack."

Nolan pulled his phone from the cargo pocket of his khaki shorts, swiping and tapping until he found what he was looking for. "Sort of."

"He contacted you?"

"Not exactly." He handed her the phone. She took it,

enlarged the image, and silently read the text as he spoke. "That's a record of a transaction from today on Mack's company credit card."

The charge showed the purchase of an airline ticket.

"How did you get this?"

"I've been monitoring the account, hoping he'd use it. Any activity would at least mean he's still alive."

"But how do you know it was him? The police found his phone near his car, but not his wallet. What if someone stole the card?"

She handed the phone back. He slid it into his pocket and leaned against the nearest porch post, arms folded across his chest.

"Yeah, that's definitely a possibility."

"The receipt doesn't have any details about the itinerary."

"It's for a ten o'clock flight tonight. Dulles to Edinburgh."

"Scotland? How do you know that?"

"I have access to his airline account. Sometimes he'll call wanting me to book him a last-minute flight, like, within hours, as if I can just snap my fingers and get him a seat without it costing a fortune."

She stared at him, immediately suspicious. *Did you also make this reservation?*

"And before you even ask, I didn't book the flight for him."

She nodded slowly. "Has he ever gone to Scotland before?"

"Not for work, at least, not that I'm aware of."

"And this wasn't a scheduled trip?"

"If he planned it before I left last week, he didn't say anything to me about it. I don't log into his airline account unless he asks me to handle the arrangements. The only reason I checked today was because I saw the charge on the credit card. Honestly, I was expecting a gas station or a hotel. A flight wasn't on my radar."

"Any idea why Edinburgh?"

Nolan widened his eyes and sighed. "I have to think it's connected, but I don't know exactly how. Maybe he stole something from Fiona's and has a buyer."

"In Scotland? That's a long way to go. And it's still just speculation that Mack was interested in anything beyond the job Fiona hired him for. But there is someone else who might've wanted something Fiona had."

Nolan uncrossed his arms and slipped his hands into his pockets. "Who's that?"

"Someone who believed Fiona had something valuable that belonged to her."

"What is it?"

"I don't know. Fiona had some heirloom-quality pieces in her bedroom—jewelry and an old iron cross that may or may not have value. Amy didn't notice anything obviously missing, except for one thing."

"What?"

Before she could answer, Buddy barked from just inside the doorway. She glanced down at the dog, who was clearly eager to join them.

"Her gun," she said.

"The gun was *Amy's*? If Mack was there, he could've taken it."

If that's true, who was he shooting at?

"Are the police still monitoring Mrs. Campbell's house?"

She shook her head. "No. They were there yesterday just to let Amy in to get her belongings."

Buddy barked again, and she opened the screen door to let him out. He padded onto the porch and sat at her feet.

"Why did you come all the way from Winchester to tell me this?"

"I didn't plan to. I just needed to get out of the office. Mack's clients keep calling, and I don't know what to say to them. Sometimes driving clears my head. I ended up more than halfway here and wanted to run this by you anyway. You're the only person I can talk to about this … Oh, man, I really don't want to go to the police, but if Mack is leaving tonight—"

"It seems suspicious," she said.

"Exactly. If the police found out I knew and didn't say anything … I don't want to be charged as an accessory to something."

"But the police should know. Mack isn't a suspect that I'm aware of, but they want to talk to him."

"Mack told me you have a connection in the local police department. Can you tell them?"

"Why me?"

He let out a deep breath. "Look, what if we're wrong about this, and Mack is working a case or just took a vacation to search for the Loch Ness Monster or something? If the police pick him up because of me, I'm out of a job. He'd never trust me again."

She looked down at Buddy, who gazed up at her expectantly. His internal snack clock must've gone off.

"And now that you've told me, it makes me complicit," she said, weighing her predicament. "Even if I went to the police with this information, they'd still need to talk to you. You'd have to show them the flight itinerary and tell them what you just told me."

"I'm fine with that. But this way, if we're wrong, I can tell Mack we talked, but that you were the one who went to the police."

She gave a dry laugh. "So he'd hate *me* instead of you. Do I have that right?"

Nolan looked away. "Sort of. But he wouldn't hate you."

Buddy barked again. She patted his side, opened the door, and nudged him toward the house. When the beagle refused to budge, she sighed and gave up, letting the screen click shut.

"Okay," she said. "I'll reach out to my contact and share what you've told me. Send me a copy of the receipt. They'll want to speak with you, so stay available."

After Nolan texted her the image, they exchanged goodbyes, and he left. She stepped back inside, shut the door, and went into the kitchen, with Buddy following on her heels. She gave him a treat from the pantry, then sat at the table.

Her thoughts raced. If Mack really was leaving tonight, why hadn't he called her? By now, he had to know she'd tried to reach him. If he were alive and well, she believed he would've sent a message. Unless, of course, he'd been using her all along for some hidden agenda.

The police likely weren't monitoring Mack's financials, given that he wasn't officially a suspect yet. But Mack wasn't careless. He'd know that using his company credit card could tip someone off, especially Nolan, who clearly wasn't above turning the tables on him and going to the police. Would Mack have anticipated that move? Could it all be part of a larger plan?

Her thoughts turned to Winifred and her claim about something she believed Ruth had left for her. If Winifred had made such a long, expensive trip to try to get it back from Fiona, whatever it was had to hold some monetary value. The brooches and the iron cross in Fiona's bedroom came to mind. Both were prominently displayed and, even to Olivia's untrained eye, looked valuable. Then there was the Bible—a Campbell family heirloom, quite old and potentially rare. Such a book could fetch a hefty price at auction.

But why would Winifred care about the Bible? There was a historical marriage between the Frasers and the Campbells, but Winifred had been quick to dismiss any relation between the two families. Olivia had only skimmed the genealogy and hadn't looked closely for any branches that might suggest otherwise. But even if there were a connection, what then? How could a family Bible warrant such a dogged pursuit?

She recalled the brief conversation she'd had with Winifred yesterday. Winifred had clammed up the moment Olivia brought up her and Clare's visit with Fiona. It had seemed suspicious then, and even more so now.

After pulling her phone from her pocket, she dialed Preston's number. First, she'd fill him in on Nolan's news. Then, she had an inkling of a plan that might get her a second look inside Fiona's house.

CHAPTER 23

Compared to last night, the inn's lobby was as quiet as a glen at dawn. A handful of guests had gathered around a woman seated near the coffee cart as she demonstrated knitting techniques, weaving her needles and crafting intricate patterns with yarn. Beside her, a round table displayed tartan scarves and winter hats for sale. The rhythms of a fiddle, frame drum, and tin whistle played through the speakers, filling the air with a jaunty jig that could tempt even a mannequin to dance.

After calling Preston to share what Nolan had told her, Olivia had found the Peabodys' home number in an old-school directory. Every year, the phone company delivered the latest edition, leaving the hefty book on the ground by the mailbox. She hadn't cracked one open in at least five years. But with the Peabodys' number unavailable online, her father's insistence on always keeping the newest edition had finally paid off.

She'd called Dorothy to ask if she could borrow Fiona's house key under the pretense of wanting to search for Shadow. That wasn't entirely untrue. Olivia genuinely wanted to find the cat, though she knew Shadow wouldn't be in the house. But Dorothy didn't know that, and if Olivia happened to take another look around inside, maybe check out Fiona's bedroom again, so be it. Dorothy had suggested Olivia come by the next day to pick it up, since she and Floyd were heading out to dine at the inn. Rather than wait until tomorrow, Olivia had asked if she could meet them there in thirty minutes.

At five o'clock, only a handful of other early birds were out for dinner. The Peabodys sat at a table for two, already eating their meal. As Olivia approached, Dorothy tapped Floyd on the arm. He glanced over his shoulder, then turned back to the plate in front of him.

"Hi, Mr. and Mrs. Peabody," Olivia said with a polite smile.

"Lovely to see you," Dorothy replied warmly. "Would you like to join us?" She gestured toward the breadbasket. "They gave us so many rolls, I'd hate for them to go to waste."

Even if there had been an extra seat, she would've declined. "No, but thank you. I don't want to interrupt your evening out more than I already have."

"We'll take them home," Floyd said. "I can use them for toast. This Scotch pie is good. What kind of meat is this?" he asked Dorothy.

"Minced lamb."

"It looks delicious, Mr. Peabody. And are you also getting into the Highland spirit with your soup?" Olivia asked Dorothy.

"When in Rome, or at an inn that's turned Scottish for the week, you go with the specials. This is Cullen skink. It's made with smoked haddock, potatoes, and onions."

"The wife tried to trick me into ordering haggis," Floyd said, smirking. "I'm not eating sheep parts nobody was ever meant to eat."

"Not by you, maybe," Dorothy corrected.

"That's all I'm concerned with," he replied, taking a bite of his pie.

"You beat the crowds," Olivia said. "I was here last night, and it was packed. Two events were going on. Even without them, I think there would've been a waiting list after six."

Dorothy set her spoon down. "That's why we wanted to come early. Afterward, we're going to Tales and Treasures to pick out some children's books for the little library at the new playground. I want to stock it for Sunday's dedication."

"I've got plenty of books at home we could've used," Floyd grumbled, cutting into his pie. "I don't see why we have to buy more."

Dorothy sighed and shook her head. "Because five-year-olds aren't exactly clamoring to read westerns."

"That's a great idea," Olivia said. "It might even encourage parents to donate from their own collections.

Going to a playground and leaving with a book sounds like a good day to me." Eager to get moving, she pivoted to the reason she'd come. "I don't want to keep you from your meal. Thanks for letting me meet you here."

Dorothy reached for her purse on the table and unzipped it. She pulled out a key and handed it to Olivia. "I hope you find Fiona's cat. What will happen to her if you do?"

"I'm not sure," Olivia said, attaching the key to her Loch Ness Monster key ring. "Maybe Craig will take her or help to find her a home through adoption."

"I'd take her, but Floyd is allergic."

"My eyes swell up like hot-air balloons."

Dorothy zipped her purse. "But you always had dogs growing up."

As the conversation turned to the differences between cat and dog dander, Olivia politely thanked the Peabodys for their time and left the dining room.

A woman stood at the lobby desk with a leashed golden retriever sitting calmly at her side. Curious if she was the search and rescue volunteer, Olivia approached her with a smile.

"Does anyone normally staff the front?" the woman asked.

"Yes, I'm sure they'll be back shortly. Are you by chance Summer King?"

"That's me," she replied, her tone upbeat.

She looked a few years younger than Olivia, with medium-length brown hair pulled back into a ponytail.

Dressed in lightweight field pants, a purple T-shirt, and sturdy hiking shoes, she looked trail-ready.

"I'm Olivia Penn. I'm very close with Detective Hills, and the man you were looking for is a friend of mine." *At least, I think he is.*

"I'm sorry we didn't find him. Abby picked up his scent right away but lost it near the road."

Olivia glanced down at the golden retriever. The dog's thick, glossy coat and soulful dark-brown eyes made her smile wider. "I understand the theory is that the man you were tracking got into another vehicle, and that's why the trail disappeared."

Summer nodded. "That seems to be the case. I've seen it happen before."

"Thank you for coming all this way to help with the search. We wouldn't know half as much without your efforts. Are you still here in an official capacity?"

"No, but I'm staying until Sunday. A friend came up here with me. She has some business in the area. I want to take Abby out for a little exercise today, and I was hoping someone at the front desk could recommend a place with plenty of space for her to run."

"There's a park nearby called Lake Crystal. She'd have lots of room there."

"Lake Crystal. Sounds perfect." Summer gave the dog a few affectionate chin scratches. "What do you think, Abby? Ready to play?"

The dog popped up immediately with her tail whipping like a fan.

"I think she understood that," Olivia said with a light laugh.

"Abby, say hi."

The golden retriever padded over to Olivia and stopped in front of her.

"Is it okay to pet her?"

"When she's off duty, yes."

Olivia held out her hand, letting the dog sniff it before giving her a few gentle pats on the head. "I have a beagle, but he's nowhere near as well-behaved."

"Have you ever thought about training him for search and rescue?"

"I'm not sure he has the same discipline as Abby."

"How old is he?"

"About two."

"He's still young enough to train. As long as he has the right temperament and drive. Beagles aren't used as often as German Shepherds or retrievers, but they have exceptional noses. They're curious and high-energy, which is exactly what you want in a tracking dog. Plus, their smaller size helps them get into spaces bigger dogs can't. If you ever want to see if he has potential for search and rescue work, call me, and I can help you get started. Let me give you my number."

Olivia took out her phone and entered the number into her contacts, though she had a hard time imagining Buddy focusing on anything that wasn't a treat.

After a few more minutes of small talk, they said their goodbyes, and Olivia drove home. By the time she parked in the driveway, it was already six thirty. Meal prep would be quick and easy. During the summer, they often had salads for supper made with fresh produce from their garden. Tonight, her father would have a bowl of tomatoes paired with several slices of leftover pizza from his two-for-Tuesday deal at Bella's. She would have a more traditional salad, rounded out with store-bought produce and leftover grilled chicken.

Once inside, she moved quickly, pulling everything together. By a quarter after seven, she and her father were sitting down for dinner.

"Are you working tomorrow?" he asked, taking a bite of pizza.

A loud thunderclap drew her eyes to the window. The sky was darker than it should've been at that hour. A streak of lightning flashed, followed almost immediately by another.

"That was ominous," she said. "Looks like we're finally getting some rain. I have a staff meeting in the morning. It's just a video call."

"Do you think you'll be free around eleven?"

"Why?"

"I'm meeting with Jacqueline at the cafe to go over some financials for the bakery."

She set her fork down, narrowing her eyes. "Did you speak with her again?"

Before he could respond, rain began pounding the roof as if all the clouds had let loose at once. Willow, startled by the noise, scampered into the kitchen and huddled at Olivia's feet.

She bent down and gently brushed the cat's cheek. "It's okay, sweetie. It won't last long."

"Jacqueline called me. There's one person she's waiting to hear from before the final approval. If they say yes, then everything is set. The other backer might be with her tomorrow. I'd like you to come and speak with them so you can see for yourself that this is real. I told her about you and your concerns, and she said she'd be happy to discuss everything with you."

Olivia knew there was no talking him out of this scheme. All she could do now was debunk the scam in person. Despite everything else going on, this took priority.

"Okay. I'll be there. I want to meet Jacqueline Delacroix myself." *And tell her to stay away from you.*

With that settled, their conversation shifted to the investigation into Fiona's death. Olivia shared what she could, including what Nolan had told her about Mack's flight reservation. Preston and a deputy had driven to the airport and planned to wait near the gate to see if Mack tried to board. They couldn't stop him from leaving, but they wanted to question him, and this was the best lead they'd had so far. She wasn't expecting to hear from Preston tonight. He probably wouldn't be back in the area until close to midnight, so any updates about Mack would have to wait until tomorrow. She also told her father about getting Fiona's key from Dorothy and her plan to take a closer look inside the house after dinner.

When she finished, he asked, "Do you want me to go with you?"

There wasn't any danger, and they wouldn't be breaking and entering. They had a perfectly reasonable explanation for being there, and two sets of eyes were always better than one.

"Okay, dear Watson," she said with a small smile. "You're on the case. I need you to keep an eye out for a cat."

CHAPTER 24

The rain eased on the drive to Fiona's house. Summer storms often behaved like spigots in a curious toddler's hand: pouring down full force one moment, then trickling to a drip the next. Olivia parked in the driveway behind the Cadillac, grateful for the brief reprieve that spared them a soaking.

The home was dark, as were the streetlights on Raven Lane. She hadn't expected the porch or lamppost lights to be on unless they were set to automatic timers. Lightning streaked across the sky, followed by a rumbling boom of thunder.

"All this rain will be good for the garden," her father said.

Olivia opened her door. "The weeds will love it too."

He grabbed the umbrella she always kept on the passenger-side floor mat. "Do you want this?"

"No, it's a short walk. It seems to be letting up."

They both got out and hurried to the porch. Once there, Olivia unlocked the door, and they stepped into the pitch-black house. She flipped the switch near the entryway. No lights.

"The storm could've knocked the power out," he said.

"Possibly." She glanced up at the ceiling fixture. "The streetlights are out too. It could be the bulb, or maybe Craig had the electricity shut off. Stay here. I'll check the lights down the hall."

She pulled out her phone, turned on the flashlight, and went into the sitting room. There, she tried the desk lamp, tugging on its short chain.

"No power," she called out, scanning the room with the light.

"I can use my phone too."

"I've got a couple of flashlights in the car," she said, walking back toward the entryway. "I'll grab them. They'll be brighter."

After retrieving them, she returned, handed one to him, and closed the door.

"I want to check down here and in the kitchen, then I'm going upstairs," she said, already heading back down the hall.

He followed, and once inside the sitting room, they swept their lights around like twin guard tower beams searching for an escaped prisoner. He stepped toward a wall of framed photos and leaned in for a closer look.

"I bet this is Fiona's sister," he said.

She studied the photo, then aimed her light at the picture beside it. "I think you're right. They look alike, don't they? Check this one out. If that's Fiona, she couldn't have been much older than ten."

"Do they have another sister?"

"No," she said, pointing at one of the girls in the photo. "I bet that's Winifred. She's the same age as Ruth, but Fiona was a few years younger."

"Do you really think Fiona had whatever it was that Winifred wanted?"

"I do. I think that's why she came on Tuesday. And that's why I want to take another look in Fiona's bedroom."

He shifted his light toward two oil paintings on the wall. One depicted a serene loch, its glassy surface reflecting the surrounding mountains and sky. The other was of a weathered cottage perched on a windswept cliff with waves crashing below.

"These are beautiful landscapes," he remarked. "I've always wanted to visit Scotland."

"Me too," she said, shining her light around, illuminating a sofa, a television, and a laptop on the desk. "I'm going to check the kitchen."

She left the room and headed down the hallway, passing two closed doors on her right. One, she guessed, was a bathroom. The other was likely a coat closet. In the kitchen, she checked the cat's food bowl, finding it untouched. She hadn't expected otherwise, but she wanted to be sure.

Walking back toward the sitting room, she stopped in the doorway. "I'm going upstairs. There's a cat carrier on the porch. Can you check if it looks like it's been used?"

"Got it, boss. I'll look around the bushes too. Maybe Shadow is hiding from the storm."

They split up at the base of the staircase, each on their own mission. Olivia climbed the creaking steps and paused at the top, taking in her surroundings. To her right, a small alcove led to a single door. Curious, she opened it and looked inside.

A stool sat in front of an easel holding an unfinished watercolor of the inn. She swept her light across the room, revealing other canvases: scenes of the town square in different seasons, pastoral landscapes like the ones downstairs, and portraits of Shadow lounging in every imaginable pose.

She lingered for a moment, imagining Fiona there. The studio felt suspended in time. The stillness, the absence, the beauty of what remained. She'd felt the same way walking into her mother's cottage after moving back home. Fiona's paintings, like her mother's writings, lived on as a quiet legacy, connecting those who'd passed to those left behind.

After one last look, she stepped out of the studio and gently closed the door behind her.

Thunder rattled the windows, and rain pattered against the roof. At the top of the staircase, she looked down toward the open front door. Wanting to make sure her father wasn't giving off prowler vibes to anyone passing by, she hurried down the steps and onto the porch. There she found him in the yard, shining the flashlight under the bushes and over the flowerbeds.

"Dad, come on, get out of the rain. It's picking back up."

"I think I saw her."

"Shadow?"

"Yeah," he said, directing the light near a boxwood. "Right here. I saw something scamper across the walkway, but I didn't get a good look."

A bolt of lightning lit up the sky, striking a little too close for her comfort.

"Okay, come inside. You can't be out here with this lightning."

He reluctantly joined her on the porch, and they went back into the house.

"Stay in here, but leave the door partially open," she said. "If it was Shadow, maybe she'll wander in on her own."

"How about I put some food right by the entrance? We could lure her in."

"That might not be the best idea. If it wasn't Shadow, we could end up with a raccoon or a fox in here. She might get spooked if you're standing near the door. Go into the sitting room and keep an eye out from around the corner. If some other animal comes in, scare it off."

"I can do that."

Satisfied, she headed back upstairs while he took up his lookout position. This time, she proceeded straight down the hallway, passing an open bathroom, Fiona's bedroom, and a closed door she assumed was a closet.

Lightning flashed through the window at the end of the hall, momentarily illuminating the doorway to the spare bedroom. She went inside, sweeping her light around. Staged like a basic guest room with a bed, a dresser, and a full-length mirror, the space was tidy but lifeless. There were no personal touches, no adornments on the walls, and no creature comforts for Shadow to suggest Fiona spent much time there.

Backing out of the room, she passed the hallway closet and entered Fiona's bedroom. She went to the bed, sat down, and picked up the Bible. Opening it carefully, she turned to the Campbell genealogy. Then she pulled out her phone and snapped photos of the records, title page, and publication details, checking each to make sure the images were bright and the writing clear. With her first task done, she closed the Bible, returned it to the nightstand, and aimed her flashlight above the dresser.

The cross was missing.

She shot up, hurried across the room, and dropped to her knees to look under the dresser to see if it had fallen. Finding nothing but dust bunnies, she stood and directed her light at the jewelry case. The brooches were gone.

Her thoughts leapt to Amy, possibly the only other person besides Craig with a key to the house. Could she have taken the cross and brooches before Olivia arrived that afternoon? Had she given them to Mack? Had he planned to leave the country with them? As far-fetched as it sounded, the pieces seemed to be falling into place that way.

A boom of thunder jolted her, followed by a soft *thunk* from somewhere nearby.

She pocketed her phone, turned toward the door, and stepped into the hallway. "Dad, was that you?" she called out.

Lightning flashed, and rain lashed against the window. She went back down the hall and looked outside. Fallen branches lay scattered between the house and the garage.

I bet a limb fell on the roof.

She lingered at the window, watching the driving rain blur the edges of the yard. There was no avoiding it now. She would have to call the police. Sneaking in and out unnoticed, with only Dorothy aware she'd come here, had been the ideal plan. But with Preston at the airport, she'd need to quickly prep her father on what to say to the police.

Stepping back down the hallway, she passed the closet and stopped at the entrance to Fiona's room. After sweeping her light around once more, she turned and glanced toward the spare bedroom. A dark spot on the carpet near the base of the closet caught her eye. She hadn't noticed it before, but then again, checking the floor hadn't exactly been on her agenda. She retraced her steps and crouched in front of the door.

"Looks like mud," she whispered.

As she brought the light closer to inspect the quarter-sized splotch, the door burst open, slamming into her head and knocking her backward. She crumpled to the floor, stars exploding behind her closed eyes. Pain shot through her skull as she lay motionless, stunned and lost in a fog.

The stairs cracked rapidly as someone ran down them. With a groan, she rolled onto her stomach and crawled toward the flashlight, which had landed a few feet away. She grabbed it and aimed the beam at the staircase, but it was too late. Everything was unfolding in slow motion. Her brain felt half a beat behind her body.

"Dad," she said, her voice thin and strained.

When no answer came, panic gripped her. She pressed her palm against the wall for support as she struggled to her feet. The effort was too much. Her legs wobbled, and she staggered sideways, slamming into the opposite wall before sliding down to the floor.

Breathing heavily, she stayed seated and shouted, "Dad!"

"Yes?" he called calmly from downstairs.

Relieved to hear his voice, she winced, touching a bump already forming on her forehead. The stairs creaked as he slowly made his way up. When he reached the top, his flashlight beam hit her square in the face.

Shielding her eyes, she waved a hand at him. "Off. Get it off me."

"What happened?" he asked, lowering the light and hurrying toward her. "Are you okay?"

"Did you see them?"

"Who?"

She took a few deep breaths, trying to collect herself as her thoughts cleared. "Somebody was up here hiding in the closet. I saw mud on the carpet, and when I went to check it out, I got whacked by the door."

"Do you want me to call an ambulance?"

"No. I just got blindsided."

"Did you see who it was?"

"No. It happened too fast. But some things are missing from Fiona's room. Her cross and brooches. Whoever was hiding in the closet must've taken them."

"They had to be here the whole time. I didn't hear anything. I was in the sitting room when I saw something run down the hall into the kitchen. I thought it was Shadow, so I went to check, and that's when I heard you calling me. They must've gone out the front door. I'll call the police."

"Wait. Quiet. Don't move."

Slowly, she got to her knees and pushed to her feet with her father's grip steady on her arm. She aimed her flashlight toward the stairs, angling the beam to light the wall. The faint glow revealed two tiny eyes reflecting back at them.

"It's Shadow," she whispered, switching off her light. "I'm going to try to get her. Use your flashlight. Just shine the way, but don't point it at her. We don't want to spook her."

With slow, deliberate steps, she started toward the cat. "Hi, Shadow," she said with the same playful tone she used with Willow. "We've been looking for you, sweetie. I'm so happy to see you."

The cat turned and crept down two steps.

"It's okay, Shadow," she said softly. "Let's get you some food."

At the top of the staircase, she nearly lunged forward to grab the cat but held back, knowing she wasn't in the best position if she missed.

"How about some treats?"

As she leaned down with her arms outstretched, thunder shook the house, and the cat darted down the stairs.

"No!" she cried, racing after her.

By the time Olivia reached the bottom step, the cat had already slipped out the open front door. She hurried onto the porch just as Shadow streaked across the yard and vanished into the trees bordering the property. Rain poured down in torrents as the sky unleashed its fury. She stood with her hands on her hips, teeth clenched in frustration. *So close.*

Her father joined her, shining his flashlight around the yard. "Did you see where she went?"

She pointed toward the trees. "That way. But we'll never find her now. Not in this weather."

"At least we know she's alive."

"And that she's coming back to the house at night. What time is it?"

He pulled out his phone and checked the screen. "Nine thirty."

"Preston is probably still at the airport. I don't want to call him while he's in the middle of dealing with things there. But we have to call the police. Everything just got more complicated. Remember, when they question us, we were only here looking for the cat. Nothing else."

He nodded. "Got it, boss. That's my story, and I'm sticking to it."

CHAPTER 25

Olivia leaned closer to the dresser mirror and brushed her hair aside, revealing a bruise above her left temple. The lump had gone down overnight, but her skin was still tender. She'd slept like a log and woken Friday morning without a headache or any signs of a concussion. All things considered, she was no worse for wear, though she was determined to find out who'd slammed the door into her head. The panic she'd felt in the moment, fearing for her father's safety, had made the attack personal. She wouldn't have brought him along if she'd suspected any danger. The idea of someone hiding in a closet hadn't crossed her mind, but she didn't berate herself for the oversight. She could defend herself if needed, but if anyone threatened the people she loved, she wouldn't hesitate to strike back.

Willow was serenely loafing on the ledge of her reading nook. Many of her mornings over the past eight months had started just like this, but today felt different, knowing Willow was here to stay. Crossing the room, she gave the cat a few affectionate pets. Then she changed into a T-shirt and jeans before heading downstairs to see if their houseguest was still there.

She slipped quietly through the living room and paused at the kitchen doorway. Preston stood at the counter with his back to her. This was the kind of morning she could get used to, waking up and starting her day with him nearby.

Last night, Jayden and Cole had come to Fiona's house to question her and her father about the incident. Before the deputies even finished their interview, Preston had called to check on her. He was still at the airport, though Mack had failed to show. She told him what had happened, adding a few more details than she'd shared with the deputies, including her theory about why Winifred had visited Fiona on Tuesday. Preston listened without judgment, but he remained skeptical that Winifred had any connection to Fiona's death. Olivia had tried to protest his plan to come over once he returned to Apple Station, but he insisted. He was staying the night, and that was that.

She'd fallen asleep on the sofa waiting for him, only waking when he arrived around one. He recapped his uneventful trip to the airport, and she filled him in on what Amy had said about Craig's gambling. Less than an hour later, fatigue got the best of her. After finding him a pillow and blanket for the couch, she went upstairs to bed.

Now she watched him a moment longer before stepping into the kitchen. "I could get used to this," she said.

Startled, he turned, setting his coffee cup on the counter. "I didn't hear you get up."

He crossed the room in a few strides and wrapped her in a tight hug.

She settled into his arms for an extended embrace, resting her head against his chest. "How did you sleep?"

"No complaints. I can sleep anywhere, and your couch is more comfortable than mine. How are you feeling?"

"Fine. Where's my dad?"

"He said he had to go into town."

She glanced at the wall clock as they pulled apart. Just after eight. Her father was rarely out this early unless it involved a doctor's appointment. That meant today's outing probably had to do with his bakery scheme. "Ugh."

Preston gently brushed her hair aside, examining the bruise. "What was that for? And this doesn't look fine."

"I'll heal. And it's a long story."

"Tell me over a cup of coffee."

"I could use the coffee, but shouldn't you be at work? Don't you want to head home and grab a change of clothes?"

He opened the cabinet, took out a cup, and poured

from the carafe. Reaching into the refrigerator, he asked, "Almond milk?"

"Yes, thanks," she said, sitting down at the table.

He added it to the cup, then returned the jug to the refrigerator. Lifting the lid off the container of sugar substitute, he glanced over his shoulder. "Two?" She nodded, and he tore open the packets and dumped them in. "I didn't want to leave you alone until I knew you were okay," he said, stirring the coffee. "I called the station and let them know I'd be in late." He set the cup in front of her.

"Thanks. Do I need to tip you?"

Leaning down, he brushed her lips with a tender kiss. "That'll do." He grabbed his coffee from the counter and sat across from her.

"Did you eat? I can make you something."

"No, I'm good. So tell me, what's going on with your dad?"

She related her father's grand idea of opening a bakery and the morning's meeting with the supposed affluent backer, Jacqueline Delacroix.

When she finished, he offered, "Do you want me to come along for backup?"

"At this stage, I can handle it."

"What if this woman's offer is legit?"

She slouched, resting her arms on the table. "It all sounds quaint, but I think he'd be biting off more than he can chew. I haven't had time to look into her, and with only a name, I don't know how much I could even find.

If what she says is true—that he doesn't have to invest any of his own money and just has to manage it until the start-up costs are covered—then maybe. He's enamored with the idea, but running a bakery is nothing like making a few cakes and cookies at home whenever the fancy strikes."

"Didn't you say part of that course he took in Oregon involved starting a bakery from scratch?"

"Yes, but that was a tiny portion of the program. People who open bakeries usually have decades of experience."

"How hands-on would he need to be?"

"I don't know. I can't see him getting up at three a.m. to prep the day's doughs. He'd probably take on more of a managerial role behind the scenes. But I know he'd love to be out front in the shop, chatting with customers." She paused, wincing as if saying it out loud physically pained her. "The best part? He wants me involved."

"Doing what?"

"No clue. But apparently menu writing is on the table."

"Would you want to? Work in a bakery, I mean. I'd say you're overqualified for writing menus."

Over the past few months, she'd been seriously considering a career change, but boxing up pastries and pies wasn't exactly what she'd envisioned. Then again, neither was working for Carolyn, and yet here she was, giving both ideas serious thought.

"There's another possibility," she said.

His phone buzzed on the counter. He turned, grabbed it, and glanced at the screen. "A text from Jayden. Amy Winters isn't answering her phone, and she's not at home."

"She told me her gun was missing. Do you believe that? If she went back to Fiona's house Tuesday night, maybe she's the one who fired it. For all we know, she has it at her apartment and just made it look like it was taken. Did you get a warrant to search her place?"

He set his phone down, took a slow sip of coffee, and kept his expression unreadable.

"Never mind," she said with a small huff. "I know you won't answer that. Let me guess, you'd say the police don't have probable cause. Fine. How about this? Do you think Amy was the one hiding in the closet last night? You can speculate about that because it involves me."

He let a trace of a smile slip through. "Not sure that's a legally valid argument, but I'll bite. I think it's possible. We know she had a key. But so did Craig. And honestly, someone else could've picked the lock. It wouldn't have been hard."

She leaned back in her chair, sliding her coffee cup closer. "That house isn't Fort Knox. If it was Craig, though, why steal the cross and brooches? Isn't everything technically his now?"

He shrugged. "The house, the accounts, all the big stuff—yeah, that's his. But you never know. Fiona's will might've left specific items to other people. Sentimental pieces, maybe. And depending on how much cash was immediately accessible, pawning small valuables could've been a stopgap to cover gambling debts." He tapped his fingers on the table. "There's another possibility."

She didn't even need to ask. "Mack."

He nodded. "His Houdini act? The accident, getting into a second vehicle at the crash site, and then no-showing at the airport. It adds up."

"You think he orchestrated all this?"

"We might've played right into his hands. Making that reservation was like sending up a flare, broadcasting where he'd be. He had to know we'd send officers to the airport."

"Which shifted the focus far off Fiona's house."

"Exactly. And that's how it played out."

"If only I'd gotten a glimpse of whoever it was last night." She sighed, gently touching her bruise. "But a door to the head doesn't really help with that."

"You should take it easy today. What are your plans?"

"I have a video conference this morning, and then I'm meeting my dad in town at eleven."

He took a sip of coffee. "You mentioned another job possibility."

She shook her head. "It's nothing."

"It must be something if you brought it up. Unless you don't want to talk about it."

Her reluctance to discuss Carolyn's offer wasn't about him. He knew who Carolyn was and the kind of work she was involved in. Olivia hadn't yet sorted through her thoughts enough to articulate them. The decision was hers alone, but its impact on their future together couldn't be ignored. And they were at the stage in their relationship where such things mattered.

"No, it's not that. On Tuesday, I ran into Carolyn in town, and she offered me a job."

His face tightened. "Doing what?"

"It's an analyst position conducting research and writing reports for the field ops." She left it there, unsure if she could disclose the location of Carolyn's operation.

His phone buzzed again, pulling his attention. He picked it up and looked at the screen.

"You really should go," she said, nodding toward the phone.

He shook his head, typing a quick reply while speaking. "Deputy Simmons just finished talking to Dorothy Peabody. She doesn't know if Fiona gave a house key to anyone else."

"I bet that's the first time she's ever been questioned by the police."

"I don't know. She might've been wild in her youth."

"The job is local," Olivia said, steering the conversation back to the offer. "No relocation involved. And the work isn't anything like what Sam does."

He raised a skeptical brow. "Are you sure about that?"

"Quite sure. Carolyn believes that if I went into the field, I wouldn't last a day." She smiled, hoping the humor would ease his worries. It didn't.

"I don't want that tested," he said firmly. "Are you seriously considering this?"

She nodded. "I am. I'm intrigued, and the salary is impressive."

His phone buzzed again, and he grunted, grabbing it off the table.

She pushed her chair back and stood. "You have to go. We can talk more about this later. Thanks for staying over last night."

He got up and turned toward the sink, cup in hand.

"Leave it," she said. "I'll take care of it."

He set the cup on the counter and stepped over to her, holding her in a hug. "What are you doing after the meeting with your dad?"

"I'm coming back here."

"And taking it easy?"

She gave a reassuring nod as they pulled apart.

"If Mack or Amy were at Fiona's house last night, they would've seen your car in the driveway. We have to assume they knew you were there."

He gently kissed her bruise. His touch was warm and soothing, and she really wished he didn't have to go.

"I know you're concerned about Mack because of your past with him," he continued. "But at this point, there's enough evidence to treat him more as a threat than a friend."

CHAPTER 26

After Preston left, Olivia cleaned the cups, grabbed a quick breakfast, and checked on Willow and Buddy. Willow was curled up on the top level of the cat tree, so she let her be. She'd grown used to taking the cat out to her office in the mornings. But with this new favorite napping spot, she might be heading to work solo more often.

Buddy was in a subdued mood, lounging on her father's recliner. The beagle had never routinely sat in the chair, but after Willow modeled the behavior, he'd apparently caught on. Olivia often joked it was only a matter of time before she and her father ended up on the floor while their furry companions claimed the prime seats.

By the time she made it out to her office and logged onto her computer, the conference call had already started. She wasn't worried about being late. These company-wide meetings typically had hundreds of attendees, and nobody ever took roll. After listening for a few minutes to one of the higher-ups drone on about budgets and new subscription models, she lowered the volume to a faint, white-noise level.

With no solid leads to pursue regarding Mack, she felt at a loss for what to do next. After dealing with the likely scam involving the bakery financier later that morning, maybe she'd take it easy, as Preston had suggested. His warning to consider Mack a threat seemed a little overblown. Preston was protective, but perhaps he knew something she didn't. If it really had been Mack in the closet, then he'd intentionally tried to harm her, and that thought left her unsettled.

She pulled her phone from her pocket and opened the photos she'd taken of the Bible pages last night. With all that had happened, she hadn't had a chance to look at them until now. The ink recording the earliest entries in the Campbell genealogy had faded, but with magnification, many of the names, dates, and places remained legible. Judging by the penmanship, she gathered multiple individuals had contributed to the family history, though one person's handwriting stood out. That individual had documented both recent and older ancestors. The last entry written in that distinctive hand was the one just before Ruth's death. Her passing and burial location had been recorded by someone else, most likely Fiona.

The lineage traced thirteen generations, beginning with the marriage of Angus Campbell to his wife Catherine in 1723. Their daughter Elizabeth married

James Fraser at nineteen. The couple had one child, but James passed away a year after their wedding. In the margin next to Elizabeth and James' wedding date, there was a note that read: "Ten Scots acres of Inverness, from the loch to Wicker Glen, bounded by Broadland Burn on the west and Dorran Hill to the south, with all rights to fishing and grazing."

She briefly turned up the volume on her conference call to check the current topic. Someone she didn't recognize was discussing policies and best practices regarding social media accounts. Satisfied she wasn't missing anything urgent, she lowered the volume again and returned her attention to the Campbells' ancestry.

The records fascinated her. Few people could trace their family history in such detail, going back so far. Almost all the names included death dates and burial sites, most of which were in Inveraray. Elizabeth Campbell's burial location appeared to have been added more recently by the same person who had recorded the death of Ruth and Fiona's mother.

Olivia reread the note in the margin next to Elizabeth's marriage date. Curious, she opened a browser on her laptop and searched for "Scots acre." As she suspected, it was a Scottish land measurement, slightly larger than a standard acre.

She entered the entire note into the search bar, trying to discern its significance. After a few clicks, she found a similar entry in an heirloom Bible preserved in the National Museum of Scotland. From this, she learned the note likely referred to a land transaction, including rights to game and other resources within the specified boundaries.

Unfamiliar with Scotland's geography, she opened a mapping site and searched for Inveraray, the most frequently mentioned burial location in the Campbell records. Near the west coast of Scotland, Inveraray lay northwest of Glasgow, close to Loch Fyne. Notable landmarks in the area included Inveraray Castle, Kilmalieu Cemetery, and a hotel-spa. Most of the burial sites were listed in kirkyards around Inveraray and the broader region of Argyll and Bute.

Given the repeated references to Inveraray, Olivia wondered if it had been a Campbell stronghold during the medieval period. A quick search and study of a Scottish clan map confirmed her guess: Inveraray had indeed been a seat of power for the Campbells. In fact, the territory controlled by the Campbells seemed rivaled only by a few other families, including the Mackenzies and the MacDonalds. The Frasers of Lovat, whom Olivia assumed James had been associated with, controlled much of Inverness.

She read the faded note beside Elizabeth's wedding date again, then looked at the map. The land mentioned was in Inverness, which made sense, given that Elizabeth had married a Fraser. It seemed likely that if she hadn't already been living there, she would've moved to Inverness after marrying James. Inverness and Inveraray were quite far apart. Inverness lay in the northeastern Highlands near the famous Loch Ness, while Inveraray sat farther west, closer to the coast. By modern routes, the two areas were nearly 140 miles apart, a trip that would take about three and a half hours by car.

Her ears perked up when someone on the conference call introduced her new editor. She turned up the volume and listened as Jordan Sykes spoke for several minutes, mostly about how excited he was to lead such a fine staff of writers. It was all very rah-rah, and while she tried to keep an open mind, she couldn't imagine forming the same camaraderie with him that she'd had with Angela. Gone were the convivial back-and-forth moments during her Q&As and their lighthearted chats over the ho-hum cafeteria offerings whenever Olivia went into the office.

At least Cassandra would be there. Though their paths wouldn't overlap much, Olivia could see them meeting up for lunch or dinner when she was in D.C. A year ago, the thought would've seemed impossible. They'd never been close until that fateful day at Grove Manor. Now, they were as tight as if they'd been friends since preschool.

When her new editor finished his spiel, she lowered the volume and swiveled her chair, staring at the sun-streaked cat tree. Everything seemed to be changing around her. Angela and Cassandra were moving on. Her dad, in his seventies, wanted to start a bakery of all things. Even Cooper was on a new path, one that might eventually have him following in Cassandra's footsteps.

She turned back to the Campbells' genealogy. Elizabeth, too, had moved on after James' death. Four years after their son Patrick was born, she remarried and eventually had two more children. As far as Olivia could tell, Ruth and Fiona were descended from Elizabeth's second marriage. Patrick married and had four children, but the records of his descendants stopped after two generations.

At some point, Elizabeth must've returned to Inveraray, as she was buried in St. Andrew's Kirkyard in Argyll. It seemed unlikely she'd still been living in Inverness at the time of her death, only to be transported such a considerable distance back to her family's ancestral land. Then again, it was possible she'd been buried in Inverness initially and reinterred later in Inveraray.

Olivia scrolled through the images that came up in her search for Inverness. One photo—a two-lane road curving around a picturesque loch, with a quaint restaurant overlooking the water—captured her imagination. The thought of escaping it all. No pressure, no schedules, no to-do lists. Just picturing it softened her shoulders and settled her more deeply in the seat. She mentally noted that if she ever made the trip, a visit to Loch Ness would be a must. Maybe she'd even join a nighttime tour in search of the famed Nessie, just for fun. Searching for shadowy creatures in the dark sounded far more entertaining than chasing monsters in the light of day. She continued scrolling and clicked through photos from a traveler's alpaca trekking adventure along Loch Ness. The animals' adorable faces made her smile, and she instantly added the guided outing to her imaginary itinerary.

At almost ten o'clock, the conference call was due to end. She turned the volume back up just in time to catch the managing editor thanking everyone for their attendance and yada-yada-yada. With that, she left the meeting and closed the app.

Other than learning some fascinating facts about Scotland's geography and the Campbell family's detailed history, she wasn't sure why the Bible held much value beyond its rarity as a seventeenth-century artifact. The most recent entry was Ruth's death five years ago, likely documented by Fiona. Curious, Olivia searched for Ruth's obituary and found it immediately. Ruth had been eighty when she passed away at a nursing home in Glasgow, though she was buried in Inveraray.

Gladys Henderson had also been eighty when she died in the care facility in North Carolina. Olivia hadn't thought much more about the connection between Amy and Gladys, unsure if there was an angle to pursue. But if Mack had made a note of it, there had to be some significance. She tried to imagine how he might've investigated the link. The most logical method would've been to call someone close to Gladys with a plausible story and subtly dig for details.

Being local to the facility in North Carolina, Linda Lacoste was likely the most informed about her mother's care. Olivia searched again for the school where Linda worked, and her browser history brought it up right away.

With two clicks, Linda's contact information appeared on the screen.

Olivia knew how dubious it would sound to be contacted by a stranger asking questions about a loved one's death. A private investigator would've spun a story, maybe claimed to be checking a reference from a résumé.

That could work.

She debated whether to e-mail or call. Since it was summer and school wasn't in session, she rolled the dice on the more direct approach and dialed. The school secretary answered, and after Olivia gave her name, she asked to speak with Linda about her mother. She hoped the nature of the request would spark enough curiosity for Linda to take the call.

After a brief hold, the secretary transferred Olivia.

"Hello, this is Linda Lacoste."

"Hi, my name is Olivia Penn, and I'm calling from Apple Station, Virginia. I was hoping you might have a few minutes to speak with me about someone your mother knew from the care facility where she stayed. I'm sorry. I know your mother passed away there."

"Who, exactly?"

She winced, grateful the conversation wasn't face-to-face. "I'm looking into the background of a home health aide who lives in my area. She worked as a nurse at the facility, and you are listed as a reference. Her name is Amy Winters." She didn't fully believe her own story, so she leaned into it. "I'm trying to find a home health aide for my dad, and Amy is a candidate."

"You're the second person who's contacted me about her."

The other must've been Mack.

"There were so many nurses and aides, but I know who you mean. Amy was one of the nicer ones. My mom liked her, and that says a lot. She didn't mince words."

"So you'd give her a positive recommendation?"

"For Amy, yes. For the facility she worked for, no."

"Oh, I'm sorry to hear that."

"I should clarify. Most of the staff were fine. But my mom died suddenly one night, and nobody could explain what had happened."

"That must've been awful. No one should have to go through that." Her inner sleuth was itching to ask more, but she knew it would be wildly inappropriate.

"I had just seen her a few hours earlier," Linda continued, as people often do when grief pulls words out unasked. "I was visiting, and she was getting ready for bed, so I left. Then I got a call around three in the morning from someone at the facility saying she'd passed away. I went there immediately, but no one could tell me what had happened. The hospital did an autopsy, but the results were inconclusive. They cited natural causes. I remember Amy was on shift that night, and honestly, she was more broken up about my mom's death than anyone else there."

"You must've been devastated. I can't imagine your heartbreak. Thank you for sharing this with me. I know it's very personal."

"I was equally sad and mad for a long time. But my mom wouldn't want me carrying that anger forever. If Amy is looking for work, based on my experience with her, I'd give her a good recommendation."

"Thank you. That's very reassuring."

After a few polite exchanges and goodbyes, the call ended.

She glanced at the clock. Thirty minutes until the meeting with her father and the mysterious backer. She stood and stretched, unsure if the call had swayed her opinion of Amy. Linda's impression aligned with her own, but the lingering question of what had caused Gladys' sudden death remained. Was it a coincidence that Amy had been on shift that night, then left the facility and nursing altogether shortly after?

For now, those questions would have to wait. Olivia's focus turned to protecting her father from a scammer and proving that Jacqueline Delacroix's offer was little more than smoke and mirrors.

CHAPTER 27

Olivia sat at a table near the front of the cafe with a small Americano in front of her. Though she'd already had coffee that morning, the aroma of freshly ground beans proved too tempting, so she ordered something to sip while waiting for her father. The breakfast rush had passed, and the lunch crowd was still an hour away from descending on the town's go-to spot for a quick bite. A soothing jazz mix played over the in-house speakers, accompanied by the occasional mechanical rhythm of the espresso machine.

She'd arrived a few minutes before eleven, but her father was running late. He'd texted that he was at Jed's Auto Body getting an oil change and would get to the cafe as soon as he could. He added that Jacqueline Delacroix knew Olivia would already be there waiting.

She took a sip of coffee, then pulled out her phone and searched for where to report financial scams in

Virginia. The top result led her to the Attorney General of Virginia's website. She navigated the site and found a list of red flags for fraudulent schemes. At the top was a familiar warning: If it seems too good to be true, it probably is. She copied the page's URL and pasted it into a text to her father. Before she could hit send, she sensed someone standing just over her shoulder.

Dressed in a white pantsuit, Carolyn stepped from behind her to the other side of the table. The sheer audacity of wearing all white in a coffee shop spoke to her supreme confidence. If Olivia ever dared do the same, every cup of coffee in the cafe would line up, eager to spill itself all over her. Carolyn set a cup of lemonade on the table, then sat down.

Olivia's focus darted to the door, checking for her father. He was due any minute, and the last thing she wanted was to introduce him to Carolyn, or worse, have to explain who she was.

"Carolyn," Olivia said, keeping her voice neutral. "I hope you're not here for some kind of ongoing operation."

"I enjoy the lemonade." She draped an arm on the table and leaned back, settling in like she had no intention of leaving. "Have you given more thought to my offer?"

She hadn't expected this conversation today, especially not here. "I don't have time to get into this right now. I'm meeting someone in a few minutes. It's flattering that you asked, but I don't think I'm the right person for the job."

"And you believe you're the best person to determine that?" Carolyn's reply was as calm as it was cutting.

"Ah, yeah," she said, fumbling slightly. "I do. I don't have any training in what you deal with. I think you're overestimating how my skills could benefit your team."

Carolyn tilted her head just enough to signal doubt. "Are you questioning my judgment?"

"No. Not at all." Olivia took a long breath, wishing she'd thought this through more carefully. She glanced toward the door just as her father walked in. *Great timing, Dad.* She sighed as he waved to her and headed over. "Look, I can't get into this just now. My dad is here, and we're meeting someone."

Her hope that Carolyn would get up and go was wishful thinking. Carolyn picked up her drink and took a sip, as though she hadn't heard a word Olivia said.

"My offer won't stay open forever. I will find someone else."

"Hi, honey. Sorry I'm late," her father said, reaching the table.

Carolyn looked at him, and his face brightened with a wide smile.

He glanced between Olivia and Carolyn. "Oh, great, you found each other."

"Bill, it's good to see you again." Carolyn's tone turned suddenly warm. "And your description of your daughter was spot-on. She's every bit as lovely and charming as you said."

What's happening here?

"See, Olivia? Jacqueline Delacroix is a real person."

Her breath caught. If she hadn't been sitting, she might've ended up on the floor. She stared between them, her focus bouncing from one to the other. Words escaped her, even if she'd had the air to speak. The gentle hum of the cafe faded, overtaken by her pulse hammering in her throat. When the initial shock lifted just enough for her to form a coherent thought, she pointed at Carolyn and managed, "This is Jacqueline?"

Her father nodded cheerfully. "Of course." He turned to Carolyn. "Did your investment partner arrive yet?"

"Bill, I'm sorry," Carolyn said, cutting in before Olivia could react. "Something came up, and I have to go."

Olivia's thoughts scrambled, struggling to process what was unfolding in front of her.

Her father's grin faded. "Oh. Okay, I understand." He glanced around the cafe. "Is the other backer still coming?"

Carolyn gave Olivia a Mona Lisa smile. "As a matter of fact, Bill, I've just met with her. I only need to hear a yes, and we can get things moving."

The ground beneath Olivia might as well have vanished. Her throat tightened, unable to swallow the implications of what had just become painfully clear.

How long had Carolyn been orchestrating this? The manipulation. The precise timing. Olivia might've called it masterful if she and her father hadn't been the targets. She closed her eyes briefly, letting her thoughts congeal.

So my dad gets a bakery if I work for you? Oh, hell no. That's not happening.

"Maybe if I talk to your co-backer, I could help convince her," he said.

Carolyn's gaze stayed locked on Olivia. "I think she knows exactly how much this means to you."

Olivia's mind shifted into overdrive, calculating the fallout of financing the bakery herself. She had savings, plus a decent chunk in her retirement account. The penalty for early withdrawal from her IRA would hurt, but it was manageable. Maybe she could get a bank loan more easily than her father. One thing was certain—she wasn't letting him risk his retirement funds. He was on a fixed income. She had decades to rebuild her savings.

The decision was made. She'd pour everything she had into going into business with him. Even if it meant draining every dollar she'd saved over the past twenty years, she'd make it work.

Carolyn stood, lemonade in hand. "Bill, you have such a delightful daughter. As soon as I hear something, I'll be in touch."

They exchanged a few more polite words, none of which Olivia registered. She needed a moment, or several months, to wrap her head around her spur-of-the-moment, completely irrational decision fueled by anger.

She was about to become part-owner of a bakery with zero experience, draining her savings in the process.

"Honey, what do you think?" her father asked. "She's impressive, isn't she?"

Olivia had been staring wide-eyed at the table. She hadn't even realized Carolyn had left, and now her father was sitting across from her.

She's impressive because she runs a black-budget team doing things I don't even want to know about. And her real name is Carolyn. And she's using you to get to me.

But none of that made it out. Instead, she forced a nod. "Yes, she's quite impressive." She looked out the window as Carolyn passed by on the sidewalk. "I'll be right back."

She stood abruptly, hurried out of the cafe, and jogged a few steps before calling out, "Hey!"

A man in a gray suit heading her way glanced over but kept walking, dismissing himself as the target.

She quickened her pace. "Carolyn, hold up!"

Carolyn stopped in front of the old hardware store and turned to wait for her. When they were face-to-face, Carolyn stared at her as if she'd already said everything she intended to.

"If you think you can blackmail me into joining your team so my dad gets a bakery, you're gravely mistaken."

Carolyn smiled and nearly laughed. "Blackmail? That's quite dramatic."

"Then what would you call it?" she shot back.

"Employee benefit."

The answer was so bizarre and unexpected that Olivia blanked. *What?*

"Isn't that the American way?" Carolyn continued. "You take a job, you get benefits. Health insurance, retirement plans, and so on and so forth."

"Yeah, well, believe it or not, startup loans for bakeries are extremely rare. Probably nonexistent. And you have that kind of money lying around? To fund a bakery? Just to get me on your team?"

"You flatter yourself. It's not just about you." She looked at the empty suite. "I think this place would be useful. It could serve as a cover for our operatives."

She groaned to herself. That meant her father might unknowingly become part of Carolyn's operation. And that was something she couldn't let happen. She shook her head. "No. That's my answer. Find someone else."

Carolyn was quiet for a moment. "Let me guess, Olivia. You've already calculated how much you can pull from your retirement account—an impressive sum for someone your age—to fund your father's dream."

Dang. Carolyn not only knew her finances but had predicted exactly what she was thinking. Heat rose to her cheeks as she fought back the feeling of being exposed.

Carolyn reached into her pocket, pulled out a business card, and held it toward Olivia.

Reflexively, she took it and read the details: a name, a New York address, and a phone number. "What's this?"

"I understand you have a manuscript you want to publish."

Olivia clenched her jaw. Sam must've told her.

"John is a literary agent and an old friend of mine. He's expecting your call."

Olivia stared at the name. "No. I don't want any favors." She offered the card back, but when Carolyn made no move to take it, she let her arm fall to her side. "I don't understand why you're going to such lengths. I can't be bought."

At that, Carolyn stepped closer. "Exactly. You can't be bought. Loyalty is your superpower. In relationships, that can lead to wasted years. For me, it's everything. Three months ago, a mole nearly cost Sam her life and wreaked havoc on my team. I need someone I never have to doubt. I let my guard down once. I won't do it again. I protect my team. I know who you are, Olivia. I know what you're capable of." She let the words settle before continuing. "You can keep living your comfortable life, writing pithy columns for strangers while swimming in the shallow end of the pool. But quite frankly, that's a waste of your talents. And we both know that's not what you want. Deep down, you want to make a difference. You're curious, tenacious, and dependable. I'm not wrong about you. I want you on my team. But I won't wait around forever. Decide."

With that, Carolyn turned and walked off, leaving Olivia staring at her reflection in the store window, at a loss for words.

CHAPTER 28

As noon approached, the relentless rhythm of machines and baristas drowned out the soft jazz playing inside the cafe. Olivia had rejoined her father at the table about twenty minutes earlier. He'd been going on about how lucky he was to have met Jacqueline on Monday. She nodded occasionally, saying nothing. She needed time to process everything and wasn't ready to burst his bubble about the conditions attached, ones that would almost certainly make him see things differently.

Carolyn's offer was overwhelming: the salary, the bakery, the literary agent on call. Could she even see herself following up on the latter? As her father described his vision for the shop's décor, she glanced around the cafe as if watching a foreign film. The low hum of conversation, the banter of the baristas, and her father's voice all felt slightly out of sync, dubbed over in a foreign language.

Her initial anger at Carolyn's manipulative attempt to play on her heartstrings had softened. With a clearer head, she replayed Carolyn's words, though she wasn't about to jump at the ticking-clock ultimatum. For all of Carolyn's efforts to control the narrative, Olivia held the real power. She hadn't asked for any of this. Carolyn was the one left hanging, and Olivia doubted she was used to being kept waiting.

"And I believe that wholeheartedly," her father said.

"I'm sorry, Dad," Olivia replied. "I missed that last part. It's getting noisy in here."

"I said, what you're not changing, you're choosing. That hardware store has been empty ever since it went out of business. It's a shame. That place sticks out like a sore thumb in town. Apple Station needs a bakery."

Slash, front for a black-budget team.

She pushed back her chair. "Let's go. I need some fresh air." *And a quieter place to think.*

He agreed right away, and they both stood and binned their cups. As they left, Craig, Gavin, and Kirstie were crossing the street, heading toward them.

"That's Craig and his kids," she said. "I want to say hi. I'll see you at home."

"Okay. Thanks for coming to meet Jacqueline. This is the start of something great. I can feel it."

She mustered a smile as he turned and walked to his car, parked about a block away.

When Craig and his kids reached the sidewalk, Olivia gave a small wave. Mindful that he was still under suspicion, she stayed cautious about what she shared. Where the truth lay about his gambling, she had no way of knowing, and she wasn't making any judgments.

"Hi, good to see you again," Olivia said.

Craig replied in kind and reintroduced his kids, probably more for their sake than hers.

Olivia gestured to Kirstie's shirt, which featured a black cat in a kilt playing the bagpipes. "That's adorable."

Kirstie glanced down. "Thanks. I had it made to show Aunt Fi. I think she would've gotten a kick out of it."

Craig pulled out his wallet and handed Gavin a credit card. "You two go inside and get whatever you want. Just grab me a large coffee."

Kirstie and Gavin went into the cafe, leaving Olivia and Craig alone on the sidewalk.

"Did Preston tell you about last night?" she asked.

Craig nodded, slipping his wallet back into his pocket. "He said you got hurt."

"It was minor. I'm fully recovered." Though it wasn't out of the question that Craig had been the one in the closet, she had doubts. A blow from his brute strength probably would've sent her through the hall wall, not just to the floor. "I'm sorry I didn't let you know I was going to the house to look for Fiona's cat."

"No apology needed. I don't have any issue with that. Preston said you spotted her?"

"Yes. She was within reach, but thunder struck and

scared her off. Still, it's a good sign. I guess Preston told you about the missing brooches and the cross?"

"He did. You hear about things like this. Once thieves know a house is empty, they move fast."

"That's true. I saw both the cross and the brooches when I was in the bedroom on Wednesday. The cross looked really old. Do you know anything about its history?"

"No. Preston asked me the same thing. I remember my mum had something similar that she said had been passed down for hundreds of years. I completely forgot about it until he mentioned what was stolen."

"Do you think that might've been your mom's cross?"

"Could've been. After my mum's funeral, I told Fiona to come by the house and see if there was anything she wanted. My mum didn't have many valuables, so I figured whatever she took had more sentimental value than anything else. I never asked what she chose. So yeah, it's very possible that was my mum's cross."

"What about the brooches? Could those have been your mom's too?"

He shrugged. "Maybe. She had some jewelry, but nothing much of value."

"If the cross or the brooches originally belonged to her, Winifred might know something about them, since they were close." *Maybe one of them was the reason she made the trip.*

"That's possible. I saw her before we came over. She was heading into the dining room at the inn with Clare, but we only exchanged hellos. I didn't want to hold her up."

"Which is exactly what I'm doing to you now."

"Not at all. I'm taking the kids to a local park the person at the front desk recommended."

"Lake Crystal?"

"That's the one. A group of us is going out there to get some training in for the weekend. We stopped by to fuel up."

"Then I won't keep you."

After they said goodbye, Craig went into the cafe and Olivia started toward her car. Looking across the town square at the inn, she debated whether another conversation with Winifred was worth it. She would've bet her bottom dollar the cross in Fiona's room had once belonged to Ruth. If that was true, Winifred might know something about it.

Changing course, she crossed the street, quickened her pace, and followed the sidewalk toward the inn. As she neared the entrance, two men were coming out, and one held the door open for her. She nodded in thanks and stepped inside. Bev stood behind the reception desk but came around when she saw Olivia, meeting her in front of the vase of heather and thistle.

"Tell me what you think," Bev said, reaching over the counter to grab a scarf. She wrapped it around her neck with a flourish, like she was prepping for an après-ski scene in St. Moritz.

"I think it's a little warm to be wearing a scarf."

"No, I mean, what do you think of the tartan? It's the Royal Stewart."

The pattern was a vibrant mix of red, blue, and green, accented with thin yellow and white stripes.

"It's very nice. It matches your kilt."

Bev picked up another scarf. "How about this one? It's the Mackenzie tartan."

The plaid was predominantly blue and green, with thin stripes of white and red.

"Are you planning to wear a scarf inside?"

"I can't decide between the two."

"They both look great." Olivia glanced around the lobby. A newly mounted claymore and a shield hung on the wall near two saddle-brown leather wingback chairs. "I'm really going to miss the Scottish theme when you change everything back. All you need is a terrier or a Westie as a lobby dog, and no one would ever guess they were in a small southern Virginia town."

Bev pinched her lips and adjusted her scarf like she was bracing for a sudden chill. "Hmm …"

Worried she'd offended her, Olivia quickly added, "Not that the inn doesn't look great as it normally is."

Bev scanned the lobby, gesturing here and there. "That's a very intriguing idea. In fact, that might be genius. The décor would be easy. Most of what I brought in for the Games was rented, but I could buy it outright. More paintings on the walls, the furnishings already work, and the restaurant has a full menu of Scottish recipes. The rooms would only need minimal facelifts.

Oh! I could even bring in live entertainment. Music on the weekends. How charming would that be? We could be the gateway to Virginia's Western Highlands."

She smiled at Bev's ever-optimistic marketing mind-set. "Apple Station isn't exactly close to the Highland region."

"Every small town has a run-of-the-mill inn," Bev said, brushing right past the geographic correction. "But how many can claim to have a historic *Scottish* inn?"

"First, I wouldn't call this place run-of-the-mill. And second, rebranding it as a 'historic Scottish inn' might be a stretch, seeing as we're still in Virginia."

Bev barely registered the concern. "Who doesn't love an old-time Scottish Christmas?"

"Sounds romantic," Olivia conceded with a light laugh. "Though I'm not exactly sure what that would look like."

"Rebranding wouldn't be difficult. It's all cosmetic. What do they say? Build it and they will come."

Olivia grimaced. "I don't really think that works as a general principle."

"I bet Preston would love your idea."

She held up a hand. "Not really my idea. Let's leave my name out of it."

A guest approached the desk, lingering a few feet away.

"I'll be right with you," Bev said to the woman before turning back to Olivia. "I've been trying to figure out how to breathe new life into the inn, and this just might be it. It wouldn't cost much at all. I'll need to do some research, but this could be the start of something big." She picked up the Mackenzie tartan scarf and looped it around Olivia's neck. "You take this one. It matches your eyes."

She offered a soft "thank you," hoping that, if Bev went through with the rebrand, the scarf might become a keepsake from a decision that turned out to be the right one. Then she excused herself, allowing Bev to tend to her guest, and went into the dining room.

The restaurant was about a quarter full, and with patrons widely scattered, Winifred and Clare were easy to spot. Clare had her head down, focused on her phone, while Winifred watched the server pour her a cup of tea. Olivia waited until they were alone before crossing the room to approach their table.

"Excuse me," Olivia said. "Hi. We met on Wednesday night at the gathering for Fiona."

Winifred regarded her for a moment. "Is it that cold in here?"

Olivia glanced down at the scarf and tugged on one end, slipping it from around her neck. "No, someone just gave it to me as a gift."

"The Mackenzie tartan," Winifred noted. "I had a cousin who married a Mackenzie."

"Would you mind if I spoke with you for a few minutes?" Olivia asked.

Clare looked up from her phone. "Aunt Winny, I'm going to meet up with Gavin. A bunch of people are practicing for the Games, and I want to go watch. Will you be okay here?"

"I'll be fine. Thank you."

Clare stood, offered Olivia a thin smile, and left the dining room.

Hello and goodbye to you too. Guess I have a way of clearing a room.

Olivia folded the scarf and placed it on the table before sitting. "Did only Clare travel with you from Scotland?"

Winifred sipped her tea. "Yes. She dotes on me. She doesn't have to, but I'm grateful for her help."

"She sounds like a very caring niece. Well, great-niece, that is."

"We dispense with all the 'greats' between us."

"I did the same with my great-aunt."

Of all the people who might've had a stake in Fiona's things, Winifred hadn't been on Olivia's list of possible suspects hiding in the closet. But that didn't mean someone else couldn't have been acting on her behalf.

"Since you knew Fiona and her sister so well, I was wondering if you might know anything about a few items Fiona had. I believe they originally belonged to Ruth."

Winifred set her cup down, listening intently.

"In her bedroom, she had an old iron cross and three brooches. One had a large emerald, another was a cameo on a coral background, and the third was heart-shaped with diamonds and a pearl in the center. Craig thinks some or all of them may have been his mother's.

He told me that after Ruth passed away, Fiona went to her house and took a few sentimental items."

Winifred took another sip before answering. "The cross sounds like one Ruth had. It was a Campbell family cross, dating back centuries. The brooches, I don't know. I'd have to see them. But Ruth always wore jewelry. She didn't believe in saving her best things only for special occasions."

Olivia detected no hesitation or hint of deception. "So the cross most likely was Ruth's. I'd bet the Campbell family Bible was hers as well, and Fiona probably took that too. I looked through it again, and the details are astonishing. Someone went to great lengths to trace the genealogy."

Winifred leaned in slightly. "Ruth did most of that research. It was a hobby of hers."

"That makes sense. From the handwriting, you can tell multiple people contributed over the years, but one person seemed to have recorded most of the more recent notes, along with a few from way back. Ruth's death was written in by someone else, probably Fiona."

Winifred gave a solemn nod. "Aye, that's fair to think."

Olivia pulled out her phone and opened her photos, scrolling to the Bible pages she'd photographed. "The history is fascinating—births, deaths, marriages, burial locations. It looks like most of the family was buried in or around Inveraray."

"That's ancestral Campbell land. Of course, these days, such things don't matter much."

Seeing Winifred engaged, Olivia leaned further into the family angle to keep her talking. "Where was the Fraser clan based?"

"The Frasers of Lovat, of which I'm a descendant, controlled Inverness."

"Am I right in thinking that's quite a distance from Inveraray?"

"Over three hours by car."

Olivia turned the phone toward Winifred and enlarged the image. "This is the Fraser–Campbell marriage I mentioned before. James Fraser married Elizabeth Campbell. There must be a James in every Fraser line."

Winifred pointed at the phone. "This Bible—where is it?"

"I assume it's still at Fiona's house. I saw it yesterday. There was a break-in there last night, and a few things were stolen."

Winifred stiffened. "Was the Bible taken?"

That got Olivia's attention. She'd mentioned the cross and the brooches, hoping Winifred would reveal a personal connection. But only the Bible drew a reaction. It was a rare book, yes, but still a Campbell family heirloom.

"No, it wasn't."

"Who has it now?"

"It's probably in the house, but I imagine Craig will take it."

Winifred glanced down at the table, slowly nodding. "Yes. I suppose he will."

"Have you seen this Bible before?"

"I have. Ruth wasn't the only one interested in genealogy. We researched our families together. I know many of the names on the Campbell tree." She held out her hand. "May I see?"

Olivia handed her the phone, watching as Winifred zoomed in on the section showing the marriage between Elizabeth and James.

"Elizabeth Campbell moved from Inveraray to Inverness when she married James Fraser," Winifred said. "They had one child, Patrick, before James died. In Ruth's and my research, we found Patrick Fraser also appears on my family tree."

"Oh wow. So you're a descendant of James Fraser?"

Winifred gave a small smile. "Aye. Ruth, Fiona, and I are distant cousins."

CHAPTER 29

The server came over to refill Winifred's tea, then turned to Olivia. "Anything for you, ma'am?"

She declined, waiting until the server was well clear of the table before continuing the conversation. Her thoughts were racing. When Olivia had brought up the Fraser–Campbell marriage on Wednesday, Winifred had simply implied they were two very common surnames in Scotland. She hadn't acknowledged the connection. Then again, Olivia hadn't asked directly. Craig had never mentioned being related to Winifred, and the way he spoke about her, it almost seemed as if he might not know.

Could that be possible?

Now that Winifred had revealed the family tie, Olivia intended to see where it might lead. "Craig never said you were related."

Winifred closed her eyes for a long blink. "I don't

believe he knows. When Ruth and I first found out, we kept it to ourselves. Eventually, we told Fiona." She pressed her lips together, curling her fingers around the teacup. The silence stretched until she finally spoke, her voice low and troubled. "But if it had anything to do with Fiona's death, I can't live with it on my conscience."

It almost sounded like a confession. Almost. Of what, though? How could being distant cousins be related to Fiona's death? Something in Winifred seemed to have shifted. Her poise was fraying, and her control was beginning to slip. As if the secret had grown too heavy to carry alone, and now with the slightest crack of interest, she could no longer hold it back. Whether Olivia was the right person or just the one sitting across from her, didn't seem to matter.

"Why keep your relation a secret? It doesn't seem like something that would matter, at least not in a bad way."

Winifred looked at her, a quiet breath escaping. "It's all going to come out now anyway."

The strain in her voice made Olivia sit straighter. Whatever Winifred was about to reveal sounded long buried. She didn't interrupt or press. She waited, letting the silence hold space for whatever came next.

"Can I see that picture again?" Winifred asked.

Olivia handed her the phone with the photos already open.

Winifred zoomed in on the property entry next to James and Elizabeth's wedding date, then gave the phone back. "We kept it to ourselves because of that."

Olivia read aloud, "Ten Scots acres of Inverness, from the loch to Wicker Glen, bounded by Broadland Burn to the west and Dorran Hill to the south, with all rights to fishing and grazing." She looked at Winifred, puzzled. "I don't understand."

"Elizabeth Campbell moved to Inverness when she married. How she and James ever met, I don't know. That would make for an interesting story. From letters passed down through the years, Ruth learned that Elizabeth didn't come alone. Her brother and his wife came too, along with someone we believe was a cousin. James' father sold that land to her brother to farm and tend."

"Elizabeth and James had one child, Patrick Fraser," Winifred continued. "But James died a year after they were married. With no other family in the area, Elizabeth returned to Inveraray with Patrick, her brother's family, and the cousin. Later, Elizabeth married Malcolm Campbell, no relation to her own family. It's just a common name. Ruth and Fiona were among their descendants."

"So, you're a descendant of Patrick Fraser, the child from Elizabeth's first marriage. And Fiona and Ruth trace their lineage back to her second marriage. That's incredible. You grew up together and didn't know?"

"Aye, it's true. I live in Glasgow now, but I spent many years in Inveraray."

"It must've been a shock to find out."

"It was. But Ruth and I always felt like family."

"Then what's the connection to the land? And why

would something in a family Bible have anything to do with Fiona's death?"

Winifred stirred sugar into her tea, set the spoon down, and took a sip before answering. "In Scotland, transfers of land, whether by gift or sale, were once legally required to be recorded in the Register of Sasines, which dates to the 1600s. The government is still converting those records to a modern system. But many historic properties, like the one listed next to Elizabeth's marriage record, haven't yet been incorporated. I now own that land."

"You bought the land that Elizabeth's brother once owned?"

"No. When James died and Elizabeth left Inverness, Fraser descendants gradually moved back onto it. They built homes, raised families, and tended it for generations. Eventually, it passed to me. No Campbell ever made a claim."

"Maybe because no one knew about it?"

"Aye, until Ruth and I found out."

"There must be some official documentation somewhere. What about this register you mentioned?"

"Ruth and I went to the Registers of Scotland office in Edinburgh. The earliest deed we found was from 1650, showing the land as Fraser property. We couldn't find a record showing James' father ever sold it to Elizabeth's brother."

Olivia nodded slowly, trying to follow. "Okay, so legally it still sounds like Fraser land, even with what you know about Elizabeth. But I still don't understand why you and Ruth wanted to keep the family connection a secret."

"Because of what's written in that Bible."

"A land transaction? But that can't possibly be considered a legal document."

"It's not. But if Craig found out, he might start an inquiry. And who knows what other records might exist to support a claim of sale. These days, before land is sold, the seller must prove they're the legal owner. I've had a generous offer on the property, and I want to sell it. I don't want my children to have to deal with this." She let out a long breath, as if weary of carrying a heavy load. "My solicitor says that because the Register of Sasines shows no record of a transfer, and since the Frasers have occupied and maintained the land openly for generations, it qualifies as mine under prescriptive possession. But if someone contested ownership, a legal battle could delay the sale, and the buyers have set a deadline."

"Why wouldn't Ruth tell her own son about this?"

"Because it's been Fraser land for over three hundred years," Winifred said pointedly. "She didn't feel right challenging that or taking it from me. James' father sold the land to the Campbells only for Elizabeth and her family's sake, and they were there for barely a year."

Olivia leaned back in her seat. She understood Ruth and Winifred's motives, but she wasn't sure where the legality of it lay, and it didn't concern her. What mattered was whether any of this connected to Mack. The burglar had specifically targeted the brooches and the cross, items that might seem valuable to the untrained eye. But the treasure Winifred had sought was something else entirely. The Bible wasn't just a family heirloom. It could be the only written record of the land transfer. Olivia doubted an entry in a Bible could be used to contest legal ownership of the property, but she understood Winifred's concern. If Craig found out, he might search for documents that could hold legal weight.

"Why are you telling me all this?" Olivia asked.

Winifred's shoulders sagged. "I came here hoping to put this matter to rest with Fiona. I thought she'd see reason, and we could settle this for good." She looked away and traced the rim of the cup, as if only half aware of Olivia now. "But I'm afraid everyone will know the truth soon. I suppose it was bound to come out eventually."

Olivia stayed quiet as Winifred's restraint unraveled, one thought at a time. When it seemed she might not say more, Olivia gently nudged her. "Craig told me that after Ruth's funeral, you asked him for something his mother was supposed to have left for you. That was the Bible, wasn't it?"

"Yes. While Ruth was still alive, she told me she'd left a note in the Bible with instructions that it was to be given to me upon her death."

"But Fiona took it. Did she know about the land?"

Winifred nodded. "She thought I was being silly. She said my concerns were overblown."

But they weren't, especially since Craig needs the money.

"Fiona promised that if she died before me, she'd made arrangements for the Bible to be given to me. What could I do? The Bible belonged to their family, and Fiona had every right to keep it."

"As Craig does now."

"Aye."

"Are you going to tell Craig everything?"

Winifred nodded. "I have to. I'll tell him about our relation and his mother's wishes regarding the Bible. Then it'll be up to him to decide."

"After all this time, why come here now to ask Fiona for it?"

Winifred removed the cloth napkin from her lap and set it on the table. "Clare and Gavin are good friends. She stayed with his family during a semester abroad. When she told me Craig was coming to the area, I thought he might try to see Fiona. I was worried she might have a change of heart."

"You mean tell Craig he might have a rightful claim to your land in Scotland? What I don't understand is why you think Fiona's death could be connected to the Bible. If nobody else knew about it, how could it be involved?"

Winifred paused and looked down at her hands. When she finally spoke, her voice was barely above a whisper. "Clare knew."

"About the significance of the Bible?"

"I didn't tell her why I wanted it, but I was so upset after we left Fiona's house on Tuesday. I told Clare that

Fiona had a Bible that Ruth had intended to leave for me. Later that night, after dinner, we went up to the room we're sharing. I read for a while, but Clare left and didn't come back for an hour. When she returned, she told me not to worry about the Bible anymore. She said she'd taken care of it."

"How?"

"Poor Fiona. If she died because of this, I couldn't live with that. I've kept this secret out of fear, but I can't carry it anymore."

Winifred fell silent, and after a moment, Olivia asked softly, "How did Clare take care of it?"

"I don't know. I asked her what she meant, but she just told me not to worry. She said she'd talked to Gavin, and he had a plan to get it for me."

CHAPTER 30

Driving along the sun-dappled access road to Lake Crystal, Olivia passed two cars heading out. One had a pair of mountain bikes secured to a hitch-mounted rack, while the other hauled an orange kayak on its roof. Near the narrow lane that led to Melissa Barn's house, a red fox stalked the forest line, searching for a midday meal. Overhead, a hawk glided gracefully, likely hunting similar prey from its loftier vantage. Clusters of wildflowers thrived in patches of tall grass, their yellow and purple blooms swaying in the breeze.

She parked in the lot beside a silver sedan and scanned for Craig and Gavin. Beyond the playground and picnic pavilions, a group of about thirty had gathered, practicing for the weekend events.

Winifred hadn't speculated on how Gavin might've conspired with Clare to get the Bible from Fiona, but

Olivia couldn't help imagining a disturbing scenario. Could he have visited Fiona on Tuesday, after Winifred left but before Craig arrived? Olivia had only exchanged brief pleasantries with Gavin and hadn't formed much of an impression. She was almost certain the police hadn't spoken to him. Why would they? Until now, there'd been no reason to suspect he had any part in what happened.

Had Gavin gone to Fiona's intending to get the Bible for Clare? If so, what had transpired? Fiona would've welcomed him in, no doubt. Olivia couldn't believe he had anything to do with her death, but if he'd seen her that night, he might help narrow the timeline.

Within minutes, the cabin grew sweltering, so she got out and locked up. Thinking of getting closer to the group, she headed toward the shade of the picnic pavilions. The athletes, grouped in threes and fours, took turns practicing and cheering each other on. It didn't take long for her to grasp the essence of the training: pick up something heavy, then hurl it as far or as high as possible.

The playground was a whirl of activity, with little ones swinging, sliding, and climbing while their mothers watched from nearby benches. A tiny tyke in a red dragon T-shirt stood at the edge of the playground's mulch, eyeing the athletes. He scoured the grass, found a stone, and spun three times before hurling it and tumbling to the ground. Then he popped up and gave a victorious yelp, leaving no doubt he was a Highlander in training.

Gavin stood with a few others his age, taking turns throwing what looked like a shot put. He was the reason she'd come. She wanted to ask if he'd visited Fiona on Tuesday, but hadn't yet figured out how to approach him. Just as she was about to sit under the shelter, Craig turned and started toward the lot. Spotting her, he changed course and came her way.

"Did you come to train with us?" he asked, grinning.

She stepped out of the shade and onto the grass. "Now that's a terrifying thought. I'm just a spectator. It's such a nice day, and since I was in the area, I thought I'd stop by for a preview. Do you usually practice like this before competitions?"

"If there's time. Most serious competitors train year-round."

"Do you go to a lot of these events?"

Craig placed his hands on his hips and nodded. Sweat darkened his gray T-shirt, the fabric clinging to him where it was soaked through. "More so in the past. I used to travel all over: California, Georgia, Michigan. Some people take vacations and lie on the beach. I'd rather go to the Highland Games whenever I can. My event schedule is lighter these days, so I stay closer to home."

"Does Gavin go to all the events with you?"

"Some, but not all. He's not as into the Games as I am. He came this time because Clare was making the trip."

"I see. Winifred told me Clare stayed with your family when she spent a semester abroad."

"Yeah, last year. Hard to believe how fast time flies. She was at Wake Forest, studying environmental science."

Olivia scanned the group, looking for Clare. "Does she compete in the Games?"

"No, but there's a strong contingent of women who do. Some are more competitive than the men. Why don't you come over and try something?"

Her laugh came quick as a whip. "I don't think I'm Highland material. Everyone is throwing heavy things very far, and that's not exactly my forte."

"We've got some warm-up weights you can use. When will you ever get the chance to do this again?"

She could happily live the rest of her life without giving it a go. But this would give her an excuse to mingle and maybe talk to Gavin, which was the reason she'd come.

Though her inner voice protested, she said, "Okay, why not?"

"Great! We'll start with something basic. I just need to grab a weight from my car. Give me a second, then we'll see what you've got."

It's really not much, and basic sounds good. "Super."

He crossed the lot to his SUV, opened the back, and pulled out what looked like a square kettlebell with a thick handle.

If I end up tearing my rotator cuff, this will officially be the most ill-advised thing I've ever done when no one's life was at stake.

Moments later, he returned with the weight in hand, the effort subtly outlining the cut of his biceps.

"That looks very heavy," she said as they headed toward the others.

"It's fifty-six pounds."

"Please tell me that's not what you're planning to teach me with."

"No. For you, we're going straight to the caber," he joked as they passed the pavilion.

"In that case, you'd better call an ambulance now. How much do those things weigh?"

"There's no standard, but they're usually around a hundred pounds or more."

"Do you do that event?"

"I used to, when I was a little younger."

Gavin stood with three other guys, taking turns tossing the weight and breaking down technique. He was athletic but lacked his father's bulky build. Craig was close to six feet tall and had to go a muscular two-fifty, while Gavin was leaner and at least four inches shorter. The sprightly steps she'd heard racing down the stairs at Fiona's last night didn't sound like they belonged to someone Craig's size, but they could've easily been Gavin's.

"So what are you planning to do with this monster weight of yours that, thankfully, doesn't involve me?"

Craig lifted the weight slightly, as if it were nothing more than a sack of produce. "This is for an event called Weight Over Bar. The goal is to toss it over a bar mounted between two poles. We don't have the full setup here, but it's not necessary for training."

"I've seen that before. It's impressive how high some people can get it." She looked around again for Clare. "Do you know everyone here?"

As they reached the practice area, Craig set the weight down next to a cooler. "Most, but not all. Many of us travel the circuit, so faces become familiar. We're a competitive bunch, but there's a lot of camaraderie too."

"I've been to a few Highland Games over the years. It always feels like a big family atmosphere." Her gaze shifted between all the heavy weights being hurled by people much larger than her. "So, what kind of torture are you about to inflict on me? And what injuries should I plan to leave with?"

"Hopefully none. We'll start with the Open Stone Throw. That's what Gavin and his friends are doing over there."

"It looks like the shot put."

"It's similar. The weight is called a stone, and the goal is to throw it as far as you can."

"What could possibly go wrong with that?"

"There you go, already embracing the Highlander spirit. In competition, we have boundaries we can't step over, but we won't worry about rules with you."

"I appreciate the leniency." She was already picturing

how poorly this could go. "If you're going to ask me to spin before throwing a weight, that could end badly. For me and anyone nearby."

His loud laugh turned a few heads. "No spinning necessary. That's just one technique. I use a glide, but for you, we'll stick to a shuffle."

Not sure that's much better.

He picked up a large, round stone, then grabbed a smaller one and handed it to her.

She turned it over in her hands. "That's lighter than I expected."

"For women, the stone is usually between eight and twelve pounds. That one's four. We use it to teach beginners proper technique."

She wasn't the least bit insulted. Escaping this without tendon or ligament damage was the goal.

He walked her through the motions first, then had her mimic his technique without throwing the stone. After that, he demonstrated several full-speed throws, launching his stone about forty feet.

She picked out a worn patch of grass about fifteen feet ahead. If her throw landed the stone even close to it, she wouldn't be completely humiliated. "How heavy is your stone?"

"Twenty-two pounds. Ready?"

Nope. "As I'll ever be."

He coached her through the steps one more time. Then she shuffled, heaved the stone, and watched it land with a thud, a wee bit shy of her goal. Still, she rounded up and called it a win for her first attempt.

"Beautiful," he cheered, clapping. "You're a natural."

"Nothing about that felt natural," she joked.

Gavin picked up the stone, brought it back, and handed it to her.

"Thanks. I think I used too much arm and not enough legs."

"You want to really drive it with your hips," Gavin said.

Craig slapped his son on the back. "Why don't you work with her for a while." He picked up the weight he'd carried from his car. "I want to get some throws in while I'm still loose."

She turned to Gavin. "I don't want to take you away from your training."

"I don't mind."

"Once you master this, we'll move on to the hammer throw," Craig said, pointing toward the far end of the field. A behemoth whirled a long-handled weight around his body in an up-and-down motion before heaving it with a loud yell.

"You're kidding, right?" she asked.

Craig just smiled and walked off, carrying his weight.

She looked at Gavin. "He's kidding, right?"

"My dad takes training pretty seriously. Women compete in the hammer throw too."

Her strategy for gathering information was rapidly veering into bad-life-decision territory. With a resigned exhale, she went through the motions Craig had taught her and launched the stone again. This time, it landed a smidge farther than the last toss. No snaps, no pops—so far, so good.

Gavin retrieved the stone and handed it back to her.

"Thanks," she said. "Your dad told me you and Clare are close, but that she doesn't compete in the Games."

"Yeah, no. She's way more into the fashion side." He nodded toward the stone. "That was better. Did you feel the difference when you used more drive from your legs?"

"Definitely. Maybe I'm getting the hang of it."

"Want to try a heavier stone?"

"Absolutely not. I'm good." She glanced around. "I thought Clare might be here watching you practice."

"I think she's having lunch with her aunt at the inn."

She was until supposedly coming here to watch you.

Olivia lined up for another toss, psyching herself up to give it all her welly for a personal best. With the extra oomph, the stone flew a little farther.

"Yeah! There you go." Gavin jogged out to retrieve it.

She hadn't anticipated Highland Games training as part of her day. Dressed entirely wrong for a workout, she was sweating and desperate for water. With each throw, she felt like she was tempting fate. Before she needed to schedule an appointment with an orthopedic surgeon, she aimed to get to the real reason she'd come.

As Gavin handed her the stone, she turned to face

him. "I'm sorry about your great-aunt. Did you know her well?"

He glanced down, shaking his head. "Not really. When I was younger, my family went to Scotland to visit my grandmother, and Aunt Fi came with us."

"I've always wanted to go to Scotland." She pointed to his Wake Forest T-shirt. "Are you a student or an alum?"

"Student. Third year. I'm studying art history."

"That sounds fascinating. Your aunt had some beautiful heirloom pieces in her house that you'd probably be interested in. I understand she was a painter. I saw some of her work. She had real talent. Did you get a chance to visit her?"

"No, I didn't. I feel bad about it."

"Maybe Clare can tell you about some of her paintings. I'm sure she saw some of your aunt's work when she was in the house."

"No, Clare was never there."

She didn't even have to act surprised. "Oh. I thought she went with Winifred to visit her on Tuesday. I must've been mistaken." *But I know I'm not.*

"Yeah, no. I mean, Clare went to the house, but she didn't go inside. She waited in the car while Winifred was visiting Aunt Fi. She was texting me the whole time."

"Oh, I see. Now I understand." *What?*

"Clare said Winifred wanted to talk to my aunt alone."

Olivia just smiled and nodded as though that made sense. "Old friends, old business, I suppose."

Preston had told her that both Clare and Winifred claimed Fiona was alive when they left. But if Clare never went inside, how could she know that? Winifred had already proven to be selective with the truth. Maybe she'd been the last to see Fiona alive. But was Fiona really alive when Winifred left the house?

CHAPTER 31

"Looks like you're working out a kink," Sam said from the passenger seat of the Expedition.

Olivia stopped massaging her shoulder and gripped the wheel with both hands. "I tweaked it."

"Overhead presses?" Sam joked.

"Not so pedestrian. I tried my hand at the Open Stone Throw. With a training weight." She gave a quick rundown of her first, and likely last, ill-advised dabble in the competitive side of the Highland Games.

Yesterday, after speaking with Gavin, she'd left the park before Craig could rope her into trying the hammer throw. On the drive home, she'd called Preston to share that Winifred's account of her visit with Fiona had left out one crucial detail: Clare had stayed in the car. Amy hadn't said if Clare came to the door with Fiona, but it seemed likely Amy saw Clare outside and assumed she'd soon join Winifred. Olivia had also somewhat reluctantly mentioned Clare and Gavin's meeting, careful not to speculate about their intentions. The idea that Craig's son might be tied to Fiona's death was perhaps the most unsettling possibility she'd considered.

Preston hadn't been surprised or upset by her continued digging. Questioning a seventy-something-year-old woman over tea, he'd commented, was the least dangerous sleuthing she'd ever done. He doubted that Winifred, Gavin, or Clare had anything to do with Fiona's death, but he said he'd question them all anyway.

She'd also told him that Winifred wanted Fiona's Bible, without explaining why. She only said that Ruth had promised it to her. Olivia wasn't convinced the Bible had anything to do with Fiona's death. The burglar had taken the brooches and the cross, leaving the Bible untouched. As for the history between the families, for now, that was still Winifred's story to tell.

There was nothing more she could do about Mack. He was out of touch, whether by choice or not. Unless he contacted her, showed up, or was found, her involvement in the matter had hit a dead end. All she could do was wait and hope the police investigation turned up a lead. With no angles left to pursue, she'd stepped back from it all and called Sam during breakfast to see if she wanted to go to the Highland Games. She had picked Sam up at eleven, and now they were about halfway to the venue.

Until Olivia had brought up yesterday's outing at

Lake Crystal, they'd been chatting about Melissa and Kevin's upcoming wedding, sidestepping the elephant in the room. Sam had known for months about Carolyn's plan to recruit Olivia for the team. Olivia understood why Sam hadn't said anything sooner. Looking back, she could recall several conversations where Sam had subtly asked about her future plans. Now, Olivia wondered just how much Sam knew about Carolyn's tactics and whether she'd played a role in using her father's dream of opening a bakery as leverage.

"How do you do it?" Olivia asked, glancing at Sam.

"Do what?"

"Keep your personal life and work separate. You lived next door to my dad for years, and we knew almost nothing about you. Even after we became friends, I didn't know what you actually did for a living. I only found out because I had to. If things had gone differently when the carnival came, I might still be in the dark."

"I don't completely separate my personal and professional life. You and a few trusted friends know. But the truth is, most people don't pay much attention to anyone but themselves. You pass strangers, see your neighbors, say hello to acquaintances, but for the most part, you have no idea what's going on in their lives."

Olivia had to look no further than her loose friendship with Mack to know that was true. Ruth and Winifred too. They'd agreed to keep the connection between their families a secret, even from relatives. Olivia wasn't sure if she could or wanted to play that game. If she accepted Carolyn's offer, her father and Preston would have to know. But how far would the circle of disclosure extend? She couldn't imagine leading a double life and keeping Sophia and A.J. out of the loop. But what about Bev, Maria, and Tori? Her confidantes were already few. Would she have to narrow them even more?

Their arrival at the venue cut the conversation short, which was just as well. Olivia felt guarded talking about such matters with Sam, unsure whether anything she confided would make its way back to Carolyn. She followed a line of cars into the open field parking lot, where attendants in orange vests waved flags, guiding drivers into orderly rows.

They waited in the Expedition until the people on either side had gotten out and shut their doors. Many had come for the day, toting lawn chairs, coolers, and picnic baskets. For every one person in shorts and a T-shirt, there were two in kilts. It was the kind of event that brought out the Celtic spirit in everyone, whether or not they had Scottish ancestry.

They hadn't made any firm plans about how long they'd stay, but both had packed light. Olivia wore shorts, a T-shirt, and sneakers, bringing only what fit in her pockets. Sam, tactical as ever, wore long pants, a merino wool tee, and hiking shoes, her ever-present sling bag ready at her side.

After getting out, they headed toward the ticket booth, paid their admission, and entered the venue. Just inside the gate, a table selling official souvenirs sat beside two small speakers playing a spirited reel. Rows of multi-colored canopies lined both sides of the narrow paved lane, normally used for access to the barns and the stables. Signs outside each tent displayed Scottish surnames: MacGregor, MacLeod, MacDougall, and more. Beneath the tents, tables were stacked with tartan goods, while racks of traditional clothing invited visitors to browse. Families had hung banners displaying their crests, and posters offered at-a-glance clan histories, noting famous ancestors and past glories.

Two young girls with St. Andrew's Crosses painted on their cheeks skipped past Olivia and Sam as their parents strolled behind. The children giggled as they crouched beside a leashed collie lying on a cooling mat under the Gordon clan's canopy. The Lassie lookalike lifted its head and accepted their gentle pets, clearly accustomed to attention from strangers.

Beyond the clan tents, a fenced-in grass arena served as the competition field. Spectators had gathered around the perimeter, lounging on blankets or relaxing in lawn chairs.

A robust voice over the PA announced the final competitor in the Men's Masters Hammer Throw. Olivia and Sam found an empty spot along the fence to watch. Dressed in a navy and green tartan kilt and a white sleeveless T-shirt, the broad-shouldered competitor took a few steadying breaths inside the protective cage. His mates shouted encouragement as he set his heels against the wooden trig and rolled his shoulders in preparation.

With his back to the field, he hoisted the hammer and swung it low and high in a fluid rhythm, gaining speed with each rotation. On the fourth go-around, he unwound and let the hammer fly, sending it soaring into the field. A roar of applause met his triumphant shout as the PA confirmed his winning distance.

Olivia wasn't one to live with regrets, and skipping the hammer throw yesterday hadn't changed that philosophy. In the background, bagpipe music played over distant speakers, while across the arena, the crowd erupted in applause. A woman competing in the Braemar Stone had just landed a throw announced at twenty-two feet. The event resembled what Olivia had practiced at the park, except the competitor threw her stone from a standing position, with no spin, shuffle, or glide.

"Look over there," Sam said, pointing. "They're getting the caber ready. That thing has to be at least fifteen feet long."

"Craig said they usually weigh around a hundred pounds. You know, women do the caber toss too. Seems like something up your alley."

"When you sign up, I'll sign up," Sam joked.

"Touché."

The first competitor's name in the Men's Amateur A Caber Toss was announced over the PA. A powerhouse of a man raised his hand to acknowledge the crowd, and was greeted by cheers and encouragement from his fellow competitors. Clad in a white T-shirt and a red and green kilt, he took control of the towering caber, aided by two men who steadied it upright. He braced it against his shoulder, wrapped his hands around its rough surface, and lowered himself into a deep squat, inching his grip farther down.

In one explosive movement, he hoisted it and stood tall. With short, measured strides and his neck flexed forward, he advanced, balancing the massive log against his shoulder while a spotter followed close behind. When the caber began to tilt forward, he halted, planted his feet, and launched it into the air. The thick timber flipped end over end, landing perfectly at the twelve o'clock position. The man gave a triumphant yell, and the crowd applauded as the announcer confirmed, "A perfect turn!"

"That's crazy," Sam said, laughing. "How do you even train for that? Where do you buy a caber?"

"I don't know. Craig told me the competitors take training very seriously, so I have to imagine they practice with the real thing."

"I want to watch this for a while. Try to understand the technique."

"I knew it. Give it six months and you'll be in your yard tossing around a big ol' Scots pine pole."

"You might be right."

"Well, you can fill me in on what you learn for that bank of knowledge I'll never put into practice. I'm going to take a walkabout. Get the lay of the land. I want to find something in tartan for Buddy. I'll be back in a bit."

Sam nodded as Olivia turned and headed toward the main walkway. Past the rows of family clan tents, more canopies were set up, each hosting a traditional craft demonstration. Artisans showcased weaving, leatherworking, and rope spinning. A blacksmith delighted a group of children as he hammered glowing metal on an anvil, sending sparks flying with each strike as he shaped a Scottish dirk.

At another tent, she stood behind a packed house, listening as three musicians played a lilting reel on fiddle, guitar, and accordion. The infectious rhythm had everyone clapping along in time. When the song ended, she applauded with the others and continued onward.

People of all ages packed the walkway. Many carried shopping bags or nibbled on finger foods from the food trucks farther down the lane. She thought of texting Sawyer, but there'd be time to catch up with him later. Besides, he was on work detail today, and she didn't want to distract him.

A short distance from the musicians' tent, a crowd had gathered around a large penned-in area. Inside the fencing, a dog handler worked a border collie and five meandering geese. At the handler's command, the collie herded the geese into a single group, then maneuvered them in the indicated direction. The black and white dog dashed to one side of the geese and dropped to its stomach, lying perfectly still until they turned. Then, in an instant, it sprung up and raced to the opposite side, steering them ninety degrees. With another command, the collie expertly moved them through a large tunnel and over a walkway bridge. The crowd clapped as the handler lavished the dog with praise and a small treat.

A light breeze carried the savory-sweet aromas drifting from the nearby food vendors. The scent of grilled meats and fried fish mingled with the warm, buttery notes of baked goods. Though not hungry yet, she figured it wouldn't hurt to scope out the options for lunch.

Turning, she headed toward the trailers, passing a truck boldly advertising itself as The Great Scot Haggis Spot. She might venture as far as a Scotch egg, but sheep's heart, liver, and lungs? Hard pass.

At the next trailer, Gavin and Kirstie stood at the counter, placing an order. Both wore white T-shirts and kilts woven in the deep green, navy blue, and black tartan of the Campbell clan. The vendor handed Gavin a Scotch pie wrapped in foil and a paper towel, along with a soda. He stepped aside while Kirstie waited, her small tartan backpack slung over one shoulder.

"Hi, Gavin," Olivia said. "Good to see you. Thanks again for yesterday. It was a lot of fun." Since it was a bluebird sky, she wasn't too worried about being struck by lightning for her little white lie about risking a tendon tear in the name of sleuthing.

"No problem. If you're interested in training for any other events, there are great online resources that teach technique."

She forced a smile and nodded. "Maybe I'll have to

look into them." *And pass the links on to Sam.* "Are you competing today?"

"I'm doing the Sheaf Toss this afternoon."

"That's the one with the pitchfork, right?"

"Yeah," he said, grinning. "Basically, you try to fling a sixteen-pound burlap sack over a bar. A skill for life."

She laughed. "In that case, I'd better pick up a pitchfork on my way home and fill in that gap in my education. What time is your event?"

"Two o'clock. That's why I'm fueling up now."

Kirstie joined them, carrying a drink. After exchanging hellos, she said, "Gav, I'm going to the market tents."

"That's where I was heading," Olivia said.

Kirstie gestured down the walkway. "They're right over there."

"I'm going back to the field," Gavin said.

"Good luck this afternoon," Olivia offered.

"Thanks. I'll need it."

With that, he took off, and Kirstie and Olivia started toward the market tents together.

"Are you looking for a kilt?" Kirstie asked.

"No, I want to get something for our beagle."

"There's a whole tent just for pets. They've got all sorts of cute stuff. Sweaters, leashes, collars, bow ties— you name it."

"Our dog isn't a fashionista, but I'm thinking a tartan collar or a leash would be perfect."

"This is it up here," Kirstie said, pointing to a tent

packed with racks and tables full of everything needed to adorn fur babies of all kinds and sizes.

Olivia browsed, dismissing the clothing options immediately. Trying to get a sweater on Buddy would be like wrestling a greased piglet. Attempting the same with Willow would only lead to unnecessary trauma for everyone involved. Olivia had tried more than once to put a featherweight harness on the cat, only for her to dramatically collapse as if saddled with a ten-pound vest.

She was browsing a selection of collars when Kirstie came up beside her and picked up a leash from the adjoining table.

"Score!" Kirstie exclaimed. "A Campbell leash for my lab."

"Nice," Olivia said. "So many to choose from."

"Do you have any Scottish heritage?"

"A little on my mother's side, but it's so far back I don't know the name." She picked up a collar that was bright red, with green, blue, white, yellow, and black stripes. "I was thinking of this pattern. My dad seems to think our dog's favorite color is red, even though I'm pretty sure red looks gray or brown to dogs."

"That's the Royal Stewart," Kirstie said. "It's associated with the British Royal Family. It's a good choice for people who aren't Scottish but want to wear tartan."

"Then that sounds perfect, since our beagle definitely isn't Scottish."

After they paid for their items, they left the tent.

"Thanks for your insight," Olivia said. "I'm sure our

dog will love it. Our cat will probably think it's a new toy. Have you heard any news about your great-aunt's cat?"

Kirstie shook her head. "No. It's so sad. I hope somebody finds her."

"If she's found, can someone in your family take her in?"

"I don't think so. My roommate is allergic, and my parents can't have pets because of my mom's illness. Maybe Gav could, but I'm not sure he'd want to. He's more of a dog person. Besides, he lives in a tiny apartment, and I don't know if pets are allowed there."

"I saw Shadow on Thursday, but she got away before I could catch her. Maybe someone else will have better luck."

"She's a roamer. She loves getting into all kinds of adventures."

"How do you know?"

Kirstie flipped her backpack around, put the leash inside, and pulled out her phone. After a few swipes, she turned it toward Olivia and played a video. The jerky footage showed movement across a yard, along a sidewalk, and partway up a tree, all from a low-to-the-ground perspective.

"What is this?" Olivia asked.

"Aunt Fi knew I loved animals, so she used to send me videos of Shadow. It's pretty cool seeing the world through a cat's eyes."

"Shadow wears a pet camera?"

"Yep. Right around her neck, attached to her collar.

Aunt Fi got a kick out of watching Shadow explore her world. She'd sometimes let her out in the yard. I'd be scared she'd run off or wander into the street, but Aunt Fi said Shadow always stayed close and came back when she called."

Olivia's thoughts skittered. On Thursday, she hadn't paid attention to what the cat was wearing. It had been too dark anyway, and all she'd cared about was trying to grab her. But if the cat had the camera on her collar the night Fiona died, could it have captured what really happened?

"Did Shadow always wear the camera?"

"I'm not sure."

"Do you know how it works?"

"Yeah. When I saw Aunt Fi's videos, I bought the same one for my dog. It has a rechargeable battery, and you can set it to record continuously or only when there's movement. You clip it to the collar, and the footage saves to a microSD card. Then you plug it into a computer to watch."

"How long does the battery last?"

Kirstie shrugged. "Depends on the setting. If it's always recording, maybe an hour. On motion-activated, it can last up to eight. At night, though, the battery drains fast."

Olivia's mind raced. The cat could be the key. A quiet observer in the shadows might reveal the missing piece.

"Thanks for the information," Olivia said. "I have to go. I'm sure our dog will love the leash."

After a quick goodbye, she hurried back the way she'd come. Weaving through the crowd, she pulled out her phone and fired off a text to Sam: "Have to cut this short. Sorry. Meet me at the entrance ASAP. We need to find a missing cat."

CHAPTER 32

Olivia sped down the access road to Lake Crystal, scanning for any critters thinking about darting across. On the way, she'd shared her theory about the cat camera with Sam, who was fully on board with the plan. She turned onto the lane leading to the houses just outside the park's boundary. Melissa's house was closest to the lake, but today, Olivia's target was the mobile home belonging to Jason Rotterdam.

Jason was an outdoorsman: a hunter, trapper, and tracker. He was the only person she could think of who might know how to find a hiding cat. She would've called ahead, but didn't have his number. They weren't strangers, but they weren't quite friends either. She'd helped Melissa and Mikey back in October, and in return, Jason had offered her a favor. Today, she was calling it in.

The first glimpse of his mobile home brought a

welcome sight: his truck parked on a bare patch of ground shaded by a new metal awning. She'd thought they might need to search the park or stop by Melissa's to ask if she knew where he was. But as Olivia pulled off the road onto the grass, he came around the corner of his home, carrying a five-gallon white bucket in each hand.

He was clean-shaven and a bit leaner, wearing camouflage pants and an army-green T-shirt. She might not have recognized him if he weren't standing in front of his place. As they got out, he walked to his truck without breaking stride, eyes on them, and lifted both buckets into the bed with practiced ease.

"Hi, Jason," Olivia said. "Long time no see."

As he strolled toward them, he adjusted his hat and pulled a rag from his back pocket. "Are you lost?" he asked, his mouth curving into a small smile.

"No, I came to see you. This is my friend, Sam."

He wiped his hands with the rag, then tucked it back in his pocket. "I believe we've met."

"Briefly," Sam replied.

"What can I do for you?" he asked.

"I need help finding and trapping a cat," Olivia said.

He gave a short, amused laugh. "Nobody's ever asked me to do that before. That's a tough one. Did you call animal control?"

Olivia shook her head. "No, but it's crucial we find her as soon as possible."

"Is it feral?"

"No. Her owner died earlier this week. There was a break-in at the house, and at some point, the cat got out. I think she's been staying close by. She used to roam outside, but she always found her way back home."

Jason was quiet for a moment, staring at the ground as he gathered his thoughts. "How long has it been missing?"

"Since Tuesday."

"Then it's either finding food or someone's feeding it. It's probably nearby but hidden, which makes finding it almost impossible. You might have to wait until someone takes it in. And if you're lucky, they'll check with the shelters for missing animal reports." He paused and rubbed his chin. "I've got traps we could set up. They're spring-loaded, so they won't hurt the cat. Once it steps inside, the door shuts behind it. It's a long shot, though. We could end up catching something else."

"Whatever help you can give would be great," Olivia said. "Anything is better than nothing."

Jason agreed to set the traps immediately and said he'd return that night to check them. Olivia and Sam waited in the Expedition while he loaded them into his truck. When he finished, they pulled out together, Olivia leading the way.

About twenty minutes later, they arrived at Fiona's house. Near the porch, Olivia explained that she and her dad had seen Shadow in the house Thursday night, but she'd slipped away before they could catch her. Jason surveyed the yard, then they circled the house and returned to the driveway.

"I'll set a trap on the porch and at the back door. The cat's probably used to coming in both ways." He pointed past the garage toward the closest house. "Does that neighbor know the cat is missing?"

"I'm not sure," Olivia said.

Sam turned and started across the yard. "I'll check."

"I'll get the traps and set them up."

"Thanks, Jason."

As he went to his truck, Olivia pulled out her phone and called Preston to share the latest developments.

After two rings, he answered. "Hey, Liv."

"Hi. Are you at home?"

"No. Hold on a sec." His voice lowered as he told someone he'd meet them by a trail. Returning to the line, he said, "I'm out on Riverbend Highway."

"Are you working?"

"Yeah. Two hikers found a gun in the stream near Shadow Creek Campground. A deputy recovered it, and the serial number matches Amy Winters' gun. I went out to Winchester this morning to talk to Nolan Pierce about Mack. Nolan is here with me now. He said Mack knew someone with a hunting cabin not far from the campground, and a few times a year, he'd stay there. Nolan went with him once, so he knows where it is. He's going to show me."

Jason finished setting the trap on the front porch, then headed around back with the second one.

"Well, be careful," she said. "Do you have backup for the search?"

"No. I doubt we'll find Mack anywhere near there. Besides, there was a four-car accident on the Snickersville Turnpike, so a few deputies are tied up with that. Another one went down to Amy's house to question her. Even Chief Payne came in this morning to cover the phones until someone on shift gets back."

"Busy day for the Apple Station Police Department. While I have you, any news about Clare and Winifred?"

"I talked to both again yesterday. Clare admitted she stayed in the car while Winifred saw Fiona." He gave a dry laugh. "She didn't think she misled us by saying Fiona was alive when they left because, get this, Winifred never said she was dead."

"Which isn't the same as saying she was alive."

"Exactly. Winifred stuck to the same version of events she'd given before. And you were right about Gavin. He went to Fiona's house around eight. He said he knocked, but there was no answer and the lights were off, so he left. He didn't try to go inside, so we don't know if the door was unlocked then."

"Did he say why he went?"

"Just that he planned to visit. But I wouldn't be surprised if it had something to do with the Bible Winifred wanted."

"If the door was closed, Fiona must've still been alive when he got there."

"Probably."

"Do you believe him?"

"That he didn't see her? I don't know. Seems like everyone is hiding something about their business at that house Tuesday." He sighed. "I should go. Maybe I'll manage a few hours of downtime on my day off."

"Yeah, okay."

"What about you? Are you at the Games?"

"No. I was earlier, but now I'm at Fiona's house." She explained how the morning had unfolded and her efforts to find the cat.

Sam crossed the yard as Jason came around the front.

"I never would've considered that angle," Preston said. "But I'm open to anything at this point. Keep me posted."

"Alright. Talk to you later."

They ended the call, and Olivia joined Sam and Jason on the walkway in front of the cat-shaped topiary.

"The neighbors confirmed Shadow has been coming around," Sam said. "They knew she belonged to Fiona, and they've been trying to coax her inside, but she either stays on the porch or runs off if they get too close."

"That's great to know," Olivia said.

"Both traps are set. I'll come back out tonight to check if we caught her." Jason glanced toward the driveway. "Whose Cadillac is that?"

"It belonged to Fiona Campbell, the cat's owner," Olivia replied.

"So that car hasn't been driven for a few days?" he asked.

Olivia nodded. "Probably longer than that. It wasn't used very often. Why?"

He pointed at the bushes along the side of the house. "There's a strong smell over there. Makes me think a cat's been doing its business nearby."

He went over to the Cadillac, circled it, and crouched to look underneath. He pounded his fist on the front passenger-side door, then straightened and moved to the hood, giving it a few solid thumps before pressing his ear to the grille.

"Can you get the keys to open this up?" he asked.

"They might be inside the house," Olivia replied. "I'll go check."

He went to the driver's side and dropped out of view.

"How are you going to get into the house?" Sam said.

"I have a key."

"How did you manage that?"

"I borrowed it from a friend of Fiona's and just haven't returned it yet."

Before Sam could respond, Jason called over, "Never mind." A moment later, he stood, cradling a black cat in his arms. "Is this who you're looking for?"

CHAPTER 33

"That's her!" Olivia said. "Where was she?"

Jason rounded the front bumper, struggling to keep hold of Shadow as she squirmed to get free. "She was lying on top of the tire in the wheel well. Found herself a safe place to hide close to home. Whoa, take it easy, girl. We're just trying to get you back where you belong."

Olivia met him on the walkway. "I'll take her." She slid her hands beneath the cat's belly and along her back, ready for the transfer.

"You got her?" he asked.

"I'm good."

He loosened his grip as she tightened hers, securing Shadow in her arms.

"Thank you," he said. "She's feisty."

The cat calmed as Olivia held her close and brushed her cheek. "Probably scared. Poor Shadow, you've had quite a week. We've been searching everywhere for you. You're safe now. I'm not letting you go." She ran her fingers along the collar. "Your camera is still here. Good girl." She looked at Jason. "Thanks. You're a genius."

"Cats sometimes huddle under cars or even crawl into engine compartments to stay warm," he said. "I've heard stories of cats going for long rides hitchhiking under the hood."

"I wouldn't have thought to check there," Olivia admitted. "Now we can see what, if anything, Shadow witnessed on Tuesday."

"What do you mean?" he asked.

She gently tapped the small device on the collar. "This is a camera. It might have recorded what happened to her owner that night. Shadow was probably in the house when the intruder entered. At some point, she got out, but maybe the camera caught something before she did."

Sam stepped in for a closer look as the cat rested her head on Olivia's shoulder. "It should attach straight to a computer through this port."

"Craig's daughter has the same camera for her dog. She said it records to a microSD card."

"I have a reader at home," Sam said.

"Better yet, there's got to be one in the house. Fiona had a laptop in the sitting room. I bet that's where she watched the footage."

Sam nodded. "Let's go."

"I'll collect my traps and be on my way."

"No, come on in when you're done," Olivia said. "You're part of this now."

"Alright. I'd like to see what kind of video this camera can record."

He turned and headed toward the back of the house while Olivia and Sam stepped onto the porch. Holding Shadow securely with one arm, Olivia dug her keys out of her pocket and handed them to Sam. "Can you open it? It's the key on the Loch Ness Monster ring."

Sam took the key ring, unlocked the door, and they went inside.

"The laptop is down the hall, first room on the left," Olivia said, closing the door.

Sam led the way to the sitting room and went straight to the desk. She sat down, turned on the lamp, and examined the laptop's ports.

"What if there's a password?" Olivia asked.

Sam tapped an orange note taped to the desk. "Computer password: Shadow."

"Not super secure, but maybe smart for Fiona. She probably left it in case someone needed access. That's something my dad would do. I'm going to take Shadow into the kitchen and get her some food."

"Hold on."

Sam stood, removed the collar, and set it on the desk. Then she opened the top side drawer and rummaged through its contents. Not finding what she was looking for, she tried the one below. A small device resembling a USB stick lay on top of an address book. "This is it."

"Go for it. I'll be right back."

Olivia went into the kitchen, flipped on the light, and gently set Shadow down near her food bowl. The cat immediately began munching on the kibble.

"Let's see if you have wet food in here somewhere," she said, opening the cabinets. She came across the plates first, then moved to the pantry. "Here we go. How does salmon pâté sound?"

She grabbed a can, closed the door, and popped the top, instantly catching Shadow's attention. The cat padded over and wove between Olivia's legs, letting out a few plaintive meows. Smiling, Olivia pulled a spoon from the drawer, scooped the food onto a plate, and set it on the floor. The cat began to devour it, clearly missing what must be a favorite flavor.

"Good girl. Eat up." She gave the cat a few gentle strokes before putting fresh water into her bowl. Leaving Shadow to her meal, she returned to the sitting room.

"How is she doing?" Sam asked.

"Hungry, but otherwise, she seems okay."

"What are you going to do with her?"

"I'm not sure. I'll get Craig's number and contact him, but I don't think he can take her. At least she's safe in the house. I'll leave out enough food for her overnight and figure things out tomorrow. Maybe—"

A knock at the door interrupted her train of thought.

"That's gotta be Jason," Olivia said. "I must've locked him out."

She walked into the hallway, glancing back to make

sure Shadow wasn't following her. No way was she giving the cat another chance to escape, not on her watch. With the coast clear, she opened the door and let Jason in.

"Sam is looking at the footage now," she said, closing the door behind him. "Come this way."

"Swanky house," he observed, following her into the sitting room.

Sam sat at the desk, eyes fixed on the screen. "I started at the beginning. There are hours of footage here. I'm fast-forwarding through most of it."

At twice the speed, Shadow's life played out like a madcap adventure. Quick glimpses of the yard cut to scenes of her eating, then leaping onto Fiona's dresser and bed. When Sam slowed the video to real time, the cat's day settled into a quieter, more mundane rhythm. Much of the early afternoon was spent gazing out windows and wandering the house.

"Winifred visited around three," Olivia said. "Let's see if the timestamp is accurate."

Sam fast-forwarded, and sure enough, the camera captured both video and audio of Winifred entering the home. Shadow followed them into the sitting room, lingered for a few minutes, then went upstairs to nap on the cat tree in Fiona's bedroom.

As they watched the playback, Shadow padded into the room and sat near Olivia's feet. She bent down and stroked the cat's head. "You've been missing your human, haven't you?"

"Here," Sam said. "I think this is something."

She rewound the video slightly, then let it play at normal speed. At eight-thirty, Shadow was walking toward the kitchen when a bright beam illuminated the hallway above her. The cat froze, then scampered into the sitting room and hid under the sofa. The camera cut out for a moment before reactivating, now showing someone in the room shining a flashlight around. Shadow tracked the movement, but from her hiding spot, only the intruder's shoes and pant legs were visible.

"Can you turn up the volume?" Olivia asked.

Sam did, and they listened as the intruder moved deliberately through the room. Then the figure stopped, and a sharp, unmistakable *zip* sent the cat scurrying deeper under the sofa.

"That had to be Amy's bag," Olivia said. "She left it in here. That's got to be when they grabbed the gun." She glanced down at Shadow. "Good girl. You caught them on your cam."

"Hey, here we go," Sam said, pointing at the screen.

The room went dark as the intruder left. A few seconds later, the cat emerged from under the sofa and cautiously followed the person down the hallway. The video was dark, but creaking steps revealed the intruder was heading upstairs. The cat approached the steps, but the camera only captured footage of the floor and the wall.

A woman called out, "Hello? Amy, is that you?"

"That's Fiona," Olivia whispered.

Two muffled voices exchanged words, followed by a

heavy *thud*. Shadow startled just as the front door slowly opened. The cat spun to face the door and backed down the hall. Someone stepped inside, visible only from the knees down. They paused in the entryway, then started up the stairs.

"Fiona!" a man called out.

"That's Mack," Olivia said.

His voice rose. "Hey! What the hell!"

A struggle broke out on the staircase, followed by the steps cracking, a table crashing, and then two gunshots.

Olivia leaned in closer. "Mack was the one being shot at."

The video cut away as the cat darted back into the sitting room and hid under the sofa. The intruder re-entered, quickly paced around, and yanked open the desk drawers.

"They were looking for something," Sam said.

Then, as abruptly as they'd entered, the intruder left the room and presumably the house. A faint noise was the last sound the camera recorded that night.

Sam fast-forwarded, but there was nothing more except the moment Shadow bolted out of the house and scampered toward the garage.

"That's it," Sam said. "The battery must've died."

"Rewind it to the end, just before Shadow ran out," Olivia instructed.

She did so, and they watched again.

"Did you hear that at the very end?" Olivia asked.

Jason nodded. "Yeah. Could've been a noise from outside or upstairs."

"Play it again, Sam, with the volume all the way up," Olivia said.

She rewound the footage, then pressed play.

"That almost sounds like a grunt," he said.

"Or maybe Fiona calling out or groaning from upstairs," Sam suggested.

"One more time," Olivia said, leaning in as close as she could, eyes shut, focusing solely on the sound as the video played. Then, as if day had turned to night in a blink, she bolted upright and gasped. Her thoughts collapsed in on themselves. "That was a sneeze." Her stomach seized, her breath lost its way. "Oh, no."

"What is it, Liv?" Sam asked.

Panic gripped her throat, and her pulse pounded like a string of sonic booms. "Oh God, no. Preston."

CHAPTER 34

Olivia pulled out her phone and called Preston.

"What's wrong?" Sam asked.

She pressed a hand to her forehead. "The sneeze. Oh, no. Answer." The call went to voicemail. She hung up, cursing under her breath.

Sam stood. "What about the sneeze? What's going on?"

She dialed again. "I think that was Nolan in the video —Mack's assistant."

After three more rings, she ended the call with another muttered expletive. "He's not answering."

"Who's not answering?" Jason asked.

"Preston."

"Why are you calling him?" Sam said.

"Preston Hills, the cop?" Jason clarified.

Olivia nodded. "Preston is with Nolan right now. We've got to go."

She started for the hallway, but Sam gently caught her arm.

"Whoa, back up, Liv. Tell me what you think is going on."

"Nolan is allergic to cats. It all makes sense now." Her breath came fast, and her words tumbled out. "That's why he never wanted to come here with Mack. He was in my house for no more than ten minutes before his allergies flared. He knew Fiona had valuables and that no one was supposed to be here last night."

Sam let go of her arm as Jason asked, "Who are Nolan and Mack?"

Olivia was about to redial but stopped herself, knowing the result would be the same. "Long story. The short version? Mack is missing, and I think Nolan is responsible."

"I don't know, Liv. A lot of people are allergic to cats. And the sneeze, if that's even what the noise was, might've had nothing to do with an allergy."

"No," she insisted. "He's been circling the periphery of this from the beginning. He's the one who told me about Mack booking the last-minute flight out of town. But Nolan had access to Mack's account. He made that reservation. Not Mack."

"Why would he do that?" Jason asked.

"Misdirection," Sam answered. "Put all eyes on Mack."

Olivia looked at Jason. "Thursday night, there was a break-in here. Some of Fiona's possessions were stolen."

"And you think it was this Nolan, the same guy in the video?"

"Yes," Olivia said.

"How would he have gotten in?" Sam asked.

"I don't know. Picked the lock? The front door doesn't have a deadbolt, just a key and a chain. And the chain couldn't have been engaged. Nolan was the first one to cast doubt on Mack and Amy."

"Who's Amy?" Jason asked.

"Fiona's home health aide," Olivia answered. "Her gun was taken from her bag in this room Tuesday night. Fiona left her money in a life insurance policy, and Nolan suggested that Amy and Mack might've been working together for mutual gain."

"If Mack was the one being shot at, like you said, where is he now?" Jason asked.

Olivia couldn't help herself. She redialed, pressing the phone to her ear as she spoke. "Mack is either missing or intentionally staying off the grid. He texted me Tuesday night. It must've been after he left here and before he crashed his car."

The call went to voicemail again. She exhaled sharply and hung up.

"Do you think Mack also believed it was Nolan here on Tuesday?" Sam asked.

"I don't know. If he had, I think he would've said so in his text. As far as he knew, Nolan was out of town. That's why I thought he texted me that night instead of him."

Jason crossed his arms. "If Mack was shot at, crashed his car, and now can't be found, I hate to say it, but he's probably dead."

Olivia shook her head, unwilling to accept that, though she knew it wasn't out of the question. "A search and rescue dog picked up a scent trail near the crash site. The police believe it was Mack's. The dog followed the trail to another road, but the scent ended there. The theory is that Mack got into a vehicle and left the area."

"Why is Preston with Nolan now?" Sam asked.

"He was questioning Nolan this morning in Winchester when he got a call about a gun found by hikers in a stream near Shadow Creek Campground. Nolan said he knew a cabin out that way Mack frequented. He was taking Preston there."

"That must be Hank Satterfield's cabin," Jason said. "It's close to the campground."

"What are you thinking, Liv?"

She looked at them, trying to piece it all together. "Preston went out there to search for Mack."

Sam's eyes narrowed. "If Nolan shot at Mack, and now that gun was found in a stream near this cabin, why would he take Preston there?"

"Nolan floated the theory early on that Mack staged the crash as part of some scheme."

"You think Mack and Nolan planned this together?" Sam asked. "To frame Amy?"

"Maybe Nolan double-crossed him," Jason added.

"Shooting at someone is a risky ploy, even if you mean to miss."

"If they're working together, maybe Nolan is leading Preston away from where Mack is hiding," Sam said.

"Or straight into an ambush," Jason countered. "We should call the police."

Olivia's thoughts raced. How could Nolan, on his own, overpower an armed cop? Nolan no longer had Amy's gun, but that didn't mean he, or someone else, didn't have another. "They're short-staffed at the station. Preston didn't even wait for backup. And what am I supposed to tell them? That I think something's wrong because of a sneeze and the fact that Preston isn't answering his phone in an area with probably sketchy service?" She turned to Jason. "Would you be able to find the cabin?"

He pursed his lips, puffing out his cheeks. "It's been a long time since I've been out that way. There's no road directly to it. Hank always parks either in the campground lot or in a turnout used for horseback riding, then hikes in. The campground is maybe fifteen minutes from here. Honestly, I'd be guessing on the direction."

"If you can get us to the general area, I can get help fine-tuning the trail." She opened her contacts and called Summer.

After Olivia relayed the bullet points of what was happening, Summer agreed to bring Abby right away. As Jason gave Summer directions to the campground, Olivia hurried down the hall and into the kitchen, with Shadow on her heels. She rinsed the cat's plate and turned off the lights.

Dropping to a knee, she scooped Shadow in for a quick hug, more for her comfort than the cat's. "I'll be back as soon as I can. Be good tonight." She stroked the cat's cheeks, then stood and rushed to the front door where Jason and Sam were waiting.

"We're ready," Sam said. "Summer is en route with her dog. We'll follow Jason. Let's go."

Once outside, Olivia raced to her car, started the engine, and shifted into gear while Sam locked the house. By the time Sam climbed into the passenger seat, Jason had already backed out of the driveway and was on his way.

Traffic was light, and both she and Jason ignored the speed limit, weaving around slower cars without hesitation. Olivia forced herself to focus on the road, pushing back panicked thoughts swirling like debris in a tornado. Preston could hold his own in a fair fight, but she feared he was walking into an ambush.

"We'll find him, Liv," Sam said.

She tightened her grip on the wheel and drew a shaky breath as moisture pooled in her eyes. "I should've suspected Nolan from the start."

"You couldn't have known."

She swallowed hard. "What if Nolan already killed Mack, and now——"

"You know Preston. You know what he's capable of."

She took a deep breath, Sam's steady tone grounding her. She glanced at Sam's bag. "Do you have your gun?"

Sam reached down, lifted the sling off the floor, and set it in her lap. "Almost never leave home without it."

Up ahead, Jason crested a hill and dropped out of sight. As Olivia followed, her eyes locked on a black pickup parked in a turnout off the road. Jason sped past it, but she slowed, leaning forward for a better look.

"That's Preston's truck," Olivia said. "I don't see him. Do you?"

"No. They probably started in while we were at Fiona's."

She pulled into the turnout just as Jason made a U-turn and came back their way. After an abrupt stop, she unfastened her seatbelt, flung open the door, and jumped out. Jason pulled up alongside and lowered his window as Olivia raced toward the F-150.

"This is Preston's truck!" Olivia called to him.

She tugged at the locked doors as Sam joined her, circling the vehicle.

"No signs of a struggle," Sam said.

After Jason parked, he got out and hurried over. "You sure it's his?"

"No doubt," Olivia said, looking into the passenger window.

An SUV approached from down the road, slowing as it neared. The driver passed them, pulled onto the shoulder, then reversed, stopping just short of where they stood. Summer got out and jogged over.

"I recognized you as I was passing," Summer said to Olivia. "My GPS had the campground farther up the road."

"This isn't the campground access," Olivia said. "But this is Preston's truck."

Jason looked toward the forest. "There are horse trails back in there. They lead to the cabin, if you know which one to take."

"Which none of us do," Olivia said.

Summer glanced at her SUV. "If two people walked in together, Abby will find them faster than a map ever could."

CHAPTER 35

"We have to go after them," Olivia said, stepping toward the forest.

"Wait, Liv," Sam cautioned. "We don't know for sure what's going on or what we'd be walking into."

Olivia pointed at the F-150. "That's Preston's truck, and he's not here, which means he and Nolan are back in there somewhere."

"I think there's enough uncertainty to call the police," Jason said.

Sam pulled out her phone. "I'll do it."

"You can call them, but I'm not waiting," Olivia shot back. "I'm heading in."

"If you do that, you'll make it harder for the dog to track their scent," Sam warned.

Rationally, Olivia knew that. But she couldn't just sit on the side of the road and leave Preston's fate to chance.

Hoping for the best wasn't a strategy. If there were any opportunity to act, she would.

"Every minute we waste standing here is one less Preston might have. It could take thirty minutes for the police to get out here, if they even come." Her voice sharpened. "Do you really think they'll send in the cavalry just because we found his truck parked near where he said he'd be?" She turned to Summer. "I can't ask you to take Abby in without the police present. We don't know who else might be in there or if they're armed."

"Volunteer search and rescue teams don't usually enter areas where violence could be a factor," Summer said. "And if the police show up expecting danger, they probably won't let me and Abby search. Right now, all we know is that an armed officer is on foot with another male. The scent cloud will be more complicated, but if they're together, Abby won't have trouble tracking them."

"What if they get separated?" Sam asked.

"Abby may prioritize one scent if it's stronger. But I'm willing to go in with her."

Olivia turned to Sam and Jason. "I'm going in with or without you."

"I'm with you," Jason said, his tone leaving no room for debate.

They both looked at Sam, who met their eyes one by one, weighing their resolve.

"If we do this, we have to follow the dog's lead," Sam said. "I'll be right behind Summer. Liv, stay close to me.

Watch for movement off the trail. Jason, you've got our six. The moment I sense any danger, we fall back." She locked eyes with Olivia. "All of us, Liv."

"Understood," Olivia said with a firm nod. "Would it help Abby to have a scent item? Preston's jacket is in his truck. If she needs it, I'll break the window."

Summer shook her head. "Not necessary. Abby is trained to air-scent. She'll detect any recent human presence in the area. We can't be more than—what, thirty minutes behind them? If there's a trail, she'll pick it up. It's got to be Detective Hills and Nolan." She stepped back toward her SUV. "I'll get her ready."

As Summer turned, Jason went over to his truck. While Sam called the police, Olivia hit the lock button on her key fob, prompting a chirp from the Expedition.

Summer let the dog out of the rear of the vehicle, opened a large duffel bag, and pulled out an orange vest. Abby gave a sharp, excited bark, fully aware of what was coming. She shifted from side to side, her tail whipping wildly, as Summer set a bowl on the ground. The dog circled her handler, thumping her tail against Summer's legs before barking again. When Summer slipped the vest over Abby, the dog's ears perked and her eyes widened.

Speaking in a playful, encouraging voice, Summer amped up Abby's energy even more. She filled the bowl with water from a jug and let the dog drink. Abby lapped up a healthy measure before Summer poured out the rest, stowed the bowl, and shut the SUV door.

Jason returned holding a tire thumper stick.

Olivia nodded once at the dark hickory club. "I'm guessing you don't actually use that to check tire pressure."

He mimicked a swing. "It's better than nothing for defense. You should keep one in your car."

"The police are on their way," Sam said, approaching. "They know the situation, but I didn't tell them we're starting the search."

"If you don't want to be told no, don't ask," Olivia said.

"Exactly," Sam agreed.

Olivia glanced at Sam's sling. "You set with what you need?"

"Loaded. Ready for a quick draw. I've also got first aid supplies, just in case."

Summer, now wearing a large hip pack, hurried over with Abby. The dog let out several short huffs and a small whine, barely containing her eagerness.

Summer rubbed the dog's side vigorously. "Yeah, yeah, I know. You're ready to go." She looked at the forest. "We're probably in bear territory. I'm keeping her on a long line for safety. If we run into any mamas, they could have cubs. Do you have bobcats up here?"

Jason nodded. "Yeah, but they should steer clear, especially with the dog."

"Alright, let's go," Sam said.

Summer led Abby to the side of Preston's truck. She unzipped her hip pack, pulled out a ball, and held it up in front of the dog. "Ready to work?"

The ball and the excitement in Summer's voice sent Abby into overdrive. The dog pawed at the ground, and her tail stiffened. Summer tucked the toy away and gave the command, "Find them! Find them!"

Abby lifted her nose high, sweeping her head from left to right. The dog advanced a few feet, zigzagged across the grass, then tensed and surged ahead.

"Good, Abby!" Summer praised. "Find them!"

Abby took off at a fast pace with Summer right behind her.

"She's got the scent!" Summer called over her shoulder.

Sam fell in quickly as Olivia and Jason brought up the rear.

The forest pressed in from all sides, thick with lush undergrowth and towering trees. Branches wove together overhead, casting deep, shifting shadows across the narrow trail. The air was heavy and still, saturated with the scent of moss and rotting leaves. Fallen trees lay scattered along the path, some cleared just enough to let horses pass.

Summer shortened the lead, keeping the dog closer as the dense foliage narrowed their visibility. Abby had slowed but stayed locked onto the scent. Twisted roots jutted across the uneven trail, making footing treacherous. Creeping ferns encroached on the path, brushing Olivia's legs as she pushed through. She kept her head on a swivel, catching glimpses of Abby's golden fur flickering through the filtered light about twenty feet ahead.

At a small clearing, the terrain leveled out, and the trail split into forks. Abby stopped briefly, lifted her nose, and scented the air. Then, she snapped back into motion, leading them along a path that veered around the massive roots of an uprooted pine.

Moments later, they were back beneath the canopy. Sunlight barely touched the forest floor, save for scattered shimmers when the breeze stirred the branches overhead. On either side, tangled thickets and prickly catbrier hemmed them in, discouraging any stray step off the trail.

They moved quickly, stepping lightly. Between the pace and the heat, sweat trickled down Olivia's back. She glanced over her shoulder at Jason. He held steady, unfazed, as if he could go all day if needed. Though the wildlife sensed their presence, the forest still breathed with sound. The harsh, raspy calls of blue jays cut through the quiet like a blade, followed by the low, haunting *coo-OOO-oo-oo-oo* of a mourning dove.

Twenty feet ahead, Abby froze, ears pricked and tail rigid. Summer let out a sharp, short whistle. The dog's head snapped toward her handler as Summer gave a silent hand signal—one finger to her lips, then a flat palm moving down. Abby sat, perfectly still, eyes locked on the brush.

Sam moved forward and exchanged a few whispered words with Summer. She unzipped her sling bag, drew her gun, and advanced cautiously. When she was five feet from Abby, the underbrush rustled and a branch snapped.

Sam rushed in front of the dog just as a white-tailed doe burst from the thicket, crossed the trail, and disappeared into the woods. She lowered her weapon, turned, and waved the others onward.

Abby started following the deer's scent with her nose low to the ground. Summer whistled again, sharper this time. The dog stopped immediately and looked back.

"Leave it!" Summer ordered. "Back to work. Find them! Find them!"

Abby lifted her head, scented the air, then stepped back to the middle of the path. In a burst, she caught the trail again and took off. Summer and Sam jogged to keep up, with Olivia and Jason a few steps behind.

They pushed forward at a quick clip until the trail narrowed and angled up a gentle slope. When Abby reached the top, Summer whistled and gave her a hand signal. The dog stopped and waited.

Summer and Sam climbed the slope, closing the distance. As soon as they reached Abby, Sam ushered Summer behind the thick trunk of an oak, then gestured for Olivia and Jason to stay low. They crouched, slowing as they moved up.

At the top, the cabin came into view. The structure, old and weathered, had a sagging porch and two dark, uncovered windows. It sat in a small clearing surrounded by dense forest, no more than twenty yards ahead. From a distance, a casual passerby might not even notice it. Olivia's pulse pounded as she scanned for Preston. No movement. No sign of anyone.

"Is that the Satterfield cabin?" Sam whispered to Jason.

He nodded. "I could go up and see if anyone's there. I look like I belong out here more than any of you."

Sam shook her head and turned to Summer. "Think Abby still has the scent?"

The dog whined.

"There's your answer," Summer said. "She knows she hasn't finished the job."

Sam studied the cabin for a moment longer. "You okay continuing forward with Abby?"

"Yes." She unzipped her hip pack and pulled out another leash. "I'll put her on a shorter line."

Sam nodded. "You and I will move forward, using the trees for cover. If Abby leads us to the cabin, I'll check the front. The second she alerts, you and Abby fall back. Jason, while we move in, circle around the far side and get eyes on the back. Stay out of sight."

"Got it," he said.

"Liv, you stay here. Watch for anyone coming in from another direction."

All agreed. Jason started his route toward the rear of the cabin.

Olivia's heart thundered, her breath quick and shallow. Until now, she hadn't let herself believe Preston might be hurt, or worse, but as the thought surfaced, she buried it and forced herself to focus.

At Summer's command, Abby charged toward the porch as if she'd never been interrupted. Within twenty feet, Summer and Sam had to break cover to keep up. Then everything happened in a flash.

The dog bounded up the steps and went straight to the door. Sam was right behind her. She glanced at Summer, who gave a quick nod. Sam waved her back, and Summer gave Abby a sharp whistle. The dog hesitated, but at Summer's firm hand signal, she came down the shallow steps.

With her gun drawn, Sam peeked through the window, using the frame for cover. In a beat, she shifted to the door and gripped the knob. Locked. She threw her shoulder into it—once, twice. No give.

Summer and Abby were already back under the cover of the trees, hurrying toward Olivia's position. Sam darted to the window, shoved her gun into her waistband, and ducked down to grab the handle of a long shovel lying on the porch. In one fluid motion, she rose, swung it, and shattered the glass.

Olivia's fear spiked. Someone had to be injured inside.

Without thinking, she took off, sprinting toward the cabin as Sam knocked out the remaining shards.

Then—movement. A figure bolted from behind the cabin, disappearing into the trees in the opposite direction from Jason.

Olivia pulled up short, hesitating for a split second.

Damn it.

With no sign of Jason, she veered off course and tore after the runner.

CHAPTER 36

Olivia shot forward, cut through the trees, and picked up the narrow trail leading away from the cabin. Dips and mounds riddled the hard-packed ground, making her footing dicey. The fleeing figure was fast, but she was gaining. Thin branches lashed her arms and legs as she dashed, scanning for hazards ahead.

Her heart galloped, each shallow breath feeding doubt about how far her legs could carry her. As she closed the gap, she made out a man wearing a hat and a backpack. The dense forest blurred around her, shadows shifting as she chased him down the twisting trail.

The ground dipped, and her foot caught on a hidden root. She stumbled, barely recovering, as her quarry leapt over a fallen tree and vanished behind a thick wall of green undergrowth. She cleared the tree without breaking stride. Her quads burned, and her throat was raw from the all-out sprint. Pushing through fronds and encroaching brush, she found herself even closer now. When he chanced a glance over his shoulder, her suspicions were confirmed: Nolan.

Suddenly, he tripped and went down. She barreled forward, breath ragged and eyes locked on him as he hit the ground. As he pushed to his knees, she surged, reaching him just as he got to his feet.

"Stop, Nolan!" she shouted, grabbing the backpack handle. "You can't get away!"

She yanked hard, pulling him back a step. He twisted, shrugged off the pack, and wrenched free. Before she could react, he bolted again, disappearing around the bend just ahead.

She hesitated for only a second before dropping the bag and sprinting after him. Rounding the corner, she skidded to a stop. Her chest heaved, each breath thick with the damp reek of forest decay. The trail stretched clear for thirty feet, but he was nowhere in sight.

No way he could've gotten that far.

Then—a sharp snap.

Before she could turn to look, he burst from the underbrush and tackled her into a tangle of brambles on the other side of the trail.

Thorns pricked her arms and legs like tiny knives. She clenched her jaw and swallowed the pain, reaching for his shirt. But he broke her grip easily, scrambled to his feet, and took off.

With a sharp inhale, she tore free of the clawing brush and got up. He was nearing the far end of the trail now, close to the next bend. Though she didn't know where he was headed, she aimed to keep him in sight. If she lost him, at least she'd have a direction to give the police. She was almost certain he wasn't armed, or at least not ready to turn a weapon on her. Confident that his only goal was to escape, she pushed forward, chasing as far as her legs would take her.

She raced down the path and adjusted her stride to round the corner, then nearly ran straight into him. He stood motionless, his back to her. Just twenty feet ahead, a black bear and her two cubs blocked the trail.

A different fear gripped her now. Thoughts of Preston, apprehending Nolan, or learning Mack's fate vanished in an instant. In this moment, only one thing mattered: putting distance between herself and the bear. Her pulse pounded as she tried to remember the difference between black and brown bear encounters. Don't run. Don't play dead. If it attacks, fight back.

The bear fixed its gaze on them and took a few steps forward. Nolan shifted, starting to turn, but she grabbed his arm and held him in place.

"Don't run," she whispered between quick breaths.

"Hey, bear!" he shouted.

The bear rose onto its hind legs, towering close to seven feet tall. Behind her, the cubs played in the undergrowth, oblivious to the threat they faced or the one their mother posed.

She tightened her grip. "Don't yell at it. Stay calm. Walk back with me slowly." In a gentle but firm voice, she called out, "Hey, bear. Just passing through. Leaving you alone now."

The bear dropped onto all fours, turned slightly sideways, and looked at her cubs.

"Nice bear," he murmured.

They eased backward, step by step, until they rounded the bend and slipped out of sight. The moment they were clear, he twisted free of her grip. She shot back, putting space between them.

Sure as the tide, he had only one way to run. She was slightly taller, but he had at least thirty pounds on her. She couldn't overpower him, but she could be an obstacle—trip him, block his path, or stall him until help arrived.

"You're not getting away," she said, widening her stance, bracing for his move. "There's nowhere to run."

He held up a hand, breathing hard. "You have to understand. It wasn't my fault. I just took a few things. None of this was supposed to happen. I didn't mean for anyone to get hurt."

Face-to-face, she saw him clearly. The intruder from Fiona's house. The one who'd slammed the closet door into her. Maybe even the one behind Mack's disappearance. Right now, though, only one question mattered.

"Where's Preston?" she demanded, her voice low, furious, and laced with adrenaline.

Sweat streaked down his face as he pressed his lips into a tight line. He dropped his shoulders, then lunged at her. She grabbed his shirt, and they both went down hard. He reached his knees first, but she stretched and grabbed his ankle, holding on as she lay flat on her stomach. He planted his free foot, pushing to stand, then started kicking. One. Two. Three. Her hold weakened until he broke free.

"I don't think so, buddy," Jason growled.

She looked up just as Jason caught Nolan in a strangling headlock, using the tire thumper to secure the hold. She pushed to her feet, wiping dirt from her palms onto her shorts.

"Are you okay?" Jason asked, keeping his hold tight as Nolan tried to pry free.

"Yeah, I think so."

"Stop squirming, you little runt, or it's going to be lights out."

"I can't breathe," Nolan said, struggling for air.

"Let him breathe," she said, stepping in front of Nolan and meeting his panicked, watery eyes.

Jason loosened his hold just enough for Nolan to gasp a few short breaths.

"Where's Preston?" she demanded.

Nolan looked away.

Her voice sharpened. "Where is he?"

"Answer her," Jason barked.

"In the cabin."

"Go," Jason said. "I've got him. I'll make sure he gets back one way or another."

CHAPTER 37

Thirsty, hot, and exhausted, Olivia took off for the cabin, running in short bursts before slowing to catch her breath. Red pinpricks dotted her arms and legs, the skin still stinging from the bramble thorns.

She hadn't wanted to ask Nolan what he'd done to Preston or whether he was okay. If Preston was hurt, or worse, she didn't want to hear it. Not there. Not in the middle of the forest, staring at the man responsible. If he'd harmed Preston, she probably would've grabbed Jason's tire thumper and used it as intended.

With every step, she clung to the hope that Preston was all right. But Sam's desperation to break into the cabin suggested otherwise. She forced herself not to spiral. It couldn't be that bad. It wouldn't be. She refused to consider the alternative.

Up ahead, Nolan's backpack lay where she'd dropped it, but she ran past without stopping to look inside. Whatever it held was evidence now, better left to the police.

The cabin soon came into view, its back side in the shadow of the surrounding pines. She pushed herself harder, each step heavier, every breath more strained. The panic she'd kept at bay surged as she closed the distance.

She cleared the final stretch of trail and caught her first glimpse of the cabin's front. Summer tossed a ball, and Abby chased after it as if nothing had happened. The playful scene jarred her. She'd been expecting the worst, but for a moment, it looked almost normal.

Her focus snapped to the porch. Preston sat on the top step, looking dazed but not seriously injured. Sam stood at the bottom of the steps with her back turned. For a beat, Olivia couldn't move. Relief surged through her in a dizzying rush. Her shoulders dropped, and the knot in her stomach loosened. He was alive. The worst hadn't happened. She let out the breath she'd been holding and broke into a jog, her legs suddenly light beneath her.

When he saw her, he started to rise, but Sam pressed a hand to his shoulder, keeping him down. Olivia knelt on the step in front of him, and they embraced. When she felt him, something in her finally let go. The pounding in her chest eased, but her breath stayed shallow. When she pulled back, her eyes locked onto a gash at his temple. A thin line of dried blood marked the length of a split in his skin.

"Your head," she whispered. "You're hurt."

He gave a wincing half-smile. "I'll be okay. What about you? Did Nolan hurt you?"

She shifted to sit by his side and rested a hand on his thigh. "No. But you're not okay."

"Where's Nolan?" he asked.

"Jason has him. He's bringing him back."

Preston moved as if to stand. "I should go."

"That's not a good idea," Sam said. "You were just coming around when I got to you."

"Stay down," Olivia said firmly. "Do you remember what happened?"

"It's a little fuzzy. Nolan said he knew a shortcut through the woods. Then—I was on the porch. Next thing I knew, Sam was standing over me."

"He probably hit you with the shovel I used to break the window."

The thought of the metal blade cracking against his skull made Olivia nauseous. A blow like that could've killed him. She wrapped her arms around him, grounding herself in the fact that he was still here. That he was okay.

"I really should go help Jason," he said.

"No," Olivia and Sam insisted in unison.

"The police are on their way," Sam added. "They called from the turnout about ten minutes ago. I gave them directions, so they should be here soon. I'll make sure Jason is okay and Nolan gets back here."

His brow softened as he nodded. "Thanks, Sam."

She turned and took off toward the trail behind the cabin.

Nearby, Summer kept playing with Abby. The dog bounded after the ball with endless energy, blissfully unaware of the lives she'd helped save.

Now alone, Olivia and Preston held each other's eyes for a long moment. She let out a slow breath, the fight or flight in her finally fading. They leaned in almost at once and met in a kiss of quiet relief.

"When I realized it was Nolan, and that he'd led you out here …"

He wrapped an arm around her, pulling her close. "If you hadn't figured it out, I don't know how this would've ended."

"Thank God Summer was still in town. It was Abby who found you. Jason knew about this place, but he wasn't sure how to get here. Abby followed your trail perfectly."

"They make quite a team." He rubbed his eyes as if clearing away cobwebs. "What happened when you went after Nolan?"

Before she could answer, four deputies crested the hill and approached the cabin. Cole broke off to speak with Summer while the others headed toward them.

"I'll tell you later."

"Let me get up."

"Stay down. They'll come to you. You have to go to the hospital."

"No, I'll be fine in a few minutes."

Jayden and the others reached them, but before they could speak, Olivia said, "He needs an ambulance."

Preston shook his head. "No, I'm okay."

"He has a concussion. He has to go to the ER," Olivia said, leaving no room for argument.

Jayden glanced between them, giving a small, wry smile. "Sorry, Detective, but I think she's pulling rank."

Stepping back, Jayden called dispatch on the speaker mic attached to her ballistic vest.

Preston gently took Olivia's hand and lowered his voice. "I need to talk to them."

She squeezed his fingers in understanding. Leaning in, she kissed his cheek, then stood. She was about to step away when his next three words stopped her cold.

"Mack is inside."

She looked toward the open doorway, then back at him. His expression was unreadable. But when she took a slow step toward the cabin and he didn't stop her, she knew he wouldn't let her walk into someplace she shouldn't be.

As she went inside, the exchange of orders and questions between Preston and the deputies faded into the background. Her eyes needed a moment to adjust to the dim interior. The floorboards creaked softly beneath her steps, and a faint smell of hickory smoke lingered in the air. With only the light from the doorway and the windows behind her, she stepped around a small table for a better view. Just beyond the kitchenette, a sofa, a TV, and a wood-burning stove furnished the modest living area. At the rear, a door stood open with a jacket hanging from a hook. She guessed Nolan had used it to slip out when Sam, Summer, and Abby were on the porch.

"Mack?" No answer. She said again, louder, "Mack?"

A small pillow fell from the sofa as someone rolled onto their side, then sat up.

"The woman of the hour," Mack said with a faint, playful smirk.

She crossed the room and crouched in front of him. He looked exhausted but not seriously hurt. His scruff was overdue for a shave, and the dark circles under his eyes were visible even in the low light. Any doubt she had that he might've conspired with Nolan vanished, just by looking at him.

"I've never been so relieved to hear your voice. I thought you might be …" She couldn't bring herself to say it.

"Dead? The thought crossed my mind more than once these past few days."

"You don't look okay."

"Probably look worse than I feel. I've actually been semi-well-fed in my captivity." He glanced toward the door. "I'd be out in the land of the living, but they told me to wait in here."

She stood, dragged a folding chair closer, and sat. "Have you been here the whole time?"

He nodded, scratching at his jaw, the rasp like fine-grit sandpaper. "Yeah. Sam said it's Saturday. I thought it was Friday. It was hard to tell if it was day or night locked in that back room with no windows. Pretty sure I lost some clients this week."

"Nolan said you've been here before, that you would come a few times a year."

He shook his head and leaned back against the worn sofa, shifting until he found a reasonably comfortable spot. "Never been here before this nightmare. Nolan is the one who comes here. I think it belongs to a cousin of his."

"What was Nolan planning?"

"I don't know. He wanted to make a deal. He said he had taken some things from Fiona Campbell's house and planned to sell them. He offered me a cut if I kept my mouth shut."

"Do you know about Fiona?"

His eyes lowered for a moment as he drew a slow breath. "Nolan told me. Poor woman. She was so kind-hearted. How'd she die?"

"The first responders think she might've had a heart attack."

"I was there that night. I saw her lying in the hallway."

"I heard you."

"Come again?"

"Fiona's cat had a camera on her collar. It recorded much of what happened. No faces, but I recognized your voice."

"I'll be. Cat cam. That's a new one. Might come in handy in the future."

She leaned in slightly. "You have no idea what's been going through my head the past few days. What happened that night?"

Before he could answer, footsteps on the wooden floor made them both turn as Deputy Simmons stepped inside.

"Excuse me, Ms. Penn, but I need to speak with Mr. Mack."

"Of course." She stood, keeping her eyes on Mack. "We'll talk later. I'm beyond relieved you're okay."

"Thank you, Olivia. I might not be if it weren't for you. I knew I could count on you."

"Always." She gave him a warm smile before going outside.

Once on the porch, she lingered just out of sight of the doorway with one ear turned toward the conversation inside. Near the trail in front of the cabin, two deputies were leading Nolan away in handcuffs. Preston followed behind, carrying the backpack with a gloved hand. She made a mental note to mildly scold him later for not waiting on EMS before traipsing around.

Her focus shifted back to the cabin while Mack recounted what had happened. He'd gone to Fiona's house Tuesday night and found the front door unlocked. Concerned, he entered and went upstairs, where he saw Fiona collapsed in the hallway. Before he could check on her, a masked intruder rushed him, and they fought on the staircase. Mack fled down the steps and slipped at the bottom, knocking over the entrance table. As he ran outside, the intruder fired two shots. He made it to his car, but the attacker gave chase, forcing him off Old Mill Highway and into a ditch. Fearing for his life, he ran into the forest, trying to lose his pursuer. Eventually, he reached a dirt road where he tripped in a hidden hole, fell face-first, and knocked himself out. When he came to, his hands were bound, and Nolan stood over him with a gun. Nolan forced him into the trunk of a car, then drove to the turnout, marched Mack to the cabin, and secured him inside.

Mack didn't mention texting Olivia, and she had her own questions about that. As he continued answering the deputy's questions, Jason and Sam approached. Olivia peeled away from the doorway and met them at the bottom of the steps. Summer, with Abby at her side, joined them. She gave a quiet command, and the dog obediently sat.

"Is everyone okay?" Summer asked.

Olivia nodded and crouched in front of Abby. "Yes. Thanks to the two of you. Is she officially off duty?"

"She is," Summer said.

Olivia scratched the dog's chin and cheeks. "You're a hero, Abby. You're something special." She glanced up at Summer. "I can't thank you enough. You and Abby saved the day."

"She's amazing," Sam added, kneeling beside Olivia to give Abby a few more pets.

The dog gave a soft, satisfied huff and leaned into the praise, her tail thumping a few times against the ground.

Summer turned the ball over in her hands. "Thanks. She knows she did a good job."

Olivia stood and looked at Jason. "If you hadn't been there, Nolan might've gotten away. We wouldn't even be here if you hadn't found Shadow. I owe you big time."

He gave a small nod. "I'd say we're even."

"Did Nolan give you any trouble?" Olivia asked.

"Not a peep. He knew he had nowhere to run."

As Sam stood, Olivia pulled her into a quick, grateful hug. "I can't thank you enough."

"Always," Sam said with a small smile before easing back.

Simmons and Mack stepped out of the cabin and came down the steps. As they reached the bottom, the deputy got a call over his radio from Preston, saying Cole was already on his way back to escort Mack to the turnout. Simmons acknowledged the order just as Cole appeared over the hill.

"I guess that's my date," Mack said. He glanced around at the group, his usual wise-guy act faltering for a moment. "Thank you. All of you. I owe you my life." With that, he turned and headed toward Cole.

Simmons pointed his notepad at Sam and Jason. "I need to speak with the two of you. Ms. Penn, Detective Hills says he'll question you himself."

As Simmons talked to Sam and Jason individually, Olivia joined Summer in rewarding Abby for a job well done. They took turns tossing the ball as the dog raced after it, soaking up the praise. With each throw, Olivia's gratitude deepened, knowing how differently the past hour could've ended. She wouldn't forget the fear she'd felt for Preston's safety or the relief of finding him okay. Every day with him from now on would be a gift, made possible by her friends and two four-legged heroes with big hearts: Shadow and Abby.

CHAPTER 38

Sunlight streamed through the window, warming Olivia's skin on Sunday morning. She felt surprisingly good considering yesterday's tumble into the brambles. Sipping her coffee, she looked at her Expedition parked beside Preston's truck in his driveway. A squirrel scampered across the yard, pausing every few feet to stand upright and twitch its tail. Birdsong mingled with cicada calls, creating a serene soundtrack for the new day.

Yesterday, Preston had undergone testing at the hospital, which confirmed a mild concussion but no other serious injuries. The doctor treated the cut on his head and released him with the instruction that someone monitor him overnight. Preston had tried to address some police matters before his CT scan but struggled to concentrate. After driving him home, Olivia avoided discussing the day's events. He was still foggy and unlikely to remember much anyway.

Jayden and Cole had returned Preston's truck, checking in with Olivia around six. At the time, he'd been resting, stable since his release. Later, she ordered takeout, and after eating, they watched TV until he got sleepy around nine.

Her father stopped by after Preston went to bed, bringing her a change of clothes. Though she'd already spoken with him earlier, he stayed a while, listening again as she recounted what had happened. Proud of her actions, he wanted to meet Jason to thank him personally. By ten, she insisted he go home, promising updates in the morning. She then settled onto the sofa and stayed awake most of the night, checking on Preston hourly.

"I could get used to seeing you there," Preston said.

She turned away from the window as he came downstairs, dressed in jeans and an untucked denim shirt.

"Hey there, cowboy," she said with a smile, meeting him halfway.

She set her mug on the end table and eased into his arms for a long hug.

"How are you feeling?" she asked, looking at the narrow adhesive strips holding his cut closed.

He kissed her forehead. "Good at seeing you first thing in the morning."

"Any dizziness? Drowsiness? Headache?"

"No, doctor," he teased as they loosened their embrace. "Did you get any sleep?"

Not a wink. "Plenty, though your couch isn't as comfy as mine."

"Told you so."

"Coffee is ready. Want a cup?"

He yawned and nodded. "Yeah, that sounds good."

"I'll make it. It's nice outside if you want to sit on the porch. How about something to eat?"

"Just coffee for now, thanks."

He picked up his phone from the end table, where she'd left it last night to make sure he wasn't disturbed or tempted to look at it. The doctor had recommended limiting screen time until his symptoms cleared. He stepped onto the porch while she went to the kitchen for his coffee.

When she joined him outside, he was scrolling through missed texts. She handed him the coffee and settled into a Windsor rocker beside him. The August morning was pleasant, the temperature cooler than usual for late summer. The forecast called for the break in the heat to last another five days, thanks to a Canadian high-pressure system bringing clear skies and drier air.

"How's your memory from yesterday?" she asked.

He took a sip, then leaned forward and set his phone on the porch railing. "I remember most of it except for the knockout blow."

She reached over, resting a hand on his arm. "When I realized it was Nolan and couldn't reach you, I was so scared. Why do you think he led you back to the cabin?"

He covered her hand with his for a moment. "I don't know. He probably figured we'd search the area where Amy's gun was found and come across the cabin. The cross and the brooches were in the backpack, so he must've stashed them there. Maybe he thought he could snatch the bag and make a run for it."

"He could've killed you, knocking you out like that. How about early retirement?" She rubbed his arm, then pulled her hand away.

He smiled. "Maybe the day you stop chasing dangerous people through the woods and fending off bears."

"'Fending off' is generous. We just had a conversation."

"Still, it was brave of you to go after Nolan."

"I just reacted. I thought he might get away before Sam could take up the pursuit. That's more her thing than mine."

He took another sip, then set his mug on the porch floor. "Are you sure it wouldn't be more your thing if you worked for Carolyn?"

She nodded slowly, not ready to tell him about Carolyn's idea of using her dad and the bakery as a cover for their operatives. "Positive. Her assessment of my most redeeming qualities puts me behind a desk, not in the field."

"Where do you stand with that?"

She hadn't thought much more about it, though she knew she'd have to soon.

"I'm not sure. It's intriguing. Remember that manuscript I buried on my hard drive? She gave me the name of a literary agent in New York. She said he'd be expecting my call. Seriously, who is this woman?"

"That sounds like a good deal. Sometimes, when opportunities come your way, you have to take them. Knowing someone with those kinds of connections could be beneficial, but I bet she has a lot of enemies too."

"We'd both be going after the baddies."

"As long as you're not in danger, I'd be okay with that."

They sat in comfortable silence for a few minutes, both lost in thought. Olivia's drifted to the idea of a life with him, savoring coffee on the porch together every morning when the weather was just right.

His phone buzzed, rattling against the railing. He glanced at the screen but didn't reply.

"I heard you on the phone with Craig yesterday at the hospital," she said. "What did he say about Nolan's arrest?"

"He was relieved and wanted to know what charges Nolan would face."

"Do you have any idea what they'll be?"

"That still needs sorting, but it'll be a long list."

"What about attempted murder? On you."

He picked up his mug and rested it on his thigh. "That'll be up to the Commonwealth's Attorney. They'd have to prove intent to kill, but there are other related charges. Assault with a deadly weapon. Aggravated assault. Both would fit."

"What about Fiona's death?"

"When the chief called to check on me at the hospital, he said Nolan swore he never touched Fiona. Nolan claimed he went upstairs looking for something to steal, saw her collapse in the hallway, and thought she'd fainted. He said he was about to check on her when Mack came in, and then he just panicked."

"From the video, it looked like he wasn't in the house long enough to take anything before Fiona heard him. After he shot at Mack, he ran back to the sitting room and rummaged through the desk drawers before he bolted. He didn't even know what he was looking for and probably didn't find anything. But I was the one who told him about the cross and the brooches in the bedroom, so on Thursday night he knew exactly where to go."

"It's not your fault Nolan came back for a second try."

"So maybe the paramedics were right. Maybe Fiona did die of a heart attack. But Nolan was there and didn't do anything. Could that still make him responsible?"

Preston took a sip and lifted his mug slightly. "Thanks for this. It tastes better when you make it." He rocked his chair back. "The Commonwealth's Attorney will take a hard look at the circumstances. Nolan says Fiona collapsed when he saw her, but who knows if that's what really happened. The preliminary ME report points to a heart attack, but the final results are still pending. Here in Virginia, we have a felony murder rule. If someone dies during a felony, like burglary, the person committing it can be charged with murder, even if they didn't directly cause the death. Depending on what else we get from Nolan or what the evidence turns up, involuntary manslaughter is also a possibility, though less likely. By the time it's all said and done, he'll be looking at enough charges to keep him locked up for a long time."

"How did his alibi clear him initially?"

"On the surface, his travel records checked out, and he wasn't close enough to Fiona to raise any red flags. With no clear cause of death and no sign of forced entry, there wasn't much reason to question him further."

She figured the brooches, and maybe the cross, had some value, but probably more sentimental than monetary. The real treasure was Fiona's Bible, not just for its family history but for the personal stake Winifred had in it. Confiding in Preston, she told him about the land issue between the families and the real reason Winifred had come.

He took it in, quiet for a moment. Then he said, "Even though Craig is my friend, I would've handled it the same way you did. That's family business. It's up to Winifred to tell him they're related."

"Did you ever find out why Craig lied about where he was on Tuesday before he went to Fiona's?"

"He said he took a drive to work up the nerve to ask her for a loan. He's been betting on horses, trying to make quick money. He wins some, loses some, but he was convinced he had solid information on some upcoming races."

"I don't think Fiona would've given him money for that."

"That's why he framed it as a loan. He planned to pay her back with interest."

"I don't know if that would've worked. Betting on horses feels about as risky as hitting a slot machine."

"You've got that right." He stretched out his legs, crossing one over the other. "The grass really shot up after Thursday's storm. I'll have to mow one evening this week."

"Ours did too. The rain was good for the garden."

"And it helped lead us to Nolan."

She looked at him. "What do you mean?"

"After Nolan locked Mack in the cabin on Tuesday, he panicked about keeping the gun with him. So he ditched it inside a hollowed-out tree that was lying partly in the stream near the campground. The rain must've flooded the area, dislodging it and carrying it downstream to where the hikers found it."

"Huh. How about that. An assist from Mother Nature. I wonder what Nolan was planning to do with Mack."

He shrugged. "If Mack wouldn't go along with him, Nolan might've felt like he had only one option. Have you talked to Mack this morning?"

"No, but I was thinking of stopping by the inn before heading home. It was nice of your mom to put him up for the night."

"You know my mom. Once she heard what had happened, she wanted to feed him, and then that turned into an overnight stay."

"I would've thought he'd want to get home and into some fresh clothes."

"She took care of that too. She keeps a stash of lost-and-found clothes people leave behind. What doesn't get claimed, she donates. I'm sure she found something decent for him."

"Nice. He needed a night of luxury and some good food. And *you* need to take it easy today. If you're not up to coming to the playground dedication, everyone will understand."

"I feel fine. Three o'clock, right?"

"Yes. Do you want me to pick you up?"

"I can drive."

His phone rang, and he reached for it. "I want to swing by the station to take care of a few things." He glanced at the screen. "It's my mom."

She stood. "You better answer that. She's already called twice this morning."

He raised the phone to his ear. "Hey, Mom … Yeah, I'm okay, don't worry … She's still here. Hold on a sec."

Pressing the phone to his chest, he gently took her hand as she turned to go inside.

"Thanks for staying last night," he whispered.

She leaned down and kissed him softly. "Anytime."

"Love you."

"Love you too."

She kissed him again, then smiled. "Now talk to your mom."

CHAPTER 39

At noon, Olivia left Preston's house, giving them both time to take care of what they needed to before the playground dedication. She planned to cut through town on her way home, stopping at the inn first, then swinging by Fiona's to check on Shadow one last time. She still had Dorothy's key but knew she'd need to return it soon.

Cruising along, she lowered the window and let the cool breeze flow through the cabin. She'd driven this stretch of road to town countless times over the years. For nearly a decade, she'd traveled it as a visitor—a native returning to see her father for just a few days at a time. But a little over a year ago, her world had turned upside down. Now, she was a local, heading home after sharing the morning with the man she wanted to spend the rest of her life with.

Moving back to Apple Station hadn't been easy. In the immediate aftermath of Paige's death, nothing about her professional life had changed. The job in New York had still been hers for the taking, and the tiny apartment she'd rented still sat empty, waiting to become hers. But everything about her personal life had shifted. The decision to stay had been swift, clear, and without regret. Breaking her lease had come at a cost, requiring negotiation with the landlord. Her would-be employers in New York had pushed back when she rescinded her acceptance of their offer. None of it had mattered. She'd never once dwelled on what could've been. Instead, she was living a better life, one she hadn't searched for but had simply allowed to unfold.

As she neared a four-way stop and her turnoff into town, her thoughts drifted to the week ahead. On Tuesday, she'd be traveling to D.C. for a meet-and-greet with her new editor, a trip she wasn't exactly looking forward to. She'd mapped out her writing schedule, hoping to power through a few extra columns over the coming days to give herself a little flexibility for time off at the end of the month.

Maybe today she'd start on the article for Ellen about Fiona and her contributions to Apple Station. She wouldn't go into the family history or the circumstances of her death. Instead, it would be a tribute and a celebration of a life well lived.

She reached the intersection just as a familiar white Fiesta approached it from the road leading out of town. Cassandra waved, then turned and pulled alongside her.

With no cars coming in either direction, both lowered their windows.

Cassandra leaned out, grinning. "Penn, I heard the news about the arrest. Thanks *ever so much* for keeping your bestie in the loop."

Olivia checked the rearview mirror. "We're *besties* now?" she teased.

"At least when it comes to breaking news."

"You're in the big leagues now. What goes on in Apple Station is just small-town stuff."

Cassandra glanced behind her, put the car in park, and got out. Olivia checked her mirrors again before doing the same, figuring there was plenty of room for anyone to go around them.

"I remember nearly running into you about here when you first came back," Cassandra said, standing in front of her. "I can't believe that was already over a year ago. It's a full-circle moment. I'm leaving, and you're staying."

"But look at us now, both so much better off, and friends to boot. Are you coming to the playground dedication?"

"Unfortunately, I'm going to miss it. I'm heading into D.C. to look at the apartment I'm ninety-nine percent sure is the one. I won't make it back until after it's over. But tomorrow, I expect the exclusive scoop on everything that went down yesterday. It'll be my last big story for *The Times*."

"A fitting dénouement to your prestigious career at

the paper, and the perfect launch into your next chapter."

"Whenever you're in D.C., call me so we can get together. You'll always have an open invite to stay at my place. I don't know many people in town, so seeing a friendly face will be great."

A worn-out pickup truck pulled up behind Cassandra. They both turned as the senior driver slowly passed, tipping his hat as he went by. They waved in return, grateful for his patience.

"This December, we'll have to go see *A Christmas Carol* at Ford's Theatre," Olivia said. "It was one of my traditions when I lived there."

"I'll plan for it."

Olivia glanced over her shoulder. "We should probably stop blocking the road."

"Yeah, you're right." Cassandra paused, looking down for a moment. "Liv, I just want to say, I wouldn't be standing here if it weren't for you. I'll never forget what you did for me that day at Grove Manor. I'll always, always owe you."

As they embraced, Olivia said, "You don't owe me, but I'll gladly crash on your couch from time to time. I'm so proud of you. You're going to take the world by storm."

They pulled apart, both a little teary-eyed.

"You will too, Penn."

"Drive carefully."

"You too. See you tomorrow."

They got back into their vehicles. With a final wave, Olivia turned toward town, and Cassandra continued on her way to D.C.

With the Highland Games in full swing up the road in Berryville, parking in town was plentiful. She found a spot right in front of Tales and Treasures, got out, and strolled to the inn.

The lobby looked like a tourist shop in a Scottish hamlet during the offseason: tartan everywhere, a stocked souvenir table left unattended, and a basket brimming with scones on the beverage cart. Bev stood at the concierge desk, finishing up checking in a lone guest. Spotting Olivia, she stepped around the counter to meet her.

"You saved my son," she said, wrapping Olivia in her arms.

"Summer and Abby are the real heroes. Without Abby, we would've been lost." As they pulled apart, she added, "Sam led the charge, and without Jason, we never would've figured any of it out."

"Preston said he was okay, but is he really?"

"He seems so. His headache is gone, and he's showing no lingering signs of a concussion. I wouldn't have left him alone if he had been."

Bev nodded. "Of course you wouldn't have. I knew right away, from the first time I saw you, that you two would end up together. I've never seen him happier than he is now, and that's all because of you."

Olivia smiled, a little embarrassed and probably as

red as Bev's kilt. But she couldn't argue with the prediction. She felt the same about her life with him. Despite the events of the past week, there was a quiet steadiness to her days now, as if her life had finally clicked into place.

"Everything has changed since you moved back here. All for the good." Bev glanced around the lobby. "And I've decided I'm doing it. I'm rebranding the inn."

"Wow, that's a huge decision. Congratulations."

"It's going to be marvelous. We'll be the gateway to the Virginia Highlands. I've already started the research. I had no idea how many people from Scotland immigrated and settled in Virginia." She paused, took a deep breath, and drew her shoulders back. "It's a big step, though. It scares me a little, if I'm honest. Of course, now I've got a dozen tabs open on my computer and a to-do list a mile long. But it feels good to be changing course."

Olivia simply nodded, knowing Bev would make it work. "I think it'll be a goldmine for you."

"You're the first person I've told. I'm glad you stopped by. Are you hungry? How about some lunch?"

"No, thanks though. I've got some things to do before this afternoon. Are you coming to the playground dedication?"

"Yes. Zoey is at the Games, but she'll be back by two to take over here for me."

"Do you know if John Mack is still here? Preston mentioned you put him up for the night."

"He is. What he went through this week was just dreadful. I haven't forgotten how he misled me back in December, but if Preston thinks he's okay, that's good enough for me. I saw him eating lunch not too long ago."

"Alright, thanks. I'd like to catch him before he goes. I'll see you this afternoon."

With a wave, Olivia turned and went into the dining room. Mack sat at a table near the fireplace, head down, looking at his phone. As she approached, he glanced up and gave a wide grin.

"You're looking much better today," she said.

He set his phone down and rubbed his chin. "A shave, a shower, and some borrowed clothes have made me feel like a new man."

She sat across from him. "How long are you staying?"

"I'll be on my way this afternoon. Bev generously offered me another night, but I really should get home."

"Do you need a ride?"

"No, but thank you. A rental agency is dropping off a car around two. I called the garage where my car has been sitting. They're going to appraise the damage, but the mechanic thinks the insurance company will total it."

"Ouch. I'm sorry to hear that."

"Yeah, me too."

Since they were well out of earshot from anyone, she wanted to talk shop. He'd brought her into this, and she intended to find out why. She scooted closer and leaned in. "When you sent me that text, I thought you'd made a mistake"

He tapped the phone. "I saw all your texts and missed calls."

"I didn't know what to think. I couldn't come up with a solid reason you'd ask me to do something like that. But the fact that you did—"

"Made you curious."

"And concerned. I went to your office, took pictures of everything in the file, but left it there because I had no idea what was going on. When I saw Amy's name and learned how she was connected to Fiona, I thought you wanted me to follow the trail."

"I knew I could trust you. I dictated that text while fleeing for my life down the highway. Thank goodness for modern technology. I really thought that might be it for me. If I didn't make it, I wanted someone to connect what I was doing to Fiona. Of course, I didn't know it was Nolan at the time. I thought he was out of town. That's why I contacted you."

"Why not call the police right away?"

He leaned back and lowered his shoulders. "I didn't know what was happening, and someone had just shot at me. It's not exactly easy to explain to the police—while doing seventy on the highway—that I'd just been in a house with a possible murder victim and was now being chased. I didn't want to die, only to be accused of whatever happened to Fiona. In every scenario, I'd be pinned as a suspect."

She tilted her head. "It did look bad."

Amused, he asked, "Did you think I was involved?"

"The thought crossed my mind more than once, but I couldn't believe it. You're not that kind of person."

"I appreciate your belief in me. Honestly, no one else would've gone as far as you did."

"Well, you went just as far for me in May at Spring Hills."

He picked up his glass and took a sip of water. "Whatever happened to those parrots?"

"They all survived. They were placed either in sanctuaries or in homes where they're now living their best parrot lives."

He gave a sharp nod. "That's great. We make a heck of a team."

"A dangerous one at that," she said with a light laugh. "Speaking of which—Nolan." She blew out a breath. "I thought you two were tight."

"Goes to show you, huh? Nolan isn't a murderer. Yeah, he shot at me twice, but I think he just panicked. The whole time I was at the cabin, he brought me food and water. He could've killed me, but instead, he kept trying to talk me into making a deal. I'm sure he thought the house was an easy target. Slip in, grab a few things, and get out unseen. He'd been talking recently about wanting to buy a new car. Probably thought stealing a few things and pawning them would help finance that. I don't think he meant for anyone to get hurt."

A server approached and placed a cup of tea in front of Olivia. "Courtesy of Mrs. Styles," he said.

"Thank you."

"Sir, would you like anything else? Dessert?"

"No, I'm done here."

The server cleared Mack's plate and left.

She took a sip, guessing it was Earl Grey. "Were you investigating Amy because Fiona had concerns about her?"

"Fiona was simply doing her due diligence. She only ever spoke highly of Amy, but she wanted to be sure about who she was leaving such a large sum to."

"As far as I could tell, Amy's departure from her last job wasn't tied to any misconduct or negligence involving Gladys Henderson's death."

His lips eased into a smile. "How do you know about that?"

"I spoke with Gladys' daughter, Linda. She told me there were unanswered questions about her mother's passing but still gave Amy a positive recommendation."

"You talked to the daughter? You never cease to amaze me. How'd you get her to open up?"

She shifted in the seat. "I'm not proud of it, but I told her I was looking for an aide for my dad and that Amy had listed her as a reference."

"I'd believe that coming from you. I like the way you think. I spoke with Linda, too, and a few of Amy's former colleagues. The impression I got was that she was burned out. Losing another patient was the final straw, so she left nursing altogether."

"So Fiona knew nothing about Gladys?"

"No. Is all your curiosity satisfied now?" he teased.

"Craig Campbell."

"What about him?"

"His name was in Amy's file with just one note: 'unaware.' Very mysterious. You know, if you want people to follow your trail in the future, maybe include a little more context."

That earned her a laugh. "I'll remember that. I called him and said I was an administrator with the agency Amy worked for, just doing a routine check to see if he had any concerns about Fiona's care."

"But Amy wasn't from an agency."

"Campbell didn't know that. He barely knew anything about Amy. He was 'unaware' of her employment history."

"When I brought your name up to Craig, he didn't recognize it. I figured you must've used an alias."

He nodded. "Of course. Oliver Penn."

She burst out laughing. "No, you did not."

"Okay, I didn't. But from now on, that's my go-to alias."

She took another sip of tea, then leaned back. "Why did you return to Fiona's house on Tuesday?"

His phone rang. Without picking it up, he declined the call.

"I meant to go earlier but got delayed. I wanted to wrap things up with Fiona. I knew she went to bed early, but I thought I'd try anyway. When I saw the lights were off, I checked the door to make sure it was locked. I do it for all my older clients. It's a habit. As a kid, I lived across the street from my grandmother, and every night at nine, I'd go over to check her door because sometimes she'd forget to lock up."

"That's so sweet. Who knew you had such a tender streak?"

"Let's keep that between us."

"Did you get in touch with your other clients about your sudden disappearance?"

"Most of them. I explained, without going into details, that I'd been detained beyond my control. They understood."

"So, without Nolan, what's in store for Mack and Associates?"

"First, I'm taking some time off. I'm heading to the Caribbean for a few weeks to figure out my next move. If I reinvent Mack and Associates, version two-point-oh, I'll need a partner. Someone I trust."

Knowing where he was going with that, she simply nodded. "You deserve the time away. For what it's worth, you're good at what you do. Maybe just avoid associating with dangerous people."

He laughed. "That means I'd have to stop talking to you."

She waved her hands, grinning. "I'm settling down. No more danger for me."

"I'll believe that when I see it. You're good at what you do too. And I'm not just talking about your column, though that's fine work. When I get back, I'd like to have a conversation with you about the future."

Maybe we will. I could be off chasing spies by then, though being a PI does sound kind of fun.

He lifted his glass, and she raised her teacup.

"Cheers," he said.

"To new beginnings." She sipped her tea, then stood. "I should be on my way."

He offered his hand, and they shook.

"Until we meet again, Olivia Penn."

"Take care of yourself, John Mack."

CHAPTER 40

Craig opened Fiona's front door, just as surprised to see Olivia as she was to find him there. Dressed in athletic shorts and a Highland Games T-shirt, he looked ready for his turn at the Weight Over Bar. "Olivia, hi," he said with a broad smile. "Come on in."

He closed the door after she stepped inside. She still had the house key but decided against handing it over to him. Dorothy had loaned it to her, and Olivia intended to leave its fate in her hands. The Campbell Bible sat on the entryway table, with a cardboard box of folders and papers below it.

"I'm glad I caught you here," she said. "I didn't know if you'd already be at the Games."

"I'm heading there soon. I stopped by to grab some paperwork I need to take care of Fiona's affairs. How are you? Preston told me what happened yesterday."

"I'm good. I'm still worried about him, but he seems okay."

"Yeah, sounds like he took quite a blow. He tried to downplay it, but getting knocked out isn't exactly all in a day's work, even for a cop." He gave a thin grin. "Good thing he's got a hard head sometimes."

She laughed. "I'll let you be the one to say that, not me. When will you be back in town?"

"Maybe next month. I want to get things settled here as soon as I can. We'll have to spend more time together then."

"That would be nice."

Shadow sauntered out of the sitting room and padded over to her.

She reached down, stroking the cat's back. "It's good to see you, Shadow."

"As soon as I walked in, she came running up," he said. "I think she was expecting Amy or Fiona."

"Poor kitty. It's been a difficult week for both of you." Her eyes drifted to the Bible. Curious to learn its fate, she said, "That looks really old."

"Remember when we talked about that thing Winifred said my mum left her but wouldn't tell me what it was? Turns out, it was that. I had breakfast with her this morning, and I couldn't believe it, but she told me we're related. She said Fiona had a family Bible with a record of the genealogy. When I got here, I found it on Fiona's nightstand. It's really incredible. The records go back to the 1700s. I don't know why my mum never told me."

She raised her brow and widened her eyes, dialing up shock like a pro. "Wow. What a surprise to find out. Maybe it was one of those long-lost-cousin-twice-removed kind of things."

"Exactly. I can't remember ever seeing that Bible growing up. I found a folded note tucked inside the Book of Ruth. It was written by Fiona and said that, upon her death, the Bible was to be given to Winifred or her descendants."

"Huh. Did Winifred say why she didn't tell you the Bible was what your mother had promised her?"

He shook his head. "No, and I didn't ask. I figured it was something personal between them. Not everything has to be shared. Both my mum and Fiona wanted her to have it, so that's fine by me. I'll make sure she gets it before she leaves."

There was no need to ask any more questions. Whether Winifred had told him about the land issue would remain a mystery. It wasn't Olivia's story to tell, and the legalities were murky anyway. Nothing Winifred had done was criminal, and the legal details would sort themselves out. More importantly, two families were reunited after generations, all because of a note written long ago: "Ten Scots acres from the Loch to Inverness."

Shadow meowed, rose onto her hind legs, and gently placed her forepaws on Olivia's shins. As Olivia bent over to pet her, the cat lowered herself, then sprung into her arms.

"Jeez, okay," she said, laughing, cradling the cat. "Wasn't expecting that."

"She's been hesitant to come around me."

"She's the reason I stopped by. I wanted to check on her and make sure she had food and water for the day. I'm glad I caught you before you took off."

"Her food bowl was empty, so she must've been hungry."

She brushed the cat's cheek. "What are you going to do with her?"

"I thought about rehoming her in North Carolina, maybe asking friends or neighbors if they could take her. But I decided a shelter might be the best option. They might have an easier time finding her a family."

She looked at Shadow, curled up and purring in her arms. The thought of the cat sitting in a cage waiting for someone else to love her after losing Fiona was unbearable. The decision came in an instant, without an ounce of doubt.

"I'll take her," she said. "If that's okay with you. I already have a cat and a dog, so she'll be in good company."

His face lit up with a relieved smile. "Yeah, that'd be great. Thanks. That's a load off my mind, and clearly, she's taken with you."

I hope Willow will be just as taken with her. She wasn't

worried about Buddy, who welcomed any new friend. As for her father, well—surprise. Still, she was confident he'd be fine with it.

"It's settled then," she said. "Shadow, sweetie, you're coming home with me."

"Do you want any of her things from here?"

"I'll gladly take whatever you're willing to part with. Having her own things will make the transition easier."

Over the next thirty minutes, they gathered enough of Shadow's things to help her settle in. Craig offered to bring over anything left behind the next time he was in town. He loaded her car with two litter boxes, a cat tree, food, toys, blankets, and scratchers. She secured Shadow in a carrier and placed it on the front seat, within reach so she could comfort the cat during the ride. In Fiona's paperwork, he found a folder with all Shadow's medical records and gave it to her. With everything packed, they said their goodbyes and promised to catch up next month.

By the time she got back home, her father had already left for the playground dedication. She brought the carrier into the house straightaway and set it gently in the living room, keeping Shadow inside. Buddy padded over, sniffing the carrier and peeking through the holes. She stayed for a moment, making sure Buddy didn't spook Shadow, who remained curled in the corner, seeking comfort in the enclosed space.

"Be nice, Buddy," Olivia warned. "Don't scare her."

She scanned the living room for Willow, but the cat

was nowhere in sight. With little time before she needed to leave, she hurried outside to grab just enough supplies to keep Shadow comfortable for the next few hours. On her last trip back in, Willow appeared, hugging the kitchen's edge with her body low, ears back, and eyes locked on the carrier with unblinking suspicion.

"I know, Willow," she said. "You smell her, don't you? It's okay. Everything's fine. I hope."

Planning to keep the cats separated at first, she took the carrier upstairs to her father's bedroom. It was already cat-proofed, and there was no way she could shut Buddy and Willow out of her own room, not if she wanted any peace.

With the door closed, she set up a litter box, a blanket from Fiona's, and a few toys to help Shadow settle in. Then she placed two bowls on the floor—one with food, the other with water. When everything was ready, she sat down and opened the carrier.

The cat hesitated, sniffing before cautiously creeping out. She padded around the room, nibbled some kibble, then circled back to Olivia for comfort. Just as Olivia stroked her back, scratching sounded at the door, spurring Shadow to climb into her lap. Buddy whined outside while Willow's small white paw poked in under the door.

"No, no, Willow," she said, gently tapping it. The cat withdrew her paw, only to immediately stick it under again.

"Curiosity is going to get the best of both of you."

She needed to be on her way, but not until there was some kind of temporary peace. "Okay, we'll try a little face-to-face time. But if you two can't tolerate each other, the door stays closed."

She carefully set Shadow on the floor, stood, and cracked the door open. Willow scampered back to Olivia's bedroom, but Buddy stayed put, tail wagging like he was on a grand adventure. She stepped into the hall, closed the door, and headed downstairs to grab the pet gate from the living room. It was sturdy enough to withstand Buddy's nudges and tall enough to keep Willow from jumping over.

Once back upstairs, she shooed Buddy a few feet away, went into the bedroom, and placed the gate in the doorway. Buddy immediately pushed his nose through the bars, while Willow crept closer. Shadow inched toward the doorway. The two cats sniffed each other, close enough to investigate, but just out of swiping range.

"At least neither of you is hissing," she said. "That's a good sign."

Olivia stayed in the room for another twenty minutes. Eventually, Willow wandered off, and Shadow curled up on the blanket from Fiona's house. With a temporary détente in place, Olivia quietly left, keeping the door open and the gate secured.

It was already a quarter to three. She hurried to her bedroom to change. As she pulled fresh clothes from a drawer, her eyes landed on the framed photo of Paige she kept on top of the dresser. She smiled, imagining Paige cracking a joke about her becoming a cat mom again.

"I'm stopping at two," she said aloud. And in her heart, she heard Paige's infectious laugh.

CHAPTER 41

Olivia pulled into the playground lot and parked beside Preston's truck. After getting out, she headed toward the picnic pavilions, where most of the adults had gathered. The party was in full swing, and the playground buzzed with children, many using walkers or wheelchairs while their parents stood nearby, phones in hand, capturing their adventures.

A wide, level walkway forked into two paths: one leading to the playground, the other to the shelters. At the point where the sidewalk split, Dorothy was arranging books in the little library while Floyd sat on a bench beside it.

"That looks fabulous," Olivia said, nodding toward the library, designed like a quaint country cottage. "What a great idea to put it here."

"Are you almost done?" Floyd asked Dorothy. "I'm hungry."

"Go on ahead," she said, pulling a few picture books from a tote bag on the bench. "I'll be right there."

He huffed, waved his hand, and folded his arms. "No, I'll wait."

Smiling, Olivia wondered if she and Preston might one day be like the Peabodys, inseparable as a pair of mourning doves. She fished her keys from her pocket, removed Fiona's, and handed it to Dorothy. She'd already decided not to bring up yesterday's events. Today was for celebrating. The news would spread soon enough.

"Thanks for lending me Fiona's key. Good news. We found Shadow, and I'm going to look after her. Craig was going to put her up for adoption, and since I already have a cat, I figured, why not two?"

Dorothy gave a wide grin as she placed the key in the tote bag. "How wonderful! Fiona would be so happy to know Shadow will be well taken care of. I'm sure she'll miss her old home, but she'll adjust. The Belles are going to keep the flowers tidy around Fiona's house until her nephew sells it. Fiona wasn't one to tolerate a weed, so we'll do our best to keep it as she'd like. You know, you should think about joining the Blooming Belles. We could use someone young like you with more energy and technical skills. We voted at our last meeting to start a newsletter. Helen says it's all the rage, but none of us has the faintest idea how to do it."

"Maybe someone over by the food knows," Floyd said.

"You hush," Dorothy teased. "I said, go on over."

Olivia imagined herself gathered with the other Belles, chatting about tulips and warning Helen not to plant phlox every spring. "I don't know much about flower gardening, but I'll think about it. At least I can help you with the newsletter."

After a few more minutes of conversation, she exchanged a warm goodbye with the Peabodys and left them to finish stocking the library.

Up ahead on the sidewalk, Tori and Tyler were slowly making their way toward the playground.

When Tyler saw Olivia draw near, he tapped his mother's leg and pointed excitedly. "Auntie Wiv! Auntie Wiv!"

Grinning, Olivia crouched and scooped him into a bear hug. "Ty-guy, my little buddy! How are you?"

When she let go, he spun around and yelled, "Watch me!" He dropped into a sprinter's stance, then dashed toward the playground.

"Wow, he's fast," Olivia said as she stood.

"Tyler, slow down!" Tori called after him. "Watch where you're going!"

"Could you have imagined the day when you'd be telling Tyler to slow down?"

"Never. It's been quite a year for him. When he was born, the doctor told me he'd never even walk, and now I can't get him to sit still."

Tyler stopped to play with Mikey, who was spinning

large plastic cylinders marked with X's and O's as if they were Buddhist prayer wheels.

"He proved them wrong," Olivia said. "I'm glad I got to see him grow."

"I just hope he doesn't grow up too fast. Now he wants to play soccer."

"When you're a parent, the worrying never ends."

"Truth."

Tyler ran over to the slide and started climbing the steps.

"Tyler, wait for Mommy!" Tori called. She turned back to Olivia, shaking her head. "I swear, he's going to be the death of me."

"You better go, Mommy."

"Yeah. Chat later."

Tori jogged ahead and caught up with Tyler as he reached the top of the slide. Olivia looked over toward the picnic pavilions. Preston, Carolyn, and Sam were deep in conversation. Just as she took a step their way, A.J. passed Tori and headed toward her on the sidewalk.

"Fashionably late?" he joked, pulling her into a hug.

"I had a few things to do this morning." As they separated, she glanced around the gathering. "Everything looks great. You couldn't have asked for better weather."

"Lucky, Liv," he said, ruffling her hair.

She swatted his hand away with a laugh. "I'm so proud of you. You've completely transformed this property. It's hard to even picture the manor anymore."

"That was the goal. I wanted to tear it all down and start fresh, so from now on, people will leave with only good memories." He lowered his voice. "Before construction started, I went into the woods where I'd set up that stupid moonshine still. I know the police looked for it, but they never found it. I had it hidden well. I wanted to get rid of it before anyone started hiking back there and stumbled across it. But someone beat me to it. It was already gone."

She nodded, warmed by thoughts of the risk Preston had taken for her by making the evidence disappear. "Huh. Sounds like that was for the best. Well, you're a different person now than you were then."

"So are you. Remember when we were kids and camped out in your parents' backyard during the summers?"

"Of course. Those are some of my favorite childhood memories."

"We used to talk about what we wanted to be when we grew up. You always said you wanted to be a writer. I know this isn't exactly what you pictured, being here in Apple Station. You were so excited when you got that promotion in New York. No doubt, you would've taken the Big Apple by storm, but I've got to say, I'm really glad that never happened."

She smiled, her gaze drifting toward Preston, the man she never saw coming but completely fell for. "Me too. Sometimes when life throws you curves, it's not about stopping. It's about course correction."

"And look at you now. You're the happiest I've ever seen you."

"I can agree with you on that."

"We'll have to camp out again sometime, so we can plan for what we really want to do when we grow up."

"In my dad's backyard?"

"Of course."

"Not without an air mattress, though."

"Have you become a glamper?"

"With a capital G."

"I love you all the same, Liv."

"Ditto."

A.J. glanced toward the picnic pavilions. "We're doing the name drawing in about half an hour. Be there."

"Aye aye, Captain."

He threw her a mock salute. "Until then, dismissed."

She gave his forearm a warm squeeze, then joined the gathering. Several tables, draped with plastic cloths, held a generous spread of food and desserts. She greeted June, then waved to Maria and Josefina, who were making sure everyone's plates stayed full. The smoky aroma from the nearby grills hinted that the party was just getting started. She was about to grab a soda when a sharp bark drew her eyes to the walkway. Summer and Abby were heading toward the lot.

Hurrying after them, Olivia called, "Summer, hold on!"

Summer turned as Olivia caught up.

"Are you leaving already?"

"Yes, I'm on my way back home. The inn's owner told me about the party here. I didn't know she was Detective Hill's mother. I just wanted to stop by and see how he was doing."

"Because of you and Abby, he's doing well. I can't thank you enough. I don't think we would've gotten there in time if it hadn't been for the two of you."

A smile spread across Summer's face. "I'm glad we could help."

Abby faced the parking lot and barked.

Summer glanced over her shoulder, then waved and called out, "Hey, Wren! I'll be right there."

Olivia looked toward Summer's SUV, where a woman a few years younger leaned casually against the passenger-side door. Dressed in black jeans, a white T-shirt, and dark sunglasses, she had an air of confidence and an edge.

"Do you have a long drive home?" Olivia asked.

"No, not too far. I live about an hour south of here in a small town just like Apple Station."

Abby whined, shifting restlessly as she took a few steps toward the lot.

"Alright, alright," Summer said, laughing.

As soon as she unclipped Abby's leash, the dog bolted toward Wren. She crouched, greeting Abby with eager pets and a warm hug.

"They get along well," Olivia observed.

"Wren is good with animals."

"Does she work with you?"

Summer shook her head, her smile fading slightly. "She's a good friend. She came up here looking for someone."

"Did she find them?"

"No." Summer let out a quiet, weighted breath. "But that won't stop Wren. She'll keep searching. Some people just don't want to be found, and maybe that's for the best." She coiled the leash. "I'd better get going and take Abby home. It's been a long week for her."

After Olivia thanked Summer again, they parted ways. She lingered for a moment, watching Summer walk to her car. Abby bounded happily back to her handler—two heroes, one unaware of just how many lives she'd changed yesterday.

Olivia turned back toward the pavilions as the aroma of barbecue stirred the first rumblings of hunger. Carolyn came toward her on the sidewalk, effortlessly polished in cream linen pants and a navy short-sleeve shirt.

Olivia slowed, offering a polite smile as they met. "I didn't expect to see you here."

"Sam briefed me on yesterday's events. I stopped by to offer your detective any resources necessary for the prosecution."

"Thank you for that."

Carolyn simply nodded. "Good day, Olivia."

"Wait, you're not staying? There's quite a buffet set up. A true-blue American picnic."

"Hot dogs are dreadful."

Olivia couldn't help laughing. "Okay, maybe we can agree on that."

Without another word, Carolyn stepped past her and headed for the parking lot.

Olivia continued toward the pavilions, taking in those gathered—her father, Preston, Sophia, Sam, A.J., Tori, June, Bev, Maria, and Josefina. These were the people she loved. And this moment, this scene, never would've played out had she not returned home to visit her father on that Monday, two Mays ago.

Originally, she'd planned to arrive a day later, but she'd wrapped up her packing for New York sooner than expected. That single shift in timing had changed everything. If she hadn't come on Monday, she would've missed seeing Paige one last time. A.J.'s life would've taken a far different turn. She wouldn't have grown even closer to her father. She never would've become a cat mom—twice over. She never would've fallen in love with Preston or realized just how much home truly meant to her.

It had all come down to choices. Many difficult, many risky. But in making them, she'd trusted herself, her abilities, and her heart to know what was right.

She paused, glanced back, then turned. "Carolyn."

Composed as ever, Carolyn faced her, waiting patiently as Olivia stepped forward.

Taking a deep breath, Olivia checked for any doubt. Finding none, she made her choice. "I want in."

A pleased smile crossed Carolyn's face. "Excellent. Welcome to the team, Olivia."

"One thing, though. My dad has to know the truth about the bakery deal. And there are a few people in my life, those who matter most, who'll need to know what I'm doing."

Carolyn nodded. "I trust your judgment. I'll see you tomorrow morning. We have a developing situation involving stolen classified information from China Lake, the Naval Air Weapons Station in California. Sam and Mark will bring you up to speed. Enjoy the rest of your afternoon."

Olivia sidestepped the bombshell of getting her first assignment the moment she was hired. No doubt, many such surprises were in store for her in the future. "You too."

With that, Carolyn walked away, and Olivia turned back toward the picnic pavilions. And just like that, she'd ended one career to start another, with no idea where this choice would take her. Though it took but a second to say yes to Carolyn, the decision had been over a year in the making.

She laughed to herself, recalling a prediction from Madame Morgana, a carnival tarot card reader she'd met in May: "Something must die before something can live again." At the time, the ominous musing had left her unsettled. Now she saw it as a reminder of a universal truth playing out on this day.

Once among those gathered around the pavilions,

Olivia mingled for a bit before seeking out her father. He was seated at a table, speaking with Bev, with a full plate of food in front of him. As she approached, he stood, excused himself, and led her a few steps away from the others.

"I saw you talking to Jacqueline," he said. "I didn't want to interrupt, but did she say anything about the bakery?"

Soon, she would sit him down and tell him the truth, starting with the fact that Jacqueline's real name was Carolyn. She still groaned at the thought of the bakery doubling as a front for a black-budget Spec Ops team. She could already picture their future dinner conversations filled with shop talk and intrigue.

"Let's talk about it tonight," she said. "In the meantime, I'm partial to Penn's Sweets and Treats."

"I love it." He pulled her into a hug, planting a kiss on her cheek.

"Everyone, come on over!" A.J. shouted. "It's time for the drawing!"

Her father grabbed his drink and moved toward the front of the shelter. Preston came up behind Olivia and wrapped an arm around her shoulders.

"How are you feeling?" she asked him.

"Good now that you're here."

The crowd gathered around A.J., with Maria, Josefina, June, and Sophia standing front and center.

"I want to thank everyone for coming out to help celebrate the opening of the playground," A.J. said. "A special thank-you to Sophia, who was instrumental in working with the designers and contractors. And thanks to everyone who bought a raffle ticket. The proceeds will go a long way toward the playground's maintenance." He clapped his hands. "Alright, let's do this! Sophia will use a random number generator on her phone. All entries have been assigned a number. Maria has kept them under lock and key and will pull the winning envelope. The winner doesn't need to be present. I feel like I had to say that."

Laughter rippled through the crowd.

"Sophia, do your thing," A.J. said.

Holding up her phone for everyone to see, she tapped the screen and announced, "Eighteen."

Maria opened a box on the table, flipped through the envelopes, and pulled one out. "The winner of the naming rights is … Cooper McCarthy."

"Yeah!" Cooper shouted from the back. He hurried forward, parting the gathering like the Red Sea. "Winner, winner, chicken dinner!"

Olivia and Sophia exchanged a look, then glanced at A.J., whose expression was pure dread.

Now standing at the front, Cooper struck a triumphant pose with his hands on his hips. "Yahoo! I won!"

"Sí, congratulations," Maria said before handing the envelope to A.J.

He tapped it against his palm a few times, sighed, and passed it to Olivia.

"You do the honors," he said, sounding resigned.

Taking the envelope, she shook her head playfully and mouthed, "It'll be fine."

She tore it open, bracing herself to smile no matter what ridiculous name Cooper had chosen. But as she read the card, her breath caught, her smile faltered, and moisture pooled in her eyes.

She looked at Cooper, and they shared a knowing nod born of friendship and grief.

"Come on, Liv," A.J. said. "You're leaving us hanging."

She cleared her throat and turned the card around. "This playground will be forever known as Paige's Palace."

A hush fell over the crowd, followed by cheers and applause.

Olivia went over to June, who had started to cry. A.J. pulled Cooper into a tight hug, clapping him on the back.

"It's perfect," June whispered through her tears as she embraced Olivia.

"It absolutely is," Olivia agreed as they pulled apart. "Paige is doing cartwheels right now."

"I wasn't expecting that at all," June said.

Cooper joined them and waited respectfully as June wiped her cheeks. "Mrs. Warner, I hope the name is okay with you. If it's not, I'll withdraw it. Paige was a dear friend, and I miss her every day. I thought this would be a good way to honor her memory."

"Please, call me June. And I think it's a beautiful name. Thank you."

While June and Cooper talked, Olivia stepped back, her heart full at the sight of them—two people connected by love and loss.

"That turned out well," Preston said over her shoulder. "I was a little worried."

She faced him. "I was a lot worried."

"Thanks again for staying over last night," he said, resting his hands on her waist.

"I'm not sure I'll ever do that again," she said, settling her hands on his shoulders and feigning a stern expression. "I didn't even get a tip for making your coffee."

He chuckled, then leaned in, kissing her tenderly.

"How's that?" he whispered.

"That'll do. Turns out you're a good tipper."

He ran his hands along her arms before letting go. "I saw you talking to Carolyn."

"Yes, we had a brief conversation. How about we grab some food, and I'll fill you in."

"Sounds good."

"Go ahead. I'll be right there."

As Preston headed for the buffet, Olivia stood still for a moment, taking it all in—love, laughter, home.

Everyone who mattered most was here, yet two of the dearest were not. Gone but never forgotten, her mother and Paige lived on in her heart. She and Paige had once promised to be friends forever, no matter where life took them. Olivia had traveled far, only to return home to where she needed to be. And with every step along the way, she still heard her mother's voice, reassuring and steady, reminding her she'd be okay.

She'd been through so much since moving back to Apple Station, and now, a new chapter was about to begin. Wherever the road led from here, she would follow her heart and, without a shadow of doubt, stay true to herself.

Forever a daughter. Forever a friend. Forever Olivia Penn.

The End

ACKNOWLEDGMENTS

My heartfelt thanks go to those who have played an essential role in bringing this story to life.

To my brilliant editor, Serena Clarke, your insight, patience, and unfailing encouragement have guided this story to its best form. I'm grateful for the care you bring to every page and your polish that makes each story shine.

To my meticulous proofreader, LaVerne Clark, your keen eye, thoughtful feedback, and steady support have been invaluable time and again. You've saved me more than once, and I'm thankful for every single time you have.

To the talented team behind the cover design, thank you for capturing the spirit of this story so beautifully.

A very warm thank-you to the bloggers who have championed my work, especially Dru Ann Love of *Dru's Book Musings*, whose steadfast support has meant so much. I'm also grateful to Anna of *Cozy Crime Reads* and Sarah of *Sarah Can't Stop Reading* for their generosity in sharing and celebrating *The Olivia Penn Mystery Series*.

And to my readers, you've been companions on this

journey from the first page to the last, and I'm deeply grateful for every moment you have spent in Olivia Penn's world.

Dear Reader,

Thank you so much for reading *Without a Shadow of Doubt*. I hope you enjoyed unraveling this mystery alongside Olivia and her friends.

If you'd like updates on new releases, a peek into my writing life, and the occasional special promotion, you can sign up for my newsletter on my website. I'll never share your e-mail address, and you can unsubscribe at any time.

If you enjoyed *Without a Shadow of Doubt*, I'd be truly grateful if you left a review on your favorite retail site or review platform. Reviews are one of the best ways to help other mystery lovers discover my books.

I'd be delighted to know if you found this book in your local library. My own love of reading began with endless hours in the library as a child, discovering new worlds and dreaming of countless adventures. Libraries continue to be such important spaces for sparking curiosity and imagination, especially in young readers. If you'd like, recommending my books to your library is a simple but powerful way to support my work and connect me with new readers.

And please don't hesitate to reach out through my website, social media, or e-mail if you fancy a chat. I love hearing from readers and being part of this wonderful book-loving community.

With gratitude and warmest wishes,
Kathleen

www.kathleenbaileyauthor.com
Instagram: @cozycrimewriter

WORKS BY KATHLEEN BAILEY

OLIVIA PENN MYSTERY SERIES

Where the Light Shines Through

Silence Says the Most

Under the Cocoon Moon

When the Carnival Came

Without a Shadow of Doubt

The Case of the Broken Heart (Prequel short story)

ABOUT THE AUTHOR

Kathleen Bailey is the award-winning author of *The Olivia Penn Mystery Series*. She writes mysteries with heart and humor that keep to the traditional and cozy sides of crime. For over twenty years, she worked as a pediatric physical therapist with children who have special needs, drawing on degrees in English, psychology, and physical therapy. She now writes in Virginia with her feline assistant, who insists on supervising every draft. When she's not writing, Kathleen can usually be found covered in cat hair, surrounded by far too many sticky notes, and plotting new twists to keep readers guessing. She is a member of Sisters in Crime. Visit her online at kathleen-baileyauthor.com.